Captain of Rome

Also by John Stack

MASTERS OF THE SEA
Ship of Rome

MASTERS OF THE SEA

Captain of Rome

JOHN STACK

HarperCollins*Publishers*

HarperCollins*Publishers*
77–85 Fulham Palace Road,
Hammersmith, London w6 8jb

www.harpercollins.co.uk

Published by HarperCollins*Publishers* 2009

1

A catalogue record for this book
is available from the British Library

ISBN: 978 0 00 728525 9

This novel is entirely a work of fiction.
The names, characters and incidents portrayed in it are
the work of the author's imagination. Any resemblance to
actual persons, living or dead, events or localities is
entirely coincidental.

Set in Minion by Palimpsest Book Production Limited,
Grangemouth, Stirlingshire

Printed and bound in Great Britain by
Clays Ltd, St Ives plc

Mixed Sources

Product group from well-managed
forests and other controlled sources
www.fsc.org Cert no. SW-COC-1806
© 1996 Forest Stewardship Council

FSC is a non-profit international organisation established
to promote the responsible management of the world's forests.
Products carrying the FSC label are independently certified
to assure consumers that they come from forests that are managed
to meet the social, economic and ecological needs
of present and future generations.

Find out more about HarperCollins and the environment at
www.harpercollins.co.uk/green

To my children,
Zoe, Andrew and Amy,
with affection and gratitude.
I love you.

CHAPTER ONE

'Battle speed!'

The *Aquila* sprung to life at Atticus's shouted command, the ram-tipped bow of the Roman trireme slicing cleanly through the wave tops as the galley accelerated to seven knots, the drum master's beat commanding the actions of two hundred chained slaves, a multitude working as one. The order was repeated on the aft-decks of the galleys surrounding the *Aquila* and the captain noted with satisfaction that the once inexperienced crews of the ships flanking his own now moved with alacrity and purpose. There were thirty galleys in total, each one based on the new cataphract design, although the *Aquila* bore subtle differences that set her apart and spoke of her experience; healed scars from forgotten skirmishes, timbers weathered by a hundred storms.

'Two points to starboard!' Atticus commanded.

Gaius, the helmsman, adjusted the *Aquila*'s trim, lining her up with the centre of the harbour mouth.

The Carthaginian-held port town of Thermae was nestled neatly beyond the enfolding headlands that protected the inner waters, her docks home to a fleet of enemy galleys and transport ships, their number beyond counting. Atticus moved to the side rail of the aft-deck, leaning out to look beyond the *corvus* boarding ramp that now dominated the foredeck of the *Aquila*. He instinctively cursed the unsightly device, its bulk out of place on the otherwise unobstructed foredeck, the arrow-like lines of the galley distorted by the new addition.

'Masthead . . . report!' Atticus shouted, his green eyes drawn upwards to the lookout and the figure of Corin standing precariously over the lifting yard fifty feet above. The youngest member of the crew was a fellow Greek from the city of Locri. His eyesight was akin to an eagle and he paused before replying to confirm his estimate.

'No more than ten galleys! One quinquereme! Roughly twenty transport ships!'

Atticus nodded and turned to search for Lucius, his second-in-command. The familiar figure was striding across the aft-deck, his restless eyes continually ranging over the deck of the *Aquila*, noting every action of the crew, his forty-five years resting easily on his solid frame.

'You there, Baro?' he roared as he went, 'One cubit on the starboard aft running line.' The crewman reacted instantly, two additional men rushing to his aid as the sail was given an extra degree of tautness.

Atticus nodded to Lucius who immediately came to his captain's side.

'What's your assessment Lucius?' he asked, drawing on the older man's experience; a knowledge that seemed to encompass many lifetimes.

'It's exactly as reported. One squad. Minimal activity.' Lucius replied with a scowl, his expression troubled.

'And . . .' Atticus prompted, sensing the unease.

'When have you ever known a report to be so exact, Captain?'

Atticus nodded, considering Lucius's unspoken opinion. Since the Roman victory at Mylae three months before, all enemy activity on the northern coast of Sicily had dissipated, both on land and sea, and the Roman transports plying weekly from Brolium to Rome sailed unhindered through empty sea lanes.

Atticus looked to port and the rapidly rising sun an hour above the eastern horizon. It shone white behind a veil of light cloud and the surface of the sea split the morning light into a million shards, glare upon glare until Atticus was forced to look away, blinking rapidly to clear his vision. He looked starboard to an equally empty western horizon, the shoreline bleeding away until it was lost behind the curve of a distant headland. It was as if the Carthaginians had all but abandoned northern Sicily to the Romans.

'Well, Captain?' Atticus heard, turning to see Titus Aurelius Varro, the tribune and commander of the attack fleet of thirty galleys, crossing the aft-deck towards him, leaving a huddled group of four senators in his wake.

'Enemy numbers as reported, Tribune.' Atticus replied, the tone of his words voicing his underlying uncertainty.

'Excellent!' Varro replied, slapping his hands together, not understanding the sub-text. 'Well then, ready the ship for battle.'

'Yes, Tribune.' Atticus saluted, his face betraying none of his inner thoughts.

Titus Aurelius Varro was a young man, not yet twenty, but his father was a senior senator and magistrate and it was rumoured amongst the fleet commanders that he had paid a king's ransom for his son's commission. Atticus could only marvel at how fast fortune had transformed the Roman navy. Less than six months ago it was a provincial force of a dozen galleys and the sailors and marines who served in her ranks were treated with contempt by the vaulted legions of the Republic. Now the *Classis Romanus*, the Roman Fleet, numbered over two hundred galleys, both Roman and captured Carthaginian and the command of her forces was sought after by the elite of Roman society. It was for this reason also, Atticus suspected, that Varro had chosen the *Aquila* as his flagship, no doubt hoping to emulate the success of Gaius Duilius, Consul of the Roman Senate, who had sailed on the *Aquila* at Mylae.

Atticus turned to Lucius and repeated the tribune's order. Within a minute the lifting yard of the mainsail was lowered and the huge canvas was furled and made secure. The lifting yard was quickly re-raised to half mast and swung through ninety degrees to be fastened parallel to the mainmast. The galleys surrounding the *Aquila* noted the action, the signal of commitment to battle and they followed suit, the order rippling down along the line.

The fleet of thirty galleys tightened up as the harbour mouth approached, an unconscious movement that sharpened the thin edge of the arrow head formation, the manoeuvre bunching the ships together, coiling the energy of their advance, a deadly force that would be unleashed on the un-prepared enemy at Thermae.

The rhythmic beat of ten thousand footfalls filled the valley floor, the sound overlain with sporadic clinks of metal on metal as equipment and kit swayed with the repetitive march of five thousand legionaries. Forty maniples of the Ninth Legion had been assigned the task of securing the town of Thermae. They were the 'Wolves of Rome', a legion of men who carried with them a near fanatical lust for revenge against the Carthaginian foe who had humiliated them at Makella only months before. The *Punici* had brought the Ninth to their knees under the double burden of starvation and pestilence, isolating them in hostile territory. The Carthaginian blockade of Sicily had cut the legions off from the supplies of Rome and it was only the naval victory at Mylae that released the stranglehold, and freed the soldiers.

With the threat of starvation lifted the Ninth had slowly regained its strength, the influx of men and equipment, of food and supplies, sweeping away the last vestiges of weakness and vulnerability. The legionaries had kept the wounds open however, constantly picking at the scab to reveal the raw flesh beneath, never allowing the pain to abate fully less they forget the measure of revenge owed to them. Their wound could only be cauterised in the heat of battle, sealed with the blood of their enemy.

Septimus Laetonius Capito, marine centurion of the *Aquila*, marched with the IV maniple. At six foot four inches and two-hundred and twenty pounds, he stood tall in the front rank but his stride was marked by a slight limp, an injury suffered at Mylae when his demi-maniple of sixty legionaries swept the main deck of the Carthaginian flagship in that bitter and hard-won fight. After the battle Septimus had been amongst the first relief column to reach Makella and rescue the Ninth, the fulfilment of an oath to the man now marching beside him, Marcus Fabius Buteo, centurion of the IV and Septimus's old commander before he had transferred to the marines. Marcus had a dozen years and a hundred battles on Septimus but his stride matched the youngest men of the legion and his will and discipline outstripped them all.

'Anything?' Marcus asked, noticing Septimus's gaze sweep the hills on either side of their approach, trusting the younger man's eyesight over his own.

'Nothing,' Septimus replied, his voice betraying his unease. 'No sign on either flank.'

'Bloody cavalry!' Marcus spat, he like Septimus keeping any comment of disquiet to himself, knowing his men behind him were in easy earshot.

'There's still time,' Septimus remarked as if to himself.

5

Marcus grunted a reply in agreement, both men lapsing back into silence.

Septimus shifted his gaze to the head of the column and the mounted figure of Lucius Postumius Megellus, legate and commander of the Ninth and Second legions in Sicily. He rode with his back straight and his head upright, his gaze to a casual observer seemingly transfixed on the town of Thermae now less than a mile away. Septimus knew however he had to be searching surreptitiously for the outriders of the cavalry detachment that protected the flanks of the marching column. They had ridden in as each mile of the approach was covered, reporting each time that the flanks were clear for the next mile of advance. Now they were overdue.

Hamilcar Barca rode with his chest a mere inch from the withers, his body moulded to the shoulders of his mount as horse and rider moved as one. At full tilt the wind rushed in Hamilcar's ears and the coarse hair of the mane whipped his cheek as his senses were filled with the warm smell of horse sweat and leather. He crooked his head and looked over his shoulder, blinking rapidly to clear the windswept tears from his eyes. Behind him rode five hundred of his men, Carthaginians all, riding with the same fury as their leader, but unable to match the pace of Hamilcar's Arabian mare, a light horse bred in the desert for speed and stamina, an animal with a proud and fiery temperament that set her apart and above from the other races of horse.

Hamilcar returned his gaze to the ground ahead, judging the lie of the land with a skilled glance before shifting his weight slightly left, a signal to his mount to veer up the gentle slope that screened the Carthaginians from their enemy, the riders behind him matching their commander's course. A sudden blaze of shame washed over Hamilcar as he rode but instead of suppressing it he nurtured the flame, holding it close to his core where his hatred for the enemy lay. Hamilcar had commanded the right flank at Mylae and had witnessed at first hand the staggering reversal of the once invincible Carthaginian fleet. It was he who issued the general order to retreat, a command both shameful and necessary that dishonoured him and his men. The anger he felt had been partly assuaged when he crucified Hannibal Gisco, the foolhardy and maniacal commander of the fleet, but now it returned anew at the thought of the Roman enemy just beyond his field of vision and he pushed his mount to increase her speed as she fought against the slope of the hill.

'Captain, signal the fleet, full attack.'

'Tribune?' Atticus replied perplexed, spinning around to face the younger man.

'Full attack, Captain!' Varro repeated, his expression animated, his eyes restless as his gaze swept the inner harbour.

'But Tribune,' Atticus began cautiously, trying to read the young man's intention. 'The Carthaginians are heavily outnumbered. If we sent an envoy forward alone it is possible they will surrender without a fight.'

'Surrender?' Varro replied, his expression one of genuine shock. 'Why would we wish for them to surrender? Where is the glory in that? We have come here for battle and by the gods we will have it. Order full attack.'

Atticus nodded but felt it necessary to point out one other important element, wondering if the tribune had considered it. 'And a rear-guard, Tribune?' he said, 'I suggest five galleys from the third squad.'

'A rear-guard?' Varro asked, his tone now laced with impatience. 'The enemy are there, Captain,' he said, pointing forward.

Atticus made to reply but Varro cut him off – 'Order full attack, Captain. Now!' he snarled, his expression no longer friendly, his eyes cold.

Atticus hesitated, every instinct of his experience calling on him to counter the asinine command. He was stunned by the tribune's words, until suddenly realisation swept over him. Varro was looking to make his name in battle and he was going to force an all out battle if necessary. Atticus weighed up his options for a heartbeat longer. He had none.

'Lucius, signal the fleet!' he ordered.

Varro smiled once more and returned to the group of senators, talking animatedly as he went, expounding the genius of his strategy.

'This is madness,' Lucius said quietly beside Atticus. 'We could take Thermae without a fight and I don't like entering a hostile port without someone watching our backs.'

'I agree,' Atticus remarked, his own gaze shifting to the Carthaginian galleys. For fifteen generations the Punic navy had been masters of the Mediterranean, their seamanship and naval tactics second to none. The *corvus* had surprised them at Mylae but it was the only tactic the Romans could deploy. As Varro was going to force a fight, the Roman legionaries would have to board in strength, they would have to carry the fight to the enemy. It was going to be a hard fight, but more than that, Atticus knew it was going to be a waste of men's lives, a pointless attack where none was required. He moved aside from the tiller and walked forward to look over the assembled legionaries of the *Aquila* on the main deck. On this day, their blood would be on Roman hands.

'Form lines! Deploy the skirmishers!'

Marcus automatically began to relay the order from the front of the column to his maniple, an innate reaction borne from over fifteen years in command. The men moved with disciplined intent as they manoeuvred into the *triplex acies* formation, the three line deployment with the light *hastati* troops in the front line, the more seasoned and heavily armoured *principes* in the second and the older veteran *triarii* in the third. The lightly armoured and more independent *velites* broke off as skirmishers, their javelins light in their hands as they ranged over the ground immediately in front of the deploying legionaries.

Septimus moved without hesitation into the second line although he was no longer one of the *principes* of the IV maniple of the Ninth as he had been at the Battle of Agrigentum. As he did so he examined the sudden command of the legate to deploy into battle formation. Thermae was less than two hundred yards away and seemed completely devoid of activity. This in itself was not surprising given that the advancing Roman legion would have been seen from over a mile away and would have prompted every civilian to flee into the interior of the town. What was unusual however was that the outriders of the Roman cavalry had not reappeared, and since the legion was in enemy territory, albeit to subdue a town that was reported to be sparsely defended, it seemed prudent to deploy for battle rather than advance without proper reconnaissance. Legate Megellus was a cautious man, Septimus thought.

Within five minutes the forty maniples of the Ninth had deployed into battle formation and the air grew quiet again as they waited patiently for the order to advance. Septimus blinked a bead of sweat from his eye, overcoming the urge to lift his hand and wipe his face, the ingrained discipline of the legions still strong in his blood. His gaze shifted left to right at the skirmishers who were now reaching the outskirts of the town, the closed shutters of the low whitewashed buildings revealing nothing to the advancing soldiers. He watched as one of the *velites* negotiated his way around a tethered dog, the sharp bark of the mongrel breaking the silence before a yelp of pain cut the sound short. In the centre of his vision, the approach road to the town was crowded by a detachment of the *velites*, their commander signalling orders as they prepared to advance into the town proper.

Septimus dropped his gaze, ignoring the unspoken order of eyes front as he sensed a tiny vibration beneath his feet. His mind registered and processed the sensation within a heartbeat, triggering a memory and a corresponding sense of alarm. As if to confirm his dread a sound began to fill the air around him, a sound like distant thunder to the uninitiated, but unmistakable to a veteran. His mouth began to form the warning but a dozen other men in the rear ranks beat him to it, their uncoordinated voices overlapping into a jumble of sound, but their warning nonetheless distinctive.

'Enemy cavalry to the rear!'

The low sun blazed into Hamilcar's eyes as he crested the hill and he blinked away the momentary blindness, his eyes taking in the entire vista before him in an instant. To his left, a mile away and less than two hundred yards from the town, the Roman legions seemed to be in disarray but Hamilcar's military eye could see they were deploying into a battle formation, their cohesion evident even at this range. His gaze did not linger long on the enemy however, but shifted to a point directly across from his own on the other hill flanking the valley approach to Thermae. He was half way down the slope, his men following en masse behind, before he spotted the second attack force breach the top of the hill, the second unit of five hundred cavalry that would link with his own on the valley floor.

Hamilcar wheeled his horse into the centre of the valley and his men formed a line of battle on his flanks as they continued at the gallop. He straightened up in the saddle, shifting his weight and locking his legs against the barrel of his mount. His horse, a veteran herself of many battles, sensed the shift and, raising her head slightly, allowed Hamilcar to guide her with his legs, thereby freeing his hands from the reins. He reached behind and drew his sword from the scabbard strapped to his back, drawing the blade in a high arc, a fluid motion that signalled to his men the commitment to battle.

Hamilcar set his gaze firmly on the Roman formation a thousand yards in front of him. He had prepared for this moment for the past three months, from the day he had watched Hannibal Gisco suffer and die on the cross, punishment for the arrogance that had been the Carthaginians' undoing at Mylae. He had marshalled his forces and then almost immediately concealed them, hiding them from the Roman enemy who sailed unopposed across north-eastern Sicily. He had surreptitiously watched their every move, expecting and then confirming the imminent attack on Thermae and with tempered hate he had laid his trap. Now Hamilcar's eyes glazed over as he muttered a prayer to Anath, the Carthaginian goddess of war, for her favour in ensuring the enemy had approached unawares. With her good grace he prayed the Roman fleet had advanced under the same veil of ignorance and arrogance. As his vision cleared, the enemy ranks, although still eight hundred yards distant, seemed to fill his vision. A visceral war cry reared up within him and he roared his defiance at the Romans, a shout that was taken up by the thousand men who followed him without question.

*

'Attack speed!' Atticus commanded.

The whip cracks below decks intensified at the order as the two hundred slaves of the *Aquila* worked to get the trireme up to eleven knots, the drum beat intensifying, the heightened rhythm triggering the adrenaline to rise in Atticus's veins at the anticipation of battle. The Carthaginian line was less than three hundred yards away, nine triremes and one quinquereme in line abreast formation perpendicular to the dock, their hulls pointing directly at the Roman advance.

'Captain . . .' Lucius remarked slowly, standing at Atticus's shoulder.

'I see it . . .' Atticus replied, his mind racing. The enemy decks were swarming with activity but Atticus noticed they weren't getting underway. In fact, they were showing no signs of advancing.

The Carthaginians' strength was in ramming their enemy. For that they needed sea room and that space was rapidly being eroded by the Roman vanguard advancing at speed. In less than a minute it would be too late and they would be sitting ducks.

'Or the perfect bait,' Atticus realised suddenly. He whipped around to look out over the aft-rail to the headlands encasing the harbour and the entire fleet of Roman galleys now enclosed within them. 'Poseidon protect us!' he whispered.

'Masthead lookout!' Atticus shouted, 'Check out approach, beyond the harbour mouth!'

Corin immediately turned from the impending battle and looked out over the low lying headlands. From fifty feet below Atticus could clearly see the sudden look of alarm on the lookout's face and dread filled his stomach.

'Enemy ships approaching from the east!' Corin roared, pointing to the harbour mouth and the rush of Carthaginian galleys entering at battle speed.

Atticus was already running to the main deck as Corin shouted the alarm, the captain seeking Lucius out amongst the throng of men surrounding the mainmast. He spotted him immediately, his bull-like stature pushing through the legionaries as he too sought his commander.

'Lucius! Get aloft. I want a full count including formation!' Atticus ordered, knowing the inexperienced Corin wasn't up to the vital task.

Lucius nodded and dashed to the running rigging, grasping the rope with his calloused hands and nimbly climbing arm over arm to the head of the mainmast.

'Drusus!'

Immediately the acting centurion was at Atticus's side.

'Have your men form up on the foredeck behind the *corvus*. Once you have control of the enemy main deck I want you to fire her and retreat. Don't engage below decks.'

Drusus saluted, his clenched fist slamming into his chest armour. He turned and issued terse orders to his men, the soldiers breaking ranks to reform on the fore. Atticus hesitated a moment to watch him. He was an *optio* of the Fourth legion who had been drafted to the marines as Septimus's second-in-command. With the centurion absent, Drusus was in full command of the marines, a position he had never held before in a naval battle. He was a quiet man who kept his own counsel, but Atticus knew him to be a strict disciplinarian and he followed orders to the letter, never questioning a command or commander. But he lacked experience and Atticus realised he would need to guide both galley and marines in the fight to come.

'Thirty enemy galleys!' Lucius roared suddenly from the masthead and Atticus lifted his gaze. 'Three quinqueremes in the van! Moving in arrow formation!'

'Captain!' Varro shouted, breaking Atticus's concentration, 'What's going on?'

'A trap, Tribune,' Atticus said brusquely, not looking at the Varro but at the Carthaginian galley to the *Aquila*'s fore, now less than a hundred yards away, 'and we sailed right into it.'

'A trap?' Varro repeated, a slight edge of apprehension in his voice, his confidence of minutes before suddenly challenged.

'Ready the *corvus*!' Atticus shouted, watching Gaius from the corner of his eye as the helmsman lined up the bow of the *Aquila*.

'What are you doing?' Varro asked, his previous command forgotten. 'We must withdraw.'

'No!' Atticus said angrily but then immediately instantly calmed his voice, needing the tribune to understand. 'We must attack, Tribune. We're too close, too committed. We need to wipe out the threat to our front before we turn. Otherwise we'll be forced to fight on two fronts.'

Varro looked away, his face twisted in uncertainty, his eyes darting left and right. Atticus turned his attention once more to the attack.

With twenty yards to go Drusus ordered his *hastati* to release their javelins, the final prelude to attack that would shatter any confluence of men on the Carthaginian foredeck. The *Aquila* shuddered as the seventy ton galley struck the unyielding hull of the Carthaginian ship and the *corvus* was instantly released, its thirty-six foot length hammering down onto the enemy deck, the three foot long spikes on the underside of the ramp crashing into the seasoned pine of the enemy fore, securing the two galleys together in a deadly embrace. Only then did the legionaries roar, their bloodthirsty cry filling their hearts with anger and courage. Within seconds Drusus led all sixty of his men across and a battle line was formed at the head of the Carthaginian galley, the interlocking four-foot *scutum* shields of the legionaries creating an impenetrable barrier against which the *Punici* could not stand. Slowly and inexorably the Romans began their advance, their swords finding the gaps between the shields, each thrust searching for and finding the flesh of the enemy as man after man fell beneath Roman iron. The noise of battle carried clearly down the length of the *Aquila* to the aft-deck; cries of anger and pain mixed with the clash of weapons. It was a sound like no other in the world and Atticus was transfixed by the sight before him, the vicious struggle that he had known half his life, first as a pirate hunter and now as a galley captain in the war against the *Punici*.

Septimus gritted his teeth as he ran, almost stumbling as he favoured his right leg. All around him the sound of officer's commands filled the air, their voices raised above the sound of five thousand men running towards the outer buildings of Thermae; their orders tightly controlling the panic that lingered just under the surface of every Roman infantryman at the thought of being caught in the open against enemy cavalry.

Septimus's vision was filled with the throng of men in front of him but his senses also picked up the advance of the Carthaginians behind; the approaching thunder that infused the very air and his mind calculated their proximity from the sound. Less than two hundred yards. They weren't going to make it and Septimus heard the legate issue a desperate order to try and check the Carthaginian charge.

'*Hastati*! Prepare to form ranks!'

Septimus ran on through the assembling ranks of the junior soldiers, each one preparing to deploy their *pila* javelins over the heads of the retreating legionaries, the decision to deploy them a desperate gamble to give the rest of the legion time to take cover. The troops were crowded together in the gaps between the buildings and on the main road into the town.

Septimus pushed himself out of the throng and into an island of calm against the bare whitewashed wall of a house. He drew his sword and immediately began to command the men at the crush points to his left and right, his voice reprimanding the soldiers who were pushing those in front, ensuring that panic did not ripple across the men frantically vying for the safety of the town. He looked back towards the approaching enemy, their primeval war cries almost drowning the orders of the centurions commanding the *hastati*. The junior soldiers stood with their feet apart, braced for the throw of their weapons against the enemy bearing down on them. It was a sight to see and Septimus felt his pride swell at the fortitude of the younger men, many of whom had never faced down a cavalry charge. His trained eye judged the distance between the forces, counting the yards off in his head. At thirty yards they would release and the *hastati* would break for cover. Whether they reached it or not depended on the enemy's courage.

Septimus instinctively muttered the command a heartbeat before the shouted order of 'Loose!' released fury upon the enemy.

Twelve hundred javelins were released as one, their trajectory almost flat at the short range and they hung in the air for a mere second before crashing into the enemy ranks, the iron point of each six foot spear slamming indiscriminately into the exposed flesh of the enemy with Fortuna's hand separating the lucky from the damned. For an instant the force of the charge was repressed, its momentum struck as horses and men fell under the weight of Roman iron. Time slowed as Septimus locked his gaze on the front ranks of the enemy. From where he stood he could see the individual expression of each man and witness the critical moment when their courage would either rear up in defiance or collapse. It passed and his body moved before his mind could fully register the outcome, his survival instinct faster than his conscious mind.

Septimus was already through the now empty gap between the houses behind him when the order for the *hastati* to break was given. Only then did he replay in his mind the sight he had just seen, the moment to which he had borne witness. The Carthaginians had never wavered. They had run over their own dead and injured without check and the air behind Septimus was ripped by the terrible sound of the enemy cavalry striking the exposed ranks of the *hastati* as they scrabbled the remaining yards to the cover that many of them would never reach.

Hamilcar roared in triumph as a spray of Roman blood fell across his face, the legionary beneath his blade pitching backward with his arms outstretched; his chest slashed open, his defiant stand when all around him fled, ended by a Phoenician blade. Hamilcar continued the swing of his blade over his head as his mount thundered on, the momentum of their combined charge bringing the sword down with savage speed onto the helmet of another fleeing soldier, the forge-welded blade slicing cleanly through the thin metal helmet, dropping the legionary instantly.

All around Hamilcar the Carthaginian line enveloped the fleeing Romans, the slaughter unopposed as the exposed *hastati* ran for cover, many of them dropping their weapons in a futile attempt to speed their flight, the front ranks left with too far to run. They paid for the precious seconds they had given their comrades with their lives. Hamilcar violently reined in his mount only yards short of one of the outer buildings of the town while to his left and right more Carthaginians continued to butcher the bottlenecked legionaries. He drew his forearm across his mouth, tasting the blood of his enemy as he wiped the stain away, his heightened senses capturing each second of his first close-contact fight with the Romans.

A cheer erupted from the Carthaginians as the last of the Romans fell or fled, the men wheeling their mounts in tight circles as they held their swords aloft in triumph. Hamilcar scanned the scene around him. Fifty yards to his rear he spied his fallen men, their number laid out in a line marking the fall of the Roman spears, their loss repaid fourfold by the number of dead Romans who littered the horse-trampled ground and the Roman cavalry so easily dispatched in ambush only an hour before. Cries and alarm cut through the cheering and Hamilcar spun around to see a flight of Roman spears erupt from the confines of the town, the untargeted volleys falling loosely amongst his troops.

'Withdraw!' he roared, his men instantly obeying, galloping out of range of their unseen foe.

'Commander!' Hamilcar shouted as he spun his mount around fifty yards from the town. A senior cavalry officer was immediately by his side.

'Re-form the line,' he ordered. 'Have your men rush any Roman who appears but do not attempt to breach the town.'

The officer saluted and galloped down the line, shouting orders as he did, the men falling back once more into a battle line that effectively imprisoned the Romans in Thermae. Hamilcar watched the officer for a minute, his gaze ranging over the extended formation, the expressions of his men still manic from the frenzied attack only moments before. They would need a firm hand to keep them in check and the uneasy stomp of their horses' forelegs betrayed the pent-up aggression of the riders. Let loose they would charge the very heart of the town, their blood lust blinding them to the danger of attacking infantry in enclosed streets where their superior speed and manoeuvrability would count for naught. He watched as discipline reasserted itself, and turned his attention back to the town. Between the buildings and on the entrance road he could see a multitude of red cloth and burnished steel, the Romans rushing across his line of sight as their officers fought to regain control of their shattered formations. Hamilcar smiled although his eyes remained cold. No fewer than four hundred Romans lay dead before him and yet the wound to his pride was still raw, his heart calling for greater vengeance. He spurred his mount and raced off towards the southern end of the town and to the flank that would take him quickest to the shores of the inner harbour. As he rode he looked back once more over his shoulder and to the cavalry that had wrought such slaughter. Their fight was fought and won. Now Hamilcar would unleash the next wave, the attack that would wipe out the Romans and restore his honour.

'By the Gods . . .' Atticus whispered as a horde of Carthaginian soldiers suddenly emerged from the hatchways of the Carthaginian galley now transfixed to the *Aquila*. There were scores of them, many more than the normal complement of a Carthaginian galley; a multitude rushing towards the thin battle line of Drusus's men. They stormed forward as one, the weight of their charge barely checked by the disciplined legionaries as they were pushed onto the defensive by a number three times their own.

A cheer emanated from the Carthaginian galley on the *Aquila*'s left flank and Atticus spun around to see the Roman line of the *Minerva* collapse under a similar assault, the legionaries retreating across the *corvus* as the enemy followed them onto the deck of the Roman galley. Atticus spun around to the waters of the outer harbour behind him. The Carthaginian galleys were forming a battle line across the width of the harbour, but Atticus noticed that they were slowing their advance and he hesitated, his mind racing to understand the enemy's rationale, why they were not attacking. He swept aside the question and turned once more.

'Lucius!' Atticus shouted, his voiced raised above the Punic war cries that carried from the *Minerva* not thirty yards away, 'All hands forward, send a runner across to Drusus and tell him to withdraw. We'll cover his retreat!'

'Yes, Captain.' Lucius replied and was away.

As Atticus ordered his crew forward, the first flight of arrows from the enemy on board the *Minerva* flew across the narrow gap between the galleys and struck the main deck of the *Aquila*. A shiver ran down Atticus's spine as an arrow swept past him and he fought to suppress it, standing resolute in the centre of his ship. He muttered his familiar prayer to Fortuna, knowing that if her hand was upon him this day he would live to see another. If not then Hades, the Lord of the Dead, would take him across the Acheron before the sun set. He felt his nerve strengthen as he ended his prayer, the initial panic every soldier felt at the start of close combat quickly subsiding within him and like countless times before, with a warrior's heart, he gave his life to fate.

Atticus looked beyond the fight before him to the buildings surrounding the docks of Thermae and his thoughts strayed to Septimus. If the fleet had been baited into a trap then surely the legion had suffered the same fate. He turned to the town beyond the inner harbour and as his eyes strayed over the whitewashed buildings he saw a fire arrow take flight, its golden orange tip followed by a black tail of smoke that stood out against the cobalt sky. Even above the noise of battle all around him, Atticus clearly heard the visceral war cry emanating from the bowels of the town and he instinctively recited his prayer once more, this time for his friend.

*

The dread war cry of the *Punici* whipped through the still air, the sound causing Septimus to turn his head to the western end of the town and the source of the cry, the men who roared it as yet unseen beyond the confines of the narrow streets now crammed with legionaries. High above his head he spied a lone fire arrow, its purpose immediately clear as a roar emanated from the eastern end of Thermae and the enemy on the reverse flank. Septimus immediately began to form the men around him, his officer's voice joining the confusing disharmony of commands as centurions and *optios* fought to bring a semblance of order to the chaos.

The Ninth had run into Thermae in confusion, the ordered formations created on the open space at the edge of the town destroyed as the men fled the Carthaginian cavalry. Septimus searched around him for the banner of the IV maniple and the men under Marcus's command but it was nowhere to be seen within his field of vision, a scene choked with men pushing and shoving to regain their own units.

The war cries to the west intensified and Septimus charged his shield in that direction, the men around him following suit, many taking their lead from the taller centurion in their midst. Septimus frantically looked for a unit of *hastati*, the sequence of defence ingrained into his command psyche but none were intact and he realised that even if a unit were available there wasn't enough room for them to deploy and release their spears in the crush of men. With a rush of under-standing he realised the brilliance of the Carthaginians' trap. A Roman legion was born and bred on an open battlefield where her ordered formations were impenetrable. In the narrow confines of a town, without room to manoeuvre, the disciplined structure that made the legions near unbeatable was lost.

The blare of a Roman military trumpet reverberated through

the streets, Septimus spinning around to find its source. An order rippled down through the street. 'Fighting retreat to the docks!' a centurion shouted and Septimus repeated the order to all within his own earshot, continuing the relay of the order. Soldiers began to push back past Septimus as they made for the centre of the town and the road to the docks while others stood confused and dazed, lost without their unit. Septimus stood firm, his eyes locked on the street ahead of him, unable to see beyond the abrupt turn to the right not thirty yards from his position. A number of *principes*, the battle-hardened core of the legion, spotted Septimus's stand and fell in behind him, creating a wedge of men that separated the flow like the cutwater of a galley.

The sound of the oncoming enemy filled the air around, their voices now intermingled with the sound of their running footfalls, the noise ricocheting off the walls of the town, tricking the ear so Septimus was forced to turn his head left and right to judge the distance of direction of the oncoming onslaught.

'Form line!' he roared, the soldiers spreading out across the twenty foot wide street to form a shield wall.

Septimus took his place immediately behind the first line, his gaze sweeping over the men around him, their insignia from a dozen different maniples marking them as strangers but their uniform making them one. The wall of sound to their front increased in intensity and Septimus focused his attention on the corner to their front.

'Steady, boys!' Septimus growled, 'Steady!'

The men in front of Septimus visibly bunched their shoulders into the back of their shields, bracing themselves against the rush of enemy that was bearing down on them.

'Here they come!'

Septimus watched with a determined expression as the first

of the *Punici* raced around the corner towards them. Their pace checked for a heartbeat at the sight of the shield wall but their expressions of pure aggression never varied and they ran headlong without pause.

'Steady the line!' Septimus shouted.

The legionaries roared a primeval battle cry in response, acknowledging the order. Steady the line. Not one step back until the enemy was held.

The Carthaginians crashed against the front line as one, their momentum absorbed and then repelled by men tempered in the forge of the Roman legions. The legionaries heaved forward against the press of the enemy, creating gaps between their shields through which they fed their *gladius* swords, the iron blade seeking a death stroke against an enemy's groin or stomach. The *Punici* battered the wood and canvas shields, hammering the iron edging, their brute strength fuelled by their hatred of the Roman aggressor. A legionary fell, then another, their place rapidly filled as Septimus fed replacements into the breach.

'Fighting retreat!' Septimus shouted. The line was strong and holding but the weight of the enemy against it was increasing with every passing second. The battle around Septimus filled his senses, the sound of iron on iron, wood and flesh, the incoherent overwhelming war cries mixed with cries of pain and death, the smell of blood and voided bowels as dead men fell beneath the butcher's blade.

'Hold!' Atticus growled to his men on the foredeck, 'Steady, boys!'

The crew of the *Aquila* were fanned out on each side of the *corvus*, with archers deployed on the forerail, the men forming a funnel through which the legionaries could retreat in order. Atticus was given a second to look around him and he spotted Varro standing near the back of the line. He stood amongst his own personal guard, commanded by a veteran of the legions named Vitulus. In front of these many of the older senators, former military commanders in their own right, had drawn their swords, their time spent in the legions commanding their actions even now in their later years.

With one fluid movement Atticus drew his sword, the iron blade singing against the scabbard, his arm instantly accepting the familiar weight of the weapon. The rear ranks of Drusus's men had reached the *corvus* and they were edging back along it. Within a minute the front rank, Drusus amongst them, were coming across the boarding ramp, his line continuously pushed by the press of Carthaginian warriors to his fore, the enemy war cries increasing in ferocity as they sought to board the Roman galley.

As the last of the legionaries crossed, the crew of the *Aquila* instantly engaged. Atticus took a step to his front as a Punic warrior pushed towards him, a battle axe in his hand. The Carthaginian swung the axe high and Atticus collapsed his body into a defensive stance, coming to his full height – again chest to chest with the enemy fighter, instantly stabbing upward and behind with his sword, the blade biting deeply into the exposed kidneys of his enemy, the man collapsing with a cry of pain. Atticus fought on without check, his instincts screaming at him to rush the enemy before they could form a coherent bridgehead on the foredeck of the *Aquila*, his heart damning any man who would dare to set foot on his galley.

Varro roared in dread-filled defiance, his voice lost amongst the roar of battle. The six legionaries of his guard stood directly in front of him, their shields interlocked in a bid to stave off the Carthaginian horde that had swept over the *corvus* seconds before. Vitulus stood to Varro's fore, methodically driving his sword through the gap between his shield and the man's to his right. Varro stood riveted to his spot, his own sword still sheathed, furious that he had been drawn into the front line of the battle, forced to advance by the senators who had answered the captain's call for all hands forward without hesitation, leaving Varro with little choice but to follow or risk accusations of cowardice. Now his mind was flooded with anxiety, praying he would survive, while struggling to understand the sudden reversal of his fate. An hour before he had watched with mounting elation as his fleet had swept unopposed into the harbour of Thermae. Fortuna's wheel had turned and the easy victory he had foreseen was transforming into bloody butchery before his eyes.

Atticus felt the pressure of the Carthaginian attack ease to his front as he heard the disciplined commands of the legionaries to his rear, their line re-forming, their sudden reverse causing even the most fearsome Carthaginian boarders to waver. Within a frenzied minute the Romans checked and then began to repel the invaders, making the enemy pay for every inch of the *Aquila*'s deck they had taken.

'Fire their deck!' Atticus shouted to his archers and they shot fire arrows across the narrow divide bridged by the *corvus* to the rigging and deck of the Carthaginian galley. The fire wouldn't take enough of a hold to consume the galley but it would certainly disable her as the crew fought to bring it under control.

'Raise the *corvus*! Full reverse!' Atticus roared, as the remnants of the now retreating Carthaginians struggled to make their way back across the boarding ramp, many of them falling into the churning waters, the ramp beneath them tilting violently. The two hundred oars of the *Aquila* dug deeply into the calm waters and with incredible skill Gaius backed the *Aquila* away from the Carthaginian galley to their front.

'Enemy galley on ramming course!'

Atticus spun around at the sound of the frantic cry from the masthead and dread filled his stomach as he saw one of the Carthaginian galleys bearing down on them at ramming speed. Only a few of the enemy ships had advanced from their line across the outer harbour, an insufficient number to overpower the rapidly disengaging Roman ships. Again Atticus was left confused by the enemy's tactics.

'Gaius!' he shouted. 'Evasive manoeuvres . . . now!'

The helmsman threw his weight behind the tiller and the deck of the *Aquila* keeled violently as Gaius fought to bring the exposed stern of the galley around and out of range of the vicious ram of the Carthaginian galley.

'Captain!'

Atticus looked around to find Drusus striding towards him across the main deck, his shield hanging loosely by his side, the boss dented and blood-stained, his face streaked with the filth of battle.

'The clarion call,' he said, his expression uncharacteristically concerned, 'from Thermae.'

'What of it?' Atticus asked, recalling the trumpet sound he had heard just after he saw the fire arrow in flight over the town.

'It was a call for full retreat, Captain.'

Atticus paused for a second as the full meaning of Drusus's concern hit home. Full retreat. For five thousand men of the Ninth. Where could they retreat to?

Septimus glanced over his shoulder as he rounded yet another corner and he smiled coldly at the sight behind him. A solid line of Roman *hastati*, their javelins held at the ready. He turned to the line again and sensed then saw *pila* javelins fly over his head into the rear ranks of the enemy attack.

The Carthaginians hesitated at the unexpected onslaught, checking their ferocity as they spotted the massed ranks of the reformed and reorganised Ninth at the end of the street. For a heartbeat indecision swept through them before a second volley of javelins was released from the Roman ranks, each iron-tipped spear finding a target in the narrow confines of the street. The rear ranks of the Carthaginians fled to take refuge in the preceding street, the front line hesitating for a second more before the momentum of the retreat behind them caused them to turn and run.

The Roman line opened to allow Septimus and his men to withdraw and the centurion scanned the mass of men behind the line. Many had escaped the initial assault, but Septimus knew the reprieve would not last long. The Carthaginians would rally and although Septimus was now surrounded by hundreds of Roman soldiers rather than dozens, the odds were still overwhelmingly stacked against them.

A wave of sea spray swept over Septimus's face as he rounded the final street to the docks, the air laden with smoke and the distinctive sounds of a naval battle. He took in the entire vista of the harbour with one sweep, his heart sinking at the sight. The docks were crammed with soldiers, their ranks still meshed together, but Septimus could now discern a semblance of order amongst the troops, the solid defensive line he had passed through bore witness to the discipline that had been reasserted upon the Ninth. At the centre of the throng Septimus spotted the banner of the legate, the rallying point for the legion's commanders, and he made his way towards the confluence of officers. He spotted Marcus as he approached, the grizzled centurion barking orders to an *optio* who ran off with a brief salute.

'Marcus!' Septimus shouted, his call causing the older man to spin around.

'Septimus you young pup, where have you been shirking?' he asked, his face betraying his relief.

Septimus smiled and punched the centurion's breastplate. 'We were held up by a wall of Carthaginians!' he replied.

Marcus nodded but his face turned grave. 'We're trapped, Septimus, completely cut off.'

Septimus nodded. He had realised as much. 'What's the plan?' he asked.

'Megellus wants to evacuate the *hastati* by sea and then he's going to lead a break-out east towards Brolium with the remaining troops.'

Septimus nodded, his mind recalling the briefing of two days before. The coast to the east was defined by a small range of mountains, no place for cavalry. He turned his head, his eyes drawn to the naval battle out in the harbour. It was chaotic, a tangle of interlocked galleys, many of them ablaze. As Septimus's gaze swept the inner harbour his heart lifted at the sight of the *Aquila*, the trireme running parallel to the shore, pulling away from a burning Carthaginian galley. Her aft-deck was crowded and Septimus could not pick out Atticus but he could clearly see Lucius, his familiar stature standing at the side rail to receive the message being relayed to every passing galley from the Legate of the Ninth.

Atticus's gaze swept over the sea of red crowding the docks of Thermae. The Ninth was completely trapped by the unseen Punic forces but even Atticus, unschooled in legionary tactics, knew that the legion's strength lay in open territory and not in the rat's maze of a coastal town. Lucius approached him from the side-rail.

'Message from the legate to the fleet,' he began. 'He requests that we evacuate the *hastati* by sea.'

Atticus nodded before scanning the entire harbour, his

mind calculating the number of men to be evacuated versus the remaining Roman galleys still capable of answering the call.

'Heave to!' Atticus ordered Gaius, 'Lucius, signal every galley in sight to clear their decks and begin the evacuation.'

'No!'

Every head on the aft-deck spun around to the aft-rail. Varro was standing there alone, his face twisted into a murderous glare.

'We will withdraw ... before it's too late!' he said, stumbling slightly as he walked towards Atticus.

'But, Tribune ...' one of the senators began, stepping into Varro's path, the young man pushing the senator aside.

'No! We are beaten. We cannot risk being attacked again, being ...' Varro's voice trailed off, his expression revealing the fear in his heart, his eyes darting to the solid wall of Carthaginian galleys spread across the harbour.

Atticus turned his back on the tribune, knowing every passing minute was vital.

'Come about three points to starboard. Prepare to dock!' he shouted.

'No!' Varro roared, 'I forbid it. We must escape while we can!'

'Tribune,' a senator said, his hand gripping Varro's elbow, 'we must help the Ninth.'

'No,' Varro repeated, shrugging the senator's grip aside, pushing his way forward again until he stood behind Gaius and Atticus.

'Steady, Gaius,' Atticus said, ignoring Varro, 'Ready to withdraw oars!'

The tribune reached out and grabbed Atticus's arm, spinning him around until his face was inches from Atticus's.

'Damn you,' Varro roared, his gaze filled with anger and

frustration, 'I order you to turn this galley around and get us out of here!'

Atticus stepped back, his fists bunched, anger coursing through his veins. Varro had rammed his galley into the gaping maw of battle without hesitation, his glory-laced dreams quickly shattered by reality in the quick of combat, the lives of many men already forfeit to his ignorance. Now he was willing to sacrifice the life of every Roman in Thermae just to save his own.

'Did you hear me, Captain?' Varro shouted, 'I order . . .'

Varro's words were cut short as Atticus struck him with an open hand across the cheek. The tribune staggered with the blow, his hand flying to his face as he tried to stand upright, the pain of his split upper lip stunning him. Atticus put out his hand to steady Varro but as he did Atticus spotted Vitulus advancing from behind the tribune, the legionary's hand sweeping across to grab the hilt of his sword. Atticus made to react when he sensed then saw an extended sword to his right as Lucius stepped forward to defend his captain. Vitulus's eyes swept from Atticus to Lucius and he halted his advance, his hand still holding the hilt of his sword but the blade remaining sheathed. He backed off a pace, turning his gaze once more to Atticus, his eyes conveying a thinly veiled warning.

'Lucius,' Atticus said, putting his hand out to lower Lucius's blade, 'Take the tribune below to the main cabin. See that he stays there for his own protection until we clear Thermae.'

Lucius nodded without a word and sheathed his sword before taking Varro by the arm, the stunned youth offering no resistance as he was led away.

Atticus sobered for a second, remembering that there were four senators on the aft-deck, each one witness to his insubordination and the crime of striking a commanding officer, a crime punishable by summary execution. His eyes caught those of the senator who had stepped across Varro's path. The senator held Atticus's gaze for a second before nodding imperceptibly, his decision made, and turned his back and looked out over the side rail. The other three senators watched his gesture intently and they each followed suit without hesitation, understanding and agreeing with his decision. Each had fought bravely when the *Punici* had boarded, moving into the battle line without hesitation. They were all former warriors who, as in countless times in their youth, shed their fear and stepped up to the fight. They had been ashamed of Varro's behaviour, the overt fear that shamed his rank, and so now they turned their backs. They had witnessed nothing.

Atticus inwardly sighed at the reprieve and turned his attention to the docks once more. He looked to his hand and found that it was shaking, a combination of anger and pure adrenaline at the foolhardy risk he had just taken. For a heartbeat he thought of Varro and the shocked demeanour of the young man after he had been struck. Atticus had seen that look many times before, the shock of physical violence from those who were unaccustomed to it. The feeling would not last and Atticus had no doubt that although the senators might deny that they had seen the strike, Varro would not forget the insult.

'All *principes* and *triarii* to stand in the defensive line. *Hastati* to form ranks at the docks!'

As the order was repeated across the ranks of the Ninth, Septimus began to make his way back to the defensive line. An outstretched arm stayed his progress.

'Where do you think you're going?' Marcus asked.

'To the line,' Septimus replied automatically, not understanding the question.

'The hell you are!' Marcus said. 'This is not your fight.'

'But . . .' Septimus began but Marcus cut him short.

'You're a marine Centurion, Septimus. Your duty lies with your galley and your men.'

Septimus made to protest again but Marcus ignored him, shouting over his shoulder, 'Signifier of the IV!'

Within seconds the standard bearer of the IV maniple was at their side.

'Septimus,' Marcus began, 'I need you to do me a favour.'

'Another one?' Septimus smiled, already realising what Marcus was going to ask.

'Take my *hastati* from the IV onto the *Aquila* and see them safely away.'

Septimus nodded, assuming the familiar mantle he had carried in the Ninth over two years before.

'Yes, Centurion,' Septimus replied, saluting the older man, his friend and former mentor.

Marcus punched Septimus's breastplate twice, his expression friendly. He turned without another word and strode off towards the defensive line, the more experienced men of his maniple already deploying under the *optio* of the IV. Septimus watched him until he was lost in the crush of men crowded along the docks. Only then did he lower his salute.

Septimus spun around to find the Signifier standing firm, the *hastati* of the IV finding their way unerringly to the standard as ranks were formed all along the dock. Septimus noticed there were no more than twenty *hastati* remaining, less than half their original number, their comrades lost in the initial charge and subsequent street fighting.

'Men of the IV, on me!' Septimus shouted as he advanced towards the water's edge, his eyes sweeping the inner harbour for the *Aquila* as the Roman galleys converged.

*

'There!' Atticus said, his outstretched hand pointing out the standard of the IV maniple. 'Do you see it, Gaius?'

'Yes, Captain,' the helmsman replied and adjusted the *Aquila*'s course. Within a minute the galley was lined up with dock directly opposite the standard of Septimus's old maniple where Atticus hoped to find his friend.

'Steerage speed!' the captain shouted, slowing the galley to two knots as Gaius brought the hull perpendicular to the dock.

'All stop!'

The blades of two hundred oars were dropped into the water, creating a drag that stopped the *Aquila* within a half-ship length. The order was given to raise oars as the ram gently nudged the dock and the *corvus* was lowered. To the left and right another six galleys followed suit, their exposed sterns protected by a screen of three more Roman galleys that kept a constant vigil against the remaining Carthaginian galleys milling around the harbour, the confluence of Roman ships with their deadly *corvi* keeping them at bay for the moment.

Atticus walked down the main deck, his eyes never leaving the head of the *corvus*, trying to discern the familiar sight of his friend amongst the throng of battle weary soldiers. He spotted him almost immediately and stood directly in his path. As Septimus approached he held his hand out, the centurion smiling in recognition. They shook hands, legionary style, with hands gripping forearms. Atticus slapped Septimus on the shoulder, the smile never leaving his face. He hadn't seen his friend since Mylae.

'Welcome home,' Atticus said, as the legionaries pushed around them, the main deck becoming ever more crowded.

Septimus nodded, his gaze taking in every detail of the galley he had served on for over a year, the rise and fall of the deck beneath his feet unfamiliar after so many months on land. He nodded. 'It's good to be back,' he replied.

The smile disappeared from his face as he looked over Atticus's shoulder to the carnage of the outer harbour.

'What are our chances?' he asked.

'We'll see,' Atticus replied. 'What are the Legate's plans?'

'He's going to break out east with the *principes* and *triarii*.'

Atticus nodded. He looked over his shoulder and counted the Roman galleys within sight. Enough to take the *hastati* but no more. The rest of the Ninth would be left to Fortuna's whim.

The *Aquila* pushed off minutes later, her full complement now supplemented by an additional eighty legionaries from the Ninth legion. The other Roman galleys unconsciously formed on the flanks of the *Aquila* as they turned from the inner harbour, their bows re-creating an arrow-head formation. There were near twenty in total and Gaius set their course for the centre of the line in the outer harbour, a course that would hopefully shatter the line and allow the greatest number of Roman galleys to escape. On their flanks Atticus noticed the loose Carthaginian galleys that had advanced to the inner harbour coming back up to attack speed, hoping to pick off individual ships from the edges of the formation. He unconsciously gripped the side rail, his grip tightening until the knuckles showed white, his mind calculating the speed and course of every galley, friend and foe. They weren't all going to make it.

Hamilcar reined in his horse as he reached the shoreline, his gaze sweeping across the entire harbour. For a brief second his expression turned to one of puzzlement. Then it slowly transformed into frustration and then into twisted anger. There were no more than forty Carthaginian galleys in the harbour, a number not much more than the Romans, the battle a nearly even contest instead of the overwhelming blow Hamilcar had planned. Where in Anath's name was the rest of the fleet? When he had left Panormus, the Carthaginians' main port on the northern coast of Sicily, over two weeks before, he had left an assembled fleet of one hundred galleys, each one fully manned and ready to sail, with orders to lay off Thermae in ambush.

Now only a fraction of that force was present and what was worse was that most were still following his original orders, forming a battle line to seal the harbour without fully engaging. That tactic was devised for a force of one hundred galleys; a force Hamilcar had been sure would coerce the trapped Romans into surrendering without a fight, but with the fleets more evenly balanced in numbers Hamilcar could see that the Romans were about to attempt to punch through the line.

Hamilcar noticed that some of his captains had had the intelligence to disregard his previous orders in light of the obvious change in the tactical situation but their attacks were uncoordinated and individual, their efforts insufficient to trigger the crushing defeat Hamilcar had wanted to inflict on the Romans. They were attacking on the flanks, picking off the exposed enemy galleys but the bulk of the Roman fleet continued without check, bearing down on the too shallow Carthaginian line.

Hamilcar's mount bucked wildly in fright beneath him and for the first time he realised he was screaming at the top of his lungs, his rage boiling over into a visceral challenge against the enemy that was going to escape annihilation and the unknown forces that had ruined his plan.

An almighty crack filled the air as a Carthaginian ram, driven by an eighty ton hull, smashed into the exposed timbers of a

Roman galley on the flank of the arrow formation, the strike accompanied by a demonic cheer from the *Punici*. The momentum of the blow pushed the stricken ship up onto the cutwater of the Punic galley and the crowded deck of the Roman galley tilted violently, throwing many of the evacuated legionaries into the churning waters of the harbour, their armour dragging them instantly below the waves. Atticus cursed as he witnessed the sight but he quickly returned his gaze to the waters ahead, watching as the Carthaginian line prepared to receive the full punch of the Roman attempt to break through.

'Aspect change, dead ahead!' Corin roared from the masthead and Atticus sought the Punic galley that had turned into their course.

'One point to starboard!' he commanded and Gaius responded with an alacrity that bore testament to the intuitive bond between the captain and helmsman.

'Punic galley on intercept course!' Corin shouted and Atticus imperceptibly nodded his head, the Carthaginian's course already obvious to all on the aft-deck.

'Prepare to sweep to port!' Atticus ordered.

Lucius rushed forward to the head of the gangway that led to the slave deck below, instantly relaying the captain's order to the drum master. He stayed on station in that position, looking over his shoulder to Atticus, his entire attention now focused on the captain, his trust in the younger man absolute.

'Septimus, prepare to deploy a shield wall, starboard side!'

The centurion arranged his men just shy of the starboard rail, their shields ready to overlap to form a protective barrier against the imminent hail of incoming missiles.

Atticus moved to beside Gaius as the helmsman lined up the *Aquila*'s hull, the finely balanced one hundred and thirty foot keel reacting to the smallest of touches. For a brief second he watched Gaius work, watching him weave the chimera that lulled the Carthaginians into thinking the Roman galley was committed to a frontal assault.

At eleven knots the *Aquila* closed the final hundred yards in seconds, the drum beat controlling her speed never changing as Lucius ordered the one hundred slaves of the starboard side to prepare to withdraw. They acknowledged the order without breaking stride, their bodies collectively tensing in anticipation of the command to follow, their minds long ago conditioned by the whip to follow commands blindly and without hesitation.

At twenty yards distance the Carthaginians screamed in belligerence, their ranks massed on the foredeck, ready to receive and repel the Roman legionaries. Atticus felt Gaius tense in expectation and he roared the order without conscious thought.

'Withdraw!'

The command crew moved almost simultaneously, Gaius sidestepping the *Aquila* to port as Lucius relayed the order below decks while Septimus deployed his ranks to the starboard rail. Within three strokes the slaves raised oars and hand-over-hand withdrew them until only the blades of the oars were exposed outside the hull.

Gaius leaned into the tiller as he re-righted the *Aquila's* course, bringing her back to a line parallel to the Carthaginian galley, not ten feet from the hull. Punic cries of alarm and rage filled the air as the cutwater of the *Aquila* struck the forward extended oars of the Carthaginian galley, the fifteen foot pine oars snapping against the relentless seventy-ton hull, the screams of the slaves manning the oars drowning out all sound save the crack of shattered wood. Many of the Carthaginians reacted instantly to the reversal of fortune, lifelong battle instincts dictating their response as they released

37

flights of arrows across a flat trajectory to the Roman galley, their volleys made impotent by the wall of legionaries' shields.

'Re-engage oars!' Atticus shouted as the *Aquila* cleared the hull of the Carthaginian galley.

The starboard oars were extended once more and the *Aquila*'s speed of eleven knots took her out of effective arrow range within seconds, the crew of the now disabled Punic ship left to scream curses across the widening gap. Atticus ignored the shouts and turned his full attention to the formation behind him, watching them as they bunched together to breach the gap the *Aquila* had created and they poured through the line.

A spontaneous cheer erupted from many of the young *hastati* on the deck of the *Aquila* as the galley breached the confines of the harbour and struck out into the open sea. It was a cheer that was not repeated by the experienced men of the galley, Atticus and Septimus amongst them as they stood together on the aft-deck. Atticus's gaze was locked on a forlorn Roman galley, the *Opis*, still fighting in the midst of hell in the outer harbour. She had been cut off from the formation and the Carthaginians were turning on her like a pack of hyenas, unleashing their fury at the escape of so many of the Roman galleys by slaughtering the few who remained, the desperate cries of the Romans diminishing as the last of them fell under Phoenician swords. Septimus was looking beyond the naval battle to the docks and thought of the Ninth legion that had long been his home and family, a bond that had been re-awakened over the past three months. Their breakout would be desperation itself, a knife edge existence between retreat and rout for the near three thousand men that remained and Septimus could not bring himself to believe that more than a third would see Brolium again.

'Raise sail, withdraw oars!' Atticus commanded, finally turning his back on Thermae. The order was repeated on the seventeen Roman galleys sailing in the *Aquila*'s wake, the remnants of a shattered fleet. The last of the adrenaline in Atticus's blood began to dissipate and he suddenly felt cold and exhausted, weary to his soul. Three months before the *Classis Romanus* had swept the sea clear of the enemy, a great victory that made all believe, even Atticus, that the new Roman fleet had reversed and destroyed the three hundred year old superiority of the Punic fleet with one fell swoop. It was a belief born from the confidence of fools and Atticus felt the bile of shame rise in his throat at the thought of his stupidity. They had not destroyed the behemoth, they had merely wounded it, and now the beast had reared its head in vengeance, a brutal retaliation that ran the waters of Thermae red with Roman blood.

CHAPTER TWO

He couldn't breathe; the fetid air was too thick, too laced with the smell of fear and human waste. His mind was filled with the sounds of despair, of men dying slowly in the pitch blackness. He tried to stand, to break out, but the ceiling closed in on him, pushing him down until he thought his back would break from the pressure. His skin began to crawl, the sensation assailing his extremities first, forcing him to draw his arms and legs until he was curled into a foetal position, the tiny filthy creatures finding every inch of his skin, feeling their way up his back and across his chest, their clicking sound smothering all other in his tormented mind. They reached his neck, and he stretched his head up with forlorn hope to escape them, their advance inexorable. The first of them touched his face, scuttling across his cheek and into his hair. It was followed by a dozen others, then a hundred, the clicking noise roaring in his ears; his face was alive with them.

Scipio shot up and screamed a cry of despair from the depths of his soul. His wife was instantly awake, her hand outstretched to touch her husband and release him from the bounds of his nightmare, the horrific dream that visited him every night without fail. He sat upright in the bed, swallowing huge breaths of air as if to cleanse his lungs, his eyes wide

40

open, focusing intently on the soft light of the lantern that was now constantly lit during the hours of darkness.

'Gnaeus . . .' Fabiola began, her voice gentle, searching for the man lost in that terrible place he had described to her only once, a place that had forever stolen part of his courage.

Scipio shrugged off her hand, throwing his feet out over the edge of the bed, resting his elbows on his knees as he rubbed the last vestiges of the nightmare from his face.

'Go back to sleep Fabiola,' he said knowing he himself would not sleep again that night. He rose and walked naked across the room, brushing aside the silken drapes that led to the cool night air of the balcony. On the lower reverse slope of the Capitoline Hill of Rome, the view from the balcony took in the flood plains of the Tiber, now bathed in the soft half-glow of a crescent moon. It was a beautiful calming sight but Scipio took no pleasure from it, his anger and shame still raw from the nightly reminder of his downfall.

Scipio had no idea how long he had been held prisoner in the lower hold of the Carthaginian galley after his capture at Lipara; weeks, a month, eternity, time had lost all meaning in the blackness of that space but one thought had always remained with him during that sentence, one thought he had coiled around his heart – revenge; a *vindicta* against the men who had robbed him of his rightful fate. Scipio's dark memories were interrupted and he started slightly as Fabiola's naked body, still warm from the bed, pressed against his back, warming the skin that had cooled in the pre-dawn air. Her arms enfolded around him and he raised his hands and encased hers in his across his chest. He knew she never slept either after his nightmares and whereas most nights he preferred his own company at this time, on this night, the night before he would take his first step on his road to vengeance, he accepted her presence without hesitation. He turned around and looked into her face, her delicate features made more beautiful by the half-light. He gazed deeply into her eyes, seeing the intelligence there, but also the cold ruthlessness that she hid from all except her husband. A smile crept onto her face and he nodded slightly, his anticipation rising at the thought of the hours ahead and the plan made possible by his wife's incredible instincts.

'Soon . . .' she whispered.

He nodded again. The word had become a mantra for him, a talisman for the time when the men who had crossed him would pay for their crime.

'Soon . . .' he replied, taking his wife by the hand and leading her back through the rippling folds of the silk curtains.

The cool blue-green water of Brolium harbour removed every thought from Atticus's mind as he swam deeper beneath the hull of the *Aquila*, her recently caulked keel illuminated by the distorted light of the mid-morning sun refracting through the gentle swell of the waves above. The pressure in his lungs deepened as he hung suspended beneath the water, his brief exhalation of air to achieve neutral buoyancy prompting his body to protest at the rationing of its sustenance. Atticus ignored the slight burning sensation in his chest, his intimate knowledge of his body's limits, tested many times, allowing him to clear his mind and take in the sweep of his galley's hull. They had hit the Carthaginian ship hard and three of the strake timbers of the bow port quarter were deeply scored where the galleys had connected. With an experienced eye Atticus surveyed the damage, searching for telltale air bubbles that would foretell a weakness but the hull was sound. A reflexive reminder to breathe interrupted Atticus's thoughts and he thumped the hull twice with his fist before striking out for the surface.

Atticus broke the water's skin just shy of the forward anchor line and he reached out for the tether, breathing the morning air deeply, the two minutes underwater refreshing him after a fitful night's sleep. He scanned the seventeen galleys clustered around the *Aquila* at the eastern end of the busy harbour, their separation from the hustle and flow of the port's normal activities a self-imposed exile to lessen the shame of their defeat.

The fleet had arrived in Brolium as dawn was breaking, their unexpected appearance drawing curious crowds to the dockside where the galleys quickly disembarked the soldiers of the Ninth before retiring to take station in deeper waters, the legionaries marching in loose formation to their encampment beyond the town. Varro, his guard, and the four senators had also disembarked, the tribune making directly for the port commander's residence straddling the hill above the town. Atticus remembered tracking Varro's departure from his ship intently, expecting the tribune to approach and challenge him on his insubordination but Varro had walked directly from the hatchway to the gangplank, and thence to the dock, never once looking back.

A rogue cloud eclipsed the sun, its passing accompanied by a light on-shore breeze that animated the wave tops and cooled Atticus's shoulders above the waterline, prompting him to strike out once more for the rope ladder hanging from the main deck. He clambered up the steps and crossed the main deck, shrugging on the tunic he had left on the side rail as he went. Septimus was on the aft-deck and Atticus nodded a welcome to him as he approached the centurion.

'Drill?' Atticus asked, noticing the weighted wooden training sword held loosely by Septimus's side.

'Definitely,' Septimus replied, his eyes ranging over the drawn ranks of the marines on the main deck, 'anything to stop their minds dwelling on the last twenty-four hours!'

Atticus nodded, smiling inwardly. It was the type of order he had come to expect from Septimus; a return to routine at all costs.

'No sign of the Tribune returning?' Atticus asked, looking beyond Septimus to the empty waters between the *Aquila* and the docks two hundred yards away.

'Not yet,' Septimus replied, conscious of his friend's unease over the inevitable confrontation that was yet to occur.

Atticus seemed not to hear the reply and so Septimus did not pursue the subject, aware of the situation from Atticus's earlier remarks. He slapped his friend on the shoulder as he passed him to leave the aft-deck, raising his sword and testing its weight as he went, his concentration switching to his marines. Septimus checked his pace slightly as he noticed the gaping holes in their ranks, gaps left by the dead and injured and he mindfully shrugged off his grief, determined as always that his men would know him only as a disciplined commander.

Scipio slowly surfaced from beneath the crystal-clear water, his right hand wiping away the vestiges of water running down his face as he lay back once more in the lukewarm bath, his breathing deep and controlled. The circular bath was positioned in the very centre of the square *tepidarium* chamber, affording Scipio a view of the three doors of the room. Two of these led to the first and third chambers of the bath house annexed to his home, the third, the one that now held his attention, led to the slave quarters. He glanced at the third door surreptitiously, his ears tuned in the tranquillity of the tiled room to any telltale sound that would announce the arrival of the bath attendant.

The door opened and a middle aged man entered. He was stooped at the waist, as if bowed over by an invisible weight and his head followed the contour of his back, his face down-cast in the ubiquitous manner of a slave. Scipio was careful not to reveal his interest in the man's arrival, conscious that any overt attention would be out of character and he suppressed the malicious smile that threatened his face as he recognised the slave. His name was Amaury, his pale skin marking him as a native of some foreign tribe beyond the great mountain range north of the Republic's borders. Slaves came and went in Scipio's household, often without stirring his attention, his indifference making them invisible. But Amaury, and one other, a stable lad named Tiago, were unique among the slaves of Scipio's household, a point discovered nearly three months ago by his wife Fabiola.

The door from the first chamber opened suddenly and Fabiola walked in amidst a cloud of steam from the scalding bath of the *caldarium* chamber. Scipio unconsciously marvelled at her poise and grace, her elegant stride acutely accentuated by the fact that she was completely naked, her innate confidence intensely alluring. She acknowledged her husband with a wry smile and slipped into the consuming waters in one fluid movement, her eyes never straying to the bath attendant who was considered nonexistent. Fabiola began to talk to her husband in light tones, her conversation ethereal, skipping from one trivial topic to another. Scipio simply nodded in reply, smiling briefly when Fabiola's words warranted the expression, his attention focused on the rehearsed question to come.

'Have you made a decision on your future in the Senate?' Fabiola asked, her tone never changing.

Scipio straightened imperceptibly, his thoughts touching briefly on how effortlessly Fabiola had introduced the topic into their conversation. He paused as if in contemplation before answering.

'I have,' he replied, his gaze never leaving his wife, his other senses intently focused on the slave in their midst. 'I will pursue the censorship.'

Fabiola nodded, feigning unspoken approval. 'So you believe you can gain the support of the *censores*?' she asked, referring to the two magistrates entrusted with bestowing the censorship.

'I am confident I can,' Scipio replied. 'I have been a consul, I am eligible for the position and with Duilius focused on the senior consulship, I will gain the *censores* implicit approval prior to the election, long before Duilius is even aware of my intention.'

Fabiola's face hardened at the mention of Duilius's name, an expression she did not have to fake.

'It is unthinkable that that shop steward, that farmer, will rise to the highest rank in the Senate,' she spat, her words not part of their carefully rehearsed conversation, her hatred for the man who had outmanoeuvred her husband temporarily overwhelming her normal self-control. She instantly regretted the slip and continued as if her invective had never been spoken.

'His power will surpass yours in the Senate,' she said. 'You will be at his mercy.'

'In all areas save one,' Scipio replied, his face also betraying the hatred he could not suppress, 'and using that all important, untouchable power the censor holds, I will make Duilius pay.'

Fabiola smiled maliciously at her husband's words and for a heartbeat Scipio forgot the charade they were playing, his thoughts focused instead on the sudden overwhelming attraction he felt for his wife, captivated by the malevolent beauty of her.

'Leave us,' he commanded brusquely over his shoulder to

Amaury. The slave withdrew instantly. Scipio watched him leave, his triumphant expression finally giving voice to his emotions. He turned once more to his wife, noting immediately her expression, one that acutely mirrored his own. He moved slowly around the bath to her side, his eyes locked on beauty, his excitement and arousal combining to create an intoxicating potion that chased every thought from his mind.

Amaury quietly closed the oak door to the *tepidarium* chamber, his shaking hand the only outward sign of his inward elation, his continually downcast face as always showing only mute servility. He paused in the corridor for a heartbeat, glancing left and right, making certain he was alone before dropping the towels in his hand to the floor, his feet already taking him unerringly to the stables at the rear of the house. A rare smile formed at the edges of his mouth as he walked, the thought of his master's gratitude causing him to unconsciously quicken his pace as his senses picked up the pungent smell of the stables and the rhythmic sound of the blacksmith's forge. He turned the corner at the end of the corridor and pushed open the reinforced door to the courtyard beyond, the white sunlight of late summer spilling past him to briefly mark his exit from the confines of the house. Again he glanced furtively left and right, conscious of his anomalous presence in the courtyard. He spotted Tiago grooming a bay foal and made directly for him, his mind wilfully forming the news he had just heard into the brief report that the stable lad would deliver before the day's end.

Varro felt a flush of shame build again in his cheeks as his eyes swept back and forward between the faces of the four other men in the room on the ground floor of the port commander's residence. They were ignoring him completely, talking amongst themselves as if he had silently departed after he had finished relaying the events of the past twenty-four hours. Twice he had interjected with a comment, his carefully prepared words dying mid-sentence as his voice was lost in the agitated debate, his opinion regarded as beneath consequence. Varro shifted once more on his feet, the deep fatigue of his body concentrated in the tormented muscles of his legs. He noticed the senior tribune of the Second Legion glance briefly in his direction and he straightened his back in anticipation, fighting the impulse to quail under the tribune's undisguised look of scorn, his shame rising unbidden again to manifest itself on his face.

Varro retreated inward as the conversation raged about him, his mind reaching back to the surety of the days and weeks before the disaster that was befalling his ambitions. He was so certain, so convinced, as his father had been, that the capture of Thermae was a mere formality, a stepping stone that would open every door in the corridors of power in Rome. The events of yesterday had reversed those aspirations. He replayed the battle in his thoughts, his mind's eye flashing images before him, his latent anger building slowly as he watched the sequence of events that had forged his fate, his pride baying for retribution as he remembered the insubordination of the Greek captain. The strike across his face was unforgivable, that blow the senators travelling with him had later claimed not to have witnessed, their confederacy with a lesser man adding grievous insult to his injury, their contemptuous looks beginning a pattern that Varro had seen mirrored in the senior tribune's face.

When the *Aquila* had pulled alongside the docks at Brolium, Varro had disembarked without looking back at the aft-deck, not sure that he could control his temper should he see the captain watching him. With the senators firmly on the captain's side Varro had realised that any accusation he levelled, without eye witness support, would likely be seen by others as a desperate attempt to apportion blame on a man who had proved himself at Mylae. It was therefore a simple matter of honour between two men and Varro's accusation would have to be followed by a challenge, a challenge the young tribune knew he could not win against a man ten years his senior and ten times his better in fighting skills. Varro had decided in the darkness of his cabin as the *Aquila* fled Thermae, that there would be no spoken accusation, no open challenge. There would be only revenge.

As Varro's gaze refocused on the present he noticed all eyes in the room were upon him and he realised they were waiting for him to answer a question he had not heard.

'I . . .' he hesitated, his expression exposing his lapse in concentration; 'I didn't . . .'

'The camp prefect asked you a question, Varro,' the senior tribune of the Ninth barked, indicating the eldest man in the room. 'When will you be ready to sail?'

'To sail?' Varro asked uncertainly, furious at himself for having drifted off from the conversation.

'For Rome man, for Rome!' the senior tribune said impatiently.

Varro's mind raced as he considered the question, realising that he had no idea how long it took to ready a galley for sea.

'We'll need to restock . . .' he began, trying to hide his lack of knowledge.

'I'll see that all necessary stores are made available from the barrack's stores,' the port commander of Brolium interjected; 'we can have the *Aquila* fully stocked before the tide turns, two hours at most.'

Varro nodded his assent but the port commander didn't seem to notice, looking instead to the senior tribune for approval.

49

'Make it so,' the senior tribune commanded, usurping Varro's position.

'We're agreed then,' the officer of the Ninth continued, turning his attention to his opposite number in the Second. 'Tacitus, you will take two thousand of the Second west on a forced march to intercept the retreating soldiers of the Ninth. I will take the remainder of the fleet on a parallel course along the coast.'

'But the fleet is . . .' Varro said, cutting himself short, instantly regretting his remark.

'Is what, Varro? Yours?' the tribune replied with a sneer. 'Your *fleet* was destroyed at Thermae. Now your only task is to sail to Rome and inform the Senate of your defeat!'

The tribune turned contemptuously from the younger man and nodded his dismissal to the prefect and port commander before saluting his equal from the Second. His gesture was returned and then all four men left the room without another word, each one passing Varro at arm's length, careful not to touch the disgraced officer for fear of tainting their own fortune. Varro stood rooted to the spot as the footfalls of the others faded along the corridor.

Hamilcar let his shield fall to the sand as the approaching skiff reached the line of breaking waves off the beach at Thermae. The two oarsmen rowed with skill, riding each wave as the current of the crest caught them, using the blades of their oars to balance the hull in the crashing surf. Hamilcar walked forward into the water as one of the oarsmen jumped nimbly from the boat, holding the bowsprit to steady the craft and allow their commander to board. Hamilcar jumped in and sat in the bow as the boat was swung around to once more face the anchored fleet in the mid-channel of the harbour, both oarsmen rapidly re-taking their positions, bending their backs into the task of sculling out through the breakers.

Hamilcar stared impassively past the two rowers to the beach he had just left and the exhausted soldiers who stood motionless along the line of seaweed that marked the furthest advance of the tide. They had fought well over the past twenty-four hours, harrying the Romans relentlessly as they retreated east along the shore. At first Hamilcar and his men could only pick off stragglers and the injured, surprised as they were by the sudden breakout of the Romans, a breakout that had postponed Hamilcar's reunion with the fleet until now. The enemy infantry's escape had been uneven and the narrow confines of the coastline had forced the Romans into an extended line of advance, a weak formation that Hamilcar's commanders had mercilessly exploited, advancing rapidly on the enemy flanks to ambush every rearguard the Romans formed. Hamilcar had personally led many of the charges, his anger at the frustration of his trap causing him to recklessly take the front in an effort to assuage his fury. His orders had been disobeyed; his fleet cut to an ineffective fraction of its original size by an unknown person. Exposing the traitor had become the dominant thought in Hamilcar's mind and with the pattern of attack established, he had delegated the pursuit of the Romans to one of his commanders, freeing him to return to Thermae to find his betrayer.

The skiff pulled neatly alongside the flagship, a quinquereme named the *Alissar*. Hamilcar leapt onto the stepladder and climbed up to the main deck, ignoring the crew assembled in his honour, his gaze instead seeking out the man he had placed in command of the fleet. Himilco stood front and centre, the captain's salute formal and exact. He stepped forward towards Hamilcar, extending his hand as he did.

'Welcome aboard, Commander,' he said, a broad smile forming across his narrow face. 'Congratulations on a great victory!'

The crew cheered on cue, their voices raised in praise of their commander but Hamilcar's stern expression never changed and as he neared the captain he noticed a shade of doubt flash across Himilco's eyes.

'Follow me,' Hamilcar said brusquely, cutting off the captain before he could utter another word.

Himilco hesitated for a second, his mind racing to comprehend Hamilcar's attitude, before he hurried after his commander.

Hamilcar pushed open the door of the main cabin under the aft-deck and walked into the middle of the room. It was sparsely furnished, as befitting a battleship, with a map-strewn table in the centre and a cot on the starboard side. A large personal chest stood on the opposite side of the cabin. Hamilcar closed his eyes and dropped his head until his chin rested on his chest, breathing deeply in an effort to control the urge to run the captain through with the blood-stained sword at his side, to wipe the asinine smile off his face. 'Congratulations,' the fool had said and Hamilcar's hand moved instinctively to the hilt of his sword. He heard Himilco's footfalls behind him and the heavy sound of the door closing. They were alone.

With a speed that defied the eye Hamilcar spun around, drawing his sword in a single swipe as he did, the blade clearing the scabbard with inches to spare, its once smooth edge nicked and scored from the previous day's combat. Himilco's reaction was measured only in his face, his every defence too slow to respond to the unexpected attack as Hamilcar covered the gap between them before Himilco's eyes could blink in surprise. The blade stopped an inch from the captain's throat; its vibrating point the only outward sign of the immense self-control Hamilcar had exercised in staying its thrust.

'Where is the rest of the fleet?!' he shouted, his anger forcing the point of the blade against the skin of Himilco's throat, drawing blood from the sallow skin.

'My lord?' Himilco asked, his confusion entangled with fear.

'The fleet,' Hamilcar roared. 'The one hundred galleys I assembled in Panormus with orders to sail to Thermae. I saw only forty here yesterday. Where are the rest?'

'Off the coast of Malaka in Iberia,' Himilco stammered, his expression one of bewilderment, his hands now raised reflexively in a futile gesture.

'By whose orders?' Hamilcar barked, readying himself to run Himilco through in anticipation of his answer.

Again confusion broke through the captain's expression of fear. 'By your orders,' he replied, a plea in his voice, 'Councillor Hanno issued them on your behalf three days after you left Panormus.'

Now it was Hamilcar's face that showed shock and the tension in his sword arm lessened without conscious thought, the point of the blade moving down to rest against the captain's chest.

'Hanno?' he said, almost to himself.

'Yes, my Lord,' Himilco replied, relief rushing through him as the answer the commander had sought was finally found.

'He told you it was my order?'

'Yes, my Lord,' Himilco repeated.

Hamilcar stepped back and sheathed his sword, his mind now ignoring the captain, its focus instead on the discovery of the man who had ruined his trap and rendered it incomplete.

'Assemble a squad and set sail for Panormus immediately,' Hamilcar said.

Himilco sensed his commander's intentions and spoke with a renewed sense of safety, conscious that Hamilcar's sword was no longer at his throat.

'The councillor sailed for Carthage the day we left Panormus,' he ventured.

'Then we follow,' Hamilcar replied after a second's thought. 'All speed to Carthage.'

Himilco saluted and left the cabin, his steps almost breaking into a run in an effort to put distance between himself and his commander's sword.

Hamilcar watched him go, replaying the captain's words in his mind as he did. In by-passing Panormus he would miss a prearranged meeting with one of his senior officers, Belus, a man to whom Hamilcar had already entrusted a vital component of a greater scheme and for a moment he worried that Hanno might have also obstructed those orders. He immediately dismissed his concern, confident in Belus's loyalty and he turned his full attention to Hanno once more. The councillor's actions were inexplicable and his subterfuge, his use of Hamilcar's authority, was an act of treachery that any man who was ranked less than Hanno would pay for with his life. The depth of Hamilcar's thoughts were undisturbed even as the dull thud of the drum beat began, its sound reverberating through the timbers of the *Alissar* as the galley got underway, her crew bringing her about on a course that would take her to the city of Carthage.

Gaius Duilius sat silently in the centre of the semi-circular forum of the *Curia Hostilia*, the senate house of Rome, his eyes ranging over the faces of the other senators of the house, their attention focused on the potent, almost hypnotic words of the speaker, Lucius Manlius Vulso Longus. Outside, the afternoon sun was suspended in the western sky; the shadows and shapes it created across the marble floor of the inner chamber transfixed in the still air.

Duilius looked upon friend and foe alike, on the undecided

and the resolute in each group, his mind calculating odds and testing scenarios. As he watched, many of the senators nodded with a practiced look of sagacity at the words Longus was speaking and Duilius smiled inwardly, awaiting the applause he knew would follow, approbation for the keynote of the speech that he had written for Longus. The senators applauded on cue and once again Duilius used the opportunity to search beyond the outward displays of approval and agreement on the senators' faces to try to divine their true intentions.

The elections were less than three days away and although Duilius was confident of victory, he was acutely aware of the limits to his knowledge, conscious that although his accession to the senior consulship was assured, the size of his majority in the secret ballot was yet unknown as were the true strength and numbers of his adversaries. As the victor of Mylae, Duilius was still exploiting the residual gratitude of the people of Rome and the Senate and he had used his influence to engineer Longus's nomination to the junior consulship, his speech a carefully crafted manifesto that Duilius hoped would win favour with the undeclared majority of the house.

As Duilius's gaze reached the far end of the forum, he swept his gaze around again, this time in search of Longus's main rivals. They were scattered sporadically amongst the 300 strong senate, each one an ear of wheat amidst the chaff, some rising higher than the others, but all members of the ancient conservative Patrician class against whom Duilius had battled during his entire career in the Senate. That contest had reached its zenith the previous year when Duilius had been junior consul to Gnaeus Cornelius Scipio, the patriarch of their pompous faction. The open rivalry had brought to the surface the supporters of each man, and by extension each philosophy, conservative verses progressive, and the house had divided along those lines with the centre occupied by a fickle majority whose votes were bought and extorted by the opposing forces. Now however, with Scipio discredited and in absentia, his supporters had dispersed and were once more hidden amongst the confusion of the malleable centre, their concealment reducing Duilius's ability to judge the outcome of each vote.

As Longus finished his speech, many in the house stood to applaud the young senator and he smiled boldly at his supporters. Duilius stood also as an overt sign of his endorsement, moving his clapping hands from left to right as if to display this approval to the entire house. He caught the young senator's gaze for a brief instant and Longus nodded his thanks, his fawning devotion evident to even the most obtuse observer and Duilius looked away quickly, hoping to wipe the sycophantic smile from Longus's face, the expression unwise given that the majority of senators believed in the tradition that each consul, both junior and senior, should be their own man, each one, at least overtly, acting as a check against the power of the other.

Longus stepped down from the podium and made his way to his seat as a rival took to the centre of the floor to make his own case for election. Duilius turned in his seat, away from the speaker but also from Longus, conscious that the young senator was probably staring across at him, hoping once again to catch his eye. The thought made Duilius uncharacteristically re-examine his decision to promote Longus as a candidate for the junior consulship. With his own victory assured, Duilius's endorsement carried significant weight and he had chosen carefully, conscious that his decision would be examined minutely by every senator. Longus had many flaws as a man, his inexperience exacerbating many of them but Duilius was sure of one inimitable quality that Longus possessed, and that was loyalty. In the maelstrom of shifting alliances and duplicitous allegiances that defined the Senate, Duilius would always be sure of Longus's support. Duilius's uncertainties dissipated as he reaffirmed his decision and he let his mind drift to other topics, ignoring the rambling polemic from the speaker at the podium. His gaze extended to the colonnaded entrance to the chamber and lengthening shadows of the day, consciously willing the sun to speed its progress to a point below the horizon. As his eyes moved over the spaces between each column he spotted the familiar figure of Lutatius, his private secretary, and the sight arrested his attention and chased every thought from his mind. Lutatius was unmoved, his gaze locked on his master and although he did not gesture, his mere presence spoke of an urgency that Duilius could not ignore. The consul stood up and walked directly to the exit, his abrupt movement causing the speaker to pause in indignation at the unprincipled insult inherent in Duilius's departure and a muttered undertone of disapproval swept through the house. Duilius was oblivious however, his attention locked on Lutatius. Sundown, the traditional close of business in the Senate, was less than an hour away, Duilius thought. What was so urgent that Lutatius could not wait for his return home?

Lutatius stepped back around the column into the full glare of the afternoon sun as Duilius approached, screening himself from the prying eyes of any in the chamber. Duilius rounded the column, shielding his eyes as they adjusted to the sunlight reflecting off the marble columns and flagstones, the residual heat of the day in marked contrast to the cool atmosphere of the Senate chamber. Lutatius looked furtively over his shoulder as his master stood before him, checking again to see if anyone was within earshot, conscious as always of how easy it was to betray oneself through carelessness.

'What news?' Duilius asked his private secretary, a man who also tightly controlled the consul's extensive web of spies across the city.

'Scipio,' Lutatius replied simply.

'He has revealed his plans?' Duilius ventured, his excitement mounting.

'Yes,' Lutatius nodded. 'Tiago brought news from Amaury this very hour.'

'And?'

'The censorship, my lord, Scipio plans to attain the censorship.'

Duilius was instantly and simultaneously flooded with conflicting emotions. Relief and triumph at having finally learned of Scipio's plans and dread at the havoc Scipio could wreak should he succeed. The two censors were elected each year from the ranks of the former consuls serving in the Senate. By tradition, one of the positions was guaranteed to a retiring senator as a sinecure recognising a lifetime's service to the state, while the other was sought through application by the more ambitious former consuls. Duilius had already taken steps to ensure an ally, Anicius Paulinus, who would be the forerunner for the second position but now, with Scipio's intentions exposed, Paulinus's appointment was far from secure.

Without another word, Duilius swept past his secretary and down the steps of the Curia, Lutatius falling in behind at a respectable distance, the business of the Senate proceeding unabated within the chamber, unaware that the most powerful man in Rome would not be returning that day.

'Skiff approaching!'

Atticus walked quickly to the side-rail to see the small boat approaching the *Aquila* from the distant quay. He instantly recognised Varro sitting in the fore of the boat, his tribune's helmet distinctive even at a distance of a hundred yards. He was alone with his guard, the senators evidently remaining in

Brolium, and Atticus found himself staring, his mind trying to fathom the thoughts of a man he did not know in any sense. Varro had been born into a life of privilege and wealth where power and command was a birthright. Atticus was born a fisherman's son in a squalid hovel in the backstreets of Locri and had clawed his way to the top of his world, a pinnacle that was insignificant to a Roman magistrate's son. Atticus tried to reverse their positions in his mind in a complex attempt to find a way for Varro to save face without Atticus losing, at best, his commission and at worst, his life.

'Forget it,' Septimus said beside Atticus and the captain spun around with a puzzled expression on his face.

'Forget what?' he asked.

'I know you too well, Atticus,' Septimus replied, standing shoulder-to-shoulder with his friend. 'You're trying to think of a way out of your problem with that young idiot Varro.'

'And?' Atticus asked.

'And I'm saying forget it. I came across his type many times in the Ninth. One hand on his dagger and the other in daddy's back pocket; every one of them an ambitious viper with an ego fit for the Senate. Whatever fate he's decided for you he'll be damned if he lets anyone change his course, especially you.'

Atticus nodded, chasing any thoughts he had of explanation and reconciliation from his mind. He walked away from Septimus and began pacing along the rail.

Before Mylae the *Aquila* had been Atticus's to command with Septimus unobtrusively responsible for the marines, their ranks equal and separate, with no higher power to answer to beyond their standing orders to keep the shipping lanes of the Republic clear of pirates. It was a task that would often keep them at sea for months, away from the rigid command structures that entangled them every time they entered port, and Atticus had always relished the independence. That freedom had been lost at Mylae however, when the *Aquila* had been absorbed into the *Classis Romanus*, a lone wolf suddenly becoming part of a larger pack, no longer hunting prey using its singular skill but as part of a group, the hunt becoming a complex power play of command and ambition, where opportunities drew men like Varro to the fray.

Atticus stopped pacing as the skiff came alongside, watching the tribune disembark with the agile ability of youth. As he waited, Atticus felt anger rise slowly within him for the vicissitudes of fate that had placed his life at the whim of a man like Varro. At Mylae, Duilius had stood on the aft-deck of the *Aquila* as commander of the greatest fleet Rome had ever put to sea and yet he had treated Atticus as an equal, their shared fight uniting them against the Carthaginians, the consul understanding that in battle, men were equal before Pluto, the lord of the underworld. Varro, on the other hand, treated those of lesser rank with near contempt and negligible respect, irrespective of their past service to the Republic. For a brief second Atticus recalled the challenges of his hard fought career and his concern for his fate fled his mind. He had fought greater foes than the young tribune who now approached him across the main deck and he'd be damned if he was going to yield without a fight, even if redemption was a forlorn hope. Atticus straightened his back and stood to attention as the tribune covered the remaining steps between them on the aft-deck and he saluted smartly.

'Make preparations for Rome, Captain,' Varro said brusquely.

Atticus hesitated for a heartbeat, waiting for the tribune's next words, but none were forthcoming. 'Yes, Tribune,' he replied, repeating his salute.

Varro spun on his heal and walked purposefully away to the hatchway that led to the main cabin below. Atticus watched him go, baffled by the brevity of the exchange. The tribune's expression had been near inscrutable, cold and determined, but Atticus had noticed something in Varro's eyes, something that alerted his instincts, a mere flicker of hostility that spoke of a deeper emotion, an unspoken antagonism that belied the calm exterior the tribune had so deceitfully presented. Atticus had fought many enemies in his life and he knew the look well, knew its portent as surely as if the tribune had challenged him openly on the aft-deck.

CHAPTER THREE

Longus walked quickly through the bustling streets of the Palatine quarter, holding a firm line of advance on the right hand side of the road, sidestepping only to avoid the crumbling piles of animal waste that had yet to be scavenged by the street urchins who would sell the dung to farmers outside the city. The crowds of people on the street seemed unconsciously aware of his presence and they moved aside to allow him to proceed unhindered. It was a capital offence to strike a senator of Rome and none would dare take the chance that an accidental collision might be construed as an attack by an irate senator on his way home from the Curia. But Longus was not heading towards his own home; instead his destination was a house he knew almost as intimately as his own, the home of his mentor and idol Duilius.

As Longus walked through the darkening streets his concern concentrated all his attention on the flight of Duilius from the chamber less than an hour before. He had been watching the consul intently, waiting for him to turn and nod his approval for Longus's delivery of the speech that Duilius had so masterfully composed the evening before; words that Longus had infused with passion and meaning, but the consul's sudden inexplicable departure had thrown Longus's elation into turmoil and instead he found himself attempting to silence the whispered censures that swept the chamber at the consul's flagrant disregard for Senate protocol. Longus's remaining time in the Senate had been torturous and twice he had made a determined move to depart early only to have his nerve fail him, realising he did not have his mentor's mettle.

Longus had never been an ambitious man and his whole life to this point had been lived by the formula dictated to him by his ancestors and the tradition of his family. At sixteen, a year after his father had died, Longus had joined the legions as a tribune and waited out his obligatory service in a quiet outpost in Campania. At twenty he had followed his father's path into the Senate and thereafter he had settled into the daily life of a Roman senator, attending speeches and votes, hosting trade delegations and variously busying himself with the minutiae of a thriving city. That plodding existence had changed with the arrival of Gaius Duilius to the Senate, a charismatic and ambitious *novus uomo* and Longus had been drawn to him like a moth to a flame, igniting a determination within him that he never knew existed, and he had supported Duilius every step of his rise to power. He had never craved the power his mentor sought, only his approval and so now he was prepared to stand at Duilius's right hand as junior consul, a position he coveted only because his idol wanted it so.

Longus was admitted into Duilius's house after only one knock on the door and he followed the servant across the meticulously swept outer-courtyard to the entranceway to the house proper. It led into an atrium where the sound of trickling water into the inner pool blended serenely with the flicking candlelight. The atrium was unadorned but careful inspection revealed the quality of the marble columns and flooring; understated evidence of the vast wealth of the owner that contrasted sharply with the heavily ornamented atria that were typical of senators' homes, where statues competed for space with precious antiques and fine tapestries. It was a simplicity that Longus had tried to emulate in his own home without success and he wondered, as often he had before, whether Duilius's humble background was the source of his unaffected modesty.

The servant led Longus through a series of rooms, adhering to the consul's earlier command to bring the young senator directly to him when he arrived. Duilius was walking slowly around a miniature garden at the rear of the house, a favourite retreat where he marshalled his thoughts and set his mind to finding the solution to every problem he encountered. The garden was immersed in shadows, the crepuscular evening light dissipated by the overhanging interwoven trellis and a servant moved discretely in the background, lighting sporadic candles that the gardener had placed with care to accentuate the beauty of the inner sanctum.

'Good evening Longus,' Duilius said, as he heard the approaching footsteps, his back still facing the entranceway.

'Consul, I came as quickly as I could,' Longus replied, his voice laced with agitation.

'I knew you would,' Duilius said as he turned, a half smile on his face, an expression Longus took as gratitude and he returned the smile ten-fold.

Duilius recommenced his easy stride around the garden and Longus watched him intently, shifting his weight from one foot to another, anxious to learn why the consul had fled the Senate chamber. Within seconds his impatience got the better of him and he blurted out the question that had plagued him over the previous hour. Duilius turned again, this time however there was no trace of a smile, only a hint of the frustration that lurked just beneath the surface.

'Scipio plans to attain the censorship,' he said simply.

Longus nodded slowly, his mind racing to find the exact reason why Duilius was concerned, eager to place his thoughts on a parallel to his mentor's. He could not discern a reason however; in fact he thought Scipio's appointment would be a godsend as it would place him further from the centre of power in the Senate.

Duilius watched Longus impassively, examining his transparent facial expressions, knowing within a minute that the young senator had not seen the overwhelming problem that Scipio's appointment would bring. He smiled sardonically to himself at the senator's ignorance. How often had he seen it before in the young pups who inherited their place in the Senate? Their casual indifference to money, their ignorance of how wealth was created and maintained, the skilled brilliance of their ancestors who created the family fortune lost and forgotten, diluted by generations who simply fed from the cornucopia.

'What are the duties of the censors?' Duilius asked, suddenly impatient with Longus and his inability to see beyond his own privileged world, a world that Duilius had entered through ambition and not the womb.

Longus was taken aback and took a second to answer, forming his reply before he spoke. 'They are mainly responsible for the census.'

'And in completing the census, what information must each citizen divulge?'

Again Longus paused, sensing Duilius's impatience, still searching for the key. 'He must register his holdings, his property both in the city and elsewhere.'

'For what purpose, what do the censors dictate with that information?'

'They set the property tax for every citizen.' Longus said slowly in answer as understanding flooded his mind. 'But surely Scipio could not target you directly without upsetting everyone whose holdings are similar?'

Duilius laughed derisively, his gaze penetrating.

'Of course he could,' Duilius replied angrily. 'He could set a separate tax on agricultural lands of a certain acreage, or those immediately straddling the city as mine are, or those newly registered in the past ten years. He could bankrupt me within a year and his decision would be inviolate, outside the control of the Senate.'

'But what of the other censor?' Longus asked. 'Surely he could counteract any aggressive policy of Scipio's, ensure that the taxation is just.'

'The other censor,' Duilius scoffed, 'will be a toothless old retiring Senator with his best years far behind him. Whoever he is he will be no match for Scipio.'

Longus paused for a moment. 'Perhaps Scipio's attempt to attain the position will fail,' he offered. 'People already speak of your ally Paulinus as if he is guaranteed the position.'

'My ally Paulinus,' Duilius thought, his mouth unconsciously twisting into a sneer of derision. Before Mylae, Paulinus, a patrician, had been one of the uncommitted of the Senate, his alliance changing with every vote, his loyalty for sale to the highest bidder. Since Mylae however, he had openly supported Duilius, a support Duilius had welcomed and capitalised on by persuading the former consul to stand forward for the censorship, but his alliance had never been assured and Duilius had planned to keep him on a tight leash.

The final decision on the position rested with the *censores*, the two magistrates, but even here Duilius couldn't be sure what influence Scipio would exert over them, monetary or otherwise and even if Duilius managed to secure Paulinus's appointment, the patrician's former avarice or even loyalty to the coterie of ancient families might eventually make him Scipio's pawn.

Duilius shook his head, amazed at the simplicity and brilliance of Scipio's plan. 'One way or another,' Duilius muttered, 'Scipio will control the censorship.'

'We must stop him.' Longus spoke without thinking.

'There is only one way,' Duilius said, almost to himself, preparing to speak aloud the only solution he had been able to find over the previous hour as he waited for Longus's arrival. 'I must attain the position myself,' he said. 'It is the only way. I can trust no other former consul in that position. There is too much at stake.'

'But the senior consulship?' Longus said aghast.

'Is a powerless title without the money to back it up!' Duilius said, his frustration boiling over, silently cursing Scipio for the hundredth time.

'I could back you, financially,' Longus ventured.

'No, my friend,' Duilius said smiling, 'you do not have the resources.'

Longus nodded in silence.

'But I could back you,' Duilius continued in a near whisper.

Scipio glanced furtively over his shoulder as his entourage turned yet another corner in the warren of streets that made up the ancient Esquiline quarter of Rome. It was two hours past sunset and the feeble light of the rising quarter moon barely penetrated the heavy shadow cast by the hill which dominated the entire quarter. Scipio's four heavily armed guards moved cautiously and silently in an effort to remain inconspicuous. Each man was a veteran of the legions, battle scarred and experienced; their courage without question and yet they moved with the trepidation of raw recruits, their swords drawn and ready in a defensive circle around the senator. Scipio sensed their nervousness and he consciously reached beneath his robe for the hilt of his own dagger, fingering the pommel lightly before wrapping his hand around the hilt. The jewelled handle was warm in his grip and he withdrew the blade an inch from its scabbard, testing the fluidity of his draw, the familiar motion calming his nerve.

The scurrying sound of feet caused Scipio to stop suddenly and his guard halted without command, all eyes turned to their right in an effort to penetrate the darkness and identify the perpetrators. Scipio turned his head slightly in order to extend the limit of his hearing but the sound had dissipated and the streets were silent once more. He began to walk warily on and his guard moved again as one, eager to complete their journey to the house that lay just beyond the next corner. Scipio felt his heart beating rapidly in his chest once more and drew in a deep breath to ease its tempo, ignoring the stench of the fetid night air. As his heart rate returned to normal he cursed once more the necessity of the late hour of his meeting, knowing that the risk of travelling through the streets of Rome at night were enormous, even in one of the most affluent quarters of the city. The darkness belonged to the roving gangs of starving poor who took to the streets at night, scavenging for food scraps and prowling for naive visitors to the city or drunks caught unawares by nightfall. They killed without hesitation or fear of retribution, the darkness hiding their vicious crime and Scipio knew he would only be safe behind the walls and stout doors that protected each house in the quarter.

As the group rounded the last quarter Scipio immediately spied the torch illuminating the door of their destination. It was the only light on the street, acting not only as a beacon for him and his men but also as a sign to the roving gangs that the gate would be in use and Scipio's guards increased their vigilance as they covered the final yards of their journey. The lead soldier reached the door and tapped it lightly with the pommel of his sword and a small, face-high panel slid open in the door to reveal a wary expression in shadow. The eyes moved left and right but settled on the figure of Scipio who stood in the centre of the group, his own face bathed in the orange glow of the torch. The panel slid shut and the door reverberated with the sound of a series of bolts being withdrawn, the grating sound of metal unnaturally loud in the deceptively quiet street.

Scipio passed first through the doorway into the dimly lit courtyard, never looking back as the door closed firmly behind him, his gaze instead searching the gloom for the man he had made the hazardous journey to meet. The courtyard was empty however, save for the doorman and a servant standing by the inner door to the house and Scipio reflected bitterly at the fall in his political status. Marcus Atilius Regulus was Scipio's equal, a former consul and member of the Patrician class, but Scipio was still in office and so etiquette demanded that Regulus should meet Scipio on the threshold of the door to the inner house. He was nowhere to be seen however, and Scipio was forced to swallow the insult in an effort to remain focused on his goal.

Regulus sat in the formal greeting room of his house, reclined on a confusion of cushions, a half-filled goblet of wine lolling in his hand. He was a heavyset man with a high colour that was accentuated by the candle and torchlight that infused the room. He stared at the doorway which led to the atrium beyond but his vision was without focus, his mind endlessly pondering a single question, 'Why did Scipio want to meet him?' The messenger had arrived earlier that day, Scipio's note brief and without allusion, the demand for a meeting thinly disguised as a request. Regulus had immediately sent word of acceptance, knowing he could not refuse the consul, even if ostensibly Scipio was a spent force in Rome.

'The consul has arrived,' a servant announced from the doorway and Regulus waved the man away as he leaned forward to stand up. He had previously decided to deny Scipio the normal respect due to a sitting consul and not meet him at the main door, but basic civility demanded that he greet him as a guest and so Regulus placed his goblet on the low table and moved towards the doorway. A moment later Scipio swept into the room.

'Good evening, Consul,' Regulus said, his voice a high pitched tone that seemed to emanate from the back of his throat, his face breaking into a forced smile.

'Good evening, Regulus,' Scipio replied, his own expression a perfect mask of friendship, a practiced skill that hid his true feelings.

Regulus motioned to the raised seating area in the centre of the room, an open-sided square of low couches around a table lain with a sprawling feast, a banquet fit for a multitude of two.

'Please,' Regulus motioned with his hand, allowing Scipio to be seated first as the guest.

Scipio nodded and took the seat vacated moments before by Regulus at the head of the table, intentionally occupying the most important position, a seat normally reserved for the host and only relinquished to the most honoured of guests. It was a subtle point but with it Scipio retook the advantage in the continual power-play that had become almost instinctive after so many years in the Senate. For an instant Regulus's expression showed disapproval but he instantly swept it aside with a smile and he sat to Scipio's right, clapping his hands lightly as a signal for the servants to enter and begin serving the evening meal.

For the next thirty minutes the two men talked of inconsequential matters, touching lightly on matters debated every day in the Senate. It was mere foreplay, courtesy and convention dictating that the more serious topics be avoided until after the meal was ended. Regulus however, was unable to contain his curiosity and he blurted out his opening question before the servants had completed clearing the largely untouched food.

'So what brings you to my humble abode after dark, Consul? Why the need for such secrecy?' he asked.

Scipio was forced to summon all his will power in an effort to remain calm at Regulus's vulgarity but his voice betrayed his inner anger as he leaned into the senator.

'Dismiss your servants first,' he breathed in a near whisper, the timbre of his voice disguising his anger.

Regulus was taken aback slightly by the request but he complied and within seconds the two men were alone in the room.

'I have come,' Scipio began slowly, committing himself fully to the plan he had devised, 'to make you a proposition, Regulus. I have come to offer you the position of senior consul.'

Regulus was stunned, disbelief robbing him of a response. Scipio was mad, surely unhinged if he believed he could offer such a thing. He was still senior consul but only in name and even that for only a few days more. His enemies in the Senate openly mocked him using the cognomen they had conferred upon him after Lipara. *Asina*, they called him, the donkey. The word made Regulus smile involuntarily and before he could stop himself he was laughing uproariously at the absurdity of the moment, a morsel of food shooting from his mouth as his face twisted in mockery.

Scipio felt his entire body tense in sudden rage as he witnessed Regulus's response. His fist clenched into a tight ball and an almost insurmountable urge swept down his arm, his anger screaming at him to ram his fist into the face across from him. He conquered his emotions once more and let Regulus expend his laughter until the room lapsed once more into silence.

'My apologies, Scipio,' Regulus said with false sincerity. 'Since your request for a meeting I have searched my mind for the reason. Believe you me, this was not one I envisaged.'

'Nevertheless,' Scipio said, as if Regulus's reaction had not occurred, 'I am in a position to offer you the senior consulship.'

Regulus made to respond but he stayed his words. He searched Scipio's face for signs of duplicity but there were none and he forced his mind to ignore the absurdness of the proposal and examine it anew. Scipio was still a powerful man, a patrician with enormous wealth and, before Lipara, a man with a fearsome reputation in the Senate. It was probable that he still held sway over many of the junior senators, and history had shown that men could recover from calamitous defeat in battle, but again Regulus was wary. Surely it was too soon for Scipio to rise again, to have regained the support of the senior senators and yet Regulus could sense the utter conviction in Scipio's offer. He continued to stare at the senior consul and for the first time a rueful frown appeared at the corner of his eyes.

'How?' Regulus said, all trace of joviality now gone from the room. 'The election is in two days and Duilius currently stands unopposed.'

Scipio nodded as if the fact was tiresome.

'And with good cause,' Regulus added. 'His victory at Mylae gives him the support of every senator in the house.'

'Not every senator,' Scipio replied cannily.

'Granted,' Regulus said after a moment's pause. 'There are

some, maybe even many who would prefer that a "new man" did not become senior consul, but none will challenge him openly, not when defeat is certain and their challenge would gain them a powerful enemy.'

'But what if he didn't stand for election?' Scipio asked.

Again Regulus made to scoff, but he suppressed his natural reaction and continued instead to search Scipio's hard gaze.

'Go on . . .' he said, trying to draw out Scipio's reasoning, the specific information he so obviously had.

'If Duilius did not stand, you could put your name forward for nomination. You have held the position before. You are renowned and well respected. With Duilius's name removed from the ballot the Senate would favour a senior patrician.'

'But what of Longus?' Regulus asked. 'He is Patrician and his nomination for junior consul is foremost. He would almost certainly strike for the higher position *if* Duilius withdraws.'

'Longus is Duilius's puppet.' Scipio scoffed. 'A vote for him is a vote for Duilius and every senior senator knows it. You are by far the better man.'

Regulus nodded politely at the superficial complement, but he struggled to remain guarded, a creeping ambition taking hold within him at the thought of once more holding the highest office, a position he had held when his star was at its zenith many years before. Since then he had become a peripheral figure in the Curia, content to rest on his achievements. Or so he had believed before Scipio's offer was revealed. He sat forward, his mind already calculating the possible outcome of an imagined vote.

'You believe the Senate will choose me over Longus?' he asked.

Scipio nodded. 'Over the years I have amassed considerable credit with many of the junior senators of the house, many of whom owe me dearly despite my current state.' Scipio said slowly, knowing he had to reveal his innermost hand if he was going to commit Regulus to his cause. 'I have already called in each of those favours and alliances and to a man they have each put their vote secretly at my disposal.'

Regulus remained silent, his mind examining Scipio's proposal from every angle.

'And the senior senators will vote for one of their own,' Regulus said almost to himself and again Scipio nodded.

Regulus turned the proposal over again. Only one obstacle remained, one insurmountable barrier that Regulus was sure could not be overcome, even by a man as cunning as he knew Scipio was.

'How will you guarantee Duilius will not stand for election? His withdrawal would be the act of a madman.'

'He will withdraw' Scipio said with utter certainty.

'But . . .' Regulus began, unable to assure himself despite Scipio's conviction.

'He will announce his withdrawal tomorrow in the Senate and when he does I will look to you.' Scipio said, his gaze penetrating, intimidating, his force of will filling the space around Regulus. 'You will have your proof that my plan is sound and I will expect your full cooperation from that point onward.'

Regulus lapsed into silence once more and his gaze shifted from Scipio's face, his eyes ranging into the candlelit spaces behind the consul as if he was chasing some elusive doubt. His gaze settled on Scipio once more.

'You would do all this for revenge?' he asked.

'It is reason enough,' Scipio said and Regulus nodded imperceptibly in agreement.

'Then I accept,' he said simply.

Scipio stood almost immediately, his sudden movement helping to mask the traces of a smile of triumph creeping onto his face. Regulus stood also and escorted Scipio from the room, this time giving the consul the full deference his position had always commanded. The two men walked into the courtyard and Scipio's guards formed up around their master, each one visibly tense at the thought of the return journey through the dark treacherous streets. Only Scipio seemed at ease and he bid Regulus farewell with a brief conspiratorial nod, struggling to contain a laugh as Regulus returned the gesture in kind. Once on the street and out of earshot of the senator however, Scipio gave full vent to his pent up triumph. Regulus had been easily swayed, happy and ready to believe that Scipio's motives were entirely based on revenge against Duilius. They were in part, but Scipio's ambitions sat well above mere retribution. They were as always set on only one objective, an aspiration that fate had cruelly wrenched from his grasp at Lipara but one which Scipio was determined to regain at any cost. Absolute power in Rome.

CHAPTER FOUR

Day dawned for the *Aquila* ten miles south of Naples, with an offshore breeze blowing lightly over the aft-deck, the air laden with wood-smoke and waste, the deep musky smell of unwashed streets in the cramped innards of the teeming port. Atticus closed his eyes and opened his mouth slightly as the faint smell washed over the foredeck and he was immediately transported back thirty years to the slums of Locri and the struggling existence of his childhood. He opened his eyes again slowly and drank in the sight of the open sea around him, whispering a silent thankful prayer to Fortuna for the guiding hand that had led him so far from that life.

Atticus's gaze picked out a dark spot against the strengthening light in the east and he focused his attention on the sky over the low coastline a mile away, watching the silhouette intently as it slowly took shape into the familiar profile of a sea eagle and Atticus found that he was holding his breath in anticipation as the bird approached his ship. At two hundred yards distance the moment came and the bird suddenly withdrew its wings and tucked them tight against its body, the swift change sending the eagle into the beginnings of a graceful dive that transformed the once benevolent profile of the eagle into a deadly spear.

The sea eagle hit the water at an incredible speed and she was immediately swallowed by the calm sea, the ripples of her entry instantly swept away and her existence lost until a second later she broke the surface again with a fish trapped in her beak, the water cascading from her feathers to be caught by the light of the rising sun. She soared heavenward once more, however her success went unacknowledged as Atticus shifted his gaze to a flash of colour immediately behind where the bird had struck. The *Aquila* was almost past the point, her seven knot speed pushing her inexorably northward and Atticus spun around to look to the masthead. Corin was there, his gaze fixed dead ahead, scanning the waters for the trading ships that would soon emanate from the port of Naples. Atticus looked to the sea once more, the half-image he had witnessed lost once more to the rolling waves. He hesitated for a mere second longer.

'Hard to starboard,' he roared. 'Come about east-south-east.'

The balanced hull of the *Aquila* swung instantly beneath his feet as he traversed the main deck towards the aft, his eyes locked on a reference point on the coast and as he reached Gaius at the tiller he ordered him to straighten the galley's course.

'Steerage speed, lookouts to the fore!' he ordered and the crew scrambled to the task, Lucius reiterating the order as the Aquila settled low in the water, her two knot speed giving her a gentle headway against the off-shore breeze. Septimus approached Atticus with a quizzical look on his face.

'Something in the water,' Atticus said in answer, 'two hundred yards off the bow.'

'Understood,' Septimus nodded and made his way to the foredeck to inform the lookouts stationed there.

Below deck in the main cabin, Varro felt the sudden change in the galley's course and her drop in speed. He sat up in his cot and planted his feet firmly on the deck, his sudden action triggering a scurrying sound on the floor as cockroaches fled the unexpected movement. Varro reached up for the porthole above him, pulling back the shutter, allowing the early sunlight to flood the narrow confines of the cabin and he caught sight of the last of the ubiquitous insects as they fled for the dark recesses of the room.

He stood up slowly and rubbed the fatigue from his eyes, digging his knuckles in deeply until his vision exploded with tiny stars before returning to the gloom of the twilight world below deck. He had barely slept, the constant motion of the world around him still completely alien, the confines of the room and the sudden inexplicable sounds that punctured the darkness keeping him constantly on edge. It had been one of the longest nights of his life, his mind filled with nightmarish visions of everyone he had ever known turning their back on him in vile condemnation, their faces haunting him even now in his waking hours and he cursed his fate and the ship that bore him anew.

Varro dressed quickly and mounted the steps to the main deck, squinting in the dawn light as looked about him to the frenzied activity of the crew. The majority of them were looking over the side- and forerails, shouting instructions to each other as they searched the waters around the galley. Varro moved quickly to the side-rail, pushing a crewman aside to see out over the water but he saw nothing in the empty sea. He turned to the aft-deck and his eyes sought the captain, seeing him instantly as he stood beside the helmsman, his easy confident stance evident, even from a distance, and Varro felt a resurgence of his hatred. He was about to stride back to the captain when a shout cut through the cacophony of voices on deck.

'Two points starboard. Someone in the water!'

All eyes on the *Aquila* spun to that point, Varro following the gaze of others as he sought the point indicated. It was there, fifty yards off the bow, a small mass of indeterminate shapes in the gentle swell, hidden one moment and exposed the next but amidst the tangle Varro could see the shoulders and head of at least one person.

'All stop,' Atticus shouted and he ran the length of the galley to the foredeck, not noticing Varro as he passed him by, his attention firmly fixed on the figure of Septimus standing by the rail, his arm outstretched in indication of what Atticus had spotted minutes before from afar.

'One survivor,' Septimus said as the captain reached them. 'Lashed to some debris.'

Atticus nodded and turned to the crewmen beside him.

'You two, over the side,' he said and the men instantly obeyed, each one swan-diving into the sea eight feet below to surface once again a couple of yards short of the inert people in the water. The crewmen were both able swimmers, as was every man on the *Aquila*, a skill Atticus strictly ensured that every sailor who joined his crew was taught. It was an ability that many of the more traditional sailors who found themselves serving on the *Aquila* thought irrational, believing it better that a sailor should die a quick death if his ship was sunk rather than suffering a lingering struggle before the sea inevitably claimed you.

'He's alive but unconscious,' one of the crewmen shouted and they struck off towards the *Aquila* again without command, each man swimming with one hand while the other dragged the makeshift raft behind them. Two more sailors jumped overboard as the group reached the hull of the *Aquila* and the survivor was quickly cut from the debris and hauled by rope up and over the side-rail. The crew formed a rough circle around him as he was laid on the deck but it parted again for Atticus and Septimus, the centurion kneeling down and listening intently at the unconscious man's chest, his knowledge qualified only through years of experience in the military.

Atticus was given a moment to study the man as Septimus's steady hands searched for the signs that would indicate the strength of his life-force. The man was dark, almost certainly Roman, his young angular features made prominent by the sea water that had seemingly washed the very blood from his face, his skin stark against the deep red of the tunic which had caught Atticus's eye.

'He's dehydrated and suffering from exhaustion,' Septimus said without looking up, putting his head to the man's chest once more. He stood up. 'He'll need rest and fresh water.'

'Will he live?' Atticus asked.

Septimus nodded. 'He's young and strong,' he said, and as if bidden the man stirred slightly, his hand rising and falling again across his stomach.

Atticus instantly ordered the crew to pick him up. 'Take him to the main cabin,' he ordered without thinking, suddenly catching Varro's eye at the edge of the circle, the tribune looking up with an aggravated expression, 'with your permission, Tribune.' Atticus added.

Varro nodded curtly and spun around, his exit creating a gap in the circle through which the crewmen carried the man to the main cabin below. Septimus followed, the young man now in his charge.

Regulus stepped warily through the throng of senators on the floor of the Senate house, catching the eye of many as they nodded a greeting. The men were clustered in groups, talking animatedly before the familiar hammer of a gavel, signalling the beginning of the first session of the day, would hasten them all to their seats. Their discussions were almost frenetic in their tempo, as if the dreary debates scheduled for the day could be mitigated by a couple of minutes of interesting conversation about the consulship elections that were due on the morrow.

Regulus engaged with no-one, skirting the groups to avoid being dragged into a discussion. His gaze sought many of the senators however, surreptitiously watching them, eavesdropping on their conversations as he moved past, trying to guess which ones might be the junior senators that Scipio claimed to secretly control. As he reached the edge of the throng, Regulus spotted the consul seated alone in the centre of the semi-circular seating that framed the central podium of the chamber. Scipio sat with an emotionless expression, his eyes scanning the room, ever restless. Regulus made to approach but thought better of the idea, turning away instead to make his way to his own seat.

A loud hammering sound filled the vaulted chamber and the three hundred senators took to their seats, the men sitting as individuals, loose confederations and close-knit factions, the fluid ever-changing political landscape placing former confederates beside current adversaries. Regulus sat on the right hand of the speaker, a side increasingly associated with the Patrician class of the ancient Roman families although it was near impossible to gauge the loyalties of every senator and dividing lines were only as stable as the last vote taken in each session.

'Senators of Rome,' the speaker of the house called as the chamber came to order, the underlying murmur of a hundred conversations dissipating in the still morning air. 'Before we begin the business of the day, Gaius Duilius,' the speaker continued, as he nodded towards the junior consul seated firmly in the centre of the left, 'the junior consul, has requested a brief audience with the chamber.'

Duilius stood and acknowledged the speaker with a nod, his unscheduled request prompting a light patter of applause that rose in intensity as Duilius made his way towards the podium. Regulus's heart skipped a beat at the sight and he clapped unconsciously, his mind racing to the conversation he had had the night before with Scipio and the premonition made that was transpiring before his very eyes. He looked briefly to Scipio but the consul's gaze was firmly fixed on his enemy.

Duilius walked with a determined stride and many of the senators sat straighter in their seats in anticipation, the comfortable slouch they had adopted for the scheduled debates thrown off as expectation filled the chamber. He whispered a brief thanks into the speaker's ear as he took to the podium, the old senator nodding gravely as if his consent to allow Duilius to speak was anything more than a mere powerless formality.

The junior consul stood with his arms straight, his hands gripping the sides of the podium, his upper body leaning forward to convey the significance of his words.

'My fellow Senators,' he began. 'It has been my esteemed honour to serve you and the city of Rome as junior consul this past year.'

A brief applause broke the silence before it was engulfed again by the palatable tension of the chamber.

'It has been a significant year for the Republic, one which has seen our city embark on a new frontier, a bold courageous endeavour which has, I have no doubt, brought pride to the hearts of our ancestors, the men who built this mighty city and who, even now, look down upon this chamber from Elysium.'

Again the senators clapped politely at Duilius's words, many willing the consul to get beyond the self congratulatory preamble to the crux of his speech.

'I have been fortunate to have been part of Rome's success

in her first naval battle,' Duilius continued, his words neatly ignoring and condemning to oblivion the disaster at Lipara, and for a brief heartbeat his gaze rested on Scipio before ranging over the expectant faces of the entire chamber, 'and I hope I have done my duty as your consul.'

Loud applause and sporadic cheers filled the chamber at these words but Duilius raised his hands for silence, his request immediately obeyed as the senators sensed the point of Duilius's speech was at hand.

'My duty done,' Duilius said, pausing for a second as if the words were hard to articulate, 'I hereby withdraw my nomination for the position of senior consul and instead I will ask to be considered for the post of censor.'

The final words of Duilius's sentence were lost in the uproar that followed as both ally and foe were taken completely unawares by the sudden turn of events, the entire Senate thrown into confusion with Duilius standing steady in the eye of the storm. Only a select few remained calm, their foreknowledge of the announcement insulating them from the maelstrom of questions and confusion.

Scipio remained seated amidst the turmoil, his eyes veiled, his head tilted back slightly as he drank in the utter chaos his plan had wrought, the sudden disorder that panicked the lesser men of the Senate, leaving them crying out for direction, for leadership. He lowered his head and steadied his gaze to a point on the right of the chamber, instantly catching the eye of Regulus and the older senator nodded imperceptibly. He was committed.

Scipio's thoughts were broken by the slowly surfacing sound of Duilius pounding the gavel against the podium. By degrees the chamber returned to order although many of the senators remained standing, their agitation preventing them from retaking their seats.

'My fellow Senators,' Duilius began again, conscious that this last statement was all important and he paused once more to ensure the chamber was quiet enough for all to hear his words, 'in withdrawing my nomination so close to the election I realise that the elections scheduled for tomorrow stand in disarray, not least as there are no other nominations for senior consul.'

A dark murmur of censure met these words but Duilius ignored them, concentrating instead his will on his allies and the undecided majority, ignoring those who now, for the first time, were emboldened to stand openly against him.

'I would therefore,' Duilius said aloud, once more waiting for the chamber to come to order, 'I would therefore like to nominate Lucius Manlius Vulso Longus to stand in my stead, a man who will lead this Senate with the same sense of duty that has been the hallmark of my service.'

Duilius pointed to Longus as he spoke those final words and the senator stood to receive the applause of the Senate, both polite and enthusiastic. The cadre of senators surrounding him, each one an ally of Duilius, shook his hand and slapped him on the shoulder, and Longus raised his hands to still the Senate once more, clearing his throat as he did to make the gracious acceptance speech he and Duilius had crafted the evening before. As the chamber became quiet however, another single voice silenced Longus's opening words before he could utter them.

'Senators of Rome!'

All eyes turned to see Regulus standing tall.

'Less than an hour ago this chamber stood poised to elect Gaius Duilius to the position of senior consul on the morrow. It was a fitting decision, an endorsement by this house of the achievements of a man who has served Rome well.'

There was a murmur of agreement and Regulus paused.

'But,' he continued, 'following his withdrawal I believe this election must not become an automatic transfer of votes but must be open to all. Longus is a fine senator; a dutiful servant of Rome.' Regulus paused and looked directly at Duilius. 'But our city, our republic is at war and in times of war it is better to be led by the solid hand of experience, not the impulsive hand of youth.'

A murmur of agreement swept across the chamber.

'You all know me,' Regulus continued. 'The senior members of this Senate know my reputation. I have held this highest of offices before and I am ready to lead again. I therefore humbly nominate myself for the position of senior consul, ever conscious that the Senate will decide wisely and elect the most suitable candidate accordingly.'

The Senate chamber was once more enveloped in deafening sound as Regulus retook his seat. Longus stood motionless as the waves of sound crashed over him, furious that his own moment of triumph had been swept away by Regulus's sudden entry to the fray, and he desperately turned to his benefactor for guidance.

Duilius remained standing at the podium, the knuckles of his hands white from the intensity of his grip on the stand. He was speechless, his mind flooded with anger and confusion, and he gazed intently at Regulus, waiting for the movement he knew must occur. It was inconceivable that Regulus was acting alone, that he spontaneously formed the idea to run against Longus, that he was not forewarned. Duilius knew that human nature would cause Regulus to seek out his confederate at their moment of success, if only to share a silent triumphant glance, a secret congratulatory nod. Regulus turned to his left and Duilius immediately scanned the three quarters of the Senate on that side of him. He unconsciously discounted allies and focused on his known enemies, but none seemed to catch his gaze; their faces instead turned all directions as individual debates raged across the Senate. Duilius swept the chamber one last time and as he did, his heart plunged as the identity of Regulus's associate suddenly became apparent, not because the man was looking back at Regulus but because his gaze was fixed intently at the podium. As Duilius watched a malicious smile spread across his enemy's face.

Atticus walked swiftly down the gangway that led to the main cabin at the stern of the *Aquila*. Below decks the sound of the drum master's beat was amplified and transmuted into a dull repetitive thud that seemed to emanate from every surface, the heartbeat of the galley heard from within. The hull moved slightly under Atticus's feet and he put out his hand against the bulkhead to steady himself, the course corrections becoming more frequent as Gaius wove the *Aquila* through the busy shipping lanes of Naples. The timber felt smooth beneath his palm and Atticus let his hand linger for a second, feeling the grain of the wood, the lines of a once vibrant tree felled and shaped and made alive again as part of a Roman galley.

The sound of voices could be heard through the main cabin door and Atticus hastened his last remaining steps, stepping through the door without check, the familiar space made welcoming again knowing that Varro was still top-side on the aft-deck. The man who had been rescued by the *Aquila*'s crew was seated on the cot on the port side of the cabin, his head bowed, but his back straight and the single hour he had spent so far on the *Aquila* had immeasurably revived him. He looked up, pausing in his conversation with Septimus as Atticus closed the cabin door. The man stood, his legs unsteady and he kept one hand on the edge of the cot to help him balance.

'I am Quintus Postumius Camillus,' he said. 'Boatswain of the trading galley *Fides* out of Ostia.'

'Captain Perennis,' Atticus replied, placing a hand on the man's shoulder, a simple request for him to be seated once more. 'Tell me what happened.'

'We were en route to Taras when we were attacked,' Camillus began.

'Attacked?' Atticus said.

'By pirates, Atticus,' Septimus said, nodding towards Camillus. 'He has already filled me in on some of the details.'

Atticus sat back against the table in the centre of the cabin, his mind flooded with questions. 'Where did the attack take place?' he asked of Camillus.

'We were a day's sailing south of Naples, just short of Centola.'

'And the pirate ship?'

'She was a bireme, sailing under a banner of Egyptus. She was travelling north and as she crossed our bows, she suddenly changed course and swept out starboard oars.' Camillus fell silent for a moment. 'I'd never seen a galley move so fast,' he muttered, shaking his head, his disbelief an unconscious absolution for him and his crewmates having been caught unawares.

'They boarded us in overwhelming strength, at least a hundred men. We never had a chance,' Camillus continued, his voice trailing off as his mind relived the horror of those desperate minutes.

'How did you escape?' Atticus asked after a moment's silence, allowing Camillus time to fight his demons.

Camillus looked up as if suddenly woken from a nightmare.

'When our defence collapsed I dived over the stern,' Camillus began, his head bowed in shame at having fled from the fight. 'By the time I resurfaced, the undercurrent had dragged me twenty feet from the galleys. I caught hold of some of the severed oars and kept low in the water.'

'What of the fate of the other members of the crew? Did you see any others escape?' Atticus asked.

'There were no other survivors,' Camillus said in a near whisper as he looked up, his face once more haunted by the images of his mind's eye. 'They slaughtered them all, every last man, even after they surrendered. I saw them, on the aft-deck, at least twenty of the crew. They threw down their swords and begged for quarter but the pirates, they just . . .' Camillus's words trailed off to silence and Atticus and Septimus were left to imagine the butchery that the pirates had wrought.

Atticus stood up abruptly, his fists balled in futile anger. 'They're swarming again,' he spat, 'with the war in Sicily, they know we're stretched too thin to cover the coastline here.'

Atticus began to pace the cabin, his anger seething just beneath the surface. Before the current conflict with the Carthaginians he had spent his career hunting down the pirates who plagued the Ionian coastline of southern Italy. As captain of the *Aquila* he had caught many and each time he had ordered his crew to put the entire pirate ship to the sword. No trial, no quarter, no mercy. Revenge for the countless victims who had fallen prey to the vultures. They were a disease; a pestilence, and Atticus had devoted his life to removing their existence, their stain, from the shores of Italy. Now they had crept once more out of the shadows.

'And what of the *Fides*?' he asked of Camillus. 'Where did they sail her to? What course?'

'They didn't take her,' he replied, the colour draining from his face once more. 'They put her to the torch.'

'And the slaves?' Atticus asked, confused.

'They went down with the ship, every one of them,' Camillus replied, remembering the tortured, desperate screams of the doomed slaves, the sound forever trapped within his memory.

'I don't understand,' Atticus said almost to himself. 'Why

would they sink their prize? The galley alone was worth taking, but the slaves would be worth a fortune on any market.'

'Maybe they were looking to stay mobile,' Septimus suggested, 'taking only what they could carry.'

'Then why not take the slaves?' Atticus countered. 'It doesn't make sense. Pirates often sink trading ships after they take what they can from the hold. But with a galley, the cargo is generally small; the real prize is the slaves manning the oars.'

'They must have had some reason,' Septimus said.

'Whatever it was,' Atticus said, almost to himself, 'it's something unique. I've never heard of pirates sinking their prize before. Never.'

CHAPTER FIVE

Hamilcar's heart soared as he caught sight of the walled citadel of Byrsa high above the city still hidden from his vantage point on the foredeck of the *Alissar*. The late evening light was reflecting off the wind-blasted fortifications, turning the entire fort into a beacon which seemed to draw him closer with every stroke of the galley's oars. Hamilcar had not seen the city in over a year, but his memory guided his eyes instinctively, his gaze sweeping left and right as the tops of the taller temples started to appear on the horizon ahead and he quietly recited their names, his mind's eye adding detail to each one until they merged into a single entity. Carthage.

Within minutes the massive wall that encircled Carthage dominated the view, a defence which had stood against every enemy in the city's history, a colossal carapace that protected the heart of an empire within. The *Alissar* keeled hard to starboard as she approached the city, her bow finding a new course that would take her into the manmade harbours on the southern approaches. Hamilcar remained restless as the drum beat slowed in the confines of the first harbour, the commercial centre of a maritime empire, and the *Alissar* advanced onwards to sweep gracefully through the porticos that guarded the entrance to the military harbour, the helmsman ordering near dead stop in the crowded waters, the galley resting easily in the calm swell.

The military harbour was circular in shape, a manmade wheel with a raised island as its hub. Covered ship-houses on both the outer perimeter and the inner island dominated the space, an incredible sequence of slips, dry-docks and work-shops that could house over two hundred galleys. The *Alissar* quickly docked and Hamilcar strode purposefully down the gangplank, pausing briefly at the end before stepping once more onto the sacred land of his home city, a renewed deter-mination taking hold of him as he felt the power of the city course through his veins. He set off without a backward glance, his feet taking him unerringly through the ancient teeming streets to the Council chamber in the shadow of the Byrsa citadel.

Hamilcar slowed as he approached the Council chamber, his eyes ranging over the groups of men standing near the entrance to the chamber, searching for the familiar figure of his father. He was not to be seen however and Hamilcar continued on into the inner chamber, his vision quickly adjusting to the gloom within. He spotted Hanno almost immediately, holding court amongst a group of fellow councillors. He had a massive frame, made all the more imposing by a habit of flaying his hands about before him as he spoke. Hamilcar approached without hesitation, his military uniform and the metallic jangle of his personal arms drawing the attention of many in the chamber, all of whom recognised the young man. Hamilcar could see that Hanno had spotted him out of the corner of his eye but the councillor continued to speak uninterrupted, his face showing neither surprise nor expectation.

'Councillor Hanno,' Hamilcar called, immediately opening the circle around Hanno.

'Hamilcar Barca,' Hanno replied, his deep, booming voice friendly as the group around him opened their ranks further to allow Hamilcar to stand before the councillor. 'How is the campaign on Sicily progressing?'

'It is going well, Councillor,' Hamilcar answered evenly although his eyes were now hostile, a look only Hanno could see and one which had not escaped his notice, 'although,' he continued, 'the disposition of my forces has suffered from meddling from a civilian outsider.' Hamilcar spat the last word and as he did a shadow seemed to pass over Hanno's expression. The councillor drew in a deep breath before exhaling slowly, the smell of his breath washing over Hamilcar.

'Meddling,' Hanno said, with a definite edge to his voice. 'A very unfortunate choice of words.'

'But an appropriate one,' Hamilcar said, the other councillors around him forgotten as he struggled to rein in his temper.

Hanno seemed ready to reply but he hesitated, his eyes darting left and right to the group of councillors surrounding them. This was not the forum to reveal his plans to every prying ear.

Hanno laughed suddenly, the outburst throwing Hamilcar off balance, 'You are your father's son,' his congeniality almost convincing. 'Come, Hamilcar, let us discuss this matter you speak of in more detail,' he said, stepping forward and taking Hamilcar by the elbow. Hamilcar resisted for a second before allowing himself to be turned and he walked with Hanno to the quiet of an ante-chamber. Once there Hanno looked over his shoulder to ensure they were alone.

'You would do well to temper your words, young Barca,' he spat, his face becoming mottled with anger as he brought his full will to bear on Hamilcar.

'By what right do you change my orders on Sicily?' Hamilcar

shot back, 'Because of you, total victory was snatched from us at Thermae.'

'Thermae,' Hanno said in disgust. 'What do I, what does Carthage care for Thermae, or Sicily for that matter?'

'But . . .' Hamilcar said, thrown slightly by Hanno's casual attitude to the war.

'By what right do you summon our fleet from Iberia to fight your war on Sicily?' Hanno accused, cutting across Hamilcar, neatly turning the focus of the confrontation.

'I need those ships to reassert our control over northern Sicily,' Hamilcar replied, now on the defensive.

'Those galleys are needed to protect the shipping lanes of the empire. They are not yours to personally command!'

Hamilcar hesitated, his mind searching for a way to turn the argument once more in his favour. He suddenly recalled Hanno's sudden inexplicable laughter moments before and how he had led Hamilcar away from the other councillors. Hamilcar gambled. 'Does the Council know of your interference?' he asked.

Hanno hesitated for a mere second before he recovered. 'What the Council does or does not know is none of your concern, Barca,' he replied, a hard edge of anger once more infusing his words.

'But it is my father's concern,' Hamilcar replied.

'Have a care Barca,' Hanno said menacingly. 'These are matters far beyond your reach. I would caution you. A few well chosen words by me in the right ears might reignite a debate amongst the Hundred and Four about your summary execution of Hannibal Gisco.'

Again Hamilcar was forced to hesitate. The Hundred and Four was a council of judges that oversaw all military matters in the empire, including the appointment and dismissal of commanders. By right, only they could condemn a failed commander to death, a decision Hamilcar had usurped after the defeat at Mylae. He had escaped censure however, a pardon he was sure his father had secured.

'Now if you'll excuse me,' Hanno said, making to brush past Hamilcar, 'I have more important matters than your tantrum to attend to.'

Hamilcar shot out his hand and grasped Hanno's arm, holding him firm, his fingers biting into the soft flesh.

Hanno shot around, his face twisted in fury.

'You dare strike a member of the Supreme Council of Carthage?' he growled. 'Take your hand off me before I have you and your family flayed alive.'

Hamilcar withdrew his hand immediately, knowing he had gone too far, pushed too hard. Hanno shot him one last look of pure contempt before he strode away leaving Hamilcar standing alone in the ante-chamber, drained by the encounter, the elation he had felt upon returning to Carthage shattered in the very heart of the city.

A complete hush descended upon the entire Senate chamber as the leader of the house slowly made his way towards the podium. He moved at a torturous pace, the seniority of his years that had warranted his appointment to the position of *princeps senatus*, a ceremonial and near powerless apolitical position, forcing him to shuffle forward and an audible moan escaped the more impatient senators as they waited in anticipation.

The vote for the senior consulship was now in its third count, the first two inconclusive votes merely adding uncertainty to an election that Duilius had split wide open the day before. The first vote had been an open show of hands as each of the two names on the ballot was called in turn, Regulus and Longus. It instantly became apparent however that the vote was too close to call, the scattered raised hands for each candidate across the house impossible to count and so the *princeps senatus* called for a second vote, a division of the house, where the senators would physically move to the side of the chamber occupied by their preferred candidate, Longus on the left, Regulus on the right. Both sides claimed victory as the final seats were taken but again it was impossible to discern a clear majority on either side and so a third vote was called, an actual count by the leader of the house of each individual senator's vote.

'Senators of Rome,' the leader called out, 'I have counted the votes for each candidate and I can now inform you that one of the candidates has achieved a majority.'

A half-hearted cheer escaped from some of the younger senators before the silence in the chamber quickly reasserted itself. Duilius looked across at Regulus before shifting his gaze to the senators surrounding him, the division of the house still in force. Scipio was there, two levels behind Regulus and to his right, a distance that spoke of a complete separation that Duilius knew to be false.

Duilius vividly recalled the anxiety he had experienced the day before when he had spotted Scipio staring at him, suspecting instantly that he was behind Regulus's nomination. It had struck him like a hammer blow but he had tempered his alarm, knowing that to suspect Scipio on instinct alone was pointless. His proof had come later however when Appius, his spy master, reported that both Amaury and Tiago, the two spies he had placed in Scipio's house, had disappeared. After that there could be no doubt save for one question. Did Amaury and Tiago voluntarily betray him or were they somehow exposed by Scipio and tricked into delivering false information? Either way they were dead men.

Now as Duilius watched Scipio intently, he cursed his own

naivety. It had been a perfect trap, the bait impossible to ignore, the threat to his fortune a flawless strike at his weakest point. He saw Scipio turn towards his side of the house, his enemy's eyes sweeping the chamber until his gaze came to rest on Duilius. He stared impassively, his expression unreadable, and Duilius matched his gaze as both men awaited the next words of the leader of the house.

'I am honoured to announce,' the leader continued, 'that the new senior consul of Rome is Marcus Atilius Regulus.'

The Senate erupted as the announcement was made, the leader's following words of congratulation lost amidst the cheers of the right. Scipio simply smiled and Duilius turned away. He had been outmanoeuvred by the very foe he thought he had beaten and the realisation steeled his will. He would not be so complacent again.

Atticus left the aft-deck and walked forward along the main, sensing the mood of many of the men as he went, their expressions animated and distracted as they continuously glanced over the side rails. Atticus tried to identify his own emotions as he mounted the foredeck and walked forwards to the bow rail to get a better view of the teeming waters ahead. The *Aquila* was approaching Ostia, the port town of Rome, and although she was still two miles distant the sea lanes were crowded with all manner of vessels, each vying for the limited sea room available so close to port. Gaius held a steady course, adjusting it only slightly to circumnavigate the lumbering transport ships under sail, the oar power at his command affording him greater manoeuvrability and he moved through their wakes or under their bows with barely an oars-width to spare.

Atticus noticed that many of the trading galleys did not adjust their course to swing wide of the *Aquila* and the four-foot bronze ram that sliced the water before her. He smiled to himself, remembering a time, in fact only a few months ago, when the sight of a Roman military galley was enough of a rarity to open a channel in even the busiest shipping lane. Now the *Aquila* passed like a ghost through the sea lane, almost unnoticed and completely undistinguished, a once exceptional sight that had become as common as the white horses of the waves themselves.

Within fifteen minutes the outlying buildings of Ostia came into sight, the low lying houses of the traders who fed off the daily bounty delivered from the four corners of the Mediterranean to Ostia. These dwellings gave way to the taller trading houses and warehouses of the town proper, an almost solid line of buildings that encircled the docks. The *Aquila* maintained a course parallel to the shoreline as she passed the commercial docks of Ostia, her course taking her across the inward and outward path of every other vessel and curses spoken in a dozen languages floated across the water from crews forced to slow or adjust their course to avoid the determined path of the war-galley.

The *Aquila* was heading for the *castrum* on the northern edge of the port, the military barracks that had once housed the tiny coastal fleet that protected the sea trade to and from the city. Now it was home to the *Classis Romanus* although the majority of the fleet was stationed a couple of miles north at Fiumicino. Atticus's mind was flooded with memories as the *Aquila* neared the military docks.

Atticus had been granted a place of honour at the right hand of Gaius Duilius during the triumph that followed the great naval victory in Rome. It had been heady wine and the lasting impression of that day had further clouded and entangled Atticus's attitude towards the city that now dictated his destiny.

97

Atticus recalled the sea eagle he had seen at dawn the previous day. At the time the sight had triggered something in his mind, a thought he had pushed aside when he spotted the survivors from the *Fides* in the water, but now he remembered lamenting that bird's fate. It was a creature trapped between two worlds, relying on the land for its home but on the sea for its food, its life force, its very reason to exist. Cut off either land or sea and the sea eagle would perish.

Atticus had never believed his own existence was as interdependent. He had been born into grinding poverty, into a world where the sea offered the only means of sustenance and the land offered nothing in kind. His only happy childhood memories revolved around the sea and his time spent fishing with his father and grandfather and so at fourteen he had readily joined the crew of a military galley, the promise of open water and a life spent hunting the pirates his grandfather had taught him to hate, enough to sever his ties to Locri, a city which had never given him comfort or succour. For any given year since then Atticus could count the number of days he had spent ashore on his hands alone and he had truly come to consider the sea his home, tied only to the land through ancient bonds of ancestry and loyalty. That belief had been challenged by Rome.

For hundreds of years Rome had been a land based power, a republic surrounded on three sides by water. Its ambition to control Sicily however, was transforming that sphere, extending the reach of the Republic into the seas that had once held her fast and that ambition had quickly enveloped the small fleet of ships that had always acted independently on her behalf. The *Aquila* had been one of those ships and Atticus had been submerged into a culture that had previously existed only on the periphery of his life. This quickly created loyalties within him, firstly through Septimus and his bond with the legionaries trapped on Sicily and then through men like Duilius, new men of Rome who ignored the ancient lineage of a citizen and took their measure of a man by his deeds alone. Beyond these bonds of loyalty was Hadria, Septimus's sister and it was her presence in Rome, more than any other, that caused Atticus to realise for the first time in his life, that the land promised many things the sea could not give.

The *Aquila* hove to with a gentle touch from Gaius and the starboard oars were withdrawn, allowing the galley to swing parallel to the docks. Mooring ropes were thrown and the *Aquila* was made fast before the gangplank was lowered onto the quayside. Once again Atticus found himself comparing the sights before him with his memories. The original *castrum* consisted of a standard barracks house with an enclosed court-yard set fifty yards back from the edge of the dock and where once it had stood almost forlorn and devoid of life, it was now alive with activity, a constant flow of military personnel passing through the arched entranceways that led to the inte-rior. Atticus noticed an officer approaching the *Aquila* at the head of a *contubernia* of ten legionaries.

'What galley?' he called as he arrived at a point directly across from the aft-deck.

'The *Aquila*,' Atticus replied.

The officer quickly consulted his list, his head rising and falling as he read it through twice. 'I have no record of your galley here,' he shouted up, his expression now one of annoy-ance. 'State the reason for this unscheduled arrival!'

Atticus nearly smiled. Bloody Roman paperwork, he thought. 'We're of the Thermae attack fleet,' he said. 'We . . .'

'Captain!'

Atticus spun around to find Varro standing with his guards behind him.

'Back to your station, Perennis,' he spat. 'I'll address this.'

Atticus stepped aside and Varro approached the side rail. On the dock the officer's face showed surprise at the unexpected sight of a tribune and he immediately snapped to attention before saluting. Varro indicated the gangplank with a nod and the officer saluted once more, marching his squad to the foot of the gangplank while Varro mirrored his approach with his *praetoriani* on the *Aquila*.

Atticus watched from the aft-deck as Varro descended. The tribune issued terse orders and within seconds two of the legionaries were dispatched back to the *castrum*. As Varro continued to talk, Atticus noticed the officer's eyes flash towards him. The legionary nodded twice as the tribune's orders continued, his gaze still fixed on the aft-deck and Atticus felt a sudden instinctive flare of warning. Rome was Varro's domain, where his power was at its greatest, where an order to arrest him for insubordination and striking an officer would be followed without question.

Atticus braced himself for the inevitable as he watched Varro stride off to the *castrum*. The officer remained and instead of boarding to make an arrest, he strode once more along the dock until he was parallel to the aft-deck.

'Captain, you are to disembark your entire crew immediately,' the officer shouted, a hint of disdain in his voice.

Atticus was confused by the order. In what way was the crew involved?

'And what of my men, the marines?' Septimus asked, standing at Atticus's shoulder.

'Your full complement as well, Centurion.'

'And my ship?' Atticus asked.

The officer smiled derisively. '*Your* ship will be sailed by a reserve crew to Fiumicino.'

Atticus made to protest but Septimus stayed his words with a hand on his shoulder.

'Save your breath, Atticus,' he said. 'There's no latitude here.'

'But I don't understand. What is Varro playing at?' Atticus asked, completely bewildered.

'I think I know,' Septimus replied and he turned over his shoulder to issue the necessary orders to Lucius and Drusus. The *optio* responded immediately but Lucius looked to Atticus for confirmation. The captain nodded without comment. There was no other option but to obey.

With each passing street and each familiar sight, Hamilcar began to feel his heart rate and his mood return to normal. These were the streets of his childhood, his teenage years before he reached the age of majority and every corner ignited long forgotten memories. A year ago, when he had last walked these streets, they had been shrouded in darkness, a hurried visit to his father's house in the midst of his journey from Iberia to Sicily. Now he took the opportunity to drink in every sight, absorb every sound and smell until his heart felt once more like that of the boy he had once been.

With pride Hamilcar noticed the prosperity that infused every aspect of the street, the bustling stalls and storefronts, the haggling traders and customers, money changing hands over handshakes and platitudes, his mind and senses automatically ignoring the beggars and street urchins that swarmed about his feet. Carthage was an empire built on trade and Hamilcar was always fascinated by the multitude of minute transactions that took place every day in almost every street across the city's domains, triggering events and decisions that shaped the very empire.

As Hamilcar moved up and around the hill of Byrsa, the

streets became less crowded, the stalls more sporadic and the loud drone and buzz of the streets gave way to near silence so Hamilcar could once more hear the hobnails of his sandals on the cobblestones beneath him. These were the streets of the military families, the ancient nobility. They were all descendents of traders but now the wealth of each family was handled exclusively by agents, men who traded on their behalf. It distanced men like Hamilcar from the daily grind of commerce and he knew little of how the wealth of his family was generated and maintained. He did however know intimately the power that wealth wielded and the respect for money that was passed down father to son was strong in the Barcid family.

Hamilcar arrived at a modest but stout wooden door midway along one of the narrow streets. He paused for a second, touching the door lightly, feeling the grain beneath his fingers. He knocked with a clenched fist and then stood back. The door was opened within a minute by one of the senior servants, whose face lit up as he recognised his master's son. Hamilcar returned the smile, touching the servant lightly on the arm as he brushed past him into the outer courtyard.

The house within the walls was sprawling and lavish. It had been expanded many times over its lifetime and the diverse mix of extensions and ancillary buildings spoke to the house's long service over the lifetimes of many generations of the Barcids. Hamilcar moved inside, his ears picking up the sounds of excitement within and he marvelled as always at how fast the servants could transmit news across the house. As he crossed the main atrium he caught sight of his mother and father entering from the other side. His mother rushed to greet him while his father, Hasdrubal, approached with a measured stride, his hand extended, his expression warm with an undertone of surprise and curiosity at his son's unexpected visit.

Hamilcar was led by his parents into an informal family room, an area bedecked with couches and low tables, with doorways in every wall leading to inner courtyards and gardens. They talked easily for an hour about inconsequential matters, a year's worth of daily life and talk compressed with ease and in comfort. Hamilcar's mother soon recognised a subtle turn in the conversation however, as her husband began to touch on matters in Sicily and she rose to make arrangements for the evening meal, kissing her son fondly before leaving the room.

'What news of the campaign?' Hasdrubal asked, sitting forward, his face taking on an expression of intense concentration.

Hamilcar relayed the entire events of the previous three months. His father knew of Mylae, but only through dispatches, and he took the opportunity to question his son extensively on the causes of their defeat. He then listened in silence as his son outlined his preparations for ambush at Thermae, nodding approvingly in places, his respect for his son's abilities further reinforced. Hamilcar then spoke of how his well laid plan was thwarted by Hanno's interference and he told his father of his confrontation with the councillor earlier that day. Again Hasdrubal listened in silence but his expression changed to one of anger and then concern.

'Hanno,' he said, almost to himself, 'we must step carefully around him.'

'Why, father?' Hamilcar asked. 'Surely many would think his interference borders on treason.'

Hasdrubal smiled although there was no humour there. 'There are many that believe the city's campaign on Sicily borders on treason.'

Hamilcar's expression became puzzled, prompting his father to continue. 'Hanno is the leader of a faction within

103

the Supreme Council which is opposed to the war against Rome.'

'Opposed? Why?'

'They believe the empire's destiny lies in Africa and that the conquest of Sicily is a misguided venture, a waste of our resources.'

'But Sicily guards our northern flank and the island sits astride the northern Mediterranean sea-lanes,' Hamilcar protested. 'If the Romans are not held there, there is no telling where they will strike next.'

Hasdrubal nodded. He knew well the dangers inherent in allowing Rome control over Sicily. Hamilcar could sense the weariness in his agreement, as if he had said those exact words a thousand times in the council chamber to no avail. The two men lapsed into silence.

'Can we thwart Hanno's efforts to disrupt the war in Sicily?' Hamilcar asked after a minute.

'We must,' his father replied, 'and soon. Hanno will strike for the position of Suffet next year. If he successfully becomes the leader of the Council he will withdraw every resource from Sicily and the campaign will be strangled to death.'

Hamilcar nodded, sensing his father had already devised a solution. 'What can I do?' he asked.

'Hanno's faction was in the minority before the defeat at Mylae. Now it is steadily gaining numbers. What I, and those opposed to Hanno need, is a significant victory in Sicily, something to inspire the people and the council into backing the war fully once more.'

Again Hamilcar nodded, a knowing smile spreading across his face.

'Then you need not worry,' he said, marshalling his thoughts so as to outline the plan in detail to his father, a plan that he had already put in motion and would certainly deliver the victory that Carthage desired. In fact, he smiled as he began, if the plan was entirely successful, Sicily would be the least of the prizes won.

'So why are we here?' Atticus asked, his head propped up on his forearms as he looked out the chest high window onto the courtyard of the *castrum*. The sun was falling away to the west and more than half of the courtyard was in shadow, but the hectic activity of the *castrum* continued unabated. Atticus turned to face Septimus, who was sitting on one of the two cots in the tiny room. The centurion had shrugged off his leather breastplate and was tracing the imprint of an eagle on the leather with the tip of his finger. He looked up, pausing briefly as he picked up the voices of many other men, their words muted by the thick walls that separated the rooms. The entire crew of sailors and marines were locked in similar rooms, some larger than others but all with stout wooden doors that were locked from the outside.

'Why do you think?' Septimus asked.

'I don't know,' Atticus replied frustratedly. 'I can understand Varro wanting me arrested but why are the rest of the crew here? They weren't complicit, they were following my orders. And you, you weren't even on the *Aquila* when I hit him.'

Septimus chuckled, 'This isn't about you, Atticus. From what you've told me, and Varro's reaction when he came back on board at Brolium, those senators who witnessed you hit Varro at Thermae will deny the incident so I don't think you'll face formal charges. In any case you're not Varro's biggest problem at the minute.'

Atticus nodded, almost but not quite feeling sorry for the tribune. Bearing news of a defeat was something every commander dreaded.

'What's happened since we arrived?' Septimus asked.

Atticus thought for a second, recalling the events of the previous few hours in his mind. 'We were escorted off the *Aquila*,' he said, 'practically rushed here, locked up and we haven't seen anyone since.'

'Exactly,' Septimus said. 'We haven't seen anyone. We're in isolation.'

'Isolation? Why?'

'Where is Varro now?' Septimus asked.

'Varro?' Atticus replied, perplexed, 'I don't know.'

'I'll tell you where. He's preparing to stand before the Senate tomorrow morning. He's preparing the speech that will decide his future in Rome.'

'So? What has that to do with us?'

'My family have never been part of the Senate,' Septimus said, 'but every Roman knows how the Senate works, how the system works. Varro's version of events has to be the first to be heard. It's the only way he can control the Senate's reaction. He'll have to stick close to the truth but the bias he uses, the slant he puts on the events will be all important. His version has got to show him in the best light.'

'So he can't have us wandering around telling everyone our version of the defeat before he gets a chance to deliver the news his way,' Atticus concluded.

'Exactly,' Septimus nodded.

Atticus was silent for a couple of minutes as his mind dwelled on the other issue. 'So with Varro embroiled in all this political trouble, you think I'm off the hook,' he said.

'That's not what I said,' Septimus replied, 'I said there'll be no formal charges, but there's no way Varro will forget or forgive what's happened. Would you?'

Atticus shook his head. Not a chance. He turned to the window once more, propping his chin on his forearms again as he gazed over the twilight lit courtyard. Tomorrow's dawn would see Varro fighting the political battle of his life and for one day more Atticus knew he would be forgotten. Beyond that it was only a matter of time.

CHAPTER SIX

Belus stood with his sword drawn but the blade hung loose by his side, his shield similarly lowered, strapped to his left forearm. He was breathing deeply, his chest heaving beneath the metal breastplate of his armour. The armour was heavily scored and Belus winced slightly as he felt the bruise swell on his chest beneath the mark. It had been a good strike, and if he had not being wearing armour, as so few were on the pirate galley, he would surely be dead. Instead his attacker lay slain at his feet, his final expression of violent aggression forever etched on his face.

Belus stepped over the body, and then many more as he made his way aft where Narmer, the pirate captain, was ordering his men to assemble the surviving crew of the Roman trading galley. The Roman merchantmen had fought like demons, like men possessed, like men who knew that death walked amongst them and that none would be spared. It created an intensity to fighting that Belus had never experienced before, even at Mylae, where his own ship had survived a full assault against the Roman legionaries because of his men's sheer refusal to yield. Belus had now fought in five of these pirate attacks and he was yet to get used to the level of ferocity that marred each encounter.

Belus sheathed his sword as he reached the confluence of men on the main deck. The pirates had circled the disarmed survivors, like a pack of baying wolves, their bloody swords still drawn and charged against the doomed Romans. Belus felt a sting of shame as he watched the spectacle, his honour sullied by the barbarity. In his fifteen years as a captain of a Carthaginian trireme he had always held to the code his father had taught him. The enemy were to be fought until beaten but quarter should be given to those who surrender. On board his own galley these captured Romans would already be in irons, chained to an oar for their eternity. Here their lives were forfeit, a crime against honour he had been ordered to commit and one the pirates did not pause to perpetrate.

Suddenly one of the Romans bolted for the side-rail, a head-long rush, his shoulder lowered in an attempt to break through the circle. The pirate he aimed for sidestepped the charge and swung his drawn blade under the Romans shoulder, slicing clean into the man's exposed side. The Roman fell with a cry of pain and the pirate instantly spun around, slashing his sword down in a blur of movement, slicing through the Roman's neck, killing him instantly. The rest of the pirates roared as their blood lust was enflamed once more and they instinctively began to edge forward against the remaining terrified Romans.

'Enough!' Belus shouted, causing some of the pirates to hesitate, while others continued, oblivious to the Carthaginian's orders. One of the pirates darted the tip of his sword forward, striking one of the Romans on his thigh and the man screamed in pain, his leg buckling beneath him. His crewmates grabbed him by the shoulders and dragged him back, the circle ever collapsing, their line of retreat non-existent.

'Captain!' Belus shouted, looking directly at Narmer. 'Tell your men that's enough!'

Narmer looked over his shoulder at the Carthaginian, a look of disdain on his face. He turned around once more, watching his men as they continued to close the vice, the bloodlust in his veins calling for slaughter, sick of the game this Carthaginian was making him play. Another Roman was struck and the pirates laughed as the terrified men finally ran out of room, squeezed into a pitiful huddle, their arms outstretched in a plea for mercy. Narmer felt the men around him ready themselves to surge forward and for a second he craved to issue the order to release them, to finish the fight as they always had, always, that was, until he made a deal with the Carthaginians.

'Hold!' he shouted, rage in his voice. For a heartbeat the men wavered and Narmer felt their hesitation. He whipped his sword down on the outstretched blades of the two men to his right, the unexpected strike knocking the swords from their hands. 'I said enough!' he roared.

His men backed off, anger in their expressions although Narmer immediately noticed that a few men now had a look of malicious expectation on their faces. He smiled inwardly. They knew what was coming next, and for these men, it was a lot more enjoyable than simply putting a crew to the sword. He turned once more to the Carthaginian.

'You would do well, Belus,' he growled, charging his sword forward, its tip just beneath the Carthaginian's neck, 'to remember that this is my ship and I give the orders here.'

'And you should remember,' Belus spat in reply, 'that you are in the paid service of the Carthaginian Empire and you will follow my instructions or forfeit the gold you have been promised upon our return to Tyndaris.'

Narmer lowered his sword and turned his head, spitting

onto the dead body of the Roman at his feet. Belus ignored the insult.

'Now finish your work here,' he ordered. 'Find out what you can from these prisoners and then fire the ship.'

Narmer snorted in derision but issued the orders, glancing at Belus one last time before turning his anger towards the remaining crew of the Roman ship.

Varro felt a trickle of sweat run down his back beneath his tunic as arguments and accusations raged across the senate floor around him. Only moments before he had stood down from the podium, his carefully prepared speech still clenched in his left hand. He had been unable to finish it, his announcement mid-way through of the defeat at Thermae stifling all attempts to continue, the Senate erupting into a wall of sound. His eyes darted left and right, searching for his father amongst the three hundred white robed senators. He was seated near the centre, beside Gnaeus Cornelius Scipio, the two men deep in conversation.

Suddenly, as if he knew he was being watched, Scipio turned to face Varro, the young commander holding the former consul's gaze for a minute before its intensity caused him to turn away. When he looked back Scipio was once more engrossed in conversation.

His father's censure, spoken so vehemently the night before, flooded back into Varro's mind and he tried to block the memory, the shame, the look of disgust on his father's face. He had not told him of the Greek captain's attack and had thereafter vowed to keep the event to himself, knowing his father's censure would run deeper if he knew his son had not immediately challenged his attacker. Afterwards Varro had sat in silence as his father dictated the speech he now held in his hand, the carefully chosen words that had been cut off by the uproar of the senate. Varro had tried to reassert control, tried to shout the senators down in an effort to finish his account, the skilled trap, the impossibility of perceiving the threat, his selfless actions and courage that saved the *hastati* of the Ninth, but it was for naught.

The reverberating sound of a gavel brought the Senate back to some semblance of order and all eyes turned to the podium. The speaker of the house stood tall at the rostrum, patiently hammering the gavel until he judged he could be heard.

'In light of the news delivered by Titus Aurelius Varro!' he announced. 'The Senate will recess for one hour!'

Varro stepped back to allow many of the Senators to sweep past him on their way out of the chamber, purposefully avoiding the accusatory and derisive looks that shamed him. Again he searched for his father, spotting him once again with Scipio as both men made their way towards the exit. Varro cut across the flow of the crowd, the men before making no effort to step aside and ease his passage while twenty feet away he saw his father enter a small ante-chamber adjacent to the main exit.

'It is out of my hands, Calvus,' Scipio said, his face a mask of empathy while inside he secretly rejoiced at the humbling of such a powerful magistrate. 'The fate of your son is in the hand of the senior consul. He is the supreme commander.'

'I am not blind, Gnaeus,' Calvus replied. 'It is widely suspected that you were the driving force behind the election of Regulus.'

Scipio smiled inwardly, happy that the well chosen rumours he had circulated regarding his secret alliance with Regulus were already filtering through to the right ears.

'I cannot comment on wild rumour, Calvus,' Scipio said,

allowing a half smile to creep across his face, 'but it is true that Regulus and I have a long-standing friendship. It *may* be possible to speak to him on your son's behalf.'

Calvus signed inwardly. Scipio was one of the most cunning men he had ever encountered in the Senate and like many others, he had secretly celebrated Scipio's humiliation at Lipara, glad to see his power curtailed. Now, however, it would seem the Hydra-headed former consul was once more entwined in the inner circle of power and Calvus knew the price to save his son would dwarf even the fortune he had paid to ensure his son's commission in the first place.

A knock on the door interrupted both men and they turned to see the young commander enter.

'Ah, Titus Aurelius Varro,' Scipio said, his false friendliness fooling the son if not the father, 'we were just discussing you.'

Varro coloured at implication and he closed the door behind him, the heavy oak muting the sounds of conversation outside.

'Senator Scipio,' Varro said stepping forward, keeping his tone easy, a smile on his face. 'My father has spoken of you many times. I am pleased to finally meet you in person.'

Scipio took the proffered hand, his own smile genial, a carefully constructed mask.

'And I you, young Varro,' he replied, 'although I'm sure you would wish the circumstances were different.'

Again Varro coloured but with effort he retained his smile.

'As a man who has suffered a similar fate at the hands of the Carthaginians,' Varro said gravely, 'I know I can count on your understanding in this matter.'

The smile evaporated from Scipio's face in an instant, to be replaced by a withering stare of contempt.

'Do not speak as if we are equals, boy,' he growled. 'My

capture at Lipara was the result of a treacherous plot by the enemy. Your defeat was due to sheer incompetence.'

Varro was shocked by the sudden anger from Scipio and for a moment he was speechless. His father bristled inwardly, cursing his son and his inept approach. Scipio already held all the cards and could command any price. If he became hostile however, that price would increase exponentially.

'My son is clumsy, Senator,' Calvus said, stepping forward. 'What he meant to say was; as Romans we all share the sting of defeat.'

Scipio snorted, his gaze never leaving Varro, his anger commanding him to throw the fool to the wolves. Slowly, however, his rational mind forced him to focus.

'Of course,' he said, the smile returning to his face although it did not reach his cold eyes.

Varro stepped forward again, his own anger rising at his father's dismissal, the need to defend himself overwhelming.

'I am a legionary, Senator Scipio,' he said, 'not a sailor. You are right to say that my defeat was due to incompetence, but it was not my incompetence, it was the fault of my captain, the man who should have perceived the threat and advised me, Atticus Milonius Perennis.'

Calvus was shocked by his son's announcement and again he burned with shame. It was unseemly for a commander to blame his subordinates and he turned to Scipio once more, expecting the senator to berate his son for such a blatant attempt to shift the blame. He was surprised however when Scipio's expression seemed to show understanding.

'Perennis,' Scipio said slowly, allowing the name to hang in the air for a moment. 'He was captain of your flagship?'

'At Consul Duilius's insistence,' Varro interjected although the truth was that Varro had chosen Atticus without intervention.

Scipio nodded once more. Perennis was still under the tacit protection of Duilius and as a hero of Mylae, he was near untouchable in Rome. Away from the city he was out of Scipio's immediate reach but also Duilius's protection and so for months Scipio had being trying to devise a way to eradicate the man who had sullied his honour, while remaining above suspicion. Varro could be just the puppet he was seeking. He decided to test the depths of the young man's belligerence.

'But Perennis captained the flagship to victory at Mylae,' Scipio said, his advocacy of Perennis like bile in his throat. 'Surely he is more than capable.'

'Perhaps he is, Senator,' Varro replied, committing himself to speak aloud the words that would strengthen his case. 'But we must remember he is a Greek and has no vested interest in the fate of the Roman fleet.'

'You question his loyalty?' Scipio asked, his excitement rising as he sensed the hatred of the younger man.

'I question where his loyalty lies,' Varro replied, his half-truths taking on a life of their own.

'Very well,' Scipio said, satisfied. 'Leave us now, young Varro. I must speak with your father alone.'

Varro stood to attention and saluted, believing firmly that he had found an ally in the senator. He left the room without another word.

Scipio watched him go, his mind racing as his previous plans were discarded and new ones began to formulate. He had been content to protect Varro to place his father in debt to him but the young man had put Scipio within reach of an even greater prize and it took all of his self control to keep the look of triumph from his face. He turned once more to the elder Varro, his outer consciousness listening once more to the man's renewed supplication, his expression fixed to show only indulgence while inwardly a malicious pleasure grew. He had already enacted a measure of revenge against Duilius. Now, however, with the unwitting assistance of Varro, he was ready to strike at the other man who had stolen so much from him.

Atticus sat up on his cot as he heard the key turn in the lock's brass housing. He glanced over his shoulder to the window of his cell. It was dark outside with a light breeze herding low clouds across the sky, their passing obscuring and revealing the pale light of the rising crescent moon. As he turned back to the door he caught Septimus's eye. The centurion was also rising from his cot, his puzzled expression answering Atticus's unasked question. They had been in the cell now for nearly thirty-six hours and while food had been delivered at regular intervals by slaves, they had had no other contact with the world outside.

The door opened and a black cloaked *praetorian* guard entered. He was flanked in the hallway by three others, shadowy figures in the darkness of the hallway. The man's height was increased by his helmet and he towered over the seated men, his eyes moving over both before settling on Atticus.

'Captain Perennis of the *Aquila*?' he asked

Atticus stood up and nodded.

'You're to come with me,' the guard said, his voice revealing nothing.

'Where to?' Atticus asked.

'To see my master,' the guard replied.

'And he is?'

The guard looked to Septimus again, then to the window, his gaze wary.

'Not here,' he replied, stepping aside slightly to indicate that

Atticus should pass out into the hallway. Atticus hesitated for a mere second. There was nothing to be gained from resisting. Not yet at least. He turned to Septimus and nodded, the centurion returning his gesture before he walked past the *praetorian* guard.

Atticus waited while the door was relocked and then he followed his escort down the long torch-lit corridor out into the courtyard. A stable lad held five horses ready and they mounted quickly, two men taking station in front of and behind Atticus as they trotted out of the *castrum*. It was near midnight but the commercial dockside of Ostia was still busy with activity, some furtive, as starving waifs searched for scraps of fallen and forgotten food and slaves cleared away the remnants of the day's trading, clearing the docks for the flood of produce that would arrive when dawn's light would permit the incoming ships to dock safely.

Their way along the docks was cleared without command before them, the hoof beats unnaturally loud in the silence of Ostia, their passing unremarkable to the slaves and starving whose wretched lives they interrupted. Atticus remained silent, his position in the centre of the group preventing further questions of his escort, but he sensed the men close in around him, bunching their advance and hemming him in. He smiled inwardly, wondering where they thought he was going to run to. He didn't recognise any of them but one thing was clear, whoever their master was, they were not taking any chances that he might escape.

The group left Ostia and headed east until they reached the *via Aurelia*, the great road north from Rome. They turned towards the city and increased their pace, the iron shod hooves of their mounts reverberating against the cobbles of the near-deserted paved road. As they approached the Servian wall of the city, Atticus could see the bivouacs of travellers stranded by the closing of the city gates at dusk, arriving too late to be admitted entry. They were huddled around pathetic fires, taking solace from the feeble light, a protection from the darkness that surrounded them and the preying hunters that would steal life and possessions from any who slept unguarded.

As the escort approached the Porta Flumentana, one of sixteen locked gates in the wall, Atticus's gaze was drawn upwards along the towering wall. It was capped by flaming torches, beacons that created semi-circular patches of flickering lights on the battlements and accentuated the black darkness of the wall beneath. The gate within a granite arch rose twenty-five feet, solid oak with heavy iron bands spanning and securing the timbers every two feet. In the light of day they would be thrown back in open invitation to all, but now, in the half light of fire, in the depth of night, they stood impenetrable to the stranded travellers.

The horsemen halted as they reached the gate and the guard commander dismounted. He withdrew his sword and hammered the pommel on the wooden barrier, creating a deep resounding thud that echoed off the silent walls and alerted every traveller within earshot. A small face-high panel opened and Atticus watched as the *praetorian* conducted a terse conversation with an unseen guard on the inside. The panel closed again and the commander re-mounted. For a minute nothing happened and then suddenly the still air was wrenched with the grating sound of metal on metal. The gate was drawn back six feet and a troop of legionaries emerged, the six of them fanning out with their shields charged. The two mounted *praetoriani* behind Atticus drew their swords without command and again bunched in behind him, preventing him from turning his mount, their swords charged and ready. Again Atticus frowned at their over-cautious steps to prevent his escape, but he ignored them, his attention taken by the gust of sound in the darkness behind him.

The sound of the opening gate had roused those travellers closest to the gate and they came forward at a rush, many dragging their possessions while others tried to quickly harness their pack horses and ponies. The *praetorian* commander trotted forward through the gate without looking back, Atticus following in his wake, but the legionaries remained forward facing, their spears now levelled against the oncoming rush of people. Atticus could hear the desperation in their voices as they cried out for entry and he looked back over his shoulder to witness their forlorn attempt. They were fifteen feet from the legionaries when a flight of arrows suddenly struck the ground before them, loosed from the hidden parapets above and the crowd stopped short, their headlong rush transformed into halting steps, the sight of the arrows embedded into the ground before them causing all to hesitate.

The gate obscured Atticus's vision of the road outside as he passed through and as the *praetoriani* behind him followed suit, the legionaries backed through the narrow aperture before it was closed with an echoing thud, cutting off the last of the pathetic voices of the travellers outside.

The escort continued through darkened streets, the pitiable moonlight offering little assistance and Atticus was left to reflect on what he had just witnessed. It was inconceivable to believe that the gates of Rome were opened each time a troop of soldiers arrived, *praetoriani* or otherwise, and Atticus was convinced that the man commanding these guards had to be powerful enough to overrule an age-old law that commanded the closure of the gates during darkness.

The horsemen moved quickly and Atticus was struck, as always, by the sense of the pressing humanity around him, the multitude within the walls and at each passing side street he felt the presence of a dozen eyes on his back, observers hidden in the darkness. Within fifteen minutes the men arrived at a featureless gateway in an affluent quarter of the city. They had risen up the side of one of the seven hills of Rome but Atticus could not discern which, unfamiliar as he was with the layout of the sprawling capital. There was a marble nameplate encased in the wall next to the gate. It was shrouded in shadow with only the last two letters exposed to the ambient light, 'us.' Atticus tried to make out the preceding text but he could not and his heart rate increased despite his resolution to hold fast until the person who had summoned him was revealed.

The gate was opened without command or call and the men led their mounts into the outer courtyard. The details of the house inside were lost in darkness but Atticus could nevertheless sense its vastness. He dismounted, handing the reins to a stable lad who quickly corralled the horses and led them away, leaving Atticus standing amidst the *praetoriani*. They moved off towards the entrance to the house proper and again Atticus fell into step although he could sense that the men escorting him had visibly relaxed their guard. Once in the atrium the guard commander turned abruptly to Atticus and spoke to him for the first time since leaving Ostia.

'Wait here,' he commanded, before nodding to his men to follow him down a torch-lit passageway.

Atticus looked around him, perplexed at being left alone after the close attention on the ride. His gaze scanned his surroundings, recognising the signs of wealth that adorned the candle-lit atrium and as his eyes ranged over the various entranceways he spotted the shape of a lone figure framed in an arch. The man walked towards him and before his face was revealed, Atticus recognised his stature and gait. He walked forwards to close the distance, his mind thinking back on when he had last seen the man, when they had stood beside each other on the steps of the Curia and the aft-deck of the *Aquila*. He came to a stop and stood to attention as the man's face was finally illuminated. Atticus saluted formally but the man dismissed the gesture, extending his hand in friendship instead. Atticus took it without hesitation, his face breaking into a smile.

'It is good to see you, Atticus,' the man said.

'And you, Consul Duilius,' Atticus replied.

Duilius nodded, continuing the handshake, his other hand clasping Atticus's upper arm.

'Come,' he said and he led Atticus from the atrium into a well lit reception room.

'I am glad to see you safe,' Duilius said, proffering Atticus a goblet of wine. 'I have heard of your "altercation" with Varro at Thermae and I feared he might try to take his measure of reprisal outside the confines of the *castrum*.'

Atticus took a minute to recover, recalling the caution of the guards on his journey to Duilius's house, their drawn swords outside the Porta Flumentana when Atticus had noticed the rush of people in the dark. They had not been acting to prevent his escape, they had been guarding against an attack on his life. Atticus looked to Duilius once more, amazed at how far the senator's knowledge extended.

'Varro is a young fool,' Atticus began. 'He was ready to condemn over a thousand men to save his own skin.'

'He is young and he may well be a fool,' Duilius said seriously, 'but his hand and actions are guided by his father. And he is no fool. That is why I advocate caution.'

Atticus nodded again, marking the warning from his former commander.

Duilius indicated a low couch in the centre of the room and Atticus sat down.

'I have heard a full account of the battle from my source,' the senator said, taking a seat opposite Atticus, 'however I would like to hear your version.'

Atticus recounted the attack in detail, conscious that Duilius was an avid student of naval warfare.

'It would seem the enemy grossly underestimated our numbers, otherwise their fleet would have been larger,' Duilius remarked.

Atticus nodded in agreement. 'Their mistake allowed for the escape of eighteen of our galleys and the majority of the *hastati*. Outnumbered, we would not have broken out.'

'However fortunate your escape,' Duilius said, 'Thermae is a significant defeat. There will be repercussions.'

'Varro?' Atticus ventured.

'He is disgraced, but his father will certainly deflect a severe censure, using his influence amongst the patricians. I suspect Varro will retain a command, albeit one of little consequence.'

'You will not remove him from command?' Atticus asked, surprised.

'It is not within my power,' Duilius replied.

'But as senior consul . . .'

Duilius shook his head. He quickly told Atticus of his decision to attain the censorship, omitting his suspicions of Scipio's manipulation of his intentions.

'So who is senior consul?' Atticus asked.

'A man named Regulus,' Duilius said and Atticus shrugged imperceptibly. He had never heard of him. 'My own close ally, Longus, has attained the lesser position of junior consul.'

The men continued to talk, their conversation frequently touching on Thermae and what might become of Varro. Atticus told Duilius of his rescue of a survivor of a pirate attack, voicing his mystification at the pirates' tactics but as he talked Atticus became increasingly aware that Duilius would have a lesser hand in any of the outcomes they were exploring.

As a Greek outsider in a Roman world, Atticus had found a confederate in Duilius, a Roman through and through but an outsider in his own society, a 'new man' in a world of ancient families and the two men had forged a bond based entirely on mutual respect of each other's abilities. Duilius's outward support for Atticus, making him captain of the flagship at Mylae, had afforded him a level of acceptance amongst many Romans, a measure of integration into a Republic that normally thought of its non-Roman citizens as beneath consideration. With Duilius's acceptance of this new position however and his imminent exit from the military sphere, Atticus knew he would once more be exposed to the full prejudice of Rome.

'It is near dawn,' Duilius said finally, rising from the couch. 'If you wish, I will have my men escort you to anywhere in the city.'

'I do not need to return to Ostia?' Atticus asked.

'No, orders have been issued by Varro to release the entire crew of the *Aquila* at first light.'

Atticus nodded, wondering anew how Duilius got his information. The senator proffered his hand once more and Atticus took it, the solid grip of Duilius's handshake affirming their friendship. The senator left the room without another word and moments later Duilius's guard commander entered. His eyes were bloodshot with fatigue and he stood before Atticus with a weary expression.

'Where to?' he asked gruffly.

Atticus replied without conscious thought, the lure of his destination inescapable. 'The Viminal Quarter,' he said, brushing past the guard, his determined stride matching his anticipation.

*

Atticus stood for a moment at the south-eastern corner of the *Forum Magnum*, the main square in Rome, his gaze ranging over the vaulted temples and soaring statues, his mind casting back to the first time he had witnessed the magnificent vista before him. He glanced briefly over his shoulder but his escort was already lost in the throng of people feeding to and from the square from the narrow streets. He closed his eyes and breathed deeply, the faintly fresher air of the open forum washing some of the stronger smells of the airless crowded streets from his nostrils, the stench of unwashed bodies, of cooked food and human waste, the sweat and brine of a multitude crammed into the walled city. He reopened his eyes and took his bearings from the landmarks of the forum, his body turning unbidden to align his vision with the road leading to the Viminal quarter.

Atticus quickly sidestepped as a runner brushed passed him, knocking into another man as he did, invoking a murmured curse from the irate Roman. The press of the jostling crowd was increasing with every passing second and Atticus could remain stationary no longer. He squared his shoulders and pressed forward, smiling as he thought of how Gaius manoeuvred the *Aquila* through even the most crowded harbours with ease, wondering what the Calabrian helmsman would make of the teeming streets of Rome.

Climbing the gentle slope of the hill, Atticus spotted his marker on the right, a tavern, and his eyes instantly shot to the other side of the street, to the austere walls of the house of Hadria's aunt. He stepped to the left side of the street and ran his hand along the burnt brick wall, feeling the texture until it gave way to the iron-studded door that marked the centre of the wall. He paused for a second. It had been nearly three months since he stood on this spot and he savoured the anticipation of the moment. He knocked and stood back.

The door opened and he was admitted, the servant scurrying off to fetch her mistress the moment she recognised the Greek captain, Atticus following at a slower pace, finding his way into the atrium, pausing there to wait.

The radiance of the morning sun had begun to fill the open-roofed atrium, illuminating the colonnaded path surrounding the tranquil pool at its centre. Atticus watched the pool in silence, forgetting the last remnants of the sounds that had dominated the streets outside, and he slowly became aware of the near silence of the house. Then he heard it, the sound at first hidden beneath the soothing trickle and murmur of the water. It was music, the gentle notes created by a lyre, its resonance so subtle and hypnotic that for a full minute Atticus was lost in its spell, his excitement overcome by an enormous sense of well-being.

Suddenly, in contrast to its stealthy arrival, the music stopped, to be replaced seconds later by the sound of approaching footsteps, light and fast, a creature in near flight and Atticus turned to its source with a smile on his face. Hadria burst into view around the far corner of the atrium, her run coming to a stop within three paces and she stood suddenly still, her chest heaving under her unadorned tunic, exertion and emotion combining to take her breath away. Atticus studied her face, drinking in the sight; her sun-bleached light brown hair and sea-grey eyes, her vivacity that seemed to charge the still air until her presence filled the entire atrium. He took a half step forward and the movement spurred her to full flight, her agility covering the space between them in the time it took Atticus to stretch out his arms. She leapt into them and they embraced, speechless in the intensity of the moment, and he reached down to kiss her, the softness of her mouth at odds with the firm contours of her young body. They drew apart and stood locked in each others' gaze; the profound silence between them an extension of their time spent apart, their unspoken emotions implicit. They took each other's hand and Hadria led the way to her bedroom, quietly closing the door behind them, their restraint immediately abandoned in a rush to rediscover each other.

CHAPTER SEVEN

Hamilcar stood on the bow of the *Alissar* as his flagship entered the chaotic harbour of Syracuse on the south-eastern corner of Sicily, his hand gripping the side-rail for balance, the tunic beneath his leather chest-plate soaked by sea spray thrown up as the galley's ram butted through the off-shore driven waves. He looked over his shoulder to the rigging of the mainmast, his eyes darting from one lookout to the next, judging the body language of each, sensing their tension but perceiving little else. He turned to the waters ahead once more, his ears picking up the cries of warning on the wind as his warship was spotted by the outermost trading galleys in the harbour.

Hamilcar ignored the sailing ships as they turned ponderously before the *Alissar*, their captains judging the course of the dark hulled galley, the blunt-nosed ram pointing directly for the centre of the harbour. Instead he looked beneath and between their sails, searching for the arrow-like lines of galleys that sped under oars, spotting a couple skimming the wave-tops as they too gave way before the Carthaginian quinquereme. They were biremes, almost certainly trading vessels but Hamilcar scrutinised each in turn to be sure.

'Trireme! Two points off the starboard quarter!'

Hamilcar's gaze darted to the shouted co-ordinates, cursing the fat-bellied ships that obscured his line of sight. He spotted the trireme and he instantly felt his heart rate quicken. Was she a warship? He couldn't tell. The angle of sight was wrong, too deep, and the banners on the galley's main mast were indistinguishable from the multitude bedecking every ship in the harbour. He turned once more to the look-outs, trusting their younger eyes and elevated line of sight. He saw the face of one burst into a smile, followed instantly by another.

'She's one of ours!' the lookout called. 'A trader!'

Hamilcar spun around again, waiting impatiently as the progress of the *Alissar* improved the angle of sight. He smiled as he confirmed the identification with his own eyes. A trading trireme. His relief made him laugh out loud. Only a Carthaginian would turn a galley that size into a trading ship. She was probably ex-military, stripped and sold at auction after it was deemed her aging timbers were no longer strong enough for battle conditions.

Hamilcar again considered the wisdom of this unannounced visit to Syracuse. The province was openly allied to Rome, a treaty signed after the Romans defeated the Syracusans three years before at the beginning of the war. Rome had been lenient in her terms, the escalation of the conflict with Carthage drawing her attention to the western half of Sicily and so they merely commanded King Hiero to confine his army within the borders of the Syracuse and provide anchorage for Roman ships when required. It was for this reason that Hamilcar had known his arrival was a significant gamble. If the trireme had indeed been a Roman warship, the *Alissar* would have taken her easily, but Hamilcar could not afford to compromise Hiero's relationship with the Romans by destroying one of their ships in Syracuse harbour, not now that secrecy had become paramount.

The *Alissar* moved quickly through the cluttered harbour, the clear path created for her speeding her approach and Hamilcar smiled once more as his crew shouted acknowledgments to the Carthaginian crews of many of the trading vessels. The island of Sicily was a battlefield, but Syracuse remained an open port and trade recognised few boundaries, certainly not in a port that sat astride one of the busiest east-west trading routes. The *Alissar* docked quickly and Hamilcar strode down the gang-plank with a guard detail of four men. He ordered his galley to take station in the outer harbour and she was instantly away, her balanced hull turning within a ship-length, her two hundred and seventy oars striking and churning the waters as one.

Hamilcar walked quickly along the dockside, his guard detail ever vigilant behind him, their hands resting on the hilts of their swords. Hamilcar spotted a Roman trading ship unloading ahead and he swept her deck with his eyes before spotting the captain on the aft-deck. The Roman had obviously seen the *Alissar* dock and Hamilcar knew his every step was now being watched surreptitiously. He returned the scrutiny balefully and he smiled inwardly as the Roman turned away. Hamilcar knew the Roman would report the sighting but he was unconcerned. It would be days before news reached Rome and a single Carthaginian galley in Syracuse was hardly cause for significant suspicion.

Hamilcar and his men left the busy docks and threaded their way through the labyrinthine streets, the soaring battlements of Hiero's castle guiding them unerringly to their destination. The streets opened out into a large square directly before the guarded entrance to the castle and Hamilcar took the opportunity to study the east facing wall of the castle, as his first visit here over two months before had been at night. The castle was uncomplicated, a square fortification with watchtowers on each corner and Hamilcar nodded at the wisdom of its design, his military mind searching the thirty foot high sheer walls for weakness and finding none.

The Carthaginians crossed the square diagonally and their obvious military bearing ensured that their every step was watched with interest from the battlements above. Hamilcar approached the guards at the gate and spoke to them brusquely, requesting a word with the officer of the day. The officer arrived promptly and Hamilcar identified himself, requesting an immediate audience with the king. The Carthaginians were escorted to the guard-house and the officer disappeared to return within five minutes with permission for Hamilcar to proceed alone to the audience chamber.

Hamilcar glanced left and right as he climbed ever higher and deeper into the castle, the guards preceding him moving quickly, sensing the importance of the Carthaginian commander who had been granted an immediate audience with their king. Every junction and landing was guarded but Hamilcar and his escort moved through them without check until finally they came to the ornate outer doors of the king's chamber. The doors opened without command and the escort peeled off to allow Hamilcar to proceed alone along the carpeted approach to the king.

The chamber had a vaulted ceiling supported by a complex series of beams, held aloft by flanking columns that ran the length of the rectangular room and Hamilcar's eyes were drawn instinctively upward. He lowered his eyes and looked directly to the head of the room. Hiero was seated on a low stool on a raised platform, an adviser sitting on a cushion directly to his left while a detachment of royal guards stood unmoved six feet behind the king. The area was strewn with many more cushions and Hamilcar had a feeling that they had been occupied only moments before, his announced arrival prompting Hiero to clear the chamber. A wise move considering what was going to be discussed.

Hamilcar stopped a discreet distance from the raised platform and bowed his head in respect, his eyes remaining on the king's, searching for any clue to Hiero's thoughts but the king's expression was unreadable. Hamilcar straightened up and waited to be spoken to.

'You are welcome, young Barca,' Hiero said.

'Thank you, sire!' Hamilcar replied, smiling inwardly. The king was no older than himself, perhaps even a year or two younger, but Hamilcar conceded that if achievement was the mark of a man's age, then Hiero was indeed a lifetime older.

'You wished to speak with me?' Hiero continued.

'Yes, sire, I wished to inform you of my plans personally.'

Hiero's adviser rose promptly and whispered something in the king's ear. Hiero nodded his agreement before signaling Hamilcar to continue.

'As you may know, sire,' Hamilcar began, 'my forces have turned the tide once more in Carthage's favour with a victory at Thermae.'

'Not as complete a victory as you might have wished,' Hiero said, studying the Carthaginian commander's reaction. 'I understand many of the Roman galleys escaped.'

'Nevertheless,' Hamilcar countered, retaining his composure, 'victory was secured and I am now in a position to advance my army eastwards.'

'How far east?' Hiero asked, sitting straighter on his chair.

'To the borders of Syracuse, sire, in order to split the Romans' territory in two.'

Hiero nodded, appreciating the audacity of the plan, his mind's eye creating the map of Sicily, the west held by the Carthaginians, the east the domain Syracuse, the Roman territory dividing them both through the centre of the island.

'You risk a great deal by revealing your plans to me, Barca,' the king said after a pause, a smile on his face.

'No more than you have already risked, sire, by allowing my ships to use Tyndaris in defiance of your treaty with Rome.'

Hiero's smile broadened. He liked the Carthaginian's confidence. It matched his own. He had granted Hamilcar the use of Tyndaris because the outcome of the war was still very much in the balance and he wanted the eventual victor, whomever that was, to remember Syracuse as an ally.

'Nevertheless, why reveal your plans to me?' he asked.

'Because when my army reaches your border, there is an opportunity for Syracuse to throw off the shackles of Rome and form an open alliance with Carthage.'

'To jump from the mouth of one baying wolf to another?' Hiero asked.

'Carthage has long been a friend of Syracuse, sire. We are very much alike. We seek only peaceful trade, not submission and dominance as Rome demands.'

Hiero nodded, searching the Carthaginian's words for the real truth. His adviser rose once more to whisper into his ear.

Hamilcar waited in silence, cursing anew the need to reveal his strategy so soon to Hiero, a premature disclosure caused by Hanno's plans to stifle the war in Sicily, the victory required by his father needed sooner rather than later.

'And what of Tyndaris?' Hiero asked. 'I hear rumours that Carthage is employing the services of pirates in the Tyrrhenian Sea off the west coast of Italy.'

Hamilcar cursed inwardly. The king was too well informed. 'Not pirates, sire, mercenaries, who are familiar with the territorial waters of Rome.'

The king nodded, a sly smile spreading across his face. 'There is a thin line Barca,' he said, 'between pirates and mercenaries.'

'Yes, sire.'

Hiero's expression changed, becoming firm once more, an edge to his voice. 'I trust you are taking every precaution to ensure the Romans do not become aware of your activities, and my involvement.'

'Rest assured, sire, the mercenaries are acting under the strict command of one of my finest officers and his orders are to leave no witnesses.'

Hiero nodded again. The Carthaginian's assurances were hollow and he knew it was only a matter of time before the secret of Tyndaris was exposed. Nevertheless he still believed his decision was sound – if the Carthaginians had indeed turned the tide of the war.

'Very well, Barca,' he said, 'I will follow your campaign closely and if and when the time is right, my army will be committed to yours.'

Hamilcar bowed and began to slowly walk backward, keeping his head low. When he had retreated twenty paces he straightened up and turned, keeping his back straight as the doors leading from the chamber were opened once more. He passed through them and as he heard them close he halted, looking over his shoulder at the intricate designs on the door, the Greek iconography the spoke to the ancestral home of Hiero and his people. 'If and when the time is right,' the king had said and Hamilcar bridled at the failsafe approach that Hiero had adopted, the non-committal that placed the entire onus on the forces of Carthage. Succeed and Syracuse would become an open ally. Fail and Hiero could safely deny any pact ever existed.

Hamilcar's escort returned to lead him once more to the gate of the castle and he fell in behind them. He straightened his shoulders as he walked, his hand reaching for and grasping the hilt of his sword, flexing his fingers as he took a firm grip on the moulded ivory handle. To his front the Roman enemy stood, bloodied but by no means beaten. To his rear the cautious men of Carthage and Syracuse stood, demanding victory before committing fully to the war. Hamilcar and his men stood in the middle, defiant and confident; their only ally the sword and shield and Hamilcar increased the intensity of his grip at the thought, matching his will to the forged iron of his blade.

Hadria allowed her hand to drift slowly down Atticus's chest as he talked, her fingers tracing the contours of his flesh, brushing lightly over the creased skin of his scars, fascinated by them, wishing to know the story behind each one. Atticus lay on his back with one arm propped under his head, his eyes turned up to the ceiling as he relayed the events of the past three months in answer to her open questions, his voice unnaturally low in the privacy of Hadria's bedroom. Hadria lay on her side, her leg thrown across Atticus, the gentle curve of her thigh pressing lightly on him, her head resting on her upper arm. Outside the sun was reaching its zenith and the dead heat of the late summer draped the room in a sullen shroud of warmth, sustaining a sheen of sweat on the lovers' bodies.

Atticus spoke of Thermae but he did not mention his confrontation with Varro, not wanting to alarm Hadria. Finally he spoke of the journey to Rome and their rescue of the survivor from the *Fides*, his brow creasing anew as the logic of the pirates' tactics continued to baffle him.

'And what of Septimus?' Hadria asked as Atticus finished. 'Has he mentioned me to you?'

'He only came back on board the *Aquila* at Thermae,' Atticus replied. 'We've not spoken of you since our quarrel months ago outside the walls of Rome.'

Hadria's expression creased into a slight frown. 'We must tell him of our love,' she said.

Atticus turned over to face her, resting his hand on her cheek.

'Many of the servants here are from my father's household,' she continued. 'They move back and forth between the two houses and are bound to discuss this. It is only a matter of time before a loose word is overheard by one of my family.'

Atticus nodded, knowing the inevitable confrontation with Septimus would have to be faced sooner rather than later, their reunion at Thermae putting them once more at close quarters.

'I will speak with him,' Atticus said.

'No,' Hadria replied. 'It must come from me; he must know how I feel.'

Again Atticus nodded, searching his own feelings. Hadria believed Septimus's disapproval of Atticus as his sister's suitor was in response to the loss of Hadria's first husband and Septimus's best friend in battle and that he wished to spare his sister, and perhaps himself, the pain of that loss again. Atticus had understood Hadria's reasoning but he found he could not abandon the last vestiges of his own initial reaction, that Septimus disapproved because Atticus was Greek and beneath consideration as a match for Hadria. He knew it was a misplaced accusation and yet he had encountered prejudice so often before from many other Romans that his misgivings were hard to ignore.

A gentle knock on the door shattered the privacy of their world and Hadria leapt from the bed, her beauty pronounced by her nakedness and Atticus smiled anew.

'My Aunt!' Hadria gasped, fearing the worst as she shrugged on a tunic. 'She was supposed to be out all day.'

Atticus shared Hadria's alarm and quickly covered up. To be discovered now, on the cusp of revealing their relationship, would immeasurably compromise them both and he cursed Fortuna for her capricious nature. Hadria opened the door an inch and peered out, her shoulders visibly relaxing as she was confronted by one of the house servants. Atticus listened to the muted announcement, unable to discern the details. Hadria pushed the door closed and turned to him, her face a mixture of happiness and regret.

'A messenger,' she said, 'from my father's house. Septimus has returned and I am to go there at once.'

Antoninus Laetonius Capito stood tall at the head of the family room, his hand unconsciously fingering the vicious scar that marred the left side of his face. Septimus sat opposite him, a goblet of wine in his hand, the cushions beside him still crumpled from where his mother, Salonina, had sat only moments before, his forearm still sensing where her hand had pressed against his skin, a touch that confirmed to herself that her son had returned safely.

Antoninus began to pace, his movements slow but fluid, his gaze still the authoritarian stare of a centurion of the Ninth legion. In a low and hoarse voice, he began to question Septimus on the details of the battle of Thermae, his enquiries sharp and incisive, his military mind recreating the conflict in sharp detail.

'Megellus is a fool,' he said after Septimus had concluded, 'he should have held firm in open ground rather than hamstrung his command in the narrow streets.'

'The Carthaginian cavalry numbered near a thousand,' Septimus replied, protest in his voice, 'and the Ninth was under-strength.'

'Your time in the marines has softened you, boy,' Antoninus snorted derisively. 'You've forgotten the true mettle of a legion. By Mars, my maniple would have stood.'

'Then your maniple would have been slaughtered,' Septimus

spat back, weary of his father's dismissive attitude towards the marines.

'And you managed to escape by sea?' There was a half look of disdain on Antoninus's face.

'My duty is to lead my men on board the *Aquila*.'

'Your duty, as was mine, should be with the Ninth,' Antoninus said, standing rigidly across from his son, his scar vividly white on his coloured face. 'Where is your honour?' he growled.

Septimus shot up, his knuckles white around the goblet in his hand, his temper rising as he held his father's iron gaze.

'I am a centurion and my honour is beyond question,' he said, taking a half-step forward, his hand trembling and the muscles in his arm tensing, ready to be unleashed.

Antoninus saw Septimus's stance and thanked Jupiter his son was unarmed. The boy was certainly a wild one and his ferocity seemed to be barely in check. For the first time Antoninus wondered what kind of a centurion his son was and a half-smile crept across his face as he answered his own question.

Suddenly Salonina entered the room, stopping short as she noticed the charged atmosphere, the aggressive stance of both men, and she shot a look to her husband who faced her, knowing he had goaded Septimus, that he had given voice to the disappointment he had often spoken to her about. She suppressed her censure and looked to her son.

'Septimus,' she said, a forced smile on her face, 'Hadria has arrived.'

Septimus shot around at his mother's voice, her tone breaking the spell of his temper. His mind replayed the words she had just spoken and his anger evaporated further. He turned his back on his father and looked to the entrance. Hadria strode in, her cheeks flushed in her haste and she stood smiling for a second before embracing her brother. Salonina beckoned towards the couches and they moved to sit down, Hadria immediately noticing the tension between her father and Septimus.

The conversation turned towards lighter subjects under Salonina's diplomatic touch and soon all were at ease, the news of Septimus's absent brothers, Tiberius and Claudius, taking centre stage. Both were traders and between them they controlled the bulk of the family's wealth, an estate that had increased with the escalation of the war in Sicily, the demand for raw materials for ship building creating opportunities unseen in a generation.

'When will you sail again?' Hadria asked, wondering how long Atticus would be in Rome.

'I don't know,' Septimus replied, telling them of their arrival in Ostia, the seizure of the *Aquila* and their forced confinement in the barracks pending Varro's report to the Senate. They had been released only that very morning and Septimus had immediately ordered the crew and his men to proceed to Fiumicino.

'And you did not go with them?' Antoninus asked instinctively. A commander's place was with his men.

'No, father,' Septimus replied, and he quickly told them how Atticus had been taken from his cell the night before, his escort unidentified and his whereabouts now unknown. 'It's possible he has been taken under guard by Varro,' Septimus concluded, his concern evident to all.

'No, he . . .' Hadria spoke without thinking, impulsively wishing to allay her brother's fears.

'I mean, I'm sure he . . . ,' she continued, her mind racing. 'Why would Varro take him under guard?'

Septimus explained about Atticus's confrontation with Varro at Thermae, his own expression now puzzled as he thought about Hadria's initial reaction. Hadria's own face showed nothing but mounting anxiety at the danger Atticus was in, a danger he had kept from her. As Septimus concluded he stood once more as he suddenly understood what Hadria had meant to say.

'I must go,' he said, his family rising with him.

'Where to?' his father asked.

'I must find Atticus, although I now believe I know where he is.' Septimus touched his mother lightly on the forearm as he brushed past her, his determined stride taking him out of the room without a backward glance at Hadria or his father. Hadria ran after him, catching him as he stood in the atrium, buckling his scabbard, his hand resting on the hilt of his sword.

'Septimus,' she said, placing her hand on his shoulder. 'I must speak with you.'

'You were with him last night,' Septimus said as he spun around, his expression furious.

'Yes,' Hadria replied quickly. 'It was Duilius who summoned Atticus from Ostia. He was told the rest of his crew was being released this morning so he came to see me.'

'To *see* you,' Septimus said scornfully. 'That's one way of putting it.'

'We are in love,' Hadria shot back, suddenly angry at Septimus's debasement of their relationship.

Septimus was shocked by Hadria's pronouncement. He hadn't realised their relationship was so far advanced. 'He has betrayed me,' he countered. 'I told him not to pursue you.'

'You had no right to do that, Septimus. Atticus is not beholden to you and neither am I.'

'We'll see,' Septimus said and strode out into the courtyard, mounting his borrowed horse in one effortless movement. He galloped out the main gate without another word, scattering the people before him on the street, their angry cries drowning Hadria's calls for Septimus to come back.

Varro steeled his nerve as he reached for the handle of the door leading to the senior consul's chamber adjacent to the Curia. With grim satisfaction he noticed his hand was steady and he clenched and unclenched his fist a number of times, a simple distraction that helped calm him further. He had not talked to his father since he last saw him with Scipio the day before, the Senate reconvening soon after and his father not returning to the house that evening. The summons had then arrived at dawn, commanding Varro to attend Regulus's private room, forestalling any chance to confer with his father, to learn the outcome of his intercession.

Varro entered the consul's chamber with a determined stride but he instantly faltered, his step interrupted as his gaze was drawn upward towards the domed ceiling and the play of the late sunlight through the vaulted oculus, creating an uneven ellipse that tracked across the room with the passing of the day. The chamber was a perfect circle, an anomaly amongst the other ante-chambers of the Curia, all of which were square or rectangular and Varro felt overwhelmed by the impression that he had indeed stepped into the inner sanctum of power in Rome.

The tribune regained his wits and looked to the centre of the chamber where a massive marble-topped table dominated. Behind it sat Regulus, leaning forward with his palms spread flat on the featureless surface while behind him, by his left shoulder, stood Scipio, his sharp aquiline features accentuated by the light overhead. Varro strode to a point three feet short of the table and stood to attention, saluting with regulation exactness, his eyes staring at a point two inches above the seated consul's head.

'Titus Aurelius Varro reporting as ordered, Consul,' he said, his voice shattering the temple-like silence of the chamber.

'Varro,' Regulus said, suddenly standing, his voice laced with disapproval. As the consul moved to his right, Varro quickly darted his eyes to Scipio, hoping to see some expression of confederacy, some sign of alliance after the meeting with his father but Scipio's gaze was locked on Regulus.

Varro looked ahead as the senior consul continued. 'All afternoon yesterday, Varro,' he said, 'I listened to many voices in the Senate, each one more condemnatory than the last.'

Varro maintained his gaze on the wall ahead, trying to ignore the words, focusing only on the decision of his fate. Regulus continued to circle the room, until he stood directly behind the tribune. 'Throughout that debate however,' he said, 'I knew only one voice could determine your future . . . mine.'

Regulus paused for a minute, the heavy silence reasserting itself until Varro could hear only his own breathing.

The consul sat down, his hooded eyes looking up at the stoic tribune. 'Look at me,' he commanded and Varro dropped his gaze to meet Regulus's.

'You have failed Rome,' Regulus said, his voice once more laced with censure, 'and for that you must be punished. Therefore you are hereby stripped of all rank and privileges and are ordered to report to the Fourth Legion stationed in Felsina. There you will serve out your sinecure as a legionary.'

Varro's expression glazed over as the full import of this sentence struck home through his mounting despair. Felsina was at the northern frontier of the Republic, a constant battleground where Gallic clans continually challenged the boundaries of Rome. The legion stationed there, the Fourth, was the toughest in the Republic, but it was also the legion with the lowest life expectancy. As a disgraced tribune, marked as an aberration amongst the proud legionaries, his life would be measured in weeks, whether he met the enemy in battle or not.

'You are dismissed!' Regulus said.

With enormous willpower Varro drew himself to full height and saluted once more. He spun on his heel and exited the room.

'There is another option, Regulus,' Scipio said as the tribune's footsteps faded behind the door. He walked slowly around the table until he faced the consul. Regulus raised his eyebrows in question.

'You could spare Varro a full censure,' Scipio said.

'Spare him?' Regulus scoffed. 'Impossible. He must be held accountable.'

'But to what degree?' Scipio said, beginning his carefully prepared argument. 'I have heard reports from the battle that suggest that he does not bear full responsibility for the defeat.'

'Of course he does,' Regulus said dismissively. 'He commanded the fleet.'

'But there are reports of dereliction of duty that undermined his command.'

'Against whom?' Regulus asked, searching Scipio's expression for signs of deception, remaining guarded though he found none.

'Captain Perennis of the *Aquila*,' Scipio said.

'Perennis, Duilius's captain at Mylae?' Regulus scoffed. 'Who makes such allegations?'

'I cannot reveal my sources,' Scipio said, beginning once again to pace the room. 'Suffice it to say they are beyond question and it now seems clear that Varro was not entirely to blame for the defeat. In fact, he should be commended for his brave action in saving the *hastati* of the Ninth.'

Scipio kept his gaze from the consul, not willing to take

the chance that Regulus would see that he was gambling. His 'sources' were the words of Varro himself, and as such were completely unreliable, but they served his purpose and in any case he had already agreed with Calvus that he would intercede on behalf of his son, an agreement he would never reveal to Regulus.

'But what of accountability, Scipio?' Regulus said. 'The loss of so many galleys cannot go unpunished.'

'Nor can the loss of a loyal tribune from a respected family be justified to satisfy the vultures of the Senate,' Scipio said.

'Then what do you suggest?'

'Strip him of his rank of tribune but give him a lesser command, a squad of galleys in Sicily,' Scipio proposed, 'and banish him from Rome until we win the war. It will give him a chance to redeem himself.'

Regulus leaned forward once more as he contemplated the senator's suggestion. Scipio watched him in silence, waiting for the senior consul to agree to his well-crafted argument. The lure had been elaborate and the subterfuge regarding his sources ignoble but Scipio was content with his approach. He needed Varro in Sicily if his plan was to succeed but to directly ask Regulus for the favour of leniency was beneath him. Scipio preferred to plant and then nurture an idea in another man's head, bending his will without him knowing, allowing them to believe that the idea was his own before ultimately doing Scipio's bidding without even realising it.

'I disagree,' Regulus said, sitting straight in his chair once more. 'My initial judgement was sound. Varro will be sent to Felsina.'

For a second Scipio could not believe what he was hearing and it was only when he felt his fingernails digging into the soft flesh of his palms did he realise that the consul had disagreed with him.

'Regulus,' Scipio said, the bile rising in his throat as he fought to contain his anger. 'I urge you to reconsider.'

'No, Scipio,' Regulus said, no longer looking at the senator. 'I have made up my mind. The sentence stands.'

'You will withdraw the sentence,' Scipio ordered, his usual tact now abandoned, his anger making him blunt.

'How dare you!' Regulus shouted, slamming his fist on the marble table as he stood. 'I am senior consul and . . .'

'You are senior consul only because of me,' Scipio spat. 'Never forget that.'

Regulus opened his mouth to speak again but Scipio forestalled him.

'You will follow my orders, Regulus,' he said, 'or I will withdraw my support.'

'I do not need . . .' the consul began.

'Think carefully, Regulus,' Scipio said, cutting across him again. 'You may hold the title of senior consul, but you and I both know where the real power lies. Cross me and you will be impotent, a leader in name only.'

Regulus felt his temper flare but he kept it in check, the anger burning in his chest as he swallowed his rebuttal, knowing that Scipio's threat was viable and he turned his fury inwards, cursing his own pride. He had known that Scipio was using him for his own ends but he had dismissed the fact, believing their arrangement to be a partnership, deceived by his own ambition into thinking that Scipio wanted nothing more than simple vengeance, an indefensible lapse in judgement that fuelled his anger. Moreover the election had been a closer contest than Regulus had anticipated, with many of the patricians following Duilius's call to vote for Longus and so Scipio's support had been vital.

Now Regulus knew he was locked in Scipio's grip and with that realisation he felt a reawakening of forgotten instincts, the subtle political prowess that had propelled him to the senior consul position years before but which had become dormant during his time on the periphery of the Senate. He shifted slightly in his seat, forcing the tension from his shoulders in an effort to appear compliant. There would be another time to challenge Scipio and so for now he kept his head lowered, certain that Scipio would recognise the seed of defiance in his expression.

Scipio stood in front of the table, breathing deeply in an effort to regain his composure. He knew the confrontation with Regulus was inevitable but he cursed the inopportune moment, the lack of control that had destroyed his once surreptitious manoeuvring of Regulus's will. Now the consul would become harder to control, his awareness of Scipio's ambitions making him hostile.

Scipio briefly examined his motive for forcing the issue over Varro and with contentment found them to be sound. Varro had to be released back to Sicily and Regulus was the only man who could spare him. If revealing himself to Regulus was the price to pay then so be it, for what was power if he could not wield it to destroy his enemies.

CHAPTER EIGHT

Varro sat alone in the study in his father's house, his head buried in his hands, his mood dark and aggressive. In the background, hidden somewhere in the maze of rooms, he could hear laughter and the sounds of children's voices, his sister's children, their spirits high, oblivious to the sombre atmosphere that pervaded the rest of house. Varro's father had already stormed off, the final shattering of the aspirations he had had for his son too much to accept and his tirade against Varro still rang in the young man's ears.

Varro stood up and began to pace the room, cursing Fortuna for abandoning him yet again, cursing Scipio for his uselessness, cursing his father. Underneath it all however, in his mind's eye, he could see only the face of Perennis, the Greek whoreson who had precipitated his downfall. At first Varro had wanted Perennis dead for striking him. Then as defeat became reality, and responsibility and blame were levelled at Varro, he began to see a different offence emerging, one he had spoken aloud for the first time before Scipio, that Perennis was truly to blame for Thermae, that his allegiance was suspect and that he had neglected his duty as the naval commander. In the confines of the study one thought began to consume Varro: Perennis had been at fault but it was Varro who had paid for the defeat with his reputation and his career.

A loud knock halted Varro's pacing and he turned to the door. A servant entered and immediately quailed under his master's gaze. 'A messenger has arrived, master,' the servant said. 'Senator Scipio wishes to see you at his residence immediately.'

For a minute Varro stood silent, his mind exploring the cause for the summons. A tiny flicker of hope emerged within him and he instantly brushed past the servant. He left his father's house and turned into the street, his determined stride taking him the mere hundred yards to Scipio's house on the reverse slope of the Capitoline Hill and he hammered impatiently on the door. It was opened quickly by a heavily armed black-cloaked *praetorian*. The soldier stood to attention, recognising the uniform of a tribune but as Varro passed him, he noticed who the officer was and his rigidity slackened, the corner of his mouth rising in a disrespectful sneer.

Unaware, Varro continued on into the house, telling a servant as he passed to inform the senator that he had arrived. He waited impatiently in the atrium before being led further into the house, to a small enclosed courtyard at the rear of the residence, in the middle of which sat Scipio, pouring over a series of documents in his hands. The courtyard was warm and still, a small simple space, at odds with the opulence of the rooms Varro had passed through.

'Varro,' Scipio said rising, his expression unreadable. 'Thank you for coming so soon.'

Varro straightened and saluted as before but Scipio dismissed the action with a wave. He was not interested in speaking to Varro in a military tone. He gestured for Varro to take a seat opposite his own and sat down once more. Scipio smiled inwardly as he watched Varro. The boy was an open book, his anxiousness and curiosity clearly evident in his expression and body language. In this he was nothing like his father, a man like Scipio, schooled in the art of politics, where true emotions were buried deeply.

'I have spoken with the senior consul on your behalf,' Scipio said after a minute. 'And he has agreed to my alternative.'

'Thank you Senator,' Varro gushed, his relief overwhelming.

'You have not yet heard what that alternative is,' Scipio warned, although he knew his lure would be too powerful to resist once cast. 'The defeat at Thermae was considerable. The city and the Senate rightfully demand retribution.'

Varro nodded, solemn once more, although he could not think of a sentence worse than that given by Regulus.

'You will be demoted from the rank of tribune to that of squad commander,' Scipio began, watching Varro intently, 'and you are hereby ordered back to Sicily, there to remain until the end of the war.'

'I am banished from Rome?' Varro said in despair.

'Until the end of the war, yes,' Scipio said, slowly drawing the net closer. 'You have suffered a very public defeat. Your presence in Rome would be a further reminder to the Senate of that failure.'

Varro stood up, angry once more. That failure was not his fault.

Scipio sensed the perfect moment had arrived. 'There is one way to mitigate this sentence,' he said, happy with the instant response from Varro as the young man spun around, his hope reignited once more.

'You must accept the demotion. Nothing can be done about that, and the war still rages in Sicily. Again you must rejoin the fight,' Scipio said, his words solemn, his tone parental, a protector who wished to save the career of a soldier ill-treated by fate. He revelled in the deception. 'But perhaps the banishment can be lifted.'

Varro sat down again, his entire being focused on Scipio.

'I can speak on your behalf in the Senate,' Scipio said, 'not publicly, not where the wound of defeat is still open, but privately, in the ears of men who would listen, who could sway the senior consul and persuade him to rescind the decree of banishment.'

'Senator Scipio,' Varro gushed again, his face a mask of admiration, 'I cannot thank you enough. Your intervention is . . .'

Scipio put up his hand to stay Varro's words. He did not want to hear more words of gratitude, especially when he had no intention of speaking to any senator on Varro's behalf. He readied his next words in his mind, savouring them until he was poised to strike.

'There is something you must do for me in return,' he said in a hushed tone.

'Anything,' Varro said with full sincerity.

'You told me that one other man was culpable for the defeat at Thermae.'

'Captain Perennis,' Varro said instantly.

Scipio nodded, as if he needed reminding of the name. 'As a senator of Rome,' Scipio said, the anger in his voice now genuine, 'it galls me that this man, this Greek, has escaped the retribution he so obviously deserves.'

Varro nodded in agreement, his own face twisted in anger.

'But Perennis cannot be attacked in or near Rome,' Scipio continued. 'He has powerful friends, men who would investigate and proclaim Perennis's death as a crime against the state. His death must occur far from Rome, where the truth can be hidden.'

Again Varro nodded and Scipio fixed him with a steady gaze.

'You must be Rome's avenger when he is out of her reach,' Scipio said, relishing every word, every second as his revenge took shape. 'Do this, Varro, and I will see that you return to Rome with honour.'

Instinctively Varro stood to attention once more, saluting with all the passion he could muster.

'Yes, Senator,' he said.

With the order given and acknowledged there were no other words to be spoken and he strode from the courtyard with a renewed sense of honour and pride coursing through his veins, never looking back, never seeing the malevolent smile of triumph on the face of his saviour.

Atticus stood tall on the aft-deck of the *Aquila* as he looked out over the teeming military activity that was Fiumicino. In his mind's eye he pictured the simple fishing village it had once been, untouched and unsullied by the great city that sat only fifteen miles distant. Now it was home to the shipyards of the *Classis Romanus*, and the tented city that once sat astride the village now consisted of timber barracks and workshops, interspersed by stone-built blockhouses and officers' quarters that stretched behind the wind-shaped dunes and housed over five thousand of Rome's finest.

Stretching along the coastline, above the high-tide mark stood a vast array of skeletal frames, scaffolding for the new galleys that were under constant construction. Each new ship was a quinquereme, designed for five rowers on each bank of three oars, the lowest oar with a single rower, with the upper oars manned by a pair of slaves. They were Tyrian in design, based on the Carthaginian flagship captured at Mylae, and soon they would outnumber the triremes of the Roman fleet, their superior design and power a greater match for the ships of Carthage.

The sound of approaching footsteps across the deck caused Atticus to turn and he nodded to Lucius as the second-in-command came towards him. The older man looked pleased with himself, his normal sombre expression cast aside in a smile, revealing teeth more often clenched in anger when a crewman moved too slow for his liking. Atticus smiled back, liking the man. Lucius was the heart of the ship's crew, respected by all, a seaman for over thirty years and answerable to no man except for his captain. He knew the *Aquila* intimately, her every length of running rigging and every seam of timber and he placed her above every other ship in the fleet. When Lucius and the crew had arrived at Fiumicino ahead of Atticus, the second-in-command had found the *Aquila* languishing by her stern anchor one hundred yards from shore. He had immediately harassed and harangued the port commander for the choice mooring spot the *Aquila* now enjoyed at the end of a jetty, citing the *Aquila*'s importance as a former flagship. This greatly improved the speed and ease of her refitting and Lucius was enormously pleased with the result.

'We should be ready to sail by dawn tomorrow, Captain,' he said, moving to the rail beside Atticus.

'Good work,' Atticus replied and slapped Lucius on the shoulder. He looked to the main deck and the activity of the crew there. Lucius had taken advantage of the *Aquila*'s presence in the shipyards by ordering a new mainmast and rigging. Atticus had checked it earlier and had been more than satisfied. The angle of mast had been set perfectly and the flawless oak spar would serve the *Aquila* for years to come. Atticus turned once more to look along the shoreline.

'Bloody quinqueremes,' Lucius spat, seeing the focus of his captain's gaze. 'Fat sows, every last one of 'em.'

'They're good ships, Lucius,' Atticus said, a smile on his face, goading his friend slightly.

151

'Their draught is too deep and the *Aquila* would run rings around any one of them,' Lucius replied irritably.

'But they're fast and they can ram any trireme out of the water,' Atticus countered, playing devil's advocate, wishing to draw out the foundations of Lucius's argument beneath his obvious prejudice.

'Size and strength aren't everything,' Lucius said. 'The Greeks proved that at Salamis. What counts is manoeuvrability and once you get behind one of those, they're as vulnerable as any other galley.'

Atticus nodded, conceding the point, remembering that the *Aquila* had taken a quinquereme at Mylae. The argument was academic however, because right or wrong the decision had already been made by the Romans. The *Classis Romanus* would eventually be a fleet dominated by quinqueremes and so the triremes' days as a front line galley were numbered.

Lucius tapped Atticus's arm and pointed towards the beach end of the jetty where a group of riders were dismounting. Atticus recognised Varro immediately and his stomach tightened. The tribune was making his way down the jetty, his four-strong personal guard in tow with Vitulus at their head.

'Honour guard to the gangway, Lucius,' Atticus commanded without turning.

'Yes, Captain,' Lucius replied with a low growl, his dislike for Varro already deeply entrenched.

Atticus watched the men approach until the last possible second and then made his own way to the main deck and the head of the gangway. Varro was first to come aboard. He scanned the deck before him before finally coming to the captain. Their eyes met and Atticus tried to discern the level of the tribune's hostility but the gaze was too brief.

'When can you be ready to sail, Perennis?' Varro asked abruptly.

Atticus suppressed his anger at Varro's insult of omitting the title of his rank in front of his crew while beside him he felt Lucius bristle, but for another reason. Naval tradition demanded that a visitor request permission to board before doing so. To ignore the courtesy was an insult to all on board.

'The ship can be ready by dawn tomorrow, Tribune,' Atticus replied, keeping his tone even, 'but the complement of marines or their commander are not on board.'

'Send runners immediately,' Varro said. 'Inform the marines that we will be sailing at dawn.'

Atticus looked to Lucius and nodded and the second-in-command immediately beckoned one of the crewmen to his side, issuing him with the order. Varro brushed past Atticus, followed by Vitulus and three other legionaries. Atticus made to follow them but Vitulus sensed the move and turned abruptly.

'Step aside, soldier,' Atticus commanded, his patience long since gone.

'The tribune will be using the main cabin as his quarters, Captain,' Vitulus replied. 'He will ask for you when you are needed.'

'I didn't ask you about the tribune's sleeping arrangements,' Atticus replied threateningly, his right hand moving to the hilt of his sword. 'I ordered you to step aside.'

Vitulus squared his shoulders and looked hard into the captain's eyes. Atticus shifted his weight slightly in anticipation but suddenly Vitulus turned his back and strode to the hatchway six feet away, disappearing below without a backward glance. Atticus stood rooted to the spot, his fury commanding him to rush forward but his good sense telling him to hold fast. Vitulus was under Varro's command and protection and Atticus knew he would get no satisfaction from the tribune. With a furious scowl he walked past the hatchway

153

and made his way back to the aft-deck, his hand still locked on the hilt of his sword.

The languid on-shore breeze carried a cool sea mist that soon enveloped the shoreline at Fiumicino, dissipating the crimson light of the dying sun and chasing the last of the day's dead heat from the air. Atticus stood in the centre of the main deck, supervising the work of the crew as they carried supplies on board. It was a job he would normally leave to Lucius but tonight he needed the distraction and in any case, it took him away from the aft-deck where Varro and his guard commander, Vitulus, had been standing for the past hour.

When they had first arrived back on deck, Atticus had been standing at the tiller with Gaius. He had immediately tried to engage with the tribune, to ascertain the details of his orders and to find out where the *Aquila* would be sailing to on the morrow. Varro had been completely dismissive however and Atticus had felt compelled to leave the aft-deck. Not through intimidation but because he knew the obvious tension between him and Varro would be noticed by the crew and to have the two most senior officers on board at each other's throats would adversely affect their morale.

Atticus reached out to the mainmast and ran his finger down the newly sanded oak. His finger left a trail through the light sheen of moisture the sea mist had deposited there and he rubbed the residue between his thumb and forefinger. He touched the mast again, sensing the strength of the timber, a strength that was now part of his ship. The thought made him angry and he looked to the aft-deck. His ship, but now not his own. The *Aquila* had always been Rome's to command but before the escalation of the war and the *Aquila*'s entanglement into the conflict she had been Roman in name only, and Atticus had come to consider her his own. Now that autonomy was gone, replaced by anonymity, a single ship amidst a fleet and his command was set aside at the whim of privileged Romans.

'Lucius!' Atticus called and he was immediately on hand.

'I'm going ashore,' Atticus continued, overwhelmed for the first time ever with an urge to get off the *Aquila*. 'Finish the re-supply.'

'Yes, Captain,' Lucius replied, sensing his captain's frustration but withholding his counsel, knowing Atticus would ask for help if he needed it. He watched the young captain turn and walk down the gangway, sidestepping the men coming up against him and within seconds he was lost in the sea mist that obscured the shore-end of the jetty. Lucius realised his own teeth were gritted in anger and he instinctively turned to the aft-deck and the man who was the cause, a second too late to notice that Varro had also watched Atticus leave the galley.

The *Alissar* moved silently through the dark waters of Tyndaris harbour, her sleek hull cutting through the seemingly viscous waves, their crests dividing perfectly, peeling back to stroke the one-hundred and sixty foot hull before joining together once more in the galley's swirling wake. The rowers below decks worked without the aid of a drum with only every third row engaged and the other oars withdrawn to avoid entanglements. At steerage speed of only two knots their oar strokes were almost languid, their rhythmic fluid motion belying the strength-sapping effort needed to propel the one-hundred and ten ton galley through the water.

Hamilcar stood at the starboard aft-deck rail, Captain Himilco by his side, the two men looking out over the shoreline illuminated by a thousand torch lights, the frantic pace of construction continuing even at this late hour.

'Impressive,' Himilco remarked, picturing the plans he had seen in Hamilcar's cabin, overlaying them on the illuminated canvas of the shoreline before him.

Hamilcar nodded, pleased that the construction looked well advanced. It was impossible to tell in the dark but surely the end was well in sight.

A look-out approached Hamilcar and briefly indicated a point in the inner harbour. 'There, Commander,' he pointed. 'We can't see her yet but the signal has been confirmed twice.'

'Very well,' Hamilcar said, keeping his voice level. 'Helmsman, two points to port. Steady as she goes.'

It was a gamble to enter Tyndaris harbour but Hamilcar had wanted to see how far the construction had progressed, even though the necessity to arrive at night robbed him of seeing much detail. He would attend the pre-arranged meeting, knowing the man he was to meet would have a full detailed report of activities both here and further north. Then the *Alissar* would slip out of Tyndaris, long before dawn's early light betrayed her presence to the world, a passing shadow that would melt like the wake of a galley.

Atticus made his way up the beach, kicking the debris aside as he crossed the high-tide drift line until he reached the shallow dunes that marked the division between the beach and the semi-permanent city beyond. His vision extended no more than twenty feet in either direction, but all around he could hear the activities of the camp, shouted commands that were muted in the moisture-laden air, the hammer blows of carpenters that would soon cease as the last of the day's light was extinguished prematurely by the mist. He turned right towards the village, knowing it to be almost one hundred yards ahead and, as the noises behind him began to fade, he slowly became aware of how the mist had isolated him amidst thousands. He smiled at the thought, glad to feel separated from the Romans even if in reality he was not.

Within a minute Atticus reached the 'little river' from which the village drew its name. It was no more than a stream and Atticus crossed it at the natural ford created where sediment carried downstream met the incoming tidal waves. The beach on this side of the river was unchanged by the sprawling activity that had transformed the coast running north on the other side and Atticus was forced to weave his way through the beached fishing boats of the villagers, many of them upturned, exposing their underbellies, and as Atticus recognised the different varieties of boats, he silently mouthed their names. He stopped suddenly as he spotted a *kaiki*, a traditional Greek fishing boat, almost exactly like one his father had once owned. He made his way towards it and placed his hand on the bowsprit, his mind flooding with memories. With the mist narrowing the range of his senses Atticus could almost believe he was standing on the beach astride his home city of Locri and for a second he was a young boy again, standing amidst the boats of his own people. He stood silent for a minute, taking comfort from the memory before continuing on into the village.

In the months since the creation of the shipyards, Fiumicino had tripled in size, its once solitary reason for existence, fishing, now superseded by commercial activities specifically targeted to the lucrative opportunities available in having so many Romans isolated from the city. The main thoroughfare running parallel to the river, once devoid of life, was now lined by stalls and Atticus was accosted from all sides by traders selling a profusion of goods, from cooked food and cheap wine, to medicinal cures and balms. The side-streets running away from the river had also been requisitioned, the less valuable sites making those traders that bit more aggressive as they tried to steer customers from the main street, but

Atticus ignored them all, his eyes searching the buildings behind the stalls. Two of them in the centre of the street drew Atticus's attention. Above the door of the first was a sign bearing a crude depiction of Venus, the Roman goddess of love, her nakedness demurely covered by her enfolded arms. Atticus smiled at the illustration. Love was rarely found in a brothel. The second building, which looked like a former shop, had a different sign over the door, depicting the Roman god of wine, Bacchus, and Atticus made directly for it.

Atticus pushed open the door, his eyes squinting to penetrate the gloom within. A wall of sound greeted him, laughter and raised conversations from tongues made loose by drink. He grimaced slightly as he was assaulted by the overpowering smells in the dour room, sweet wine and dank sweat while in the corner a man was collapsed in a pool of his own vomit. The bar stood on the opposite wall to the door and Atticus could see where the internal partitions of the building had been removed to make way for the five large tables which ran parallel to each other across the floor, with half empty benches on both sides of each one. Atticus picked a path between two and made his way towards the bar.

Atticus looked at the faces of many of the men as he passed, his gaze returned intensely by some. These men were the shipwrights and carpenters of the shipyards, skilled labourers who originally were drafted to Fiumicino by order of the Senate but who now remained by choice. With the village off-limits to the legionaries, a man so heavily armed as Atticus was immediately noticed and marked and as Atticus reached the bar, he could still feel the gaze of many on his back.

Amidst the continuous uproar of the room Atticus had to shout his order and he was immediately handed an amphora of wine and a dirty chipped wooden goblet. He turned and searched for a vacant seat nearby, finding one quickly and sitting down heavily, the scabbard of his sword striking the bench with a heavy thud. He filled the goblet and drank the cheap acerbic wine in one gulp, belching deeply as the liquid hit his stomach. He refilled his goblet and drank again, the burning sensation lessened this time and after two more refills Atticus shifted his weight and sat back a little, the wine finally taking the edge off his mood.

Atticus surveyed the room again. He noticed an incongruous corner of the room and he immediately realised he had been wrong before. The building had never been a shop; it had always been a tavern, albeit a much smaller one, which had expanded to accommodate the influx of customers. The walls in this corner, directly beside the door, were darker in shade, blackened over the years by near continuous candle-light. A small narrow bench still remained against the wall, upon which sat three older men, their eyes hooded, their gaze downturned as they spoke together in obvious hushed tones. Atticus smiled. They were the locals, the men who had drunk in this tavern all their lives and who still clung loyally to their corner, keeping themselves to themselves.

Atticus went to the bar once more and ordered three more amphorae, gathering them up in his arms before making his way towards the local's corner. Someone in Fiumicino owed the *kaiki* boat on the beach, which meant it was possible they had once fished the Ionian coast. For Atticus, that was as close as he was going to get to his own kind tonight and he was determined to find out who the man was, if only to trade stories about the treacherous coastline that flanked the strait of Messina.

The three men looked at Atticus warily as he approached, their eyes at first drawn to his sword, but slowly rising to finally rest on the amphorae he was carrying and they unconsciously shifted to allow room for Atticus to sit down on the bench, taking the wine from him without comment, waiting for the stranger to begin the conversation, wondering what price he would require for the wine he had given them.

Septimus crested the dunes at the head of his sixty-strong demi-maniple, the rattle of their full armour loud in the early night air. He stepped aside out of formation to allow his men to pass, leaving Drusus to lead them down the beach as he inspected the ranks. Even in the semi-darkness many of the faces were familiar, but there was also a heavy mix of new men, replacements and transfers, men tested in other battles under different commanders.

The men were all legionaries, drawn from the legions and seconded to the navy if and when they were needed. While on board the *Aquila*, Septimus would endeavour to train them in new fighting techniques more suitable to the confines of a galley, but he knew his efforts would be met with resistance and would ultimately be fruitless as men were rotated out of naval duty and sent back to their respective legions. Septimus smiled in the darkness. They were stubborn men, proud of their legion as he had once been. Nevertheless, while he had them under his command, Septimus was determined to instil respect in every man he commanded, respect for the *Aquila* and in particular for the men who fought with the navy full-time.

As the last men passed Septimus he fell in behind them and then increased his pace to double-quick time, passing the entire troop before they reached the jetty at the end of the beach. He led them along the walkway, glancing at the other moored galleys as he passed until he reached the *Aquila*, her deck brightly lit by lanterns and burning braziers, her crew intensely active in contrast to the other quietened boats surrounding her.

For an instant Septimus's plan dominated his mind. He was

going to confront Atticus, at the first opportunity. For the hundredth time he searched his feelings and found his anger was still there, still smouldering from the thought of his friend's betrayal. He recalled every counterpoint to that anger, his loyalty to Atticus, the number of times they had trusted each other with their lives, and his sister's declaration of their love for each other. He knew it was not enough; Atticus would have to answer for his betrayal.

The sight of Lucius standing at the head of the gangway interrupted Septimus's thoughts.

'Permission to come aboard!' Septimus called.

'Granted,' Lucius called, his eyes seeing past the centurion to the ranks behind him.

Septimus led his legionaries up the gangway and again stepped aside to allow his men to pass. Drusus formed them into ranks on the main deck.

'Where is the captain?' Septimus asked of Lucius.

'He went ashore nearly three hours ago.'

'To where?'

'The captain didn't say,' Lucius replied. He saw the look of puzzlement in the centurion's eyes but didn't venture any further information. It wasn't his place to speak on the captain's behalf, particularly when the reason for his departure was a personal matter.

'Did he say when he'd be back?' Septimus asked, confused by Atticus's actions. The *Aquila* was due to sail with the dawn and it was unlike Atticus to be absent so close to departure, however reliable his crew was.

'No, Centurion,' Lucius said. He sensed Septimus's concern and relented slightly, obliquely citing the reason for his captain's departure.

'The tribune's on board,' he said, nodding towards the aft-deck.

Septimus followed his gaze and saw Varro standing at the aft-rail with his men.

'He's sailing with us?' Septimus asked, surprised to see Varro in command considering his recent defeat. But his presence did provide a possible reason for Atticus's absence.

'Yes,' answered Lucius, 'him and four of his men.'

'Four?' Septimus asked. There were only three men with Varro on the aft-deck.

'The other one must be below decks,' Lucius surmised. 'The tribune has commandeered the main cabin.'

Septimus nodded and turned his gaze back towards his own men. Having any high ranking officer on board always complicated the command structure, but with Varro, a disgraced tribune hostile to the captain, the problem would be exacerbated and magnified ten-fold.

Lucius watched Septimus intently, searching the young man's expression. He had always harboured a contempt for legionaries but had long ago learned to respect the Roman centurion, not least because of his obvious friendship with the captain. The thought caused Lucius to look beyond Septimus to the impenetrable mist that still surrounded the galley, its gloom intensified by the darkness.

The three men laughed heartily as Atticus finished his tale, one of them slapping him on the back as he coughed, choking slightly on his wine. Atticus laughed with them, his earlier dark mood now completely forgotten, doused in wine and good company. The initial wariness when Atticus approached the men had evaporated the minute he had enquired about the ownership of the *kaiki*, for only a fisherman could know of its name. They realised immediately they were talking to one of their own. Now, hours later, the original amphorae were strewn at their feet, their replacements lying empty beside them, drunk faster and enjoyed more by the three locals in the knowledge that Atticus had paid for them.

Atticus slowly recovered and lifted his goblet to his mouth. It was empty and he reached for the nearest amphora, casting it aside when he realised it too was empty. He stood up and immediately staggered, his fall prevented by the outstretched hand of one of the locals.

'I think you've had enough, sailor,' he said, his jovial face upturned in the shadowed room. 'You'd better get back to your ship.'

Atticus nodded, patting the man on the shoulder. He stood upright and turned to the door, taking a couple of unsteady steps before plunging out into the darkened street.

The night air, made cool by the mist, sobered Atticus a little and he turned left towards the sea, his stride steadying that bit more as he brushed past the last of the stall-owners still plying their trade. Atticus rolled his head and rubbed his eyes to clear his mind that bit more but the action had no effect, and he smiled slightly at the thought. He hadn't drunk that much wine in a long time.

Towards the end of the street near the beach a lone trader stood in the centre of the road, his palms upturned in greeting. Atticus sidestepped slightly but the man mirrored his move, placing himself once more in Atticus's path.

'You look hungry, sailor,' the man said, a bright smile beneath his dishevelled hair. 'Some food perhaps to satisfy an appetite sharpened at the tavern?'

Atticus half smiled, and raised his hand slightly to dismiss the man. The trader however stepped towards Atticus, ignoring the gesture.

'Charcoaled fish,' he said, reaching out with his hand and taking Atticus's elbow.

Atticus acquiesced slightly, the wine mollifying him. The trader pointed to his stall with an open hand and Atticus turned. It was on one of the side streets, not ten feet off the main thoroughfare. Atticus hesitated for a second, but the trader persisted, drawing his arm around him, and Atticus relented, the smell of cooked fish suddenly making him hungry.

The stall was the only one still open on the street, the darkness beyond it revealing only the outlines of others, the houses behind them silent and seemingly deserted. Atticus squinted into the gloom and smiled at the trader's persistence, staying open so late when everyone else had left. He turned to say as much when he noticed the man's smile had disappeared from his face, replaced instead with an expression of fear. The man was looking back over his shoulder, his body twisted awkwardly, his hand still holding Atticus's elbow.

A voice suddenly sounded in Atticus's mind, a cry of warning, and he spun around towards the trader, ducking his head forward as he did. The stab of pain was immediate as the tip of a blade whipped across his jaw-line, slicing the skin cleanly and opening a deep wound where, a heartbeat before, the back of his exposed neck had been.

A piercing cry split the air as the blade continued unimpeded through its arc and part of Atticus's vision registered the trader's face disappear behind a spray of blood, the knife striking him full in the face. Atticus sprang backward to face his attacker, hitting the stall with his shoulder, the hot coals of the brazier spilling across his outstretched left hand as he struggled for balance. His mind ignored the pain, focused instead on survival and his right hand went for the dagger in his belt, a spear-pointed blade six inches long, sliding out of the scabbard in a blink of an eye.

Atticus crouched slightly and tensed his legs, his eyes frantically searching the darkness for his attacker. He saw him not six feet away, his bulk obscuring the dim light of the main street behind. The trader continued to scream somewhere close at hand but Atticus ignored him, his eyes now locked on the blade in his attacker's right hand while somewhere in his mind he cursed the darkness that robbed him of the chance of seeing his attacker's eyes, knowing that in a knife fight, the eyes always revealed an attack a heartbeat before it came.

The man lunged forward and Atticus was forced to side-step to his right, his shoulder slamming into the side wall of a house, his body arched to avoid the strike. He counter-attacked immediately, fearful of being cornered, and he slashed his blade across his attacker's exposed side, his mind registering shock as the blade glanced off armour. A legionary! The man came on again, spinning on his heel, driving his blade underarm, searching for a killing blow. Atticus sprang into a lunge, hitting the soldier in the upper arm with his shoulder and he drove his knee up suddenly, connecting heavily with his attacker's left leg. A grunt of pain and Atticus was given a second's respite. He circled to his right and stumbled over the hysterical trader, thrashing and writhing on the ground.

The legionary rushed forward again and Atticus met his charge full on, his left hand reaching frantically for his attacker's right until he managed to grab hold of his wrist. Atticus raised his own blade and stabbed downward, aiming blindly for the neck but his own hand was equally stayed by an iron grip, instantly turning the fight in a battle of strength and will.

The two men became locked in a grotesque embrace and Atticus could feel the muscles in his arm burn from the effort of attacking with his right while defending with his left. He shifted his balance only to have the move countered immediately, while a second later he was forced to react in kind, the legionary trying to turn his wrist and force his own blade down. Atticus's face was on fire, the deep wound on his jawline fighting the adrenaline in his body to overwhelm his mind with pain while his left hand struggled to maintain its grip, the blisters raised by the charcoals bursting to coat his skin with blood.

From deep within, Atticus summoned the strength to push home his attack, driven on by anger at the cowardly ambush and the legionary took a hard-fought step backward. Atticus leaned in to increase the pressure, grunting heavily as he did, his nostrils filled with the smell of his own blood, the harsh smell of his attacker's sweat, his rotten breath washing over Atticus's face. The legionary's blade was an inch from Atticus's chest, locked by Atticus's grip while his own blade was further down, pointing vertically, looking to strike below the soldier's armour into his exposed groin. Atticus had the advantage and he summoned his will for one last lunge.

Suddenly the legionary stumbled backward over the inert trader, pulling Atticus forward, the pressure he had been exerting speeding his fall, the mutual lock binding them together. Atticus fell heavily on the soldier, his right hand shooting up and he felt an instant resistance against his blade as it struck his attacker. At the same instant the soldier's blade was trapped between them and it sliced cleanly into Atticus's chest, cutting flesh and sinew until it struck against his ribs, glancing off the bone as the full weight of his body turned the blade flat.

Atticus's mind registered it all in a heartbeat, the warm gush of blood over his knife hand, the acrid smell as the dead soldier's bowels voided, the warmth spreading across his own chest as his blood flowed from the open wound. With an almost detached sensation spreading through his mind Atticus rolled off the legionary, his mind hearing his own scream as the soldier's knife was drawn out of the horizontal gash across his chest. He fell onto his back, the fall knocking the air out of his lungs and he felt his strength draining away, the energy to draw breath once more escaping him. His eyes focused on the night sky above the street, the stars intermittently visible through the thinning sea mist. He tried to recognise them, but his mind was blank. A face filled his vision, then another, their mouths saying words he could not hear, frantic words of disbelief. He closed his eyes, the pain suddenly less intense, more distant, and he slipped into darkness.

Mooring ropes were thrown between the two galleys without command, quickly taken on both sides and pulled hand-over-hand until the bows kissed with a gentle thud. Within a minute they moved as one, rising and falling gently with the swell. Hamilcar stood on the foredeck of the *Alissar*, peering across through the darkness to the opposing galley, suspicious always of treachery, not willing to board until he knew the man he had seconded to the galley was alive and well. The sound of a splash nearby caused him to look left, to the lights of the town of Tyndaris, a hundred yards away. He waited for a second and then witnessed the cause as the surface was broken again by fish-hunting insects drawn to the waves by the reflected light of the crescent moon.

Hamilcar looked once more to the opposing foredeck in time to see Belus emerge from behind a group of men. He looked incongruous amongst the pirates, his armour and bearing setting him apart. Hamilcar immediately walked forward and jumped nimbly onto the side-rail. He waited a heartbeat for the decks to steady and then jumped down onto the pirate deck, landing steadily on both feet. His hand-picked guard of six men followed him without pause. Belus stood to attention and saluted. Hamilcar smiled in reply, glad to see his old friend safe, and he extended his arms and clasped Belus's shoulders, causing the older man to smile.

'Well met, Belus.'

'It is good to see you,' Belus replied, liking the commander greatly.

Hamilcar became aware of the other eyes on him and he looked beyond Belus to the assembled crew of pirates, their curiosity causing them to bunch together on the foredeck.

'The captain?' Hamilcar asked of Belus.

'Narmer,' Belus replied, turning towards the pirates.

The captain heard his name spoken and stepped forward. Hamilcar studied him closely as he approached. He was a colossus, with limbs that seemed grotesquely overdeveloped and he moved with a slow loping gait, as if he was prowling his own deck. Hamilcar looked to his face as he came closer and his features became more defined. He was a young man, his face unremarkable but his eyes immediately drew Hamilcar's fascination. They were the most pitiless eyes he had ever seen. In a society where ferocity and ruthlessness paved the way to power, Narmer had reached the highest rank of captain and Hamilcar knew that what he saw in the captain's eyes was merely a shadow of the barbarity within.

'I am Hamilcar,' he said.

'Narmer,' the captain replied with a look of disdain. 'You have my gold?'

'First I will hear my officer's report,' Hamilcar said.

Narmer bristled, but something in the Carthaginian's tone made him hold his tongue. He was used to dominating men with his presence and force of will but he knew instinctively that this one would not bend.

Hamilcar stepped forward and brushed past Narmer. Belus followed. The pirate crew parted before them and they walked onto the main deck alone. Hamilcar felt something soft under his foot and he looked down. The deck was filthy, strewn with debris: half-eaten food, lengths of rigging, a single wooden goblet rolling with the tilt of the deck. As he passed over a hatchway, a horrendous smell struck him from the slave deck below, a mix of human filth and rotting decay. Hamilcar peered down into the pitch darkness but could discern nothing and he listened for a moment to the sporadic groans and coughs that struggled upward into the night.

He looked up to face Belus, the disgust he felt sticking in his throat. The pirates were animals, and for the hundredth time his honour questioned him on his decision to use these scavengers. For generations Carthage had hunted pirates with merciless determination, abhorring their breed and enacting terrible revenge for every trading ship lost to their attacks. Now Hamilcar was using them in paid service of the city and he weighted his motives once more against the dishonour of the alliance. With disinclined conviction he renewed his determination. Rome was the greater enemy.

'Perhaps it would be safer for you if we were aboard the *Alissar*?' Belus ventured. 'These men have no honour and if they realise your importance they could try to hold you here.'

'It is better that we show these carrion that we are unafraid,' Hamilcar replied. 'In any case, the crew of the *Alissar* are fully armed and on alert.'

Belus nodded. He glanced over his shoulder to ensure the pirate crew were far enough away. He began to outline the information he had garnered so far from the Roman crews which the pirates had captured and tortured over the previous weeks. It was a gruesome report but Belus remained dispassionate, his involvement in the defeat at Mylae robbing him of the greater part of any pity he might have felt for the Roman traders. Hamilcar listened with heightened awareness, his mind quickly sifting and prioritising the information, searching for the salient parts that were so vital to his strategy.

'You're sure about the defences?' he asked as Belus finished.

'I would like to confirm the information from more sources but it seems the initial reports were correct.'

Hamilcar shook his head, wanting to believe him, but mystified by the Romans' seeming incompetence. Could they be so blind? Could it simply be their lack of naval experience? If Belus could confirm the information then Hamilcar's initial strategy remained infallible. He looked to Belus once more. Hamilcar had planned to release him from duty on the pirate ship this very night, as they had originally discussed, but Belus had foreseen the need to extend the assignment, and consented to it without command or hesitation.

'And the construction schedule here?' Hamilcar asked, nodding over his shoulder to the lights of the shoreline beyond the town.

'It is progressing well,' Belus said, 'and Hiero has been true to his word. The site is completely self-contained; with his troops allowing no-one to enter or leave. Its true purpose is still a secret.'

Hamilcar nodded. It was one aspect of the plan that could easily fall prey to exposure. A trained military eye would certainly be suspicious if they could see anything, but the site lay beyond the shore, out of sight from the water. It was vital that prying eyes were kept at bay, even if that meant keeping the construction workers imprisoned until the work was finished.

Hamilcar reached out and tapped Belus on the shoulder in thanks. His posting on the pirate galley was an unenviable assignment but his friend had done well and he was willing to remain on the galley for as long as it took to remove any doubts. Hamilcar led Belus to the foredeck where the pirate crew parted once more to let them through. Narmer was standing at the aft-rail, studying the Carthaginian galley moored to his vessel.

'A fine ship,' he said to Hamilcar, his covetousness plainly written on his face and Hamilcar got the impression that if his own crew were not so numerous and armed, Narmer would have his men over the rails without hesitation.

Hamilcar did not reply but rather looked across to Himilco on the *Alissar*. He held up his hand and spread out all five fingers. The captain nodded and then indicated to two crewmen who picked up one of two chests and carried it forward, its obvious weight betraying its contents. They manhandled it across the gap between the galleys and lay it at Narmer's feet.

'That's five hundred,' Hamilcar said as Narmer bent down to open the chest.

The pirate captain didn't hesitate as he heard the words and his hand reached for his sword as he stood fully upright. Within a heartbeat, Hamilcar's guards reacted in kind and then the pirate crew, the sound of iron on iron filling the air as swords were drawn from their metal scabbards. Only Hamilcar remained immovable, holding Narmer's gaze as the pirate captain stared balefully at him.

'What deceit is this?' he spat. 'The agreed price was one-thousand drachma.'

'I must extend the contract until the full moon,' Hamilcar said evenly.

'Belus agreed that I would be given the full amount when he made contact with his commander. You are he. The full moon is three weeks away.' Narmer stepped forward as he spoke, bringing his sword closer to Hamilcar's chest.

'I will pay you a further one thousand drachma in addition to this chest when next we meet,' Hamilcar said, keeping his eyes locked on Narmer. He saw the pirate's eyes glaze over slightly at the mention of the increased price and he smiled inside. He knew Narmer's avarice would decide the issue. In any case he also needed the pirate to remain cooperative if Belus was to succeed and the increased price was bound to placate him.

Narmer suddenly stepped back and sheathed his sword. He smiled at Hamilcar and then laughed out loud.

'It is a good deal,' he said aloud for the benefit of his crew, a show of bravado as if he had engineered the deal. They also backed off and soon not a single blade, pirate or Carthaginian, was exposed.

Hamilcar looked once more to Belus and nodded before turning to leave.

Narmer stepped in front of him and leaned in, lowering his voice so none could overhear.

'Look to your back, Carthaginian,' he hissed, 'this deal might bind me now but I will not forget this night'

Hamilcar held the pirate's gaze, a sudden wave of hate washing over him, not for Narmer in particular, but for his kind. He looked away and brushed past the seething captain, silently vowing that once Rome was subjugated, he would dedicate his fleet to wiping the stain of piracy from the seas of Carthage.

Septimus continued to pace the main deck as the ship's bell chimed the turn of the hour, a sound repeated near and far from the other galleys docked along the shoreline. He looked to the eastern sky but it was pitch black. Dawn was still three hours away. The sea mist had cleared, leaving the night cool and clear with a promise of fair weather for the morrow. Septimus turned and made his way to the aft-deck, silently stepping over the prone bodies of some of the sleeping crew, their bodies hunched up under blankets as they snatched a couple of hours.

The aft-deck was deserted except for Gaius, who lay beneath the tiller, his powerful arms enfolded across his chest, his breathing deep and even. Septimus arched his back at the sight, his own fatigue provoked by the peaceful sight but he knew he could not sleep, his mind too alert for rest. There was still no sight of Atticus and Septimus's resolution to confront him remained at the forefront of his thoughts. That plan was now blunted by the discovery that Varro would be sailing with the *Aquila*. How had the tribune escaped censure and punishment? Septimus couldn't even begin to fathom a defence the tribune could have used. And his return to the *Aquila* had to be connected to Atticus, so his friend was once more in danger. Septimus began to waver. Could he confront Atticus at a time when it could lead to a breach in their friendship? At a time when he needed someone to watch his back more than ever before?

The sound of raised voices caused Septimus to rush to the aft-rail and he peered into the darkness enveloping the beach end of the jetty, trying to decipher the meaning of the overlapping calls. Other voices were soon raised in answer from the galleys closer to shore; calls that were at first raised in anger. Septimus's stomach filled with dread as his intuition caught the tone of panic in the raised voices, the sound he had often heard before on the battlefield. Something was very wrong. The strongest of the overlapping voices suddenly became clear.

'Ho *Aquila*! Call out! Identify yourself!'

'Here!' Septimus called without hesitation, his commanding voice waking Gaius immediately along with half of the sleeping crew.

A tangle of figures emerged from the darkness and Septimus quickly identified them as three men carrying a fourth. He immediately ran from the aft-deck and within seconds he was down the gangplank and onto the jetty. He rushed up to the three men, his own sense of panic rising as he recognised the blood-stained man they carried.

'What happened?' he shouted, grabbing the nearest man by the front of his tunic, almost lifting him clear off the ground.

'We found him on the street in the village,' the man spluttered, terrified of the towering soldier.

Septimus pushed him aside and reached for Atticus, the other men stopping in their tracks.

'He's alive,' one of the others said and Septimus looked to him, a murderous expression twisting his face.

'What happened to him?' Septimus asked, the accusation in his tone clearly evident as he took hold of Atticus, his limp body falling against Septimus's chest.

'A knife fight,' the man replied. 'We heard the shouts of alarm in the tavern and rushed out to find him lying unconscious on the street.'

By now a number of the *Aquila*'s crew had rushed onto the jetty, Lucius amongst them and he pushed his way to the front. His expression collapsed as he spotted his captain, his blood black in the darkness, drenching his clothes and running down his legs.

'Is he . . . ?' he muttered.

'He's still alive,' Septimus said as he brushed past the second-in-command, carrying him quickly back up the gangway.

'Drusus!' he called. The *optio* was immediately on hand.

'Call out the guard and detain those three men,' he ordered and Drusus quickly commanded his men, the soldiers rushing down the ramp, pushing past the crew re-boarding the galley after their captain.

'More light here,' Lucius called as Septimus laid Atticus on the deck.

'Merciful Juptier,' Septimus whispered as lantern lights laid bare the full extent of Atticus's injuries. Septimus ripped opened Atticus's tunic, exposing the chest wound. His hands were immediately on his friend, probing the skin, examining the wound and a fresh trail of blood emerged from the crusted gash to run onto the deck.

'It's not deep,' Septimus said, the relief in his voice causing him to breathe out the words. He placed his hand on Atticus's forehead and gently tilted his face until his slashed jaw-line was in the full glare of a lantern. Septimus winched at the sight. It was a savage wound, at least four inches long and once again as he probed, the wound began to weep profusely.

'Will he live?'

Septimus turned to see the ravaged face of Lucius behind him.

'I don't know,' Septimus said; his own words foreign to his ears. This was his friend. 'The chest wound is not deep, more of a slash. He does not seem to be injured internally but he's lost a lot of blood, maybe too much.'

Lucius nodded, not really hearing the words.

'We need to get him below decks, to close the wounds and bind him,' Septimus continued. 'It's the only way to stop the bleeding.'

Again Lucius nodded but he did not move.

'Lucius!' Septimus snapped and the second-in-command suddenly blinked as if waking from a nightmare. He spun around.

'You two,' he said to two of the closest crewmen. 'Get below and bring up some planking. I want a stretcher to bring the captain below. Baro!'

The sailor stepped forward.

'Get your tools and then meet us below decks,' Lucius commanded.

Baro nodded and was away.

'Our master-sail-maker,' Lucius explained to Septimus. 'He has the steadiest hand and the best eye for this job.'

Septimus nodded and stood up, his concern for his friend lying unconscious on the deck suddenly giving way to anger. He pushed through the circle of sailors surrounding Atticus and found Drusus standing with a troop of legionaries guarding the three men who had brought Atticus to the *Aquila*. Septimus walked up to the eldest, a grey-haired man, his face weathered and aged.

'Tell me again what happened,' he said, his hand resting on the hilt of his sword, the muscles in his right arm bunched as if ready to strike. The man retold the events.

'How did you know he was from the *Aquila*?' Septimus asked.

'He told us in the tavern earlier tonight,' the man said. 'He bought us some wine and he talked with us.'

Septimus nodded, his suspicions evaporating. If the three men had really attacked Atticus, they were unlikely to carry him back to his ship afterwards.

'So who attacked him?' he asked.

'One of your own,' the man said. 'A legionary.'

Septimus was rocked back by the accusation. 'A legionary? You're sure?'

'He's lying dead in the street, along with one of the street-traders.'

'A street-trader?' Septimus asked. The whole thing made no sense. Why would a legionary attack Atticus? Or maybe it was the other way around? Perhaps Atticus started the fight.

'Drusus,' Septimus ordered. 'Take a squad and follow these men back to the village. I want the legionary's body brought back here.'

'Hold!'

Septimus spun around. Varro was standing behind him.

'I'll take over here, Centurion,' Varro said, his own tone one of barely suppressed anger. 'Vitulus!'

The guard commander stepped forward.

'Take two of the men and follow these villagers to Fiumicino. Do what needs to be done.'

Vitulus saluted and nodded to his men. They followed the villagers down the gang-plank and were soon lost in the darkness.

'How is the Captain?' Varro asked of Septimus, 'Will he live?'

'I don't . . .' Septimus replied, his concern for his friend overwhelming him. He shook off his misgivings. 'He'll survive with Fortuna's help, Tribune.'

'Yes . . .' Varro said, drawing out the word. He looked to the main deck where the crew were carefully transferring the captain to a stretcher.

'Centurion,' he said, turning once more to Septimus. 'Inform the second-in-command that he is to take charge of the crew for our departure at dawn. If necessary we will take on a new captain when we reach our destination.'

'You intend to sail as planned?' Septimus asked incredulously, forgetting himself and to whom he was talking. 'But Atticus, Captain Perennis, needs to be examined by a trained physician. He needs to be transferred to the field hospital.'

'Then he'd better be off this galley by dawn, Centurion,' Varro said, anger once more in his voice. 'We sail as planned.'

Septimus hesitated. To leave Atticus behind unguarded was unthinkable but to take keep him on board might equally condemn him, the uneasy motion of a galley at sea completely adverse to a wounded man.

Septimus suddenly noticed that the tribune was looking at him intently, waiting for an acknowledgment of his command.

He saluted his assent and walked away from Varro, determined to keep his stride steady even as his own anger rose within him. In the light of cold military logic, Varro was right to sail with or without Atticus for no man was indispensable. But Septimus knew that Varro's decision was not based on logic. He was taking advantage of this sudden opportunity to rid himself of Atticus, one way or another. Before tonight Septimus had looked upon Varro as a threat to his friend and he had silently vowed to watch Atticus's back when the tribune was around. Now however he marked the tribune as an enemy, his callous disregard for Atticus reinforcing Septimus's enmity.

CHAPTER NINE

Marcus straightened his back as he led his maniple through the main gate of the garrison fort of Brolium, the remnants of the exhausted Ninth legion finally reaching refuge in the Roman port town on the north coast of Sicily. These steps were often in Marcus's thoughts over the past week as the Ninth slowly retreated from Thermae, in his waking nightmares when the clarion calls of alarm sounded and the Carthaginian horde attacked once more. Each time he and his men had beaten their way through. Each time the enemy had come on again, more ferocious than before, more merciless, making the legionaries pay for every step they took closer to Brolium and salvation.

Marcus had led seventy-three men out of the cauldron of Thermae. Seventy-three men, the *principes* and *triarii* of his maniple. Now less than half that number marched in his wake, many of them walking wounded, many of them fighters in name only with spirits and bodies broken by the relentless fighting of the past week. On the third day out from Thermae, news had gotten through that the Second were marching west under Tribune Tacitus in relief. The pace of the Ninth had increased in anticipation of the link-up but the promised relief had never arrived, the Carthaginians managing to hold the

Second at a narrow coastal pass, frustrating their efforts to rescue the Ninth.

Dogged determination had soon descended into brutality when news of the failed relief force had reached the remaining men of the Ninth and the noble order of 'Steady the line,' a command that signalled that the men should stand shoulder-to-shoulder, was quickly replaced with an unspoken command that marked them all, 'March or die'. Where once before men stood over the wounded and protected them, now they left any who could not stand, the unremitting attacks forcing them ever onwards. To stand and fight was to die and it had taken all of Marcus's experience to maintain the cohesion of his maniple as retreat teetered on the brink of rout. More than once he had been a heartbeat away from summarily executing one of his own for insubordination, a measure that other centurions had been forced to resort to, but the IV maniple had held together, if only through loyalty to their commander.

Marcus gazed at the men of the other maniples as they began to draw up in the centre of the parade ground, the legate, Megellus, insisting on regulations even now, his iron discipline allowing for nothing less. Every maniple had been mauled as much as the IV, the rotation of the maniples on point duty exposing each to the brunt of the Carthaginian ambushes. At first those ambushes had been sporadic and un-coordinated but they had quickly become deadly effective, the narrow defiles funnelling the legionaries into unavoidable killing grounds. As the Ninth had come closer to Brolium the Carthaginians had resorted to frontal assaults, creating shield walls across the legionaries' advance. With a humourless smile Marcus recalled with pride that the IV had broken every line and barrier the Carthaginians had dared to put before them.

Marcus watched as Megellus accepted the salute of Tacitus, the tribune of the Second, his own men forming two sides of the square formation around the parade ground. The men of the Ninth looked balefully across at them, their sense of betrayal honed and sharpened over the days they had spent waiting for the relief that had never come. It was yesterday when the Ninth had finally come upon the bottle-neck pass where the Second were held, the Carthaginians withdrawing before they could be caught between the converging forces. The link-up had ensured the final day's march to Brolium passed with little incident, with only minor attacks on the rear-guard. Now however, as the Ninth stood across from the Second, that sense of betrayal was brought to the fore again, the near full ranks of one legion in marked contrast to the devastated ranks of the other.

'Bloody Second,' Marcus heard behind him. 'They gave the *Punici* an easy day's work.'

There was a general murmur of agreement.

'Silence in the ranks, eyes front,' Marcus hissed as he glanced over his shoulder. The expressions of his men were murderous, many ignoring their centurion as they continued to stare across at the Second.

'I said eyes front,' Marcus snarled, his own undirected anger rising and the men sensed his mood and complied. Marcus felt his fingers ache and he suddenly noticed that he was still gripping his sword tightly in his hand. He looked down at the battered blade, both its edges tarnished and nicked, the guard cracked in two places from forgotten blows. With an almost detached mind he turned it over in his hand, examining the weapon and with a wry smile he realised he had never thought to sheath it, not even now in the safety of the garrison fort. He couldn't remember when he had last put it down.

The camp prefect shouted the order to dismiss and it was instantly repeated by every centurion, all save one. The maniples of the Second and Ninth began to disperse but the IV remained firm, the men waiting for the confirmation of the order from their own centurion. Marcus spun around to face them. They met his gaze, knowing what Marcus was saying without the words being spoken. They stood taller, proud men. Not for having survived, for that was in the hands of Mars, but for having done what was expected of them by their commander. Marcus nodded to his men and then sheathed his sword.

'Dismissed,' he ordered.

They saluted in unison and dispersed. Marcus watched them walk slowly back to their quarters, proud to see that their backs were straight. The IV might be a broken command, its shattered strength robbing it of its ability to act as a fighting unit, but the men remained strong and determined. They would have to be, Marcus thought.

With their victory at Thermae the Carthaginians were poised to advance on every front.

The sun reached its zenith in a cloudless blue sky, its solitary presence in the heavens foretold by the play of the weather the night before. The wind however had shifted north-west to its habitual course, running smoothly down the Tyrrhenian Sea off the west coast of Italy, filling the mainsail of the *Aquila* with a constant press that begged her to take flight and become the creature for which she was named. The air contained a promise of the season to come, its touch made cooler by the moisture it carried, a foretaste of the cleansing autumn rains that were but weeks away.

Beneath the aft-deck the porthole hatchways remained tightly shut in the tiny starboard cabin, jealously guarding the fetid air inside from the fresh wind sweeping past the hull. Septimus sweated stoically in the half-light created by the lantern that illuminated the infernal space, his brow creased with worry as he gazed down at his friend. Atticus was barely recognisable, the vivid scar on his jaw-line in marked contrast to his pale ashen grey skin, his hair matted with sweat as the fever of infection racked his body. He was stripped to the waist on the narrow bunk, the wound across his chest heavily bandaged, the linen cloth already soaked through with fresh blood.

For the hundredth time Septimus checked the barely perceptible rise and fall of his friend's chest, placing his hand on Atticus's skin, fighting the urge to recoil from the searing skin that radiated such incredible heat. The infection had taken a strong hold, the loss of so much blood making Atticus all the more vulnerable.

'Twenty-four hours,' Septimus heard Lucius whisper and he turned to the older man, seeing the worry he felt reflected on the sailor's face. 'Then we'll know.'

Septimus nodded. He looked to the gash on Atticus's face again. The stitching was incredibly neat, a testament to the skill of Baro the sail maker and the wound had remained clean. However the chest injury had become infected somehow and although it wasn't deep it could kill him just the same. Septimus had seen weaker men survive greater injuries and stronger men succumb to less. Atticus might be a born fighter, but Septimus knew this battle was in the hands of Fortuna alone.

'He's still alive?'

'Yes Commander,' Vitulus replied, his own disappointment self-evident, 'I've just spoken to one of the crew. But it seems that the wound has become infected. He's not out of the woods yet.'

'That fool Quintus,' Varro spat. 'If he had carried out his orders . . .' He stood up suddenly and pushed away from the table in the centre of the master-cabin of the *Aquila*. He paced to port side and peered out of the hatchway, his fists balled in anger. 'You had no trouble disposing of his body?'

'No, Commander,' Vitulus replied. 'I had those three villagers help us take his body, and the street-trader's, out to sea in one of their boats.'

'And?' Varro prompted. He had been on deck when Vitulus had arrived back at the *Aquila* just before dawn and had been unable to question him on the details.

'We weighted both bodies and dumped them about a half-mile from shore.'

Varro nodded. 'And the villagers?' he asked.

'We took care of them when we got back to the beach,' Vitulus replied. 'With luck their bodies won't be discovered until at least tomorrow.'

Again Varro nodded. The whole thing had turned into a fiasco and even now there were too many loose ends. Varro knew the plan had been arranged in haste. He had remembered Scipio's warning, that the Greek was not to be attacked near Rome but the sight of Perennis leaving the ship alone had proved too great a temptation and he had dismissed the senator's caution, secretly dispatching one of his guards, Quintus, in pursuit with one simple command. Ambush and kill the Greek. Quintus however had somehow managed to fail in his attempt and Varro cursed him anew.

Last night, as he waited for Quintus to return, Varro had had visions of standing before Scipio on this day, proudly telling him of Perennis's death and lifting the sentence of banishment from over him before he had even left the city. Now he was sailing south as planned, with Rome in his wake.

Varro turned from Vitulus and stared out of the hatchway again. He spoke a silent petition to Quirinus, the God of his family's household, to intercede on his behalf with Fortuna, asking her to take her hand from Perennis but as he did so a vicious elation overcame him. He realised suddenly that he could afford for the captain to recover, for if he did, Varro would try again and again until Perennis was dead. If this time Fortuna favoured the Greek then the next time the wheel would turn in Varro's favour.

Belus spat over the side-rail of the pirate ship as he tried to clear his throat of the foul taste of butchery from his mouth. He watched his spittle strike the blood-stained water ten feet below and his eyes shifted left to gaze at a body floating face down in the sea. It rose and fell gently with the swell of the waves, before sinking slowly beneath the surface. Belus watched the burial without remorse, his compassion for the enemy long since cauterised from his heart.

The horrific cries from the sinking galley not twenty feet away were reaching a terrifying crescendo and Belus looked upon her once more. She was sinking quickly by the stern, the floodwaters of the sea rushing through the gaping maw where the pirates' ram had struck home. Nearly two hundred men were below decks, chained to their oars with tempered iron and Belus watched as pleading hands appeared in the rowlocks, the faces of the slaves barely visible behind them, their terror robbing them of every vestige of dignity. Belus turned away, not wishing to witness such a terrible death, knowing that Tanit, the Phoenician Goddess of fortune, might one day decree such a fate for him.

The screams faded and then suddenly died as the Roman galley finally slipped beneath the waves, the waters above her churning; a memory of the horrific struggle of the doomed men within her hull. Belus did not mark her disappearance, he had seen enough enemy ships condemned to the depths, and he sheathed his sword as he made his way across the main deck to the hatchway leading to the main cabin below. Only six of the Roman crew had been captured alive, the untamed savagery of the pirate crew claiming the rest before Belus had been able to stop the slaughter. Crucially however, for the first time, one of those captives was the captain and Belus had immediately ordered that he be taken below. The remaining five were still on deck and Belus stopped as he reached the cowering group. One of the pirate crew stepped forward, his face matted with another man's blood, his eyes alive and furtive.

'Can we begin?' he asked, a fleck of spittle escaping his mouth, his excitement barely contained.

'Yes,' Belus said with disgust. 'But this time make sure they answer your questions before you go too far.'

The pirate grunted in reply and then turned to his comrades, a demonic grin on his face. He nodded and they rushed forward as one, manhandling the bound Romans to their feet, their laughter drowning out the cries for mercy of the captured men.

Belus turned his back on the scene and went below decks. He pushed open the door of the main cabin and went inside.

'Stop!' he shouted, his hand as always instinctively reaching for his sword. Narmer hesitated for a second and then slowly withdrew the tip of his blade from where it was poised over the Roman captain's left eye. He slowly ran the point down the man's cheek, drawing a neat line of blood along the flesh. The Roman winced and pulled away but his bounds held him fast and Narmer adjusted the pressure, keeping the blade in contact until he reached the jaw-line. Only then did he remove his knife.

'He is my prisoner, Narmer,' Belus scowled.

'And this is my ship, Carthaginian,' Narmer spat.

'This ship is in the service of Carthage until we return to Tyndaris,' Belus countered and he waited until Narmer stepped away and sheathed his knife.

Belus looked at the Roman captain. It was impossible to judge his age given his weathered features but his eyes seemed to show the presence of mind of an older man. He looked at Belus with a contemptuous expression and the Carthaginian smiled inwardly. A brave man.

'What is your name?' Belus asked.

'Why is a Carthaginian officer commanding a pirate galley?' the Roman replied, studying Belus's armour and bearing.

Belus smiled, although his eyes remained cold. 'You will answer my questions, Roman,' he said, stepping ever closer.

'You can go to Hades, Carthaginian,' the Roman spat back. 'or wherever you *Punici* . . .'

A sudden thump on the deck above was followed a heart-beat later by a horrific cry. The Roman captain started, his eyes riveted to the timbers above his head. The cries were replaced by the sounds of cheering.

'Sounds like my men are getting acquainted with your crew,' Narmer said stepping forward once more into the Roman's line of sight. He grabbed a handful of the Roman's hair and yanked his head back so he could bring his face to within inches of the bound man. 'Want to know what they're doing?' Narmer asked, a malicious smile on his face.

The Roman shook his head as beads of sweat suddenly appeared on his forehead.

'Just a little game,' Narmer continued, releasing the Roman so he could continue to walk across the cabin. A second thump resounded through the deck, this time accompanied by a heart wrenching scream. Again the Roman captain felt compelled to stare up at the deck above him.

'They raise your men up to the yardarm of the mainmast

187

by the hands; a good twenty feet up, and then release them.' Narmer said, relishing every word. The Roman captain shook his head again, trying to block out the pirate's voice, bracing himself as he heard one of his men plead for mercy above. The voice was cut short as the Roman hit the deck once more, his cries becoming a scream of pain.

'The ankles break first,' Narmer continued, 'sometimes even the feet. After that it's anyone's guess, the shins, the knees, the thigh bones.'

The Roman captain closed his eyes against the pirate's voice but his mind became flooded with images, of shattered bones piercing skin, of pleading eyes begging for mercy before the rope was released once more.

'Enough.'

The Roman opened his eyes once more at the sound of the Carthaginian's voice.

'Leave us,' Belus commanded and Narmer shrugged and walked out, a smile of satisfaction on his face. Belus closed the door behind him and turned to the Roman captain. He had been tempted to stop Narmer sooner, the sound of his voice vexing him, the pirate's obvious enjoyment at the sound emanating from above deck a disgusting sight. But he realised the effect the words were having on the Roman, chipping away at his courage and will to resist, and he had therefore let Narmer continue.

'Animals,' the Roman suddenly said, spitting the blood that had trickled from his face into his mouth onto the floor.

'I am not one of them, Roman,' Belus said. 'What I do, I do for my city.'

The Roman did not reply, his face twisting into an expression of pure hatred.

Belus ignored it, knowing it would soon change to one of terror and pain. He reached to his side and slowly withdrew his dagger, bringing it up until he could examine the blade in detail. It was a fine knife, a Celtic blade seized in battle in Iberia and Belus had used it many times. He stepped forward with the knife held before him, the Roman's eyes riveted to the light reflecting off the blade. Belus steeled himself for what he needed to do next, believing that by recognising that the act besmirched his honour, he was somehow set apart from the men the Roman had called animals.

Septimus shielded his eyes against the harsh light of the early afternoon sun as he came up onto the main deck, its un-fettered light reflecting off a million wave-tops and the white canvas sheet of the main sail. He turned his face into the cooling tail-wind, drinking in its freshness, allowing it to cleanse his lungs. It had been more than eight hours since he had been top-side and the vastness of the space around him emphasised the suffocating confines of the cabin below where Atticus lay unconscious.

The sound of drill commands caused Septimus to turn and he smiled as he watched Drusus put his demi-maniple through their paces. The *optio* was a hard taskmaster and Septimus was glad he could rely on him as much as he did. Beyond the men training on the main deck, Septimus spotted Vitulus alone on the fore. He was watching the legionaries intently, no doubt studying the differences in their training from that of the standard imposed on the legions. Septimus watched him for a minute and then suddenly realised he had not spoken to the guard commander since the night before when Varro had dispatched him back to the village with the three locals.

Septimus walked around his men and made his way to the fore, nodding at Drusus as he passed, an affirmation that the *optio* seemed to ignore. Septimus smiled inwardly. Drusus was as tough as they came. The centurion walked over to Vitulus and turned to stand beside him, facing his men on the main deck once more.

'What happened last night?' Septimus asked.

'I have given my full report to the tribune,' Vitulus replied icily.

Septimus turned to Vitulus, surprised by the dismissive reply and he squared up to the legionary.

'Listen Vitulus,' Septimus said, suddenly angry. 'My friend was attacked last night and I'd like to know what happened.'

Vitulus turned to Septimus to reply, ready to dismiss him again, but he hesitated, wary of the look in the centurion's eyes. He wondered if it were better not to antagonise the marine considering he would find out what Vitulus had reported sooner or later.

'We found nothing except a dead street-trader,' he replied.

'That's all?' Septimus asked incredulously.

Vitulus nodded, sticking as close to the truth as possible. 'He was dead, knife wound to the face, probably caused by your friend.'

'And what about the legionary?'

'There was no legionary,' Vitulus said. 'The villagers were lying.'

'Lying?' Septimus said. 'Then how do you explain the captain's wounds. He didn't get those from a street-trader. Atticus is too good a fighter.'

'Before the fight your captain was drinking in the tavern. Maybe he was drunk. Maybe that's why he provoked the fight in the first place.'

'How do you know he started the fight?'

'Some of the villagers told us,' Vitulus replied. 'They said the Greek started an argument over the price of the trader's food. He turned really nasty and drew his knife. Typical Greek if you ask me.'

Septimus held his tongue. Now he knew something was wrong. There was no way Atticus would do such a thing. Either someone had lied to Vitulus or the commander was lying now.

'Did you get the names of the three villagers who brought the captain to the *Aquila*?' Septimus asked, laying the trap. 'I'd like to question them myself when we return to Fiumicino.'

'I didn't get their names,' Vitulus replied, 'and when we tried to question them, they fled down one of the alleyways. We chased them but Fiumicino is like a rat's maze. We lost them.'

Septimus nodded as if he understood and agreed but his suspicion of Vitulus was heightened. Somehow he knew Vitulus would have an excuse as to why Septimus could never question the villagers. And the story he had told. All three civilians escaping from an experienced commander and two legionaries? The odds were certainly against it. Septimus looked at Vitulus but the commander did not hold his gaze and the centurion walked away. He was half-way back across the main deck when he spotted Lucius on the aft talking with Gaius. He approached the two men.

'How is the Captain?' Gaius asked.

'No change, Gaius,' Septimus replied. 'All we can do is wait.'

Gaius nodded. Lucius had told him as much an hour before when he had come top-side.

Septimus looked back over his shoulder, spotting Vitulus still standing on the foredeck, leaning easily against the rail.

'Vitulus says there was no legionary involved last night,' Septimus said as he turned back to the two men.

Lucius nodded, 'I know,' he replied. 'I spoke with one of Varro's guards earlier. He said the same thing.'

'You don't believe their account of what happened?' Septimus asked, judging Lucius's tone.

'Do you, Centurion?' Lucius replied.

Septimus paused for a second only. 'No,' he replied.

'Then there's one other thing to take into account,' Lucius said, stepping forward and lowering his voice. 'One of Varro's men is not on board.'

'You're sure?' Septimus asked, rocked by the information.

Lucius nodded, 'Varro had four men with him last night when he boarded. Now there are only three.'

'Did you say this to the guard you were talking to this morning?' Septimus asked.

Again Lucius nodded. 'He said I was mistaken, that only he and two others were guarding the tribune on this voyage.'

'Could you have been wrong?' Septimus asked, remembering the evening before when he had seen the tribune on deck with three men. Lucius had corrected him at the time by saying the fourth man must have been below decks.

'He's not wrong, Centurion,' Gaius answered. 'I saw them too, as did half the crew.'

Septimus nodded and turned once more to look down the length of the galley. Vitulus was still there. Septimus began to think that he should challenge the commander on his version of the events of last night but he thought better of it. To challenge him meant revealing his suspicions. To say nothing gave him the opportunity of watching Varro without attracting attention. He nodded to himself as he reached the conclusion of his thought. From now on the enemy were seen and unseen, both Carthaginian and Roman, and for the first time he was given an insight into his friend's world.

Belus stepped back, panting, the bloodied knife hanging limp by his side. The Roman captain had passed out again, his ravaged face still transfixed with an expression of pain and anguish. The room seemed strangely dark and Belus noticed for the first time that the sun was setting in the western sky, its passage turning the sky a burnt red, darkening the day prematurely. Belus moved to close the hatches but he hesitated, abruptly aware of the overpowering smell in the room, the dank sweat smell of fear mingled with the sweet odour of freshly drawn blood and underneath, the acrid smell of urine from when the terror of anticipation had overcome the captain.

Belus suddenly felt suffocated by the choking air and he stuck his head out of the port-hole. The air was too fresh and he coughed violently as it struck his lungs. The wind rushing past filled his ears and he turned his head away from the flow. There were no sounds from above, no cries of pain or shouts of laughter and Belus briefly wondered when it had all stopped. He ducked back inside the cabin and lit one of the lanterns hanging from the ceiling above. The light ebbed and flowed across the cabin with the roll of the ship, at one moment illuminating only the Roman captain's legs and then showing him in the full glare of the lantern.

Belus missed a breath at the sight, the few minutes' pause breaking the trance that had descended over him as he tortured the Roman. The captain was unrecognisable from the man who had stood on the aft-deck of the Roman galley earlier that day, shouting defiance across the closing gap, issuing orders for his men to stand fast against the pirates as they boarded. The creature before Belus now was a broken shell, robbed of all dignity by hours of incessant pain. Belus raised his knife and examined the blade as he had done hours before. It was dull in the lantern light, matted with blood, some fresh, some hours old and the hand holding it was similarly coated. Belus was suddenly ashamed and he rammed the tip of the knife into the table top. He had never tortured a man personally, although he had seen it done many times, and he was acutely aware of how easily he had slipped into the role.

Belus recalled the questions he had asked and repeated over the preceding hours, sifting the information in his mind, suppressing the thoughts that reminded him of the moments when the captain had finally broken down each time. The evidence was now overwhelming and Belus consciously justified his decision to torture the Roman himself. He was the first captain they had captured and his knowledge was more valuable than any crewman. Left to the pirates they might have killed him prematurely or accidentally. Because of his meticulous approach, Belus had been able to confirm all the previous reports and fill in the missing details. That justification caused Belus to step back and nod to himself but as the lantern light once more revealed the Roman, Belus was robbed of his assuredness.

The Roman had been a man of honour, certainly ex-military given his ability to judge the implications of the questions Belus was asking him and the Carthaginian instantly decided that the captain deserved a fate better than the one that had befallen the rest of his crew. Belus opened the cabin door and ordered one of the crew to fetch two others and report to the main cabin. They arrived a minute later and upon seeing the Roman, they smiled.

'Is he dead?' one asked.

'No, he is unconscious,' Belus replied.

'Do you want to finish him off before we throw him over the side?'

'No, I want you to bring him to my cabin,' Belus said, an edge to his voice, 'and have him cleaned up and his wounds tended.'

The pirates hesitated, wondering if the Carthaginian was joking, unsure as to what to do next.

'Now!' Belus shouted, suddenly angry, 'and make sure he is treated well. I will check on him in thirty minutes.'

The pirates grumbled but they manhandled the Roman to his feet and dragged him from the main cabin, conscious that the Carthaginian was untouchable while on board and he could punish them without fear of retribution.

Belus watched them leave and then silently closed the cabin door once more. The lantern light continued to wash over the room, illuminating the now empty chair, with blood soaked bonds scattered on the floor beneath it. Belus re-examined his decision once more. He didn't know if the captain would survive, Belus hadn't considered it when he was torturing the man, but now he hoped he would. If he could grant mercy to this one man then perhaps he could regain some of his own honour, robbed from him by the pirates with whom he served, a detestable alliance that today had turned him into one of them.

CHAPTER TEN

The *Aquila* sailed into the harbour of Brolium under a full press of sail, her finely balanced hull making the turn around the protective headland within a half ship length. Gaius stood braced at the tiller, his own balance matching that of his charge and the muscles of his arms bunched and relaxed with every slight adjustment of the rudder. Atticus watched him in silence, admiring as always the easy manner of the helmsman that belied the incredible skill he commanded. The captain sat under a canvas awning, the edges of the sheet flapping in the strong north-easterly, but the awning holding firm to create a shelter from the noon-day sun.

Atticus's fever had broken the day before, two days out from Rome. He remembered waking up in the darkened cabin, feeling numb and breathless, unable to move. His mind had screamed panic in the darkness, a sudden vision of Hades sweeping through his thoughts and he had tried to scream. He could feel his arms flailing and then suddenly an unyielding hand gripped his own, holding it tightly, steadying his nerve. He drifted back into darkness and when he opened his eyes again the room was brighter, the hatch above him opened to allow in the fresh sea breeze. Atticus felt pain for the first time and his hands touched the wounds on his chest and face, his mind replaying the frenzied fight in the dark alleyway. He thanked Fortuna that the wounds seemed minor, allaying the deep fear that affected all men, that in battle they might suffer a grievous wound, the loss of a limb or worst still, loss of sight. Atticus had seen too many veterans begging on the streets of the Republic, pitiful wretches who had once worn the armour of Rome but now relied on the alms of strangers.

Atticus had tried to rise from the cot but he had been too weak and so he had to suffer the ignominy of being carried up to the aft-deck by two of his crew. He had quickly shrugged off the indignity as he took his first breath of cleansing salt-laden air and so now he was content to sit in silence.

Approaching footsteps distracted Atticus and he looked up to see Septimus walk towards him. He had not seen his friend for many days and he smiled, a gesture that was returned by the centurion.

'That scar will certainly improve your looks,' Septimus said as he crouched down beside the captain.

Atticus's smiled deepened at the gibe and his hand reached unconsciously for his face.

'You should see the other guy,' Atticus replied, a shadow passing over his face as he remembered the fight once more.

'He was a legionary, Septimus,' Atticus said, all vestige of humour gone from his face.

'I know,' Septimus replied, instinctively glancing over his shoulder to ensure they could not be overheard. He quickly relayed the sequence of events after Atticus had been carried back to the *Aquila*, concluding with Vitulus's lie the next day and the missing guardsman.

Atticus's face coloured as he listened to the words, his eyes searching past Septimus to the deck beyond, seeking out the figure of Varro. The tribune was not on deck.

'Vitulus said the villagers escaped?' Atticus asked.

Septimus nodded, 'He said they did but I find it hard to believe.'

Atticus looked away again, this time to utter a silent plea to Poseidon in the hope that the fishermen had indeed escaped.

'So the whoreson tried to have me killed,' Atticus said, unconsciously touching his face once more. By speaking the accusation aloud he set aside any lingering doubt he had that Varro was behind the attack.

Septimus nodded, 'And he's sure to try again,' he said.

'Lower sail and secure! Orders to the drum master; standard speed!' Both men turned at the sound of Lucius's shout.

Then Septimus turned back, 'Brolium,' he said. 'Now maybe we'll find out what we're doing here.'

Atticus nodded but then his expression froze as he spotted Varro emerge from below decks with his personal guard. Septimus saw his friend's face twist into an angry frown and he moved over to hide the expression from the tribune.

'Stand fast, Atticus,' he warned. 'Remember Varro doesn't know we suspect him and if we want to stay a step ahead we need to keep it that way.'

Atticus seemed not to hear and he strained to look beyond Septimus once more.

'Atticus!' Septimus insisted and the captain relented.

Septimus rose and he walked down from the aft-deck to the main. Varro was standing by the side-rail as the *Aquila* was brought to steerage speed, ready for docking.

'Your orders, Tribune?' Septimus asked as he saluted.

'Stay on station and await my return,' Varro replied. He looked beyond the centurion, spying the captain seated at the rear of the galley.

'How is the Captain?' he asked, trying to keep his tone even.

'He'll recover,' Septimus said, equally expressionless, 'so it looks like we won't need a replacement.'

Varro shot his eyes back to Septimus at the remark but the centurion looked stonily beyond him. The crashing sound of the gangplank hitting the dock caused him to turn and he gave Septimus one last look before descending, Vitulus and the others following in turn. Only when they were gone did Septimus smile before returning to the aft-deck.

Hamilcar moved slowly around the ante-chamber, occasionally looking up to glance through the open door that led to the meeting room of the supreme council of Carthage. Many of the twelve council members had already assembled, standing in small groups, their conversations never rising above a whisper.

'Speak directly to the suffet,' Hamilcar's father, Hasdrubal, said. 'His approval must be your priority. Do not look to me or any other member of the council.'

Hamilcar nodded.

'Hanno will try to disrupt you,' Hasdrubal continued. 'Do not let him draw you into an argument.'

'I will be ready for him,' Hamilcar said, a slight edge to his voice.

Two more members of the council passed through the ante-chamber and Hamilcar nodded to them both. They ignored the gesture and continued on.

'Those men will side with Hanno,' Hasdrubal said. 'Regardless of the merits of your plan.'

Hamilcar nodded again, silently cursing Hanno for his opposition. The evening before Hamilcar had outlined his plan to the One-hundred-and-four, the council who oversaw military matters in the empire. They were men like Hamilcar, every one of them former commanders, experienced and practical men who had probed Hamilcar's plans with informed questions. After hours of debate they had voted and approved Hamilcar's strategy. Now only one final hurdle remained; Hamilcar's proposal called for a dramatic increase in the size of the fleet and for a shift in the power base of its composition, from triremes to quinqueremes. For this expenditure he needed the approval of the supreme council.

'How many members of the council does Hanno control?' Hamilcar asked.

Hasdrubal looked over his shoulder to the open chamber door, wary of being overheard. He turned to his son.

'Four council members openly support Hanno,' Hasdrubal said, his voice low. 'Of the other seven members of the council, I and two others openly support continuing the Sicilian campaign while the remaining four, including the suffet, are undecided.'

'My strategy will win their support,' Hamilcar said confidently. 'The One-hundred-and-four have already given me theirs.'

Hasdrubal nodded but a frown creased the edge of his expression. 'There is one aspect of your plan that might make some of these men hostile to you.'

Hamilcar looked to his father enquiringly.

Hasdrubal looked directly at his son. 'Hanno has let it be known amongst the council members that you are using pirates to gather information on the Romans,' he said.

'But how could he . . . ?' Hamilcar asked.

'Hanno has many spies in this city,' Hasdrubal said, ensuring that his voice remained low, 'and many more in the navy.'

Hamilcar slammed his fist into his open palm, cursing the councillor anew.

'Perhaps you were unwise to use pirates.' Hasdrubal ventured, voicing the sense of dishonour many of the council members felt at knowing Carthage was associated with such animals.

'There was no other way,' Hamilcar rounded on him, suddenly angry.

'Lower your voice.' Hasdrubal hissed.

Hamilcar followed his father's gaze to the open chamber door and he turned away. 'There was no other way,' he repeated, keeping his back to his father, his anger increasing, knowing that his honour was being openly questioned. He turned once more to face Hasdrubal. 'If I had sent one of my ships north to gather the information they would have been seen, or worse captured, and the whole strategy would have been exposed. I needed men with local knowledge of the coast who could ambush Roman ships successfully, men whose loyalty could be bought.'

Hasdrubal nodded, seeing the anger in his son's face. Hamilcar made to explain further, to let his father know that he too felt the dishonour of conspiring with pirates, that he bore the disgrace for the sake of Carthage, but his words were interrupted as he noticed the suffet standing in the doorway of the ante-chamber, the elder statesman looking to both men before walking through into the council meeting room. Hamilcar watched him pass, wondering how much of the exchange the suffet had witnessed. He looked to his father, holding his gaze for a moment before Hasdrubal turned and followed the suffet into the room.

Septimus left the *Aquila* ten minutes after Varro, estimating that he had at least a couple of hours before the tribune returned, more than enough time. His first task was to find Aulus, the harbour master, and he leapt upon a pile of grain sacks to get a better view of the busy docks. The scene before him seemed chaotic, with trading ships constantly docking and departing all along the quarter-mile long quay. Organised gangs of slaves attacked each new arrival, rushing up the gangplank even before it was made secure, lumbering down seconds later under heavy burdens to deposit the supplies on the quay-side.

Septimus slowly scanned the throng, his eyes shielded against the afternoon sunlight, his ears tuned to pick up Aulus's familiar tone. He spotted the harbour master within a minute, near the centre of the docks, gesturing wildly at some unseen target, his face mottled with frustration. Septimus smiled to himself as he jumped down and he set off with a determined stride. At six foot four inches and 220 pounds, dressed in battle armour and with his hand settled on the hilt of his sword, Septimus cut an easy path through the crowd, the lines of slaves parting to allow him through and he reached Aulus before the harbour master had finished his tirade.

'No rest for petty tyrants,' Septimus said as he came to stop behind Aulus.

The harbour master spun around, his expression murderous, the previous victim of his anger forgotten. He stared up at Septimus and inhaled in anticipation of an attack but his outburst was cut short with a smile.

'Capito!' he shouted, 'I thought I smelled legionary.'

Septimus laughed, clapping Aulus on the shoulder. Once a trader and sailor himself, Aulus had no love for the soldiers; legionaries or marines. 'The *Aquila* is back in Brolium?'

'Yes,' Septimus replied, 'but for how long I don't know. We sail with Varro. I think he's reporting to the port commander right now with orders from Rome.'

'Varro of Thermae?' Aulus said with disbelief. 'Didn't think we'd see him again.'

'You know the legions, Aulus,' Septimus said sarcastically. 'Forgive and forget.'

Aulus smiled but he looked wary. He liked to know of every-thing that transpired in his harbour and the return of a disgraced tribune was important news. He was about to press Septimus further when he noticed that all humour had vanished from the marine's face and his eyebrows raised in question.

'It's Atticus,' Septimus said. 'He's been injured.'

'How badly?'

Septimus explained in as much detail as he could.

'And his fever has broken?'

'Yes,' Septimus replied. 'But now that we are in port I would like a trained physician to examine him.'

Aulus nodded. With the fever broken the odds were in Atticus's favour but Aulus appreciated the marine's caution. 'I know such a man,' he said. 'I will have him sent to the *Aquila* immediately.'

Septimus thanked Aulus and turned on his heel, his feet taking him unerringly to his next destination.

It was another fifteen minutes before Septimus reached the legions' camp outside the town. At the quayside he had been tempted to ask Aulus about the Ninth, knowing the harbour master was always well informed but he had decided to wait to see for himself. In any case, Aulus's information would not extend to the fate of individual commands.

Septimus squared his shoulders as two legionaries of the *excubiae*, the day guard, stepped out to block his way through the main gate.

'Capito,' Septimus said as he came to a stop. 'Centurion of the *Aquila*.'

The men saluted and stepped aside but Septimus noticed they did not react with the same alacrity as they normally would for a legionary centurion. He pushed aside the thought, knowing he could not confront the men on their subtle lack of respect.

Septimus walked on across the parade ground. The area

was strangely deserted although Septimus could see individual squads of legionaries in his peripheral vision. He suddenly felt tense and he increased his pace, the strange absence of normal activity unnerving him.

The legate's quarters were on the opposite side of the parade ground to the main gate. It was a dull, functional building, single storied and made from local brick. It was flanked on both sides by the officers' quarters of the Ninth and Second, equally grey buildings that were originally planned as temporary dwellings. Septimus stopped as he surveyed the buildings, comprehension replacing unease as he looked at each in turn. Outside the officers' quarters of the Ninth, the battle standards of each individual maniple were neatly arranged in a line, held aloft on iron-tipped lances. The standards of the Second and the legate himself however, were nowhere to be seen and although men were stationed at the entrance to each building, only one was occupied.

Septimus walked over to the Ninth's building and was immediately allowed access as an officer. He entered and paused for a second to allow his vision to adjust to the gloom within. The room that faced him was the largest in the building, a common room with a large table in the centre, where a number of centurions were seated, some eating, others in quiet conversation. Septimus caught the eye of one officer and he stood up, a questioning look on his face.

'I'm looking for Centurion Silanus of the IV,' Septimus said.

'Marcus?' the man asked. 'Who are you?'

'Capito.'

The centurion nodded, a thoughtful look on his face. He recognised the name. 'Antoninus's son?' he asked.

Septimus nodded, smiling to himself. A campaigning legion numbered ten thousand men between legionaries and auxiliary troops so although Septimus had served with the IV maniple in the past and again for the last three months, he never expected that any other than his own maniple would recognise him. But everyone knew of his father and the centurion looked at Septimus for a full minute, a slight smile of remembrance at the edge of his mouth, before ambling off to find Marcus.

Septimus sat down at the table to wait, his eyes ranging over the room. The atmosphere of the room was oppressive, the men subdued, the usual energy that characterised the officers' quarters completely absent. Septimus could only imagine what these men had endured on their fighting retreat from Thermae.

The sound of a familiar gruff voice caught Septimus's attention and he turned, recognising the tall, narrow frame of his friend. He rose to greet Marcus, stepping away from the table and walking towards him. Septimus extended his hand but he suddenly hesitated, the diminishing gap allowing him to see Marcus's face for the first time. The grizzled centurion was ten years older than Septimus but twenty-five years of strict legionary routine and constant physical exercise had always kept those years at bay. Now, however, it seemed to Septimus that his friend had accumulated those years and ten more in the two weeks since he had last seen him in Thermae.

The two men shook hands and Septimus was given a moment to examine the grim expression of his former commander. He stared into Marcus's eyes, searching for the iron determination that defined the man. It was still there and Septimus curbed his initial doubts. As a soldier, his friend might be in his declining years, but his fighting spirit was as strong as ever.

Marcus gestured for Septimus to sit again and the centurion took a seat beside the marine.

'My *hastati* were here when I returned,' Marcus said simply and Septimus nodded, accepting the underlying thanks.

'When did you get back?' Septimus asked.

'Three days ago.'

Septimus remained silent as he counted the days. The retreat had taken longer than he initially thought.

'Losses?' he asked.

'Too many,' Marcus replied, a shadow crossing his face, and Septimus was struck once more by how old his friend had become. Marcus described the retreat in detail, Septimus remaining silent throughout.

'The Ninth has been stood down until replacements arrive from Rome.' Marcus concluded.

Septimus nodded gravely. For proud men like those of the Ninth, to be removed from battle duty was a heavy sentence.

'And the Second?' he asked. 'They're not in camp?'

Marcus's expression turned murderous and Septimus shifted uneasily. He could not recall ever seeing Marcus look so angry.

'The cursed *Punici*,' he spat. 'While one force was bleeding us along the coast, another larger one struck inland.'

'How far?' Septimus asked.

'By the time we reached Brolium, initial reports were arriving claiming the Carthaginians had already reached Enna and the town was under siege.'

'So Megellus has marched the Second south?'

Marcus nodded, 'Too late though. Enna is four days march away and on the day the Second left, the latest reports said the town was close to collapse.'

Septimus shook his head. Enna was a fortified town in the centre of Sicily, right in the middle of Roman occupied territory.

'I don't understand,' he said aloud. 'Even if the Carthaginians managed to take Enna they're too deep in Roman territory to hold her. The Sixth and Seventh legions are based in Agrigento to the south and with Megellus advancing from the north any force the enemy send can be overwhelmed.'

Marcus shrugged, unconvinced. 'If they continue east they could cut our territory in two.'

'But to what end?' Septimus persisted. 'Once they reach the border of Syracuse, they'll face hostile forces on three fronts, Romans to the north and south and Syracuse to the east.'

Marcus shrugged again, and Septimus could see his friend's anger remained. He understood Marcus's reaction. After the mauling the Ninth had been dealt their first reaction would be to get back in the fight as soon as possible. With the Carthaginians advancing, the opportunity was at hand but the Ninth had been stood down and so Marcus and his men were left to watch other men fight in their stead.

'When are replacements due?' Septimus asked, calculating timelines in his mind.

'Within the week,' Marcus said, his mind already on the day when his maniple would be back up to full strength.

'Megellus will have engaged by then,' Septimus said; a subtle statement that the Ninth would not be needed on this occasion. Marcus recognised the subtext and he shook his head.

'The Ninth will see battle before the month is out,' he said, total conviction in his voice.

'I don't think so,' Septimus said. 'The *Punici* have over-extended themselves. They've made a mistake in attacking Enna and Megellus will overturn the siege.'

'No, Septimus,' Marcus replied, his brow creased in thought. 'The *Punici* don't make mistakes like this. Since Mylae they've been quiet. Then suddenly when we attack Thermae we're ambushed and overwhelmed while at the same time another force attacks our flank. There's no way these attacks are impulsive.'

Septimus thought for a minute and then nodded, conceding the point. Taking the two attacks together, it would seem a greater plan was in play and the strike towards Enna was more than just an opportunistic advance on the back of a successful ambush at Thermae. Whatever the strategy, Septimus was now inclined to believe that Marcus was right. The Ninth would soon face the Carthaginians again in battle.

Hamilcar held his tongue and his nerve as he heard a low dismissive laugh from one of the men facing him. He kept his gaze steady on the suffet, remembering his father's words but for a second his eyes shot to his detractor, Hanno. The remainder of the twelve man council were silent, their faces expressionless, showing neither approval or censure and Hamilcar continued without pause.

'When our forces reach the borders of Syracuse,' he said, 'Hiero's army will join ours, thereby securing our flank as our forces march to Tyndaris.'

'You trust Hiero?' the suffet asked after a moment.

'No more than any other ally,' Hamilcar replied. 'He does not know of my full strategy and probably believes we are using Tyndaris exclusively for our campaign in Sicily. He is playing both sides and so, for the moment, it is in his best interest to keep our activities from Rome.'

The suffet nodded, apparently content with Hamilcar's answer but his expression revealed nothing.

'The Romans have two legions in Agrigentum,' one of the council members interjected, 'and at least another in Brolium. Hiero's army is no match for them.'

'It is of no consequence,' Hamilcar replied. 'Once our forces sail from Tyndaris and the second part of my strategy is executed, I expect the Romans to sue for terms. The first of these will be our demand for the Romans to leave Sicily.'

Again the suffet nodded and Hamilcar prepared to step away from the podium, his strategy outlined in full.

'And what of your use of pirates?' Hanno asked suddenly.

Hamilcar made to reply but another council member, an ally of his father's spoke up. 'The minutiae of the commander's plans should not trouble this council,' he said. 'The One-hundred-and-four have already approved the viability of Hamilcar's strategy. All we need to decide is whether the plan fulfils the needs of the Carthage.'

'The needs of Carthage also include protecting the honour of the city,' Hanno shot back, his gaze never leaving Hamilcar. Again Hamilcar made to reply but he held back, knowing he couldn't win the argument and any words he spoke would further fuel Hanno's attack. The suffet raised his hand to stay any further discussion. He looked directly at Hamilcar and again Hamilcar was left to wonder how much the suffet had over-heard in the ante-chamber.

'I have heard enough,' the suffet said, his voice low and hard. 'Now we must decide.'

Hamilcar nodded and stepped back from the podium. The members of the council immediately began to discuss the matter amongst themselves and so Hamilcar was allowed a moment to study them without distraction. To his left, in the corner of his vision, Hamilcar could see his father speaking quietly with the men on his immediate right and left. Hamilcar recognised them both, for he knew the sons of each and, as he scanned the rest of the room, he identified several others, each one the head of a powerful Carthaginian family.

In the centre of the semi-circle sat the suffet, and directly to his right sat Hanno, a smile on his face as he spoke. Hamilcar felt suddenly humbled in the presence of these powerful men. Each one had paid dearly for his place on the council, openly bribing the members of the lower council for their votes.

Hamilcar had heard that the same practice existed in Rome with senators paying for votes but in contrast it was looked upon as a dishonourable practice, a necessary evil that existed but was not spoken of openly. Hamilcar had scoffed at the Romans' pretentions. In Carthage wealth was a sign of success, and to exude that wealth was to highlight that success. The positions on the supreme council therefore were open only to the wealthiest men in Carthage, men who had proven their worth and could be trusted with the reins of state.

The suffet raised his hand and the council came to order. Hamilcar fixed his gaze on the leader, marshalling his thoughts in readiness for the questions to come. The suffet rose and walked slowly around the chamber. He was one of the oldest men in the room but his back was straight and he move with ease, his intelligent eyes fixed on Hamilcar.

'Your plan is ambitious,' the suffet said.

Hamilcar did not reply. The suffet's statement was simply that. It was not a question and Hamilcar's father had warned him to respond to questions only.

'You believe it will succeed?' the suffet continued.

'If I am given the resources I ask for, Suffet,' Hamilcar replied, confidence in his voice, 'then yes, I know my plan will succeed.'

'But if it does not . . .' a voice suddenly said and all eyes turned to Hanno. 'You speak of this plan as if it is fool-proof.'

The suffet raised his hand once more to forestall Hamilcar's rebuttal.

'The One-hundred-and-four have already approved your plan,' the suffet said to Hamilcar, 'and we must trust their judgement. I merely wished to judge the depth of your conviction.'

Hamilcar nodded, although he could not judge from the suffet's words whether or not he had judged Hamilcar's conviction worthy.

'The council will vote,' the suffet said. 'Those in favour?'

Hamilcar watched as six men nodded their approval, his father amongst them.

'Opposed?'

The other five nodded, at least one of them looking to Hanno who held Hamilcar's gaze as he nodded his disapproval.

'Then my vote will decide' the suffet said. He slowly walked back to his position at the centre of the council. Hamilcar's full attention was focused on the older man. If he voted against then the vote would be tied and his voice alone would break the dead-lock, his vote essentially counting as two. He sat down and turned once more to Hamilcar, his gaze piercing as he measured the man one last time.

'Anath guide your hand, young Barca,' the suffet said. 'I approve of your plan.'

Hamilcar saluted, keeping his sense of triumph from his expression. He turned on his heel and walked from the chamber. His father watched him go, his pride for his son curbed by the reality of what had occurred. The Council had approved, but by the narrowest margin, and in that approval there was no acceptance of responsibility. His son would bear that burden alone.

Varro paused as he came to the end of the last of the narrow streets leading to the large villa that overlooked Brolium. He glanced briefly over his shoulder to the bottom of the hill and the entire vista of the docks spread out before him. From this height the throngs of people he had so impatiently pushed through on the quayside were transformed into a series of amorphous groups with steady streams of supplies passing between them before disappearing into the narrow streets and onwards to the legionary camp.

The raucous noise of the docks had prevented Varro from concentrating on his thoughts but as he had climbed the steady hill away from the quay, the noise had diminished until now it was reduced to a surging murmur, a sound that rose and fell with the gush of each breeze and the turn of each corner. Varro looked ahead once more and continued into the open square facing the main entrance to the villa, his mind now fully focused on the meeting ahead. He signalled Vitulus and the other two guards to halt in the square and he continued on alone, walking past the two legionaries who stood guard at the main gate without a second glance, ignoring their salute.

Alone in the outer courtyard, Varro came to a stop and instinctively glanced down at the sealed scroll in his right hand. He had been handed the scroll by Scipio back in Rome with orders to present it to the commanding officer at Brolium. Varro surmised that the scroll contained details of his demotion along with a general command to place him in charge of one of the naval squadrons and he bristled when he thought of the contents, not because of the words themselves, for he accepted the challenge and the specific mission Scipio had set him, but because he had learned that the legate was not in Brolium and so Varro was left with no option but to present the scroll to the port commander, an officer with a lower rank than that of a tribune but higher than a squad commander. It was an ignominy that Varro had not prepared for and he hesitated on the threshold of the villa.

The sound of approaching footsteps caused Varro to turn and he stepped aside to allow a *contubernia* of ten legionaries to pass, the officer leading them, an *optio*, saluting the tribune's uniform without recognising the man, the gesture precise and deferential. Without thinking Varro acknowledged the salute with a nod and he felt his pride stir within him once more. He tightened his grip on the scroll in his hand and continued on into the villa, gesturing to a nearby soldier and ordering him to inform the port commander that he wished to see him.

After a brief wait Varro was shown into the port commander's office. He stood in the centre of the room and proffered the scroll to the commander, standing far enough back from the desk so the commander was forced to stand and walk around to receive the scroll. Varro watched him move, his expression unreadable. The port commander was a heavy-set man in his mid-forties but he walked with such an efficiency of movement that Varro was given the impression that the commander had at one time been a trim fighting soldier.

'I did not expect to see you again so soon, Tribune,' the commander said, his tone light but questioning. Only minutes before, when he had been told that Varro was waiting outside the commander had rushed to his door to look out surreptitiously at the tribune. How had he managed to return to Sicily? Was he not in disgrace? The port commander's mind was in turmoil as he returned to his desk but as he sat down he noticed the seal in the scroll. SPQR; the seal of the Senate of Rome.

The port commander broke the seal and began to read the document. With each line the grounds for Varro's return became more apparent and the commander couldn't help but smile as he reached the conclusion of the order from Scipio and the confirmation of Varro's new rank.

Varro watched the port commander read the scroll in silence, but he studied the older man's expression closely, trying to decipher from it how Scipio had phrased the order, with regard or with derision. As he saw the commander smile, Varro felt a sudden wave of anger hit him. Whatever Scipio's tone the port commander was taking pleasure from the end result. He stood slowly, his smile remaining and Varro struggled to keep his own expression neutral.

'Very well, Commander Varro,' the port commander began, a heavy emphasis on Varro's revised rank. 'It seems I must find a squad for you.'

Varro ignored the jibe and straightened his back to receive his orders. He looked to a point directly above the commander and focused his mind on the incident that had occurred minutes before in the courtyard when the *optio* had saluted him. Varro knew that the *optio*'s respect was engendered by his tribune's uniform but he also believed his own natural bearing was a significant factor. After today his uniform might change but Varro vowed that in his mind he would remain a tribune, the minimum rank his social status demanded. In time he would fulfil his orders from Scipio and dispose of the Greek captain who had shamed both him and Rome. Then he would return to his city, reclaim his former rank and raise his head high once more in front of his father. Until then he would suffer the dismissive attitude of men like the port commander, lesser men who would live to regret their underestimation of Varro.

The *Alissar* moved sedately through the commercial harbour of Carthage as the helmsman navigated the quinquereme around the moving obstacle course of trading ships large and small. The wind was onshore and so the sail remained secured but the current of the outgoing tide eased the galley's passage and the drum beat below decks hammered out a steady four knots.

Hamilcar paced the foredeck, his excitement and impatience in marked contrast to the steady rise and fall of the hull beneath him, the moderate course changes that brought the galley ever closer to the open waters beyond the harbour. Every so often a smile creased his face and he glanced back at the entrance to the military harbour nestled beyond the commercial docks. Inside and unseen; for where he now stood he knew the area was frantic with activity, the stage of his plan backed by the supreme council now beginning to take shape under the skilful hands of a multitude of Carthaginian shipwrights and naval carpenters. They were the best in the world and the confidence they possessed in their abilities had immediately put any lingering doubts Hamilcar had about his aggressive schedule to rest.

Hamilcar turned again, this time to gaze upon the waters ahead of the *Alissar*. She had finally cleared the harbour and the drum beat was increased to seven knots as she advanced into unobstructed waters. Hamilcar looked to the horizon, his mind's eye tracing out the routes the galleys he had dispatched yesterday had taken. There had been four in total, the captain of each carrying orders Hamilcar had dictated but which also bore the seal of the supreme council. Each one had been given a specific mission and so the order would be carried to very edges of the empire, to Marrakech, Iberia, Sardinia and Gymnesiae. Within weeks the provincial fleets ordered to return would arrive in Carthage, swelling Hamilcar's command until he achieved the superiority in numbers his plan required.

Hamilcar leaned over slightly to counteract the tilt of the deck beneath his feet as the *Alissar*'s course was adjusted, her bearing north-north-east, a direct line to the south-east corner of Sicily. From there she would hug the coast, traversing the narrow strait of Messina at night to arrive at her final destination, Tyndaris. It was one of the most vital elements of the plan, in addition to being the one most vulnerable to discovery, so Hamilcar had decided to oversee the final stages of construction. In addition he had dispatched orders to Panormus for a dozen galleys to join him in Tyndaris with the intention of closing the harbour to all commercial shipping.

Hamilcar glanced back over his shoulder as Carthage began to fade in the distance. It would be mere weeks before he would see her again and thoughts of her harbour filled with all the galleys of the empire filled his chest with pride at what he was about to achieve.

Atticus leaned back against the aft-rail, keeping close to the burning brazier, its smoke keeping away the evening insects. His chest felt stiff under the tight bandages the physician had applied, and the wound felt strangely cold, the foul-smelling salve he had applied numbing the area but easing his pain. He felt tired and light-headed but he delayed his return to the cabin below, wanting to wait until the turn of the watch at dusk and curious to learn what Septimus would reveal when he returned.

The breeze shifted slightly and the smoke of the brazier cleared, revealing to Atticus the distinct underlying odours of the port, the salt infused air, the musky smell of the town where a hundred fires had been lit in advance of the night and the sour acrid smell of the bilges of the ships that surrounded the *Aquila*. The crowds were melting away from the docks as the evening advanced, the gangs of slaves already corralled back to their quarters at the southern edge of Brolium, the passage of the day a featureless event in their miserable lives.

Atticus spotted Septimus from a hundred yards, his red cape easily distinguishable amongst the predominantly white clad traders and merchants. Atticus summoned a crewman to bring wine to the aft-deck as he watched Septimus's approach with interest, trying to discern from his gait if the news he had heard was good or bad. It was hard to tell although the centurion did move with determined stride as if time was of the essence.

Atticus nodded to Septimus as he reached the aft-deck, Atticus seeing for the first time the troubled expression of the centurion.

'Marcus?' he asked, misreading the expression.

'He made it back,' Septimus said, taking a proffered goblet of wine, 'but the Ninth's losses were very heavy. They have been temporarily stood down.'

Atticus nodded gravely but remained quiet, sensing that Septimus was not finished, and after a minute's pause Septimus began to outline what Marcus had revealed and what they had discussed at length.

'So Marcus believes the Carthaginian attack is more than just opportunistic?' Atticus asked.

'Yes, and I agree with him,' Septimus replied, 'but we don't know to what end. Maybe they are trying to split our territory in two, or perhaps it's just a feint in advance of an attack to retake Agrigentum.'

Atticus nodded. He agreed with Marcus's initial belief, as did Septimus, but that conclusion had led them nowhere. Only the *Punici* knew what step was next.

Both men turned as they heard the thump of heavy footsteps of the gangway and they watched as Varro led his men on board. His eyes searched the deck and came to rest on Atticus and Septimus. He dismissed his men with a wave and continued to the aft-deck alone, his gaze never leaving the captain and centurion.

'Your orders, Tribune?' Septimus said as he saluted, focusing Varro's attention on him alone.

'We sail at dawn,' Varro replied, not correcting the centurion's use of his former title. Varro knew the crew would learn of his demotion soon enough but until then he would remain tribune, if only in name.

'What heading, Tribune?' Atticus asked, stepping forward, determined to extract the necessary information a captain was entitled to know.

Varro stared hard at Atticus for a number of seconds, 'Send one of your crew to fetch a map of the north coast of Sicily.'

Atticus complied and the three men waited in silence until the map was brought up from below. Septimus spread it on the deck and they circled around it, careful not to block the dying light of the evening sun that stood a hair's breadth above the horizon.

'We will sail east into this area,' Varro began, pointing out a rough triangle on the map. 'There we should encounter a squad of ten galleys who are responsible for patrolling that area. I will take command of this squad.'

Varro stood up as he finished and Atticus and Septimus followed suit in anticipation of further instructions. Varro however simply turned around and left the aft-deck without another word, descending quickly into the hatchway that led to the main-cabin below.

'A tribune assigned patrol duty?' Septimus asked suspiciously as he watched Varro leave.

'How is he even still in command?' Atticus said, suddenly angry, sick of the charade he was forced to play with Varro. The man had tried to have him killed and yet Atticus couldn't fight back, Varro's privileged rank and status protecting him. 'Those cursed Romans have no honour,' he spat.

Septimus spun around, a furious expression on his face. 'What do you know of Roman honour?' he asked, a hard edge to his voice, a buried anger rising to overwhelm him. 'Varro is one man. He is not Rome.'

'Who do you think is protecting him?' Atticus countered,

angry at Septimus's reaction and his defence of Varro. 'Only the senior consul could have spared that whoreson.'

Septimus stepped in closer. 'And what of Greek honour?' he asked.

Atticus frowned, not understanding.

'I told you to stay away from Hadria,' Septimus said, speaking aloud the accusation that had festered in him for too long.

Atticus was stunned, the mention of Hadria's name throwing him. 'She has spoken with you?' he asked, his anger taking a new twist as he saw the censure in Septimus's face.

'She has,' Septimus said, 'and I know of your betrayal.'

'Betrayal?' Atticus snapped and without conscious thought his hand shot to the hilt of his sword.

Septimus reacted within the blink of an eye, his hand reaching for his weapon, the knuckles of his fist white from the intensity of his grip.

Atticus held firm and stared balefully into the centurion's eyes, the urge to draw his blade screaming at the muscles of his arm, the accusation of betrayal flooding his mind. An image flashed through his thoughts, of Hadria standing in her bedroom before running off to see her brother, and Atticus clawed his anger back from the brink of attack, his hand slowly withdrawing from his sword.

Septimus saw the gesture in the corner of his eye as he struggled to contain his fury. He had played out this confrontation many times in his mind but never had he thought it would spiral to his level. He believed beyond all else that the relationship between Atticus and Hadria had to end and he had trusted his friend to end it. In exposing that betrayal he had expected Atticus to be chastened but instead he was shocked by the ferocity of Atticus's defence. He stared at his friend's face, seeing there the conflict he felt in his own resolve and he slowly loosened the grip on his sword, his previous conviction shaken. He made to speak again but he stopped himself. Enough words had been spoken and he turned and walked from the aft-deck.

Atticus never took his eyes from Septimus's back, anger and confusion striking him in discontinuous waves. He looked down to the deck, the map of northern Sicily still spread at his feet, half of it now in shadow as the daylight gasped its last. He sought to refocus his attention, to drag his thoughts from the words Septimus had spoken and from the back of his mind he recalled Varro's orders. He traced the area that Varro had described, a rough triangle that was probably one of many that delineated the patrol areas of the Roman squads based out of Brolium. One apex of the triangle was anchored in to the harbour where the *Aquila* now lay. The next apex was to the north-east, a line that ran from Brolium to strike the port of Medma on the Italian coast, the second apex. From there the line ran south-south-west to the final apex, a Syracusan-held town on the north-eastern corner of Sicily, the ancient port of Tyndaris.

CHAPTER ELEVEN

Atticus waved one last time as the *Neptunus* drew away from the *Aquila*, her captain returning the gesture before turning away to issue the order to come about. The *Neptunus* turned slowly into the north-easterly wind; the waves initially striking her broadside, throwing up a fine mist of spray until the spear-like bow came to bear, slicing cleanly into the white-horses. For a second the galley seemed suspended, the oncoming wind counter-acting the power of her oars, but slowly and inexorably the two hundred slaves below decks overcame the inertia and within a minute she was up to a steady five knots.

Atticus turned and walked slowly over to the tiller. As he did he lifted his arm, rotating his shoulder through a full circle, recalling the slight stab of pain he had felt a moment ago when he had waved at the captain of the *Neptunus*. The wound on his chest was healing rapidly but the range of motion of his right arm was still restricted and even the weight of a sword became too heavy to hold within a minute.

Atticus nodded to Lucius and the second-in-command issued the order to raise sail, the *Aquila*'s course allowing her to take advantage of the wind and the whip-crack of canvas filled the air as the trireme came to life under Atticus's feet.

'Course, Captain?' Gaius asked.

'South-south-west Gaius,' Atticus replied. 'Where the wind takes us.' And he felt an enormous sense of freedom as the galley turned neatly beneath him. The *Aquila* was his once more, Varro having transferred to the *Tigris*, the command ship of the squad, two weeks earlier when the *Aquila* had arrived on station in its patrol zone. Since then the mood of the entire crew had lifted, not least because the scrutiny of a senior officer was never welcome on any vessel.

'South-south-west Captain,' Gaius said as the *Aquila* settled on course and Atticus sensed the hopeful tone of his helmsman. He slapped Gaius on the shoulder and smiled, sharing his hope that today they would finally encounter the enemy and take back some measure of their loss at Thermae.

The past two weeks had been frustrating, with the *Aquila* patrolling at random, expecting each day to encounter an enemy galley, believing that the Carthaginians were perhaps emboldened enough by their victory at Thermae to venture east beyond Brolium. But each day had ended in frustration as the *Aquila* sailed through seas devoid of enemy ships and it was only morale that kept the crew sharp as inactivity chafed the nerves of all on board.

That frustration was compounded by the possibility that a second enemy was active in the area. The other captains spoke of reports of at least a half-dozen ships that had disappeared in the waters around the north-eastern tip of Sicily, ships that were known to be on a southerly course from Rome that had not arrived at their destination. These were the kind of reports that incensed the crew of the *Aquila* and they had accepted with relish the order that once more turned their galley into the pirate-hunter she was born to be.

'Well?' a voice asked and Atticus turned to find Septimus coming up from the main deck.

'Nothing yet,' Atticus replied, 'but the rumours from the traders the *Neptunus* has stopped are the same as before.'

Septimus nodded and stood beside Atticus, looking past him to the departing Roman galley. Atticus stood easy, his hand resting lightly on the tiller. They had not spoken of their confrontation again in the previous two weeks and the tension between them had eventually dissipated, the unresolved conflict concealed by the routine of command and friendship.

'You still think it's pirates?' Septimus asked.

Atticus nodded, trusting his instincts.

'I don't think it's the Carthaginians,' he said, reiterating his argument. 'What reason would they have for capturing or sinking such a small number of ships? More importantly, not one ship has escaped to describe their attacker which means that each one was caught by complete surprise. Only a captain with local knowledge would know the best spots along the coast to ambush a passing ship.'

Septimus nodded, accepting the argument. 'So it must be pirates,' he said.

'It must be . . .' Atticus replied, his voice low, his thoughts still forming in his mind.

'But . . .' Septimus said, sensing Atticus's hesitation.

'I keep thinking of what Camillus, the survivor from the *Fides*, said,' Atticus said, again lapsing into deep thought.

'He said the pirates sunk the *Fides* after they captured it, slaves and all. A valuable prize,' Atticus began. 'And now every rumour speaks of ships disappearing without a trace. Not found drifting with their holds empty or beached with their complement of slaves taken, just disappeared as if they too were sunk. It just doesn't make sense.'

'Whoever they are,' Septimus concluded, 'it's only a matter of time before they run into one of our galleys.'

Atticus shrugged. He was unsure if the other crews were searching specifically for the pirates. Certainly no general order to that effect had been received from Varro, but even if the Roman galleys were tasked with patrolling for Carthaginian ships, it would be unlikely that they would allow a pirate ship to pass unchallenged. Either way, up until now, Fortuna had been on the side of the pirates.

Atticus glanced over his shoulder one last time as the *Neptunus* grew smaller in the distance. Beyond her the horizon was clear as it was off all four points of the *Aquila*, a featureless seascape but one where a galley could hide if she were commanded by the right crew. In addition the ancient shoreline of Italy was littered with blind coves and headlands, a multitude of lairs for a predatory galley. To catch her, Fortuna's wheel would need to turn in the *Aquila*'s favour or Atticus would have to turn the wheel for her. Armed with a crew and a galley that had hunted pirates for years that task might just be possible.

Regulus sighed irritably as his servant announced that Scipio had arrived and was waiting in the atrium. For a second Regulus was tempted to say that he was unavailable but he immediately thought better of it. He would have to confront Scipio sooner or later and as he felt more confident within the walls of his own house, now would be the most opportune time.

Regulus had left the Curia immediately at sundown, the traditional time of day when all discussion and debate was suspended in the Senate, in the hope of postponing this confrontation but even as he left, Regulus recalled thinking how futile his efforts were. In Rome the Senate might close with the setting of the sun but the Senate's business continued regardless of the heavens and Regulus knew he could not avoid this conversation.

The senior consul half-stood as Scipio entered the room, keeping his expression neutral, matching the senator's renowned ability to hide his inner thoughts. Over the previous weeks Regulus had tried to become adept at reading Scipio's thoughts but to no avail, the senator's serpentine nature constantly making a mockery of his efforts. On this night however Regulus felt sure he knew what was on Scipio's mind and he became even more guarded, knowing that Scipio's anger was lurking just beneath the surface.

'The hour is late, Senator,' Regulus said, keeping his tone even. 'You wished to see me?'

'Who in Hades do you think you are?' Scipio exploded, his veneer of composure suddenly cast aside.

Regulus bristled at the words, his own vow to remain calm forgotten as his patience evaporated. 'I am the senior consul of Rome!' he shouted, stepping forward to meet Scipio in the centre of the room.

Scipio laughed derisively, 'You are nothing, Regulus. You are a fool who has forgotten his place.'

'My place, Senator,' Regulus growled, 'is wherever I see fit.'

'No, Regulus,' Scipio said, drawing himself to his full height, his hands bunched by his side. 'You have gone too far this time. You will withdraw your announcement.'

Now it was Regulus's turn to laugh sardonically. He turned from Scipio and walked back to his seat, taking his goblet of wine from the table as he did. He recalled the moment in the Senate only hours before when he announced that he would travel to Sicily. The campaign there was in turmoil, with the Carthaginians pushing eastward beyond Enna and the legions struggling to contain the advance in the rugged mountains, unable to bring their superior fighting skills to bear in the hostile terrain. As senior consul, Regulus had felt compelled to act and he remembered the pride he had felt when his announcement was cheered by the Senate, a spontaneous endorsement of his decision.

He had immediately looked to Scipio, knowing that his undisclosed decision would anger him, but he had been unprepared for the unbridled wrath he had seen written on the senator's face. He took a drink from his wine, feeling confident that his decision had been wise. He turned once more to Scipio, recommitting himself as he saw the hostility in the senator's eyes.

'My decision and my announcement stand, Scipio,' he began. 'Rome needs me and I have answered her call.'

'Rome needs you,' Scipio spat, a mocking smile on his face at the pomposity of Regulus's words. 'What Rome needs is for me to decide, not you.'

'You cannot hold me here,' Regulus replied and Scipio realised for the first time, as he noticed a new confidence in the consul's voice, that his grip on power was slipping. Regulus's decision to travel to Sicily was a body blow to Scipio. With the senior consul away, leadership of the Senate would pass to Longus, the junior partner and a man completely beyond Scipio's control.

Scipio was furious with himself. He had not foreseen that Regulus would become his own man and he couldn't believe that it had happened so soon. With the revelation of his true intentions weeks earlier when they had first clashed Scipio knew his control of Regulus would become more tenuous but he had thought that his initial assessment of Regulus's character was still sound, that the consul would bend to his superior will and that Regulus's aspirations did not go beyond the title and trappings of the position of senior consul.

Scipio now knew that he had ignored his own doubts about his plan when he first noticed a new hostility emerging from within Regulus. Coupled with this the consul had unwittingly begun to gain support in his own right amongst many of the senators and the Senate's endorsement of Regulus's announcement earlier that day bore full testament to that support.

Scipio silently cursed Regulus as he watched the senior consul retake his seat, but this turned to a malevolent smile as he noticed again the consul's manner, the proud bearing that was fully suggestive of his confidence. Therein lay his demise, Scipio thought and he turned to leave the room without another word, satisfied, for now, for Regulus to believe that he had triumphed.

Hamilcar Barca walked slowly along the shore, his gaze ranging over the final stages of construction, the air filled with the sound of hammering and shouted commands. He knew he should feel tired, for he had barely slept over the previous two weeks, but anticipation was fuelling his energy and the sights around him continually commanded his full attention. He stopped at the head of one of the many jetties, his mind's eye already seeing the serried ranks of galleys that would soon be moored there and again his mind ranged over the events and details that needed to transpire before that vision would become a reality. He turned in the soft sand and looked down to his feet. The beach had been churned by a thousand footfalls, the slaves' bare footprints mixed with the prints of sandaled feet of the tradesmen who had been drafted in to the site. Hamilcar traced the signs of his own hob-nailed sandals and once again he was given over to imagine when the sand would show only prints of his kind.

Over the previous two weeks Hamilcar had received one report after another, each one keeping him apace with events on all fronts. In Carthage the fleets were assembling, the military port which could house two hundred galleys already full and the navy had resorted to commandeering parts of the commercial port to house the excess. Sixty miles south-west from where Hamilcar stood, his forces had pushed past Enna and were skirmishing with the Romans, driving relentlessly eastward. They would reach the border of Syracuse within a week. One final report, received only two days before had come from Hiero through an emissary. Ostensibly the emissary had enquired about the security arrangements at Tyndaris but Hamilcar had quickly noticed that the Syracusan's eyes had taken in every detail of the port and Hamilcar had taken the opportunity to mention the progress of his fleet and land forces, knowing that Hiero would hear his words within days.

Hamilcar looked to the sun setting rapidly in the west, the drop in temperature tempting a light cloud cover to appear on that horizon while over his shoulder, in the eastern sky, the full moon was beginning her climb into the heavens. Hamilcar's thoughts drifted to Belus and his imminent return, the phase of the moon signalling the pre-determined end to his task. Perhaps he would arrive on the morrow and Hamilcar utter a silent prayer to Tanit that the information he would bring would confirm his earlier reports. Armed with that confirmation Hamilcar would be poised to strike and he suddenly felt impatient, the culmination of so many months of planning hinging on one final report.

Belus smiled in the twilight as he watched the full moon rise over the bow of the pirate galley. The moon looked unusually large in perspective and he savoured the sight that marked the end of his time on the pirate galley. Belus looked away and turned towards the darkening sea, blinking his eyes to clear them of the residual image of the moon as he once more marshalled his thoughts, sifting the information he had gathered since he had last seen his commander.

The crux of his report involved security and the perceived

opportunity to take the Romans by surprise. On this point he was now sure, the evidence overwhelming and he smiled without thinking as he imagined the reaction of Hamilcar to the news. The smile dissipated quickly as Belus was reminded of the primary source of this vital information, the Roman captain still recovering below decks. Too many times over the previous days, when Belus had gone to check on the Roman, he had found himself examining his decision to spare him. More than once his conviction had faltered, even when faced with the sight of the Roman's broken body. Rome was the enemy, the aggressor who had precipitated the conflict on Sicily until the only option left to Carthage was total war. The sons of Rome therefore deserved no mercy, whether trader or soldier, for victory could not be achieved through half-measures. And yet, more often than not, Belus knew he was right to spare the captain. He firmly believed the Romans were no better than wolves, creatures totally without honour that corrupted all they touched. If Carthage was to prevail and remain unsullied by the conflict, Belus knew her sons needed to remain honourable. The Roman captain had been a worthy adversary and Belus would treat him as such. Once the impending campaign was underway, he would release him back to his people.

The stench of unwashed skin and clothes shattered Belus's thoughts and he turned to find a crewman standing beside him.

'Captain wants to see you,' he said, his mouth a mess of broken and rotting teeth, his breath putrid.

Belus nodded and stepped passed the pirate, his eyes searching the deck until he spotted Narmer on the aft. He strode towards him, conscious of the intense stare of the pirate captain as he approached.

'A full moon, Carthaginian,' Narmer said, stepping forward.

'Then we set course for Tyndaris,' Belus replied, wishing to keep the conversation as brief as possible.

'We'll be there by noon tomorrow,' Narmer replied.

'No sooner?' Belus asked. By his reckoning Tyndaris was no more than twenty miles as the crow flies.

Narmer nodded over his shoulder to the darkening horizon. Belus followed his indication and noticed the darker smear of storm clouds.

'There's a storm rolling south,' Narmer remarked. 'We will have to stay in shallow waters and hug the coastline.'

Belus nodded. The bireme had a very shallow draft, ill suited for heavy seas, and the galley was now in open waters west of the Bruttian peninsula. They would have to sail eastwards to the Italian mainland, into the lee of the peninsula, and then south along the coast. It was unavoidable but it added considerable time to their passage and Belus allowed his irritation to show on his face.

'Trust me, Carthaginian,' Narmer sneered, seeing Belus's expression. 'I am as anxious as you to reach Tyndaris and have you, and that Roman you spared, off my ship.'

Belus stared stonily at the pirate, not deigning to reply.

Narmer stepped towards Belus, leaning forward threateningly, determined to press home his opinion. 'And remember this,' he spat. 'If my gold isn't there waiting for me, you'll die on this galley, but not before my crew string you from the mainmast.'

Belus continued to stare icily into the captain's eyes, silently marking every contour of the pirate's face before turning abruptly to leave the aft-deck.

'Another wasted day?' Septimus said with mock derision as he came up to the aft-deck.

'Not one sighting,' Atticus replied with frustration.

'Maybe the other galleys have had more success,' Septimus said, sharing his friend's disappointment although he knew Atticus's hatred for pirates ran deeper than his own, second nature for a man who had spent his life at sea.

'We'll know tomorrow,' Atticus replied, referring to the prearranged assembly of the squad in the fishing village of Falcone that was scheduled for the next day.

Septimus nodded, sensing Atticus's conviction that no other crew had encountered the pirate galley. He looked beyond the captain to the setting sun and watched as the last of the day's sunlight skipped across the wave tops. Septimus had spent most of the day in training with his demi-maniple, a welcome distraction from the seemingly endless trek across open water and even now, within a minute of watching the horizon, he became annoyed by the monotonous seascape.

'Captain!'

Septimus turned at the call, recognising Gaius's voice and he watched as Atticus walked towards the tiller and man who had called him. As Atticus approached Gaius nodded to a point high in the sky over the port rail, using only his head to indicate, his hands never leaving the tiller. Septimus turned and followed the line of sight of the captain, immediately seeing a loose flock of seagulls flying across the line of the *Aquila*'s course. He wondered at their significance and he turned again to see Atticus and Gaius in conversation, both of them occasionally looking to the northern horizon.

'What's wrong?' Septimus asked, his curiosity getting the better of him.

'The seagulls,' Atticus replied, pointing again to the dwindling profiles of the flock. 'They're heading inland.'

'So?' Septimus asked.

'It's a sign that bad weather's approaching.'

Septimus smiled at superstitious sailors but as he looked

to the north he saw the unmistakeable stain of dark clouds crowding the horizon, their height seeming to increase with every second.

'Come about east,' Atticus ordered.

'We're going to run from it?' Septimus asked, surprised. 'Surely this galley can weather an autumn storm.'

'Not with that thing on board altering the trim of the hull,' Gaius said, indicating the *corvus* boarding ramp on the fore-deck. 'We encounter heavy weather with that thing attached to the deck and we'll capsize before we have time to make our peace with Poseidon.'

Septimus looked doubtful. The *corvus* looked ungainly on the foredeck but it was dwarfed by the mainmast and he found it hard to believe it posed some kind of threat as to how the galley would fare in rough seas.

Atticus noticed the centurion's expression, 'I trust Gaius's judgement on this,' he said. 'Galleys are very finely balanced and remember the *corvus* was installed on all galleys before Mylae. That was early spring so no galley has had to sail through a storm with a *corvus* weighing down its bow.'

Septimus accepted the argument although he remained sceptical. He knew nothing of sailing and had always deferred to the experience and knowledge of Atticus and his men but in this case he couldn't help but feel that they were being over-cautious.

Narmer stood on the aft-deck of his galley, his hand resting easily on the weathered arm of the tiller, his eyes focused on the waters ahead and the brooding dark shoreline to his star-board. The helmsman lay asleep on the deck behind him, curled up against the aft-rail with a canvas tarp over his head, meagre protection against the rain which had begun over an hour before. The bireme had just sailed into the lee of the

Bruttian peninsula which protected her from the rising swell and although the helmsman knew the coastline well, Narmer was sure none knew it better than he. As the bireme moved slowly through the shallows, Narmer's thoughts began to drift. He would be glad to reach Tyndaris on the morrow and finally rid himself of the Carthaginian shackles that had held his galley fast over the previous six weeks.

Narmer's galley had taken eight Roman ships during that time, rich pickings that he had been satisfied to sink in exchange for the fifteen hundred drachmae the Carthaginians had promised him. The waters around the north-eastern tip of Sicily were becoming too dangerous however, and Narmer had already decided that his next hunting ground would be the northern coast of Africa. The pickings would not be as rich there but neither would the risk of capture be as high and Narmer recalled with unease how close to detection his ship had come over the previous weeks. His ability to avoid the Roman war-galleys was based on detecting them before they spotted his ship. In daylight this was possible because of the extremely low profile of his bireme while at night he sailed without running lights, something the regimented Roman navy galleys would never do and so they were easily seen and avoided. Even with these precautions however, Narmer knew luck was always a factor in remaining undetected and so he looked forward to the time when Tyndaris and Sicily would be lost in the wake of his galley.

'Land, bearing two-points to port!'

Atticus followed the line indicated by Corin the lookout, wiping the rain from his face and eyes as he peered through the semi-darkness formed by the struggle of the moon to be seen through the heavy but broken cloud. The north-westerly wind was picking up with each passing minute but

Atticus judged the land ahead to be no more than two miles away.

'Recognise it?' Lucius asked.

Atticus studied it again, trying to discern some detail in the ethereal half-light, knowing that the older man was testing his knowledge. He smiled and shook his head.

'It's the Bruttian peninsula,' Lucius said and he pointed out the landmarks that had allowed him to recognise the Cape.

Without command Gaius steered the *Aquila* two points to starboard, the line of her hull pointing directly off the southerly tip of the peninsula.

'Recommend battle speed until we reach the lee, Captain.' Gaius said. 'The storm is coming up fast.'

Atticus agreed and sent the order below for battle speed, sensing the changed momentum as the *Aquila* took on the extra two knots of speed.

Twenty minutes later the *Aquila* sailed into calmer waters in the lee of the peninsula. Atticus ordered standard speed and sent lookouts to the starboard rail with orders to watch the line of breakers on the shoreline less than half a mile away. The coastline here ran south-south-west, reaching out ahead of the *Aquila* but Atticus could see that Gaius was adjusting the course of the galley to match, keeping her line parallel to the shadowy shoreline.

'Ship ahead!'

Atticus moved quickly to the side-rail and looked out over the seascape before the *Aquila*. The wind was lighter here behind the Cape but it was buffeted by the land and the rain was now falling in long narrow sheets, at once obscuring and then revealing the waters ahead in quick succession. The cloud cover was also increasing and the moon's light was becoming more sporadic and feeble. Atticus could see nothing ahead and he turned his face up to the masthead lookout.

'Confirm!' he shouted and for a brief second he saw the moonlight reflect off Corin's face as he turned to acknowledge the order. Corin remained silent and within a couple of minutes Atticus was ready to put the sighting down to a trick of the light and the young crewman's inexperience.

'There!' a shout came suddenly. 'Two miles, dead ahead. A galley!'

Again Atticus looked to the waters ahead and again he was frustrated by the combination of elements that obscured his view. He turned to Lucius who was also scanning the waters ahead and he raised his eyebrows in question.

'I don't see it, Captain,' he replied but he kept his gaze fixed on the specified point nonetheless.

Atticus looked up to the masthead again.

'Corin!' he ordered. 'Report to the aft-deck.'

The young man scrambled down from the fifty foot height with ease, hitting the deck on a solid footing before running to the aft.

'What did you see?' Atticus asked.

'A galley, Captain,' Corin replied. 'A small one, possibly a bireme. Bearing directly ahead and sailing on a parallel course.'

'You're sure?' Atticus asked, suddenly not as willing to dismiss the sighting as he had been a moment before. 'We can't see it from here.'

'She's sailing without running lights,' Corin replied.

Atticus understood immediately. Looking from the deck the ship ahead was silhouetted against the dark night sky and was therefore invisible. From Corin's viewpoint however, the ship would also be silhouetted against the intermittent moonlight on the water.

'A galley sailing without running lights can only mean one thing,' Atticus said, thinking out loud. 'She's trying to avoid detection.'

'The pirate galley?' Lucius ventured.

Atticus nodded, 'It could be,' he said. He turned to Corin and placed his hand on the young lad's shoulder.

'Get aloft and let us know if you see her change course.' Atticus ordered. Corin nodded and made to leave but Atticus stopped him, 'and Corin,' he said, 'well done.' Corin smiled and spun on his heel, retracing his steps and scurrying back up the running rigging to the masthead.

'Lucius,' Atticus said, turning to his second in command. 'Douse the running lights and pass the order to the crew. No exposed flame on deck.'

Lucius nodded and left also, leaving Atticus standing alone at the side-rail. He searched the waters ahead but again he saw nothing. He smiled despite this, knowing now that a ship was there somewhere and if it was the pirate galley then dawn's early light would expose her.

Narmer turned his face up to the rain in an effort to wash the fatigue from his eyes. He and the helmsman had shared the task of keeping the galley on course during the night but even when Narmer had taken a break he had been unable to sleep and he had surreptitiously watched the helmsman to be sure the crewman was alert. The sky was turning a lighter grey in the east, with dawn less than thirty minutes away and as the darkness fled, Narmer once again checked the line of his course in relation to the shoreline. The rain had never stopped but the wind had fallen away and so now, although the galley was no longer in the lee of the Cape, the sea breathed with only a gentle swell.

The gathering light also revealed the huddled figures of his crew spread out over the deck. Narmer was tempted to rouse them but he decided to let them sleep on. With Tyndaris less than six hours away, he could afford to relax the normally brutal discipline he was forced to impose to keep his galley running effectively. Narmer's eyes slowly drifted upwards and his lenient mood was replaced by a sudden fury. The masthead lookout was asleep, huddled against the mast, a canvas hood draped over his head and face to protect him from the rain.

'Masthead!' Narmer roared and his eyes were murderous as he saw the man start with surprise. He looked immediately chastened but the captain kept his gaze upon him, vowing silently that he would flog the man raw when his watch was finished at dawn.

'Helmsman!' Narmer shouted again, his anger now spurred on by his exhaustion. The man was immediately by his captain's side and Narmer handed over control of the galley before he set off along the deck, kicking the crew awake as he did, their curses of annoyance cut short when they noticed the vicious mood of their captain. Within a minute the crew were roused and they began the daily routine that marked their lives at sea.

'Galley! Dead astern!'

Narmer's insides turned to water at the shout and he raced to the aft-rail, his mind flooded with foreboding. He saw the oncoming galley before he even reached the rail, her hull a dark arrow on the brightening horizon directly behind his own ship. She was on an intercept course, no more than three miles behind.

'Any markings?' Narmer roared as he turned to the masthead, his fury at the lookout knowing no bounds.

There was moments silence as the lookout waited to be sure but Narmer knew there could only be one answer.

'Roman!' he shouted, fear evident in his voice, a fear that rippled across the entire deck.

'Prepare for battle!' Narmer roared without hesitation. 'Orders to the rowers, battle speed!'

He looked again to the galley in pursuit. Narmer could see

237

that she was a trireme, at least four knots faster than his ship but the pirate bireme had one advantage over its bigger rival, manoeuvrability, and Narmer knew how to exploit it. Battle would soon be joined but Narmer was determined that it would be on his terms.

'She's accelerated to battle speed!'

Atticus nodded at Lucius's words, noticing the change himself.

'Battle speed!' he ordered and the two hundred slaves below decks responded to the drum master's beat without visible effort, bringing the *Aquila* up to seven knots, a battle speed that was a knot faster than the bireme's.

'She's a pirate?' Septimus asked as he approached Atticus.

The captain nodded. 'She's not Carthaginian,' he replied, 'and no other galley would have cause to run.'

Septimus nodded and looked back over his shoulder, wiping the rain from his face as he did. His demi-maniple was drawn up in formation on the main deck, Drusus to their front, the *optio* seemingly oblivious to the rain that pelted off his breast-plate.

'Then we're ready,' Septimus said, and he left the aft-deck once more, his stride determined and focused, his men equally so.

Atticus watched him go and then turned to the helmsman.

'What do you think?' he asked

'She's quick,' Gaius said, his intense gaze locked on the target.

'But not quick enough,' Atticus replied, no humour in his voice as his mind inventoried every capability of the *Aquila* and how they could be sequenced to run down her prey.

'She'll try to cut inside,' Gaius continued, 'maybe to sweep our oars or simply escape.'

'Can we cut inside her?' Atticus asked, trusting Gaius's

judgement over all others when it came to close quarter sailing. There were many different galley types, some of them unique, and it was impossible to apply a general rule of attack, the variations in speed and manoeuvrability too great. Only now, with a ship in his sights, could a skilled helmsman properly formulate an attack.

'There's only one way we can cut inside her,' Gaius said, 'and even then we need to anticipate her turn. Otherwise she's too nimble.'

Atticus nodded, as his mind narrowed the options in the face of Gaius's assessment. The manoeuvre Gaius was implicitly suggesting had been practiced many times by the crew of the *Aquila* but had never been used in actual combat. Atticus could see no other option against a galley as manoeuvrable as the pirate's.

'They'll need to be close,' he said aloud as he weighed the odds.

Gaius nodded, 'They'll never see it coming.'

'If it works,' Atticus remarked almost to himself. 'If it doesn't we'll have handed them the advantage and maybe the fight.'

Gaius remained silent as he waited for his captain to decide, glancing once more to the pirate galley, now less than two and half miles away and then back to Atticus. The choice was far from clear-cut and he didn't envy the captain's position. The sound of the rain hammering the deck increased as Atticus broke the silence and turned to his helmsman.

'We do it,' he said, total conviction in his voice. 'Make ready the helm.'

Gaius nodded, his grip on the tiller intensifying as his eyes moved once more to the enemy.

'You were on the aft-deck!' Belus roared, his gaze locked on the Roman galley in pursuit. 'How did they get so close without detection?'

'She was sailing without running lights,' Narmer spat, his anger at being caught compounded by the Carthaginian's censure.

'And the masthead lookout?' Belus said, turning to Narmer, his eyes full of accusation and contempt.

'He was asleep,' Narmer said, looking past Belus to the lookout who had just descended from the masthead by his orders.

'Asleep?' Belus growled, his anger threatening to overwhelm him. He was about to berate Narmer further when the arrival of the lookout interrupted him.

'Yes, Captain,' the lookout said, trying to sound confident but his voice was laced with panic and Belus could smell the stench of fear from him.

Narmer stepped forward. 'You were asleep,' he accused.

'No, Captain,' the man stammered, what little confidence he had tried to muster now gone. 'I just didn't see her because of the rain.'

'Do you see her now!' Narmer shouted as he grabbed the lookout by the arm and pushed him towards the aft-rail.

The man stumbled but maintained his balance and he grabbed the aft-rail for support, looking out over the water to the galley bearing down on them.

'I didn't . . .' he began, his attention captivated by the sight before him. 'She came from nowhere . . .'

He turned around to plead again and found that Narmer now stood directly before him, the captain's expression more terrifying than before, Narmer's gaze so hypnotic that the lookout only saw the blade a heartbeat before it struck. He backed off slightly, his mind suddenly screaming in panic as awareness flooded his senses and his hands shot up to his neck, the blood drenching his fingers. He tried to scream but the sound died in his severed throat and the lookout fell backwards over the aft-rail, striking the rudder as he fell before being swallowed by the wake of the bireme.

Narmer stepped forward and spat over the rail into the water as the lookout's body resurfaced, the water around him stained red. He turned to face Belus, the bloodied knife still in his hand, a silent challenge passing between them. The captain would accept no more criticism from the Carthaginian.

Belus turned away and moved to the aft-rail, watching the lookout's body until it was run over by the Roman galley advancing at seven knots. He couldn't believe that Narmer had been so inept as to be caught so easily, especially since the captain had shown incredible skill over the previous weeks in avoiding the Roman galleys that patrolled the area. Belus knew he was partly to blame. He had noticed the change in the crew the day before when the bireme had finally turned its bow towards Tyndaris. They had become complacent, the end in sight, and Belus realised he should have confronted Narmer on the issue. Now, so close to success, Belus was faced with utter failure. He cared little for his own life, it belonged to Carthage, but the information he carried was invaluable.

Belus turned once more and looked out over the crew of the pirate galley. They were good swordsmen but they fought as individuals, relying on speed and savagery to carry a fight. Against the marines of Rome those tactics would be useless and Belus remembered his own desperate fight at Mylae. To defeat the Romans he would have to change their normal plan of attack and Belus turned to Narmer as an idea resurfaced in his mind, an idea he had formulated after witnessing the enemy attacks at Mylae. The Romans might find some way to board but for the first time Belus felt a creeping confidence that maybe the vaulted marines of Rome could be beaten.

*

'Attack speed!'

The gap between the galleys was now down to a mile and as the *Aquila* accelerated to eleven knots Atticus waited for the first turn. Gaius stood firmly to his right, his feet slightly apart to brace himself, ready to throw his weight against the arm of the tiller. Lucius was stationed below deck on the shoulder of the drum master, watching the rowers intently as they pulled through the sequence of moves that defined their existence. The slaves had been forewarned of the order to come, an order no different from the many times they had practiced the manoeuvre, although this time a chain ran through the eye of the manacle on their ankles. Failure in practice had meant a lash of the whip. In the face of the enemy, shackled to the seventy-ton galley, the stakes were immeasurably higher.

The first turn came without warning, the pirate galley swinging hard to starboard. Gaius reacted without command and the *Aquila* tilted heavily underneath Atticus's feet, the captain standing with his legs shoulder-length apart for balance. He noticed Gaius did not match the turn exactly but kept the *Aquila* on a convergent course, narrowing the gap between the galleys with every oar stroke. Atticus kept his own gaze locked on the aft-deck of the pirate ship, trying to anticipate their next move. He recalled with dread fascination the scene he had witnessed minutes before when one of the pirate crew had been thrown off the stern of the bireme, his body crushed beneath the ram of the *Aquila* as she followed the wake of the bireme relentlessly. It was a sight that would have frightened lesser crews but for the men of the *Aquila*, it merely reminded them of the ferocity of the prey they were about to hunt down, a prey far more dangerous than the Carthaginians in close quarter fighting.

The pirate galley turned again, this time to port and again

Gaius matched her course. The two galleys were now less than four-hundred yards apart, the *Aquila*'s line two points inside the bireme's to further close the gap. The rain continued to fall, peppering the surface of the sea and striking the deck of the *Aquila* with a staccato beat, the sound filling Atticus's ears as he tried to single out the pirate captain on the galley ahead, the distance and the water-drenched sea air thwarting his efforts.

'Make ready!' Atticus shouted to Gaius over the sound of the rain, knowing instinctively the pirate galley was about to commit, the distance and angles near perfect.

'She's turning!' Gaius shouted, his hand steady on the tiller, his muscles tensed in anticipation. 'She's coming about!'

The bireme turned violently to port, coming about at an incredible speed, her agility a sight to behold as she turned her bow into the path of the *Aquila*.

'Centre the helm!' Atticus ordered and Gaius lined the *Aquila*'s ram up with the oncoming bireme. The two galleys were now on a collision course, ram to ram, the larger trireme tearing down the line of attack.

Atticus focused his entire attention on the oncoming galley, trying to estimate the distance between the two ships, their combined speeds devouring the gap between them. The bireme had turned with an extraordinary display of manoeuvrability and Atticus was left with a lingering doubt as to the ability of his own galley. He brushed it aside, angry at his own mistrust of the *Aquila*. She had never let him down before. He looked over his shoulder to Gaius; the helmsman braced as before, holding the tiller on a centre line but ever-ready to react. The pirate's course was suicidal and both men knew it was only a feint.

With the gap down to two hundred yards the pirate galley turned three points to port, breaking the headlong attack, a classic manoeuvre for a more agile galley that readied her for a turn into the broadside of the *Aquila*. Gaius reacted instinctively, also turning the *Aquila* three points to port, putting the galleys on parallel course to pass each other going in opposite directions at a distance of one hundred yards, the only obvious defence for a trireme of the *Aquila*'s size.

'Runner!' Atticus shouted and a crewman was instantly at his side, 'Orders to below, prepare for a turn to starboard!' The crewman acknowledged the order and ran from the aft-deck, disappearing down the hatch that led to the rowing deck.

Atticus focused his attention on the pirate ship once more. She was now on the *Aquila*'s starboard fore quarter, less than one hundred and fifty yards away and she now held the advantage.

If the *Aquila* tried to force a fight and turn into the bireme's course to strike her amidships the pirate galley's agility would allow her to cut inside the turn and sweep past the *Aquila* before the trireme could bring her ram or *corvus* to bear, perhaps even striking the *Aquila*'s exposed oars as the two galleys swept past each other. On the other hand if the *Aquila* played it safe and stayed on course, she would run past the bireme and then need to turn to pursue her once more, allowing for the pirate galley to replay the entire sequence of turns once more, never allowing the *Aquila* the opportunity to engage, trumping her speed and power with agility.

The *Aquila* sped on, Gaius holding her course, while the pirate bireme did likewise, content to pass the Roman galley with one hundred yards separating their oars. Atticus stood on the aft-deck, his eyes locked on the ram of the bireme, the rain dripping from his matted hair and soaking his tunic beneath his armour. The pirate galley seemed to slow, as if the intensity of Atticus's gaze was somehow a barrier to her advance and Atticus's eyes flashed to the bow of his own galley, judging the angles, his innate skill deciding in a heartbeat.

'Now, Gaius!' Atticus shouted without conscious thought. 'Hard to starboard!'

The helmsman threw his weight onto the rudder, swinging it fully through the half circle that would put the galley hard over. Atticus watched the pirate galley intensely as a second passed, then another, waiting for the bireme to react, to commit to the counterturn. Again time seemed to slow and Atticus was running even as he registered the turn of the pirate galley. She was turning into the *Aquila*'s line, the speed of her course change faster than the trireme's, a speed that would allow her to cut inside and negate the *Aquila*'s attack.

Atticus reached the hatchway in the time it took the pirate galley to commit fully to the turn. He roared down to the slave deck, the terrible gamble he was taking putting an edge of alarm to his voice, knowing a second's delay would cost him the *Aquila*.

'Now, Lucius!'

For a heartbeat Atticus thought the command had gone unheard but then suddenly the galley, already turning slowly to port in response to the rudder, keeled over violently as the ship accelerated through the turn.

Below him on the slave deck Lucius had signalled the manoeuvre which the rowers and drum master had been drilled in so many times before in training. At the command the starboard-side rowers had thrown themselves forward, immediately raising their oars clean out of the water within one stroke. The port-side slaves continued to row, the drum master calling for ramming speed, their top stroke. With the rudder hard over and the starboard-side rowers offering no resistance, the galley turned within a half ship length, the deck listing twenty degrees from the uneven force of propulsion.

Atticus leaned into the turn, balancing easily as the deck tilted beneath him. Within six seconds the *Aquila* had made the turn, a turn that under rudder power alone would have taken twenty.

'Re-engage!' Atticus roared to Lucius and the *Aquila*'s deck righted as the starboard-side oars bit into the water once more. The pirate galley was only twenty yards off the bow on a converging course, the opportunity to cut inside lost, the ships now too close for a counter manoeuvre.

'Centre the helm!' Atticus shouted as he turned to Gaius. 'Hit them full-on!'

'Ready the *corvus*!' Septimus roared as the bow of the pirate galley filled his vision. He had been on the main deck when the *Aquila* had made her turn and although he had been prepared for the violent and sudden course change he had nearly lost his balance with only his fighter's natural instincts saving him from a fall. Some of the younger *hastati* had not been so lucky but they had picked themselves up without hesitation, reforming ranks before Drusus had an opportunity to berate them.

Septimus led his *hastati* and *principes* to the foredeck at a run, the hob-nailed soles of his sandals giving him purchase on the rain-soaked deck. He drew his sword as he stood behind the raised *corvus*, his ears ringing with the sound of forty other blades clearing their scabbards in unison.

'Steady, boys!' Septimus growled and although there was a gap between him and his men Septimus could almost feel them pushing against him, a pent up charge ready to be released against the enemy. Septimus braced himself for impact and a second later the ram of the *Aquila* struck the bow of the pirate ship, a solid blow that did not penetrate but drove the momentum out of each galley.

'Grappling hooks!' Septimus roared. 'Release the *corvus*!'

The ramp before Septimus fell in the time it took the centurion to start his charge; his feet already on the ramp as it struck the deck of the bireme, the three foot long spikes on the underside penetrating and splintering the foredeck of the pirate ship, holding her fast in a mortal embrace. Septimus ran without issuing a command, his men following without hesitation, their guttural war-cries splitting the air, their shoulders bunched behind four-foot high scutum shields, an unstoppable charge that had them on the empty foredeck of the pirate ship within seconds.

Narmer was thrown off balance as the Roman galley struck the bow of his bireme a hammer blow, violently tilting the deck beneath him and bringing the galley to a full stop. He cursed savagely as he regained his feet, instinctively drawing his sword in anticipation of the attack to come. Only minutes before Narmer had believed the first round of battle had been his, the sharp series of the bireme's turns making a mockery of the Roman galley's attempts to gain an advantageous line of attack. He had even laughed out loud when the Romans had begun their final turn, a forlorn hope to cut across the gap separating the two ships. Narmer had immediately turned hard over, his galley responding nimbly, ready to cut inside and sweep the enemy's oars. But that laughter had died on his lips as the Roman galley completed its turn with incredible speed, matching the bireme's agility and cutting off her line of flight.

The air around Narmer was spilt by the sound of his crew roaring in defiance as the Romans' boarding ramp crashed down on to the foredeck. The sight was terrifying, even though Belus had warned him of the new tactic and for a full second Narmer was transfixed by the unholy scene. The foredeck was empty, a ploy advocated by Belus, and the Romans quickly formed a solid shield wall across the breadth of the galley. The sight enraged Narmer, the invasion of his ship, of his domain and his fury reached a fever pitch, his mind casting aside the prearranged plan as he yelled a demonic war-cry, rushing forward, his crew following with the same savage haste, each man knowing that no quarter would be granted by their attackers.

Narmer's gaze was locked on the centre of the shield wall as he rushed forward, his sword held high, his rounded Greek *hoplon* shield strapped to his forearm, the rain lashing against his face. The wall advanced to the main deck in the time it took Narmer to cover the distance and he bunched his shoulder behind his shield as he struck the Romans at full tilt. The force of the blow numbed his arm but the sensation was barely registered as his mind lost all focus except for an overriding urge to drive the blade of his sword into enemy flesh, to stain the deck of his galley with Roman blood.

Narmer slashed down with his sword, parrying a strike from between the shields before him and he stepped backed instinctively, the Roman wall pushing forward. His mind cleared for a heartbeat, the backward step triggering his reaction and he stepped back once more, this time unbidden by his attackers, remembering the plan Belus had outlined. The Romans came on and Narmer continued to give ground slowly, his men backing off at the same pace, their defence unceasing but uncommitted. Narmer saw one of his men fall, then another but he smiled viciously nonetheless as his back struck the mainmast. The Romans were fully committed, their shield wall still strong, their forward advance unrelenting. It was just as Belus had foretold.

'Advance!' Septimus ordered, his voice carrying clearly to his men over the sound of the pirates' war-cries and the rain pounding in their ears.

The line advanced as one, reaching the main deck before the pirate charge struck home, the shield wall buckling and then forming strong again as the momentum of the charge was absorbed and repelled. Septimus's face remained grim as he stood behind the front line, his eyes ranging over the attack before him. His men were well drilled, efficient and deadly, and the enemy gave ground almost immediately.

'Hold the line!' Septimus shouted, forestalling any rush forward by his men. He waited a heartbeat, 'Forward!'

The shield wall advanced again as one, its strength grounded in unity and Septimus felt his confidence rise. The pirates were savage fighters, but they were undisciplined and uncoordinated. They had foolishly missed the chance to repel the legionaries as they made their way over the *corvus*, squandering their only opportunity to engage the legionaries at their weakest moment, before they had time to deploy into line. But the foredeck had been abandoned and the legionaries had formed unmolested, creating the solid unbreakable line that was now reaching the mainmast, half the galley in their wake.

A trumpet blast filled the air and Septimus instinctively shot around to its source on the *Aquila*, the warning sound cutting through the din of battle. His gaze never left the pirate ship however, as the reason for the warning was instantly apparent, his vision filled with the oncoming attack from the previously closed hatchway at the fore end of the main deck, the charge led by an inconceivable sight, a Carthaginian officer.

'Orbis!' Septimus shouted for a circular defence, overcoming his surprise without conscious thought. 'Enemy to the rear!'

The legionaries acted without hesitation, the second line behind the wall turning on their heels to face the new threat with their centurion but they were a fraction too late, the men to the left and right of Septimus betrayed by the swiftness of the pirates' surprise attack and the enemy crashed into the unprepared line with a ferocity that immediately buckled and then shattered the Roman formation.

Septimus fought like a man possessed, his attack instantly changing from the strict discipline of the legions to the fluid movements of one-to-one combat. The men around him fought with equal desperation, but many had never been trained to fight as individuals and within thirty seconds a half-dozen legionaries were down, the cries of the wounded lost in the roar of attack.

Septimus rammed his blade home with all the strength of his frustration and anger, twisting the blade savagely before withdrawing it, the pirate falling forward as he did, his face a mask of pain and defiance. Septimus shoved him away with the boss of his shield, the pirate slumping to the rain-soaked deck and Septimus was given a heartbeat's respite. The legionaries were in the fight of their lives, the original formation now scattered across the deck. Drusus stood by the mainmast, giving ground to no man, marking the furthest advance of the line. Septimus swept the deck with a murderous gaze, searching for the Carthaginian officer who had led the surprise attack. He spotted him almost immediately, his Punic armour standing out amidst the pirate crew. Septimus raised his sword once more, the hilt slippery with blood and rain and he tightened his grip, putting his weight behind his shield as he pressed forward, roaring a challenge as he went, a challenge that the Carthaginian answered with a savage war-cry of his own.

The trumpet was loose in Atticus's hand as he watched the surprise pirate attack slam into the exposed and unready Roman line. He had grabbed the trumpet at the first sign of the attack, instinctively realising the futility of his warning but desperate to alert Septimus, his towering frame easily recognisable in the Roman line. The centurion had reacted even as Atticus had sounded the warning but within seconds he, and the men around him, were engulfed in a wave of attackers.

'Gaius!' Atticus shouted running forward. 'You have the helm. Lucius, follow me!'

Atticus drew his sword as he jumped onto the main deck, the sharp stab of pain in his chest ignored. 'Men of the *Aquila* to me!' he roared as he ran, surefooted on the wet timbers of the deck. Lucius echoed the call, drawing his own sword and shouting to individual crewmen as he ran after his captain. The twenty *triarii* of Septimus's demi-maniple were in formation on the foredeck and Atticus shouted at them to advance, unsure of legionary orders but sure they would understand.

Atticus screamed a war-cry as he ran across the *corvus*, his shout taken up by Lucius and the rest of the crew, their anger easily flamed by prospect of taking the fight to the pirates. The *triarii* followed in loose formation, battle-hardened troops who were past their prime but still possessed the strength and will to engage any enemy. The men of the *Aquila* fanned out as they reached the main deck of the bireme, their cries finally heard by pirate and Roman alike in the maelstrom of battle around the mainmast. They came out of the rain like a horde from Hades, Atticus at their centre, the raw wound on his face giving him a demonic mask as generations of inbred hate against the pirate breed was given expression on his face.

They tore into the fight with a momentum that pushed Atticus into the centre of the swarm. A legionary fell at his feet and Atticus threw up his sword to attack the pirate who had made the fatal thrust. The strike was parried and Atticus swung his blade around to block the counter-thrust, twisting his torso violently to gain the angle. Pain flooded his consciousness as he parried the blow and a warm dark stain of blood streamed across his chest, the rain-soaked tunic beneath his breast-plate clinging to the reopened wound. Atticus grunted through the pain and stabbed his sword downward; running the edge of his blade against the pirate's groin, opening a deep fatal wound that stained Atticus's sword. The pirate screamed, his face a mask of terror as he dropped his sword and fell, his blood washed from the deck by the unceasing rain. Atticus fell to his knees, his hand reaching inside his armour to be drawn out again stained red.

Septimus hammered his shield against the Carthaginian's chest twice in quick succession, roaring each time, his anger unbounded at the thought of his men falling around him. Belus answered in kind, his sword striking the boss of the Roman shield, his mind flooded with visions of Mylae and the desperate knowledge that he must prevail in order to deliver his message. Septimus registered the flood of men from the *Aquila* as they swept around him but his focus remained on the Carthaginian, the head of the serpent that had struck his line from behind, his initial incredulity at the sight of a Carthaginian officer leading the pirate charge forgotten as anger overcame reason.

Belus sidestepped to the right to gain space, his sword arm feigning a further advance before he centred his balance once more, his shield deflecting a vicious strike from the Roman. He too had seen the second wave of Romans join the fight and he knew the pirates were now hopelessly outnumbered. They had reacted so quickly, much faster than Belus had thought they would, believing that the surprise of his attack would stun the remaining crew of the Roman galley and keep them at bay until the legionaries were overwhelmed. But they had reacted instantly and attacked without hesitation, robbing Belus and his men of the precious minutes that would have led to success. He instinctively pushed forward again at the thought, a creeping recklessness beginning to control his actions as realisation swept over him. There would be no escape.

Septimus stepped back as the Carthaginian's attack suddenly intensified, his sword a blur of iron and light, rain water streaming off the tip as the Carthaginian slashed his blade in low. Septimus narrowly deflected the strike and shifted his balance to swing his shield around, slamming the brass boss into the Carthaginian's sword arm, breaking his attack and eliciting a furious cry of anger.

Belus attacked again, his skilful swordsmanship giving way to unfettered fury as he rained blow after blow on the Roman's shield, the hated enemy that had caused him to fail in his duty. He roared out a cry to Anath, the war-goddess to put strength into his sword arm, his voice rising until it blocked out every other sound, his face twisting maliciously as he felt the Roman give way under his assault.

Septimus bent his knees and prepared to strike as the Carthaginian's attack reached its crescendo, drawing his shield in close as he coiled his body behind it, drawing the Carthaginian in ever closer. Suddenly, with a strength forged in the legions, Septimus propelled himself forward, his shield crashing into the Carthaginian, knocking him back. Septimus continued his lunge, pushing his foe across the deck, waiting for the moment to strike. The Carthaginian threw his sword arm up, fighting for balance and Septimus plunged his short sword into the Carthaginian's exposed flank, striking him below his armour, a killing stroke that Septimus compounded as he twisted the blade, a rush of blood and viscera covering his hand as the Carthaginian screamed in pain.

Belus fell to the deck, his sword and shield falling from near-lifeless fingers, his hands reaching for the wound in his side as his blood stained the deck he had defended with his life. He looked up at the Roman standing over him, a younger man, the intensity of his gaze matching the ferocity of his attack, the rain streaming off his helmet and armour, his sword in his hand drenched with Belus's own blood. The Roman held his gaze for an instant longer and was gone, leaving Belus staring at the grey sky, the terrible knowledge that he had failed Carthage haunting him as his life slipped away.

Narmer roared at the men around him, driving them forward, stirring their blood and savagery into a frenzy. The pirates responded with ever-increasing cries of defiance and challenge, giving the Romans no quarter in a fight that was becoming ever more desperate for the outnumbered defenders. Moments before, Narmer had seen Belus fall, struck down by the Roman centurion who was now rallying his men for a final push that Narmer knew would overwhelm his crew. He backed away from the line of battle, the final surge of his crew affording him the opportunity to make his escape below decks and he turned and ran to the hatchway at the aft-end of the main deck.

Narmer charged his sword as he landed on the walkway in the middle of the slave deck. The rowers beside him began to clutch at his legs in panic, begging him to release them. He struck out with his sword, fearful of being overwhelmed by clawing hands and a rower cried out in pain as the blade sliced through his wrist. The others backed off and Narmer rushed to the gangway leading to the main cabin, closing and baring the door behind him as he entered.

The sounds of battle continued on the main deck above. Narmer slowly paced the room, his sword hanging loose by his side, panic rising within him as his mind sought a way out. His flight below deck would buy him another few minutes, perhaps longer, but Narmer knew there was no escape. A sudden anger welled up within him and he slammed his sword onto the table in the centre of the cabin, cursing the day he had placed himself in the midst of the conflict between Rome and Carthage. Belus had robbed him of his galley, Narmer realised that now, robbed him of his command and sailed him into waters infested with Roman galleys. Now the Romans were poised to rob him in turn, to plunder what was his and deprive him of the galley he had won through ingenuity and blood.

As Roman victory cries sounded from above, Narmer picked up his sword once more, a vow passing his lips as he examined the blade before sheathing the weapon. He had no need for it, for another blade would not stop the Romans from taking his ship. For that, Narmer would need another weapon, one more ancient and deadly, and he repeated his vow as he prepared, an oath to deprive his enemies of the galley they had dared to take from him.

'Hold!' Septimus roared, as his men began to chase after the half-dozen pirates fleeing below decks and the legionaries halted at the whip-crack of the centurion's voice, ingrained discipline overcoming their blood-lust. They stood in silent sobriety for a moment, breathing heavily, their swords slowly falling as they realised the deck was theirs and a single shout of victory quickly became many.

Septimus let them roar, the ship was theirs but to finish the task they would have to clear the remnants of the pirate crew from below decks.

'Drusus,' he called to his *optio*. 'Take ten men and secure the fore main deck hatch. I'll take the aft.'

Drusus saluted and gathered the men closest to him, leading them at a run in loose formation towards the hatch. Septimus did the same, his eyes ignoring the dead and dying, ally and foe alike, as he ordered his remaining men to stand fast on the main deck.

Septimus paused at the hatchway for a moment before clambering down, his eyes adjusting quickly to the half light of the rowing deck. Stepping back, he allowed his men to follow and they formed a defensive ring around the ladder, their shields charged outwards. A walkway ran the entire length of the slave deck, with chained rowers on either side, their pitiful cries for release deafening in the confined space. Septimus ignored them, his gaze reaching forward seventy feet along the walkway to the fore hatchway and the sight of Drusus's squad moving towards the forward cabins.

Septimus formed his men behind him and stepped towards the gangway that led to the main cabin at the rear of the galley. Its door was flanked by two others, smaller cabins to port and starboard. Septimus readied his shield and pushed the portside door open with the tip of his sword. It was a tiny cabin; no more than six foot across and it was empty. He spun around and pushed the door opposite, expecting the same but inside a man lay supine upon a low cot, his face horribly disfigured, his tunic bloodstained and torn. Septimus nodded for one of his men to step into the cabin to examine the apparently unconscious figure while he led the others to the final door, the main cabin.

A sudden eruption of shouts from the front of the galley caused Septimus to look over his shoulder as the clash of iron signalled Drusus's discovery of more of the crew. Septimus looked to one of his men at the rear. 'Report to the *optio*,' he ordered, 'find out if he needs help.'

The soldier nodded and ran back along the walkway, his footfalls heavy on the timber deck. Septimus turned his attention to the main cabin once more and as before pushed against the door with the tip of his sword. It did not open and he half turned to press his shield against the timbers, putting his weight behind it.

'Barred,' Septimus said to himself before turning to the two men behind him.

'Break it down!' he ordered and the legionaries stepped forward, reversing their swords and hammering on the door with the pommels, the hardwood spheres cracking and splintering the weathered door.

'Ready, lads!' Septimus said, preparing himself to surge forward. The door could only last for seconds more. He breathed deeply, tensing his muscles for the lunge forward, expecting to find the majority of the remaining crew behind the door. His intake of breath triggered an alarm in Septimus's mind as he sensed the underlying dreaded smell that overwhelmed the stench of blood from his sword and the reek of filth from the deck beneath his feet. It was a smell that triggered the fear that dwelt in every man who lived on the timber ships of the age, a smell that foretold of an enemy that could not be contained, one that would consume the galley and all on board.

'Stop!' Septimus shouted and he crouched down in the silence that followed. He smelled the air again. There could be no doubt. Whoever was behind the door had fired the cabin. Septimus stood up instantly.

'Back on deck. Now!' he roared, his men responding, not yet sensing what Septimus had perceived but following his order without hesitation.

'Centurion!' Septimus turned to the soldier who emerged from the side-cabin.

'This man is Roman,' he said, indicating over his shoulder. Septimus looked beyond him to the man on the cot. 'He's says he's the captain of a trader taken by these pirates,' the soldier continued in explanation. Septimus grabbed one of the fleeing legionaries by the shoulder.

'You,' he said, 'help him get this man up top.'

The soldier obeyed and between them the two legionaries carried the Roman captain up the gangway. Septimus followed them, continually glancing over his shoulder at the main cabin door, seeing the first wisps of smoke appear even as he began his climb to the main deck. The sight caused him to quicken his step and he immediately ordered men forward to command Drusus to disengage the enemy. He spotted Atticus and made his way towards him, issuing orders for his men to form up as he did.

The captain was sitting amidst the Roman wounded, his face deathly pale against his blood-stained tunic, Lucius kneeling beside him.

'The ship is ours?' Atticus asked, his voice weak but the triumph of victory strong in his gaze.

'No,' Septimus spat in anger. 'This ship is in the hands of Vulcan.'

'By the Gods . . .' Atticus whispered. 'Fire?' As Septimus nodded the first cries of panic rose up from the slave deck below, the terrifying sound ripping along the entire length of the galley in the time it took the unaware amongst the Romans to understand what was happening. Soldiers who had charged fearlessly into battle turned to flee, their eyes looking around in trepidation, searching for evidence of the fire that terrified them all. Shouts of alarm rang across the main deck as smoke suddenly billowed from the aft hatchway.

'Everyone back across the *corvus*!' Septimus shouted and he helped Atticus to stand, bearing his weight as he continued to issue orders to his men, ensuring that the wounded were all accounted for.

'Wait!' a junior *hastati* shouted from the head of the forward hatchway, listening to the cries for mercy of the slaves. 'I can hear Roman voices!'

'Hold!' Atticus roared, realising the danger but his order was lost amidst the cacophony of panic and desperation from the slave deck and he watched helplessly as the junior soldier disappeared down the hatchway to be immediately followed by two others. Atticus ran forward, the pain of his wound forgotten as saw that other legionaries were preparing to follow the first three below.

'You men stand fast!' Atticus shouted and the soldiers hesitated, looking beyond the Greek captain to their centurion, the pull of the Roman voices desperately calling for help causing them to inch forward once more. Septimus couldn't understand Atticus's command but he repeated it without hesitation, ordering his men to get back aboard the *Aquila*. Only when he reached the hatchway did he question Atticus; the endless voices of terror from below drowning out his words to all others except Atticus.

'Damn it, Atticus,' he hissed, angry that he hadn't considered the fact that there might be Romans amongst the rowers sooner. 'Why did you stop more of my men from going below? We need to be sure we rescue any Romans amongst the slaves.'

'The slaves are dead men,' Atticus replied, his eyes locked on the retreated legionaries, many of them returning his gaze balefully, 'and you condemn any man you send down there.'

Septimus instinctively looked over his shoulder, judging the spread of the fire, trying to ignore the endless cries of terror.

'There's still time,' he said. 'But the three men down there need more help.'

Atticus turned to Septimus, a look of despair on his face.

'I've seen this before,' he said, a haunted look in his eyes. 'They can't be helped.' He nodded towards the hatchway, 'Look for yourself.'

259

Septimus held Atticus's gaze for a second before turning to descend. Atticus grabbed his forearm. 'Stay out of their reach,' he warned.

Septimus nodded and started down the ladder, instinctively drawing his sword as he was exposed to the full measure of the terrible screams of panic that seemed to stem from the very timbers of the galley. He stopped halfway down the ladder, crouching down to see back along the abyss of Hades that was now the slave deck. The fire had already taken hold of the stern end of the ship, the smoke consuming the aft-end of the deck, the slaves visible in front of the grey wall dragging desperately at the manacles around their ankles that held them fast, the deck beneath them stained red by their torn skin as terror drove many to near madness.

Septimus spotted two of his men not ten feet from the base of the ladder, their bodies only recognisable from the remnants of their armour, their flesh in places torn away by the frenzied horde who had clawed desperately at them for release, robbing them of their swords and daggers, of anything they could use to free themselves, their collective panic preventing them from recognising the men as rescuers and Septimus watched in dread fascination as a slave snapped the blade of a gladius against an unyielding chain, a dozen hands clamouring for the shattered sword.

Beyond the fallen soldiers Septimus spotted the last man, the legionary who had fearlessly led the others. He was screaming at the top of his lungs, his cries ignored, terror etched upon his face as he slashed his sword at the countless hands that clawed at him. He suddenly turned in Septimus's direction and for an instant his terror cleared as he recognised his centurion, his eyes pleading for help, his instinctive half-step towards the ladder cut off before he could complete it. He roared something incoherent, his plea lost in the maelstrom of fear and Septimus could only return the soldier's gaze until the desperation of his fight forced the soldier to turn away once more.

Septimus hesitated for a second more and then turned his back on the doomed man, climbing back up the ladder and walking past Atticus without a word, the captain following the centurion back across the *corvus*, the ramp lifting behind them, separating the *Aquila* from her victim. Septimus moved to the fore-rail and stared across at the pirate galley as he sheathed his sword, his eyes ranging over the fallen legionaries on the deck, men who had given their lives for a hollow prize. The cries of the damned on the slave deck abated as the *Aquila* drew away, distance finally silencing their pleas.

CHAPTER TWELVE

Varro stood alone on the foredeck of the *Tigris* as he watched the quiet fishing village of Falcone come to life. It was a squalid little place with a half-dozen decrepit wooden huts huddled around a single jetty and the people that Varro could see from his vantage point all seemed to possess the same sullen posture that bore witness to their miserable existence. The sight disgusted him and Varro turned away from the shore to look past the assembled galleys of his squad to the open seascape beyond.

They had all arrived the day before, appearing individually throughout the daylight hours, like stragglers without conviction, with each reporting that the enemy had not been sighted. All save one, the one galley that had not arrived, the *Aquila,* and Varro smiled malevolently at the thought. Perhaps they had met the enemy and the *Aquila* with her Greek whoreson of a captain was now lost beneath the waves, or better yet, she was but hours away and Varro would be given the opportunity of having the captain flogged for insubordination. Either way, Varro relished the thought, a distraction from the news that had antagonised him since he had heard it only days before. Regulus had arrived in Sicily.

Brolium was only six hours' sailing from where Varro now

stood but he knew the senior consul might as well be in Rome given the chasm that now separated him from the most powerful man in the Republic. Over the previous days Varro had fruitlessly searched for a credible reason to approach Regulus, to finally gauge the consul's position given that since their last meeting in Rome, when Regulus had issued his order for Varro's banishment to the northern frontier of the Republic, Scipio had interceded on Varro's behalf and apparently persuaded the consul of his true loyalty and worth. Now Varro was anxious to expound those qualities in person, to reinforce Scipio's words and regain the full measure of Regulus's confidence.

'Galley approaching!'

Varro looked to the masthead and then to the indicated direction, sighting the approaching ship, its course a direct line to Falcone, its oars rising and falling with deceptive ineffectuality as if the galley was stationary in the water. It could only be the *Aquila*'s and Varro's thoughts turned seamlessly to the punishment he had decided would greet the captain of the errant galley.

'Falcone ahead!' Corin shouted from the masthead and Atticus looked up to the youth, anticipating the words to follow. 'The rest of the squad are already assembled!'

Atticus nodded and looked out over his galley to the low-lying village ahead. It was some three miles away, thirty minutes at the *Aquila*'s current speed. He turned from the side-rail and walked over to the tiller once more, his eyes unconsciously checking and re-checking the rigging and the line of the mainsail, the gentle breath of the on-shore breeze filling the canvas sheet and pressing smoothly against the off-centre drag of the rudder with Gaius's minute adjustments of the tiller keeping the *Aquila* dead on course.

Atticus's gaze came to rest on the main deck and the sight that had drawn his attention so many times since dawn's early light had given it clarity. The three men lay side by side, two legionaries and one of Atticus's own, the soldiers lying with their shields covering their chests and faces, the sailor's face covered with a strip of cloth, an act of dignity to hide their sightless eyes. They had all died of their wounds during the night, two of them succumbing mercifully while they were unconscious but the third screaming in pain until Mars claimed him, the deep wound to his kidney spilling black blood onto the deck, a stain that would never fade.

'Fifteen men,' Atticus whispered, recalling the faces of the three that were from his own crew, and with the resolution that only a commander could summon he buried the memory of them deep within his mind.

Atticus's trance was broken by the sight of Lucius before him, the second-in-command's face agitated.

'You need to speak with Albinus immediately!' he said.

'Albinus?'

'The Roman captain the legionaries found on the pirate galley,' Lucius explained. 'He regained conscious about an hour ago.'

Atticus was about to question Lucius further but he turned and walked to the hatchway leading to the cabins below, forcing Atticus to follow. He spotted Septimus approaching along the main deck, following a crewman and Atticus shrugged his shoulders to Septimus's enquiring glance before descending the ladder leading to the deck below.

The Roman captain was lying on a cot in one of the smaller side cabins. He was propped up on his elbow, a sailor assisting him as he drank a mouthful of water from a goblet, the captain coughing painfully as he choked on the meagre sip. The crewman withdrew the goblet and the captain lay down once more, closing his eyes as he drew his arms slowly across his chest and for the first time Atticus could see that all his fingers were broken, many of them sticking out at obscene angles.

'Albinus,' Lucius said, and the captain reopened his eyes. A shadow of some horrific memory swept across them before they came into focus.

'Albinus, this is Captain Perennis and Centurion Capito,' Lucius said and stepped aside to allow Atticus and Septimus to enter the cramped space. Atticus knelt down at the head of the cot while Septimus moved to the end, standing with his arms folded, anger etched on his face as looked upon the ruined body of the Roman captain.

'Tell them what you told me,' Lucius prompted and the captain nodded imperceptibly, swallowing hard as if to clear his throat of some vile taste.

'I'm Albinus Lepidus of the trading galley *Glycon*,' the captain began, his voice a whisper but easily heard in the tiny cabin. 'We were sailing to Locri when we were ambushed by the pirate galley.'

Albinus paused and was silent for a moment. 'She came out of nowhere . . .' he muttered and Atticus reached out instinctively and placed his hand on the man's shoulder. The captain seemed to draw strength from the gesture and continued.

'They captured many of my crew alive. I was taken to the main cabin and the others . . . the others were tortured to death.' Albinus said, the act of speaking of the terrible memory seemingly drawing the life force from his body.

'Tortured?' Septimus asked, 'Why?'

'It was the Carthaginian,' Albinus spat, suddenly angry and defiant. 'He ordered the men to be tortured and then the bastard . . .' He coughed violently from the effort of speaking and blood-stained spittle shot from his lips onto his tunic. The image of the Carthaginian officer on the pirate galley

265

immediately entered Septimus's mind and he remembered his incredulity; not only seeing a Punic soldier on the galley but the fact that he seemed to be in command of the pirate crew.

'Why was there a Carthaginian officer on board?' Septimus asked. 'And why was he in charge of the galley?'

Albinus swallowed hard again as regained his breath.

'I don't think it was permanent,' he said, his mind sifting through the minutes before the Carthaginian started to torture him. 'He told the pirate captain that the ship was under his command until they reached Tyndaris.'

'Tyndaris?' Atticus said. 'The Syracusan port?'

Albinus nodded.

'Why did he have the men tortured?' Atticus asked, and he sensed Lucius leaning forward behind him. 'What did he want to know?'

'He wanted to know about our coastal defences,' Albinus began. 'If I had ever encountered any patrols. If there was an active defence line somewhere south of the city. Where the majority of the galleys were stationed? What activity I had seen?'

'What city?' Atticus asked, his mind searching the coast of Sicily for the enemy's target. 'Are they planning an attack on Agrigentum?' he ventured.

Albinus shook his head and then turned to look directly into Atticus's eyes.

'No, Captain,' he said, his voice raised above a whisper for the first time. 'The Carthaginians plan to attack Rome'

Varro angrily paced the main deck of the *Tigris* as he watched the small skiff approaching. Vitulus was perched behind the bowsprit, the two rowers behind him the only other two occupants of the boat. The Greek captain, the man he had ordered

266

Vitulus to return with was nowhere to be seen and Varro looked beyond the skiff once more to the *Aquila*, now anchored a hundred yards away.

'Well?' Varro barked as Vitulus climbed up the rope ladder from the skiff.

'The captain is on board,' Vitulus began, rushing his words to explain himself before his commander could react further. 'But he requests that you come across to the *Aquila*. He has a Roman captain on board who is too weak to be moved but who has vital information that you need to hear.'

Varro stepped forward without warning, and slammed his forearm into Vitulus's chest, knocking him to the deck.

'I do not take orders from a Greek,' Varro roared, his sword suddenly in his hand, its tip held above Vitulus. 'Assemble a *contubernia* and bring this galley alongside the *Aquila*. I will deal with this insubordination myself.'

Vitulus nodded and scrambled up, moving quickly to the aft-deck and issuing the necessary orders. The drum beat started a minute later as the *Tigris* got underway, the helmsman bringing her alongside the *Aquila* with practiced skill.

The gangway of the *Tigris* was lowered onto the deck of the *Aquila* and Varro strode across, followed by Vitulus and ten legionaries.

'Where is your Captain?' he asked, grabbing a crewman by the scruff.

The sailor indicated the aft-hatchway and Varro continued on, his mind barely registering the sight of three covered bodies on the deck. He descended the ladder with one hand on the hilt of his sword and upon seeing the opened door to a side cabin, prepared to enter, the men behind him crowding the corridor.

Atticus spotted Varro the moment he appeared in the doorway.

'Commander,' Atticus began, relief in his voice, 'thank the Gods you're in time,' he said indicating the man lying on the cot. 'He is near death.'

'You!' Varro spat, drawing his sword, the movement awkward in the confines of the cabin. 'You have disobeyed me for the last time.'

'Commander!' Septimus roared, his voice deafening in the confines of the narrow room. Varro's sword immediately froze, his murderous gaze darting to the tall centurion at the end of the cot.

'It is vital you hear this man's report,' Septimus continued, the natural commanding tone of his voice causing Varro to hesitate. He shoved Atticus aside and looked down at the haggard face of the Roman captain.

'Who is he?' he barked, shaking the captain's shoulder roughly until he stirred and his eyes opened.

As if in a trance the captain began to tell his story again, seemingly oblivious to whom his audience was. It took him ten minutes to recite his report, his voice trailing off a number of times, his eyes rolling in his head as his consciousness fled to be forcibly reined in again by Varro, his impatience and mounting excitement extinguishing any tolerance he had for delays caused by the captain's weakness. He stood up as the captain finished his report and turned to face Septimus.

'He speaks of a pirate ship,' Varro said. 'Tell me what happened.'

Septimus immediately reported the events of the battle the day before.

Varro nodded, remembering the corpses he had seen on deck. 'He has made this report about an attack on Rome to you already?' he asked.

'Yes Commander,' Septimus replied. 'And to the captain and second-in-command.'

268

'And each time it has been exactly the same?'

'Yes, Commander,' Septimus said.

Varro nodded, dismissing any lingering doubt he had that the story was a delirious tale brought on by the man's obvious wounds. A feverish ramble would not be repeated so succinctly.

'Very well,' Varro said and left the cabin without another word, Vitulus and the other legionaries making way for him in the corridor before following him back on deck. Varro did not pause until he was back on board the *Tigris*.

'Cast off immediately,' he ordered the captain, 'and set course for Brolium.'

The captain saluted and roused the crew to action.

'Shall I signal the rest of the squad to follow?' Vitulus asked.

'No, order them to stand by on station here.'

Vitulus saluted and proceeded to the aft-deck. Varro watched him go before turning to gaze over the other ships of his squad, many of their crews curiously watching the *Tigris* get under way. He spotted the Greek captain and the tall centurion on the main deck of the *Aquila*; the two men in conversation. They were more than just captain and marine, Varro thought as he watched them closely, they were obvious friends and Varro was left to wonder why a Roman centurion would befriend such a man as the Greek. Whatever the reason Varro marked the friendship in his mind, knowing that when the time came the centurion's loyalty to his friend could supersede his loyalty to Rome.

Varro re-examined the information the Roman captain had given them, information that the consul would need to hear and that Varro would deliver personally, ensuring that his name was associated with the discovery of the enemy's plan. He smiled triumphantly. His rank and honour were within his grasp.

*

Varro looked upon the flagship of the consul with awe. It was a quinquereme, one of a fleet of ten anchored at the northern end of the harbour at Brolium, their massive hulls dwarfing the single trireme that Varro could see amongst them, a galley that was being used to ferry supplies and equipment between the larger ships, a stark omen of the fate that surely awaited the suddenly obsolescent smaller galleys of the *Classis Romanus*.

Varro commanded the captain to lay the *Tigris* alongside the flagship, his eyes ranging across the deck of the taller ship in the hope of confirming whether the consul was on board or not. He spotted Regulus almost immediately, the consul standing amidst a group of staff officers with the ever vigilant *praetoriani* flanking his position on the fore and aft-decks. He was easily distinguished, the consul's heavier frame in marked contrast to the leaner younger tribunes who accompanied him and Varro felt his resolve weaken, knowing the dismissive glances that would greet him from his former contemporaries on the deck of the flagship.

The *Tigris* came to rest twenty feet away from the flagship as permission was sought to come alongside and Varro waited impatiently on the main deck before the trireme closed the gap once more, the captain called for reverse oars to bring the *Tigris* to a dead stop and avoid the disgrace of accidently striking his hull against that of the flagship. A gangplank was lowered from the taller deck and Varro walked briskly across before the *Tigris* backed off once more.

Varro squared his shoulders and walked across the main deck towards the assembled commanders. They were ranged around a large table strewn with maps, their edges haphazardly weighted down with an assortment of daggers and goblets. Regulus was holding court in the centre of the group with the tribunes around him leaning over the table, affecting knowing and intelligent expressions as they agreed with the consul's deliberations. Regulus looked up by chance and saw Varro approach, the consul's expression instantly turning to one of distain. Varro was surprised by the open look of contempt. Surely Scipio's intercession had changed Regulus's opinion of him?

'Commander Varro,' Regulus said, his voice laced with condescension. 'You are not on patrol?'

'By your leave, Consul,' Varro said, his mind still trying to understand the consul's attitude. 'I bear grave and important news which I felt compelled to bring to you personally.'

A wry smile appeared at the edge of Regulus's mouth. 'Then speak, Squad Commander,' the consul said, his emphasis on Varro's rank drawing smiles from many of the tribunes.

'It may be best if we speak in private,' Varro insisted, hoping the consul would speak to him alone, knowing a personal delivery would heighten the impact and draw him into Regulus's initial reaction.

'I am sure,' Regulus began, his impatience palpable, 'that any news you might have, however important you feel it is, can be spoken of here in front of my officers.'

Again the consul's words were draped in condescension and Varro felt his anger rise at being treated with such disrespect.

'Very well, Consul,' Varro said, his voice even and emotionless, and he began to retell Albinus's report, his words slowly wiping the smiles and contemptuous expressions from the faces of the tribunes, the look of distain fleeing quickly from Regulus's eyes.

'And this pirate bireme, commanded by a Carthaginian,' Regulus asked, his voice low as his mind realised the implications of Varro's report, 'you say she has been taken and is now destroyed.'

'Yes, Consul,' Varro replied, his previous confidence returned.

'Under my orders, my squad had been hunting the pirate galley for the past week and yesterday we caught her. The Carthaginian officer died in the attack and the pirate crew fired their own galley but fortuitously we were able to rescue the Roman captain.'

'And he said the Carthaginian was operating out of Tyndaris?' Regulus asked.

Varro nodded, 'Yes, Consul.'

Regulus's expression twisted in anger. 'If Hiero has betrayed Rome . . .' he said. He looked directly at Varro, 'We sail to Tyndaris at once. Where is the rest of your squad, Varro?'

'Six hours east of here; Falcone. I assembled them there in anticipation that you would need them.'

Regulus nodded. 'You have done well Varro,' he said, meaning it. 'Signal your galley to follow my squad. You will remain on board the *Victoria* so I can discuss this report with you further.'

Varro saluted, his expression betraying nothing beyond compliance, and turned to issue the order to his own galley.

Regulus looked down and studied the map before him, picking out the port of Tyndaris on the north-eastern corner of Sicily. He stared at the inscription, his eyes tracing the letters of the name until his concentration shifted once more to Varro. He looked up once more, staring surreptitiously at the young man he had sought to ruin. Perhaps he had under-estimated him. He had believed his decision to ruin him to be sound at the time and Scipio's subsequent intervention had only served to deepen his dislike for Varro, but now the commander's apparent audacity and skill had resulted in the exposure of a Carthaginian plan to attack Rome. Varro had even resorted to modesty when he spoke of his squad capturing the pirate galley, taking none of the credit personally.

Regulus looked to the map once more as the galley lurched

beneath him, holding the table for balance as the galley swung around. The spot denoting Tyndaris stared up at him again as he replayed Varro's report in his head. If the Carthaginians were indeed planning an invasion, and Varro's actions had led to its exposure, then Regulus realised it would be honourable to admit that he had been wrong about the former tribune.

'Galleys off the starboard!'

Atticus moved to the rail and looked to the horizon, his eyes quickly assessing the dark shapes sailing in formation towards Falcone.

'Identify!' Atticus shouted up to Corin. Lucius and Septimus were standing ready beside him on the aft-deck, their gazes switching alternatively between the masthead and the distant galleys.

'Roman!' Corin shouted after a minute, and Atticus breathed out, realising for the first time that he had been expecting the worst.

Varro had ordered the squad to remain in a tactically indefensible position, hemmed in between the protective shoreline of Falcone harbour with little sea room to escape should a larger force attack. Over the previous hours Atticus had been on the brink of ordering the *Aquila* further out to sea but Septimus had persuaded him otherwise, partially because the chances of an enemy attack were negligible but primarily because Varro would be only too pleased to find the *Aquila* out of position and wilfully disobeying his orders when he returned.

'Quinqueremes,' Corin continued to shout. 'Eight to ten at least and a smaller ship at the rear.'

Atticus focused his attention on the oncoming fleet, seeing and identifying for the first time the Roman banners that Corin had spotted moments before. The lead galley was particularly bedecked, with a large standard trailing from the head of the mainmast.

'It's the consul,' Septimus said in amazement, pointing to the galley that Atticus had been studying. 'That's his standard.'

Atticus looked at it again, and as he watched the fleet changed course to run parallel to the shoreline. He had never seen ten quinqueremes in formation before and the sight amazed him. He smiled to himself. Fat sows, Lucius had called them and he looked over his shoulder to try and catch the older man's eyes. The quinqueremes were anything but sows and Atticus knew he was seeing the future of the *Classis Romanus* sail before him, a triumphant march before a fleet of on-looking triremes.

'Signal from the rear galley,' Corin shouted. 'It's the *Tigris*.'

'The *Tigris*,' Atticus remarked, 'in formation with the consul's flagship? Varro must have sailed to Brolium with Albinus's report.'

'Which means . . .' Septimus said, waiting for Corin to report the rest of the signal, knowing what was to follow.

'The squad is to fall in behind and assume battle formation!' Corin shouted, 'We sail to Tyndaris!'

Atticus nodded and walked past Lucius as the second-in-command shouted out the necessary orders to the crew of the *Aquila*, his shouts repeated on the other galleys of the squad, the ships getting underway in the time it took for the last of the quinqueremes to sail past.

Atticus looked to the main deck and the sight of a fourth corpse lying silently beside the three others. With the *Aquila* sailing to battle, the chance to bury these men on land was now lost and although for the legionaries, casting two of their own over the side would be near sacrilege, Atticus knew that his crewman and Albinus would find peace beneath the waves.

Atticus looked once more to the fleet of quinqueremes,

their aspect changing with every oar-stroke as the *Aquila* moved into position. By dawn the fleet would be off Tyndaris and only then would they know for sure if the information Albinus had provided them was accurate. Looking once more at the shroud-covered body of the Roman captain, Atticus could only hope that Albinus had been right and that the terrible ordeal he had suffered was not in vain. His body, like the others, would be cast over the side but the dark stain of their blood would remain on the deck, a stain that would put fire in the heart of the Atticus's crew. If the Carthaginians did indeed hold Tyndaris, then the men of the *Aquila* would allow none to escape their wrath.

CHAPTER THIRTEEN

Even from his vantage point on the aft-deck of the *Alissar*, Hamilcar could see that something was wrong. The patrol galley was returning early, an hour after dawn instead of noon, and she was making at least seven knots, battle speed.

'All hands, prepare to get underway!' Hamilcar shouted, his order repeated to the galleys surrounding the *Alissar* in the middle harbour of Tyndaris. The drum beat of standard speed shattered the early morning calm, its repetition across the fleet creating a staccato beat that blended to somehow signify the urgency created by Hamilcar's unexpected command.

Hamilcar steered the *Alissar* to intercept the incoming galley, his heart racing as his mind flashed to the possible explanations for the patrol's early arrival. Belus was now two days overdue, a thought that was never far from Hamilcar's mind. A storm had rolled over Tyndaris two days before, bringing heavy rain and a strong on-shore wind. In the confines of the harbour the wind had merely unfurled the banners and set them racing. Out at sea that same wind could have caused Belus to sail close to shore, lengthening his journey considerably although Hamilcar was forced to admit that even so, his old friend should have returned some twenty-four hours before.

The patrol galley slowed to steerage speed as she came upon the *Alissar*, the quinquereme mirroring her speed to allow the two galleys to pass alongside each other. Hamilcar moved to the side-rail, his eyes ranging over the approaching deck, searching for the captain. He spotted him instantly on the aft-deck, the captain's agitation palpable even at a distance of fifty yards. The final gap was closed within a minute and Hamilcar watched with dread creeping through his stomach as the captain finally caught sight of his commander and ran the length of his galley to stand opposite Hamilcar across a distance of ten yards.

'Enemy ships approaching!' the captain shouted, pointing over his shoulder to the open sea beyond the mouth of the harbour and a sudden anger rose in Hamilcar as he sensed the captain's naked fear.

'How many?' Hamilcar roared, his anger now mixed with a deeper fury that his plan, so close to fruition was in danger of exposure.

'Near twenty!' the captain shouted. 'At least half of them quinqueremes.'

'By Anath . . .' Hamilcar whispered. He glanced at the galleys flanking his own, thirteen of them in total and all of them triremes except his own. They were completely outmatched.

'Battle speed!' Hamilcar suddenly roared, his crew, shocked by the news that all had heard, taking valuable seconds to respond.

Hamilcar drew his sword, the distinctive sound shattering the trance that seized the men around him and they ran to their stations, the order repeated to the slave deck, the *Alissar* again coming to life but this time with a fierceness in her pace that drove her ram deep under the swell with every oar-stroke. The Romans were not yet within sight but Hamilcar could see them in his mind's eye, could see their approaching hulls, their decks crowded with armoured marines. It was a sight that struck determination into this heart, a sight that tensed his sword arm in anticipation of the fight to come.

'Battle formation!' he roared and this time his order was repeated without hesitation, the spirit of their commander infusing every man on board the *Alissar* with a battle hunger that could only be sated with Roman blood.

'Enemy galleys ahead!'

Varro looked along the length of the *Victoria* and beyond to the mouth of Tyndaris where a Carthaginian fleet was emerging at battle speed. He tempered his elation at the confirmation of Albinus's report, keeping his expression hard and neutral.

'It seems your Roman Captain was right, Varro,' Regulus remarked beside him and Varro turned and nodded a simple affirmation, remaining silent, savouring the unspoken approbation.

'Order the Captain to increase to battle speed,' Regulus commanded and Varro nodded again, this time walking away from the consul to the captain stationed at the tiller.

'Thirteen galleys!' the masthead lookout shouted. 'A quinquereme in the van, the rest look to be triremes.'

Varro took in this information as he passed the consul's order to the captain. If this was the sum total of the Carthaginian defence then the Roman fleet had a considerable advantage. He walked back to where Regulus was standing and stood once more at his shoulder, a privileged position that had been afforded to Varro ahead of the tribunes of Regulus's staff. With this confirmation that the enemy did indeed control Tyndaris, it was a position Varro was determined would remain his.

He felt his confidence rise with a sense that victory was

there for the taking and he smiled at how inexperienced he had once been, how the Carthaginians and the men who were supposed to be under his command had tricked him at Thermae. In the battle ahead Varro would ensure that Carthaginian slur was reversed. His courage was bolstered by the formation spread out behind the *Victoria*. The Roman ships were larger. They outnumbered the enemy nearly two to one. There was no trap this time, no hidden forces to overwhelm the Roman fleet and in leading the consul to Tyndaris, Varro had ensured his name would be associated with the victory.

The *Aquila* was positioned on the starboard flank, her speed a shade over her normal battle speed in an effort to keep pace with the larger quinqueremes in the centre of the Roman line of attack. Atticus kept his gaze locked on the approaching enemy, now less than a mile away, a lone quinquereme holding the centre line with six triremes flanking her on each side, a desperate sight given the superiority of the Roman forces. Atticus sensed the deck shift slightly beneath him but he kept his eyes on the enemy, trusting any changes Gaius might make to the *Aquila*'s course to keep her in formation.

'Any chance you'll stay on the aft-deck this time?' Atticus heard and he turned to see Septimus standing behind him.

He gave the centurion a quizzical look, not understanding the insinuation.

'That wound,' Septimus said, a half-smile on his face but an underlying seriousness in his voice as he pointed to Atticus's chest. 'I don't want you spilling more blood on an enemy deck.'

Atticus smiled, perplexed at Septimus's request that sounded very much like an order. He was tempted to point out why, on the last occasion, he had been on the enemy's deck in the first place.

'I doubt you'll get a chance this time either,' he replied, nodding to the centre of the Roman line. 'Those quins will see all of the action.'

Septimus followed Atticus's gaze and then looked across to the approaching enemy.

'Unless one or two of them attempt to break out?' he ventured.

'Any trireme will be easily run down by one of our quin-queremes,' Atticus said, but the prospect did leave him with a lingering thought and he turned to discuss the point with Gaius. If a trireme did attempt to break out, he wanted the *Aquila* to be ready.

'Attack speed!' Hamilcar roared and his voice carried clearly to the two triremes immediately flanking his own ship. They increased speed immediately and the order was carried down the line with an alacrity born of experience and age old naval discipline.

The enemy ships were less than four hundred yards away and Hamilcar's professional eye began to take in every detail. The quinqueremes were almost identical to the *Alissar*, no doubt copies of the *Melqart* that was seized at Mylae although with one glaring difference, a hideous deformity that marred the foredeck of each, the cursed boarding ramp behind which unseen ranks of Roman legionaries lay in wait.

The sight sobered Hamilcar and he realised that his order to sail headlong into battle was rooted in frustration. The fleet was near full strength in Carthage and he had planned to order it to Tyndaris in less than a week, to firmly establish the supply depot and base of operations his invasion plan so vitally needed, and await the infantry who were currently fighting their way east, a force he would be free to release to the invasion once Hiero switched his allegiance to secure Hamilcar's flank.

Now the Romans were poised to expose and destroy his preparations at Tyndaris and thwart his plan at the moment of its fruition. The thought enraged him once more and for a second he was filled with the same abandonment that roared at him to ram his galley down the very throats of the enemy and be damned, to drench his sword in Roman blood as he had at Thermae and die honourably in defence of his city. Again his mind cleared, this time at the thought of Carthage. If he was to fall this day then his city would be at the mercy of Hanno, a man who would abandon two hundred years of settlement on Sicily without hesitation.

There was still time. He could disperse his ships and flee from the Romans. They would give chase but with thirteen targets sailing in different directions the confusion would allow at least half to escape. If battle was joined then all would be lost, including the *Alissar*. As proximity increased the sound of Roman war cries, Hamilcar realised what he had to do; realised he had to commit a dishonourable act that only an honourable commander could undertake.

Hamilcar took his gaze off the approaching enemy and turned his back on them, walking slowly to the helmsman.

'Order the triremes on the port and starboard to tighten in against the *Alissar*,' he ordered and the signal was immediately relayed, the galleys minutely adjusting their course to bring them as close as possible to the quinquereme. Hamilcar nodded as the manoeuvre was completed. The captains on the triremes would no doubt be perplexed by his order, a risky manoeuvre at attack speed but they had followed it nonetheless, their loyalty unquestioning. It made his choice all the more difficult to endure and although he had made the decision he knew to be right, Hamilcar couldn't stop the foul bile of ignominy rising in his throat.

Varro roared with the rest of the crew as the *Victoria* accelerated to attack speed. She was a behemoth in comparison to a trireme and Varro felt invincible, standing on the same deck as the senior consul of Rome, a hundred marines formed in tight ranks behind the *corvus*, the beat of the rower's drum pounding out sixty beats a minute. The enemy galleys were a hundred yards away, their own decks packed with warriors, a host of spear tips and shields, impossible to count.

To the left and right the other quinqueremes were keeping pace, their hulls dipping and rising with each oar stroke, their blunt-nosed rams crashing through the white horses, creating a fine mist of spray that fell across the entire deck. On the extreme flanks Varro could see the triremes were falling behind, unable to match the gruelling pace set by the larger galleys, powered by the might of two hundred and seventy rowers.

Varro looked ahead once more. Eighty yards. He could see individual Carthaginian faces, many contorted in defiance, screaming challenges that were caught and whipped away by the wind. Fifty yards. A flight of arrows shot across from the Carthaginian galleys. Cries of pain and anger split the air. A centurion roared in command and a swarm of spears flew forth from the main deck, striking the Carthaginian force, a hail of carnage on the packed deck. Thirty yards. Varro braced his legs against the blow to come, his hand tightly gripping the hilt of his sword, the power of Rome surrounding him.

'Now!' Hamilcar roared. 'All stop! Come full about!'

The *Alissar* immediately broke ranks; her speed cut away until her bow was clear of speeding galleys on either side and the helmsman threw the tiller hard over, the *Alissar* turning away from the line of attack as the order was given for battle speed.

Hamilcar kept his eyes firmly on the enemy line, less than thirty yards away, visible through the narrow gap the *Alissar* had left in the line, a gap that no quinquereme could thread at attack speed without striking the oars of the triremes that had flanked the *Alissar*, a clash that would foil their own and break their speed.

Seconds later the air was filled with the crack of tortured timber and shattered wood as the two forces collided, the cacophony followed a heartbeat later by the lesser sound of a dozen Roman boarding ramps plunging down, a death grip for every Carthaginian trireme. War cries of anger and hate swept over the *Alissar* as she came full about, the din of battle now firmly in her wake and Hamilcar turned his back to stare straight ahead into an empty sea. An order rose to his lips, a command to turn once more into the fight, his warrior instincts roaring at him to join his doomed country- men in the forlorn battle. He swallowed the words, the taste of them foul in his throat. He had sacrificed a dozen ships to make his escape, not to save his life but to save the life of Carthage; to save her fate from lesser men. As a commander the order was his only choice. As a warrior, the order desecrated his very soul.

'Three points to port!' Atticus shouted. 'Swing around their flank!'

Gaius responded immediately, the *Aquila* maintaining her attack speed even as the other triremes on the right flank slowed their speed and held station, the battle joined in the centre was an obvious mismatch that would soon be over.

Atticus's gaze was dragged to the mêlée that was the collided lines but as the *Aquila* reached, then rounded the southern tip of the line the open waters revealed a sight that caught the attention of all on board.

'Enemy galley on easterly course!' Corin shouted.

'The quinquereme,' Atticus muttered, the galley plainly visible a half a mile away.

Septimus approached him on the aft-deck. 'What do you make of her?' he asked.

'The command ship, no doubt about it, centre of the line, the only quinquereme.'

'So why is she running?' the centurion asked.

Atticus was silent for a moment, then he suddenly turned to Septimus. 'We have to catch her,' he said and he turned to the helmsman. 'Gaius. Intercept course. Lucius!'

The second-in-command ran across the aft-deck.

'Orders to below. Maintain attack speed. Bring up the reserve rowers.'

Lucius nodded and was away.

'You want to attack a quinquereme?' Septimus asked sceptically.

'Why is she running?' Atticus asked, his eyes darting from Septimus to the enemy galley dead ahead and then to the line of the *Aquila*'s course. 'One point to starboard!' he shouted. He turned back to Septimus.

'Because she faces certain defeat,' the centurion answered.

'Then why commit to battle in the first place?' Atticus asked.

Septimus thought a moment. The Carthaginian's actions were bizarre. The quinquereme could have turned anytime before now, in fact the whole Carthaginian line could have turned and yet the quinquereme had led them into battle only to flee when every other Punic galley was committed.

'A coward?' Septimus ventured without conviction.

Atticus eyebrows raised in question. 'Have you known many Carthaginian cowards?'

Septimus shook his head slowly. Then it struck him; 'By the Gods, Atticus, whoever is commanding that galley has sacrificed the other ships to make his escape.'

Atticus nodded, 'Which means it's someone important.'

Septimus looked to the quinquereme once more. She was less than four hundred yards away and a half-mile from the line of battle, with no sign of any other pursuit.

'With only thirty men fit for duty, the best we can do is take the aft-deck and hold it until reinforcements arrive. There's no way we can push the fight to the entire ship.'

Atticus nodded again. He had surmised as much.

'Then we'll attack over the stern rail,' he said, knowing the odds of stopping the quinquereme to be near naught. 'Maybe we'll get lucky and take out her rudder,' he added, knowing only Fortuna could grant him that.

The Carthaginian galley was now less than three hundred yards ahead, the *Aquila* coming up on her starboard stern quarter, a course that would put her in the quinquereme's wake within minutes. Atticus looked to the battle once more. None of the Roman quinqueremes had broken through yet. The *Aquila* was alone.

'Roman galley still on an intercept course!'

Hamilcar turned and looked out over the stern rail for the fourth time. The enemy trireme was now directly in the *Alissar's* wake two hundred yards behind.

'Shall I increase speed?' Hamilcar turned to find the captain standing beside him.

'No,' he replied. 'Maintain battle speed. Order the archers to the aft-deck and have fifty men brought aft.'

The captain saluted and left Hamilcar to look out once

more at the Roman galley. He was sorely tempted to increase his pace but the rowers would only be able to maintain attack speed for fifteen minutes. After that they would be spent and the *Alissar* would be dead in the water and with the battle line only a mile behind, there was still time for a Roman quinquereme to emerge and give chase, a far more deadly foe than a mere trireme. Her ram would be useless against the *Alissar*, not only because she was a heavier built galley but also because the *Alissar* was travelling at eight knots away from the line of attack which meant the ram would strike her with a momentum of no more than five or six knots, not even enough to scratch her back. The only vulnerable point on the stern, and Hamilcar's only concern, was the rudder, but again, with an open seascape before him the *Alissar* could run a straight course without the rudder long enough to take her out of danger.

Hamilcar nodded to himself. The odds favoured maintaining battle speed and allowing the Roman to approach. But then, Hamilcar vowed, he would unleash fury on the impertinent trireme and release some measure of the battle lust that he and his crew had been forced to contain.

'Fifty yards,' Corin yelled.

'Shields up,' Septimus ordered at the call. 'Prepare for incoming.'

Moments later the first arrows struck home, many on a flat trajectory that plunged the arrows deeply into the weathered timbers of the *Aquila*, others lofted high to fall like deadly rain on the upturned shields of Septimus's thirty men formed up behind the *corvus*. Sporadic cries of pain rang out as exposed flesh was pierced by the murderous assault, Septimus registering the fall of one of his men behind him as he grimly stared ahead through a gap in the shield wall, measuring the distance between the converging galleys, now forty yards, now thirty.

'*Pila!*' he shouted and the legionaries emerged as one from under their defensive cover, their eight foot long spears held at the ready. The onslaught of Carthaginian arrows intensified, striking down another legionary, then another, their exposed ranks easy prey for the fury of Apollo. Septimus held firm, suppressing the urge to let fly and throw up his shield, his eyes judging the pitch and roll of the *Aquila*'s deck, waiting for the perfect moment.

'Loose!' he roared and the legionaries roared with savage revenge as they unleashed their spears. The *pila* seemed to hang in the air for a heartbeat, suspended over the water immediately behind the Carthaginian aft-deck before crashing down into the massed ranks of the *Punici*. Cries of pain and death washed over the foredeck of the *Aquila* as the spears wrought a brutal carnage, the iron shanks tearing through leather, finding the gaps between shields to impale and maim, the force of the deadly fall nailing men to the timber deck.

Atticus watched and heard the opening blows with a dispassionate stare, his mind totally focused on the aft-deck of the Punic galley, his raised hand making barely discernable gestures that triggered Gaius's hand on the tiller. All around him and on the main deck the crew of the Aquila continued to work stoically amidst the random fall of arrows, the hand of Pluto ranging over the galley to strike down the ill-fated, each casualty eliciting a shouted order from Lucius for the man to be taken below.

'Ten yards,' Gaius said aloud, cursing the *corvus* anew for robbing him of a true line of sight to the enemy rudder. 'We have her.'

Atticus nodded but kept his silence, uneasy about the bitter fight that faced Septimus and his men. Minutes before, a hundred yards out, Atticus had felt that the Carthaginian might yet run but he had dismissed the idea almost before it was fully formed, trusting his earlier deduction that the Carthaginians would try and stave off the smaller ship rather than run. That meant a desperate fight awaited Septimus, a fight that would only be relieved when reinforcements arrived.

'Steady, Gaius,' Atticus said almost to himself, the words allowing him to refocus his thoughts on the attack, the line of the *Aquila*'s ram and the enemy's rudder. 'Steady.'

'Now!' Hamilcar roared and the deck almost reared beneath him as the helmsman threw the tiller hard over a heartbeat before the Roman galley struck the stern of the *Alissar*, a manoeuvre that threw the rudder out of the path of the blunt-nosed ram. Hamilcar felt the strike of the ram against the hull through his feet but he smiled savagely, knowing the blow had done little damage and he screamed a war cry in defiance, a shout that was taken up by his men ranged across the aft-deck, a defensive line against the storm to come.

A flurry of grappling hooks flew across the narrow gap between the galleys, the men in the front line ignoring them, their eyes instead locked on the sight of the massive Roman boarding ramp that towered over the foredeck of the smaller enemy galley. A Roman command was heard above the roar of battle and a moment later the ramp began to fall, slowly at first as if a mighty hand was staying its course but then accelerating suddenly, the weight of its thirty-six foot length an unstoppable force and the front line waivered as the three-foot-long spike stabbed down into the deck.

Hamilcar screamed the order to advance even as he watched a massive centurion charge up the slope of the ramp, the unequal heights of the two galleys doing little to slow the momentum of the Roman legionaries. The Carthaginians

288

surged to the ramp and the two forces collided at the head, the centurion and then many more legionaries punching into the Carthaginian line with their massive shields to create a bridgehead on the Punic aft-deck. Hamilcar remained still, his crew rushing past him as he stood immobile, his steady gaze absorbing the Roman attack, the simple brilliance of the ramp and the savage courage of the legionaries. He stepped back, briefly looking over his shoulder, searching for the captain, finding him instantly at the head of the aft-deck, his eyes locked on Hamilcar. The Carthaginian commander smiled again as he turned once more to the mêlée only yards away. The Romans had a dozen men across, now fifteen, their bridge-head expanding, the Carthaginian defence descending into a vicious futile assault against an ever-advancing Roman wall of shields. Now they were committed. Hamilcar turned. The captain was staring at him as before. Hamilcar shouted the order, knowing his voice would not be heard above the noise of battle but also knowing the captain was waiting for this one command and Hamilcar wanted to roar out the death knell for the Roman legionaries.

'Attack speed!'

Atticus was thrown to the deck as the *Aquila* suddenly jerked forward, his instincts causing him to immediately look to the stern rail, expecting to see an enemy galley rammed into his own.

'By the gods,' he heard Gaius shout and he looked to the helmsman, the colour drained from his face as he stood trans-fixed. 'She's re-engaged her oars!'

Atticus could hardly comprehend Gaius's words and he spun around, looking once more to the quinquereme, the fury on her aft-deck now forgotten as he stared at her oars.

The *Aquila* jerked forward again, this time coming up to

speed as the initial inertia of the seventy-ton hull was over-come and within seconds she was accelerating even as her oars remained raised.

'Lucius!' Atticus roared, running forward to the main deck. 'Attack speed now!'

From the corner of his eye he saw the second-in-command run to the slave-deck hatchway, saw him mouth the shouted command. Atticus swept aside his fears that the *Aquila*'s oars would not hit the water in unison. It was a tricky manoeuvre, beginning an oar-stroke while the ship was moving. One oar out of sequence and a whole section could foul, knocking the galley off course, but it had to be done. The *Aquila* had to get up to speed under her own power.

Atticus swept men up as he ran towards the *corvus*, the crew instantly drawing their swords, ready to follow their captain into the maelstrom. He fanned them out across the base of the *corvus*, readying them to defend the *Aquila* should the Carthaginians counter-attack. They roared in answer to his command, but their shout was cut short as the deck once more shuddered beneath them and for the first time Atticus heard the scream of tortured wood. He looked to the mounting pole of the *corvus*, almost seeing the deflection of the six-inch diameter spar as the stress of maintaining the link between the two galleys took its toll. The *Aquila* bucked and shuddered again and a grappling rope snapped cleanly with a loud retort, the thick hemp rope whipping back, striking the hoplon shield of one of the crew, knocking him to the deck.

'Sweet merciful . . .' Atticus muttered and he felt the icy hand of panic slide up his spine as he looked across to the legionaries. The two galleys were going to break apart, the unequal stresses too great, the different oar stroke and sequence creating unequal acceleration even if the speeds were equal. The *corvus* was strong enough to carry men into battle, strong enough even to hold a trireme stationary in the water, but it was never designed to hold back a galley weighing over a hundred tons and travelling at twelve knots. With a realisation that struck Atticus to the core he saw that the ramp was going to fail and when it did, any Roman left on the Carthaginian galley would be slaughtered without mercy or remorse.

'Steady the line!' Septimus ordered and his men responded with a roar of affirmation, a war cry mixed with the firm resolution that not one step back would be taken. Septimus leaned into his shield once more, angling his body against the press of the enemy, his sword striking out through the gap to return with fresh blood, the deck beneath his sandaled feet already running red with only his hobnails giving him purchase. The noise around him was deafening, cries of pain and anger, of death and fury unleashed, of hatred driven to near frenzy as men hacked at each other with sword and shield. To his left he could hear Drusus ordering the line to hold firm and he nodded to himself, confident that his *optio* would not allow the line to fail.

The Carthaginian before his shield fell and Septimus was given a brief respite as he held ready for another assault. His mind triggered a forgotten thought, a minutes-old memory of the deck moving suddenly beneath him, a sensation he had felt but had ignored in the first desperate moments of the attack. Now he sensed that movement again, as if the quinquereme was moving through the water and not firmly impaled and held fast by the *Aquila*. He was tempted to look to his side, to confirm his suspicion, but he held fast, his warrior's instinct warning him to stay focused and as if in confirmation an axe hammered against his shield, knocking it back against his shoulder. Septimus's sword arm reacted before conscious thought, striking forward as he pushed back his shield, his blade striking iron as the Carthaginian parried the blow. He reversed the strike and thrust again, keeping his shield high and in formation, continuing his attack as the line remained steady.

'Baro,' Atticus shouted, drawing his own sword for the first time, 'tell Lucius I want ramming speed now!'

Another grappling line shot apart as Baro ran off.

'You and you,' Atticus indicated. Two crewmen stepped forward. 'Go aft and bring up more hooks and lines! The rest of you hold firm here.'

Atticus turned and ran up the *corvus*, his eyes searching the backs of the Roman legionaries, immediately spotting Septimus in the centre. The ramp suddenly bucked beneath him and he fell to his knees, instinctively stretching out his free hand to break his fall. He cursed loudly and put his weight on to his hand to push himself up but he recoiled instantly, the timber planking moving beneath his palm and for a second time he felt panic. The *corvus* was failing fast.

Atticus took off at a run again and gained the Carthaginian aft-deck within a second. He jumped off the *corvus* and immediately looked down at the head of the ramp. The iron spike was still embedded in the deck, however it was now preceded by a two foot long tear, the origin of the gash marking where the *corvus* had first struck. Atticus spun around, looking for Septimus again. The deck was strewn with the bodies of a dozen Carthaginian slain, their open wounds still spilling blood onto the deck, their lifeless features still screaming out the final defiance and rage that had marked the end of their existence. A half-dozen red-cloaked legionaries lay amongst them; at least two of them were still alive, but their wounds were grievous.

The Roman line was ten feet beyond the head of the boarding ramp, its furthest advance after no more than four minutes of vicious fighting. The line was fifteen men across, two deep in places and Atticus saw that they could advance no further; the Carthaginians were too numerous, too tightly packed to give way under such a thin Roman line. Atticus ran to Septimus, standing at his left shoulder, clear of his sword arm that flashed back and forward at an implausible speed. Atticus waited a precious few seconds for the moment when the centurion would not be directly engaged.

'Septimus!' he shouted above the roar of war cries. Septimus glanced over his shoulder, his mask of determination showing a flash of surprise and then another emotion, anger, as if Atticus's presence had defied him somehow.

'The Carthaginian galley is breaking free! The *corvus* is going to fail.' Atticus shouted and watched as his friend's expression changed again, this time to one of dread. Septimus looked beyond Atticus to the ramp, his eyes rooted to its head, as if he expected to see it disappear at any moment. His hesitation lasted only a second longer.

'Make ready!' Septimus bellowed and again his men shouted in affirmation, confirming that they were awaiting his next command.

'Fighting retreat . . . !'

Septimus held them steady for a heartbeat longer, vying for the perfect moment to begin the retreat, knowing that the *Punici* would surge forward at the first sign of weakness.

'March!' he shouted and the line stepped back as one, each man careful not to stumble over the men who lay dead and dying behind them.

The Carthaginians roared in attack as their enemy gave way, reclaiming their deck step by step.

Atticus ran back behind the line, stopping once more at

the head of the *corvus*. The tear along the deck was now three feet long with only a final foot of planking remaining before the aft-rail. Two more grappling ropes had given way in the thirty seconds Atticus had been on the Carthaginian galley, but as he watched four new lines were thrown and he quickly secured each one before signalling his men to pull them tight. He looked down the length of the ramp, whispering to his Gods as he saw the *corvus* buckle once more under the strain and the outer planking on one side suddenly gave way, splintering violently with a tormented crack.

Septimus kept the pressure on his shield and stabbed wildly through the gap as he stepped back, shouting constantly to his men to remain steady and slow, needing to contain any semblance of panic that might cause one of the men to flee. A hand suddenly grabbed his leg and he looked down to the agonised face of one of his *hastati*. His other hand was clutching his groin, blood surging between his fingers with every beat of his heart. Septimus watched him mouth his name, a plea lost in the clamour of battle. There was nothing Septimus could do, no second line of legionaries who could gather the wounded in retreat, no way he could help the younger man without breaking ranks and threatening the cohesion of the line. Septimus marched on, dragging his gaze from the fallen legionary as he did, torment filling his soul as he heard the soldier's scream for mercy. The Carthaginian front line stepped over him, swallowing him whole, his cries lost amidst the enemy horde.

A legionary fell, then another, the Carthaginians pressing home their advantage with terrifying ferocity, making the Romans pay for every inch of timber. The line contracted to form a defensive ring around the *corvus*, Septimus front and centre, Drusus by his side. The line was now two deep, some eighteen men strong, a bristling semi-circle of defiant steel and shield, the Carthaginians pressing in on three sides. Atticus chose two legionaries as the line compressed further, ordering them back across the *corvus*. They hesitated to run, to leave their comrades but Atticus shoved them on, needing to stave off a fatal bottleneck. They stepped onto the *corvus* and turned to descend, walking resolutely across the precarious ramp. Atticus watched them go but as he turned to select two more, the men suddenly fell from the ramp, each man struck by arrows shot from Carthaginian archers who had gained the aft-rail on the flanks. Atticus watched in horror as they fell, both soldiers striking the bow of the *Aquila*, one of the men screaming in agony, before they fell into the sea to be swept under the hull of the trireme.

'Archers!' Atticus roared across at his own crew, his fury knowing no bounds. The sailors responded instantly, letting loose on the enemy archers, drawing their fire away from the *corvus*.

Atticus grabbed three more legionaries, warning them quickly before sending them across, the three men descending backward, their shields raised in defence against arrow strikes. It was a slower retreat and Atticus waited impatiently before he turned once more to the fight. There were ten legionaries left, the semi-circle now crammed against Atticus shoulder. He grabbed two more men, the second turning defiantly, his sword raised in a trance-like rage, but he stayed his blow as he recognised the captain. Atticus pushed them onto the *corvus*, the legionaries backing down as the others had before, their shields taking strike after strike but the men protected.

Sudden whip-cracks filled the air and Atticus saw the remaining grappling lines fall, severed by Carthaginian axe blows at the aft-rail of the quinquereme. The *corvus* tore left and buckled, its laboured timbers now the only link between the galleys. The two legionaries immediately lost their balance, one falling quickly to the sea to be crushed by the *Aquila*, the other instinctively dropping his sword and shield as he grabbed onto the edge of the ramp and hung precariously over the murderous chasm between the ships. Atticus never hesitated, running unguarded down the *corvus*, throwing himself onto his stomach as he grabbed the forearms of the legionary. He held him there, the wound in chest driving shards of pain through his mind. He gasped as he bent up his arms, lifting the soldier to give him a chance to swing up one of his legs. An arrow stuck the planking beside him, then another and Atticus heard his own crew shout warnings as they intensified their rate of attack to protect their captain. The legionary swung up his leg onto the ramp, grunting heavily as he lifted his own weight and Atticus released him, coming to his feet again as he pushed the legionary ahead of him down the ramp.

Atticus turned as he got to the bottom, looking back up to the remaining five men standing, Septimus and Drusus still among them. The *corvus* was beginning to break up, the outer timbers snapping and falling away. There was no time.

'Septimus!' he shouted, watching as his friend's head suddenly jerked sideways, an unconscious acknowledgement that he had heard Atticus's warning.

Septimus screamed through the burning pain in his arm as he shot his sword forward once more, the press of the enemy never ceasing, never abating. He felt the leading edge of the *corvus* against the back of his foot, felt it slide across his flesh as it struggled to hold its grip. Atticus's call rang in his ears, the urgency in his warning. Septimus struck out once more, twisting his blade savagely to release it quickly from the sucking flesh of his enemy, an enemy that had taken nearly all of his men and given nothing in return. He had to save the rest, the men who stood beside him, the men he had led on a damned attack.

'Legionaries!' he shouted, 'Full retreat on my order.'

As always they shouted in affirmation, but the calls were without vehemence, the exhausted soldiers knowing the disintegrating ramp behind them was a treacherous path to deliverance.

'Now!' Septimus roared, and he sensed rather than saw the soldiers to his left and right turn and run down the ramp. He stepped to his right, taking the centre line at the head of the *corvus*, stepping up onto the ramp but never turning, willing to commit the last seconds of his life to save the lives of his men by giving them time to reach the *Aquila*.

A sudden void was created by the retreating Romans and a Carthaginian rushed into the gap before Septimus, his sword raised in mindless attack, the last of the Roman defenders standing firm. Septimus hammered out with his shield, parrying the untargeted blow before striking out with his own sword. The tip of the blade deflected off the Carthaginian's armour but Septimus continued the lunge, running the sword edge across the Carthaginian's exposed side, slicing the muscle deeply, putting the man down. Septimus recovered in an instant but was already too late to fend off the next attack to his left, his balance off-set, his shield too high. His mind registered the oncoming Carthaginian, screaming at his body to react quicker, to turn into the attack but there was no time and Septimus knew his fight was over.

The Carthaginian suddenly fell, his face twisted in agony and surprise as a blade ended his charge. Another rushed forward in his wake but a red-cloaked legionary stepped into the fight, protecting Septimus's flank. It was Drusus.

'Get back, man!' Septimus shouted as more Carthaginians came forward, hammering on the shields of the two men. 'The *corvus* is about to go!'

Drusus didn't answer, but held firm beside Septimus,

297

repelling the attack of two Carthaginians, striking out methodically with his sword, half a life's training commanding his arm. He put his sword arm in front of Septimus's shield and pressed him back, both men stepping up onto the *corvus*.

'Drusus!' Septimus shouted, feeling the ramp move violently beneath him, the final death throes of the *corvus*, 'I'll hold them. Get back to the *Aquila*!'

The *optio* continued to fight, ignoring his centurion; ignoring an order for the first time in his life as he held the Carthaginians off with the strength only a legionary could command. He turned to Septimus.

'We go together,' he shouted, his tone that of an order.

Septimus nodded in reply.

'Run! Now!' Drusus shouted and he lunged suddenly against the wall of attackers, his shield pushing the enemy back momentarily, throwing them off balance, creating a vital second needed to escape.

Septimus grabbed the collar of Drusus's armour and wrenched him from the fight, pushing him down the *corvus*. He hesitated for a heartbeat longer and then followed, his shield dropping away, his legs pumping beneath him, his feet finding the remnants of the boarding ramp even as the air was split by the sound of snapping timber, the spar on the *Aquila* finally giving way at the instant the spike was torn from the quinquereme. Drusus jumped onto the foredeck as Septimus desperately threw himself forward, his gaze filled with the cutwater of the *Aquila* and the ram beneath, his left hand flailing, his right never letting go of his sword. The air was suddenly blown from his chest as he struck the forward rail of the *Aquila*, the galley's ramming speed saving him from falling short and steady hands grasped his forearms and shoulders and hoisted him over the rail onto the deck.

He stood up uncertainly, pushing away the hands that

helped him, spinning around to gaze at the escaping quinquereme, ignoring the Carthaginian arrows that continued to
strike the *Aquila*'s foredeck as the enemy crew screamed curses
and taunts across at the vanquished Romans. The *Aquila*'s
speed was dropping, any pursuit futile, the rowers already
spent. The quinquereme began to pull away. Septimus watched
it go, his gaze fixed to the aft-rail of the enemy galley. He
turned suddenly to his remaining eight men, nodding to
Drusus, the *optio* returning the gesture before looking to the
enemy once more. Septimus continued to stare at his men.
Eight legionaries left from the thirty he had led across the
corvus no more than ten minutes before, the survivors' expressions a mixture of anger and shame at having lived while
others fell.

Septimus looked away to the quinquereme again and
suddenly, with all the strength of his body, with all of the rage
filling his soul, he flung his sword after the Carthaginian ship,
the blade soaring through the air before striking the stern of
the galley, the tip hammering into the timbers. Septimus
looked at it for a second longer, then to his empty hand before
turning and brushing past the men of his command. In the
distance, two miles behind the *Aquila*, the sound of trumpets
heralded a Roman victory.

Varro reached out from the skiff and climbed up the rope
ladder on the top deck of the *Victoria*. He adjusted his scabbard and then strode purposefully to the aft-deck and the
waiting figure of the senior consul.

'Well?' Regulus asked.

'The jetties as you can see can accommodate some one
hundred galleys,' Varro began, gesturing over his shoulder to
the shoreline of Tyndaris, 'while the shallows have anchor
points for at least another hundred.'

Regulus nodded, his gaze shifting to the land beyond the shore, behind the line of jetties from where Varro had just travelled, 'And?' he asked, indicating the unseen terrain.

'A supply-dump large enough to stock a significant fleet and quarters for at least twenty thousand troops.'

Regulus shook his head slowly, amazed at how close the Carthaginians had been to fulfilling their plans, how ready they were, how their surprise land-attack west now made sense, their ultimate destination revealed. And what of Syracuse? Hiero was certainly complicit in some way, allowing the *Punici* to use his port. An alliance of convenience or maybe he was fully aware of their plans. Either way Regulus vowed the king of Syracuse would answer to the charge.

'What news of the *Alissar*?' Varro asked, interrupting the consul's thoughts. The name of the Punic quinquereme and the identity of her commander had been ascertained soon after the Carthaginians' capitulation at the point of a sword and Regulus had immediately ordered two quinqueremes in pursuit. Varro had seen that they had returned as he made his way to the *Victoria* moments before.

'She has escaped,' Regulus said regretfully. 'Her lead was too great.'

'And so Hamilcar Barca, the Carthaginian supreme commander in Sicily, has escaped our grasp,' Varro added, twisting the knife of that loss in order to bait the consul.

Regulus stared at Varro, annoyance in his eyes that Varro should see the need to mention the obvious. 'The *Alissar* could not be stopped,' he said. 'She was already two miles ahead when the first of our quinqueremes broke through the line.'

'One galley should have stopped her,' Varro added, 'but they failed.'

'The *Aquila*?' Regulus asked sceptically. 'Everything they could have done, they did.'

'Even still,' Varro persisted, 'the chance to capture Barca was lost and the Captain of the *Aquila* should pay the price of that loss.'

Regulus waved his hand dismissively, 'You are too harsh, Varro. The match was too uneven, a trireme against a quinquereme and the crew of the *Aquila* were badly mauled. I am satisfied they did all they could to stop the *Alissar*.'

Varro nodded, deciding not to pursue the point, knowing that his argument was not strong, content to know that he had already achieved a great deal in only the past two days.

As if reading his thoughts Regulus turned to Varro. 'You have done well, Titus,' he said. 'If you had not revealed this plan, Rome herself could have been threatened.'

Varro straightened his back at the compliment, knowing it to be well deserved but expressing nothing beyond humility on his face. 'It was my duty to Rome,' he said modestly.

'Yes, you are loyal,' Regulus agreed. 'But you also demonstrated abilities far beyond my previous expectations, capturing the pirate galley and releasing the Roman captain. It is only because of those actions that Barca's plans lie in ruins.'

Varro nodded in gratitude, knowing now his fortune had changed irrevocably for the better.

Regulus nodded back, silently making the decision he knew to be just. 'Inform the captain, Tribune Varro,' he said. 'We sail for Rome immediately.'

CHAPTER FOURTEEN

Hamilcar paced impatiently across the ante-chamber, his eyes darting regularly to the inlaid gold on the ten-foot high doors to the king's chamber. He had been waiting for over an hour, his only company the two royal guards standing silently at either side of the door. He instinctively reached for his sword, an impulse to knead the hilt with his hand, to ease the tension in his body but he remembered that his weapon had been confiscated at the first guardhouse, an insult he had been forced to swallow before being allowed to advance to the inner castle.

The *Alissar* had arrived in Syracuse only an hour before, her crew exhausted after a four day journey down the east coast of Sicily. Hamilcar had spent the entire time trying to salvage his plan in his own mind, trying to formulate alternatives that would ensure Hiero's support and create the alliance he so desperately needed with the Syracusan. Hamilcar had also devised how best to deliver the news of the Romans discovery of Tyndaris, confident that the *Alissar* would arrive in Syracuse long before any local or Roman vessel. Now however he was not so sure. The change in the manner he was being treated did not bode well and Hamilcar's carefully rehearsed report began to unravel in his mind.

The double-doors opened suddenly, Hamilcar spinning around to see two more guards ready to escort him into the king's chamber. He followed them in, this time his eyes ignoring the ornate beauty of the room, his gaze fixed firmly on the dais and the figure of Hiero. As before, immediately to the king's left, his advisor sat, the same wizened older man whom Hamilcar had all but ignored before but whose presence now irritated him, knowing the advisor had had the king's ear for the past hour while he was kept waiting.

Hamilcar reached the foot of the raised platform and bowed as before, maintaining the same outward show of confidence he had always possessed in Hiero's company. He waited to be spoken to. Hiero made him wait, his eyes fixed firmly on the Carthaginian's, a trace of a smile at the edges of his mouth.

'What news, Barca?' he asked finally.

Hamilcar was immediately on guard, the tone of the king's voice suggesting the question was not clear-cut, that Hiero somehow knew more than Hamilcar had hoped. But how much?

'A setback, sire,' Hamilcar said, reaching for a half-truth. 'The Romans are aware that my forces have been using Tyndaris as a base of operations.'

'How did they find out?' Hiero asked and again Hamilcar sensed the king already had some knowledge of the answer.

'A skirmish,' Hamilcar said, deciding that Hiero couldn't possibly know the whole truth, not from a first-hand source, 'just west of Tyndaris. A small force of Roman ships approached and we were force to engage.'

Hiero nodded. 'And you sailed to Syracuse to inform me personally?' he asked, a note of sarcasm in his voice and Hamilcar's stomach filled with dread. Hiero knew. He had not asked the obvious question, who had prevailed? Hamilcar realised that further subterfuge was useless.

'There's still time, sire,' he said, pressing the force of his belief upon the king. 'My forces are almost at your border. If your army rises now to meet them . . .'

'Enough!' Hiero shouted, his face mottled with anger. 'You were defeated at Tyndaris. The Romans now hold the port and your plan is in ruins.'

'How . . .??' Hamilcar asked, unable to comprehend how Hiero could know so soon.

The king smiled, a vicious contortion of his anger. 'Your predecessor, Gisco, was good for one thing,' he said derisively. 'He introduced me to the Persians' ingenious method of sending reports, carrier pigeon. I knew of your defeat two days ago.'

Hamilcar struggled to retain his composure, his mind racing to find an answer, a way to persuade Hiero to commit.

'There is still a chance, sire,' he said. 'Allied together we can defeat the Roman invader. Tyndaris is only a setback, it is not defeat. It will be days yet before Rome is fully informed, maybe weeks before they react. We have the advantage if we join forces now.'

'There is no time, Barca,' Hiero said, his anger fuelled by the position the Carthaginian had placed him in. 'My complicity at Tyndaris has been exposed and my commander there has already forewarned me that an envoy from the consul has been dispatched to Syracuse.'

'From the consul? So quickly?'

'He was the commander at Tyndaris,' Hiero explained, his patience at an end, the thought of the envoy's arrival and how he could avoid the wrath of Rome consuming him. 'Now get out,' he said. 'From here on my open treaty with Rome will be my only alliance.'

Hamilcar made to protest but he held his tongue, knowing his cause to be lost, his honour preventing him from humbling himself further before the petty ruler. He bowed brusquely and backed out of the chamber, aware that he was now firmly in enemy territory and Hiero might decide that delivering the head of the Carthaginian commander would placate the envoy of Rome and the consul himself. He turned as he reached the doors, walking determinedly down through the myriad of stairwells and corridors that led to the main gate, snatching his sword back from one of the guards as he left the castle, silently vowing that Hiero would rue the day he had cast his lot in with Rome.

Longus, the junior consul, waited patiently as the servant refilled the two wine goblets. The Senate was still in session but Longus had slipped out and returned to his townhouse to update the man seated opposite him, wishing to seek his counsel before his meeting with Regulus.

'I have spoken with Seneca as you suggested,' Longus said after the servant had gone.

'And?' Duilius asked, raising the goblet to his mouth.

'He will support Regulus's strategy.'

Duilius nodded, savouring the taste of the wine, and Longus's news. 'Seneca holds sway over five other fellow junior senators,' he said. 'With their support and the others you have already confirmed, Regulus has a significant majority.'

Longus nodded but his expression remained sceptical. 'I was surprised at Seneca's endorsement,' he said, 'even with Regulus's popularity after his victory at Tyndaris. What made you believe he was no longer Scipio's pawn?'

Because now he is my pawn, Duilius thought, his neutral expression hiding his satisfaction. 'I simply believed that Seneca was ready to vote with his conscience,' he said aloud.

As censor, Duilius was responsible for the *regimen morum*, the keeping of the public morals, and he had quickly turned this responsibility to his advantage. Customarily the immoral excesses of the junior senators, the majority of whom were young men from wealthy families, were ignored by the Senate and the censors; the older statesmen seeing such behaviour as a right of passage they too had enjoyed in their youth. Duilius had reversed that traditional leniency however and he had quickly gathered a large body of evidence against many of the junior senators, a move which instantly gave him a unique power over offenders like Seneca; the young man being only one amongst many.

'I will inform Regulus that he now has a majority amongst the junior senators when I see him this afternoon.' Longus remarked. 'I expect he will publicly announce his strategy after that.'

Duilius nodded. 'Remember Longus,' he said. 'Regulus must not know of my involvement.'

'I understand,' Longus replied, wondering why Duilius did not openly back the senior consul given the support he was providing; the censor's help so far allowing Longus to secure dozens of votes for Regulus. Nonetheless he would keep his mentor's involvement a secret as instructed.

Duilius sat back and thought through his plan again, examining it in detail. Within days of Regulus becoming senior consul, he had arranged for two of his spies to become servants in Regulus's household. Their reports, along with those of his spies in the Senate chambers, had given Duilius a first-hand account of the fracture between Regulus and Scipio. At first Duilius had been suspicious, conscious of the misinformation that had been given before, but Regulus's actions had confirmed the spilt and Duilius had slowly reconsidered his initial opinion of the senior consul.

Two days earlier, when Regulus had returned to Rome, Duilius had instructed Longus to give his full and open support to the senior consul, to meet with him as often as possible and gain his confidence. Longus had obediently complied, reporting back regularly on Regulus's emerging plans. It was Regulus's strategy, and Longus's appraisal of the now seemingly independent senior consul, that had convinced Duilius that it was time to support Regulus, using the leverage he had gained over the junior senators. Duilius was not yet ready to trust Regulus completely, and so he would keep his involvement secret, but for now one thing seemed certain. Regulus had placed the needs of Rome above petty rivalries and factional allegiance and for that reason alone, Duilius felt compelled to support the leader of the Republic.

Regulus stood as the arrival of the junior consul was announced, coming around from behind the marble-topped table in the centre of his chamber. He nodded affably to Longus, his expression genuine, their meetings over the previous two days, and Longus's complete support, providing him with a reappraised view of the younger man, different from the opinion Scipio had imbued in him when he was first elected.

Longus returned the greeting, taking Regulus's proffered hand before taking a seat. Regulus returned to his own side of the table and sat down, glancing briefly to the oculus in the dome far above and the blue sky beyond.

'Well, Longus,' Regulus began, looking once more to the junior consul, 'what say the junior senators?'

'They are in favour, Consul,' Longus replied, his expression serious. 'With your victory at Tyndaris and the exposure of the Carthaginians' plans, the Senate is poised to follow any command you give them.'

Regulus nodded. His own discreet enquiries amongst the senior members of the Senate had surfaced the same support, a backing he wished to be sure of before announcing his plan.

He looked to Longus once more. The junior consul had delivered dozens of votes from amongst the junior senators, men Regulus believed were thoroughly in the control of Scipio, and although he could not conceive how Longus had achieved such a task, he was grateful for the support.

'Then we are ready, Longus,' he said after a pause, 'I will declare . . .' A knock interrupted Regulus and he looked to the door as his private secretary entered, his hands clasped together in contrition, his face downcast.

'I said there was to be no interruptions,' Regulus said angrily.

'My apologies, Senior Consul,' the secretary said. 'But Senator Scipio is outside and he insists you grant him an audience.'

'Tell him what I told him yesterday, and the day before,' Regulus shouted, looking beyond the secretary in order that Scipio should hear his words first hand. 'I will summon him if, and only if, I see fit.'

'Yes, Senior Consul,' the secretary replied but as he turned to leave Scipio slipped in, almost knocking the secretary to the ground.

'You will see me now,' Scipio shouted angrily but immediately stopped when he saw who was with Regulus.

'Longus,' he snarled, staring balefully at the younger man.

'Consul Longus,' he replied, standing straight, returning the hateful gaze.

Scipio snorted derisively. 'I need to speak to you alone,' he said to Regulus, the resolve in his voice unmistakable, his anger and impatience completely evident.

Regulus remained seated, a smile slowly emerging on his face. The sight made Scipio almost lose his temper.

'You believe this to be funny?' he snarled, standing beside Longus as he leaned over the table. 'You believe you can treat me like a common senator, that you can deny me an audience?'

'I do not believe anything,' Regulus said, a confidence in his voice that Scipio had never witnessed. 'I know that I am senior consul and as such I command the power of Rome.'

'You know nothing,' Scipio spat back. 'You think your victory at Tyndaris has made you secure, has made your position in this Senate unassailable but I wonder how many senators would support you if they knew how you gained your consulship; knew the part I played and the pawn that you were.'

Now Regulus stood, the smile he had worn cast off, his expression hard and cold.

'You may tell your story to any that will listen,' he said in whispered anger. 'But I know, as will they realise, that what you did, you did for yourself and what I do now, I do for Rome. The Senate will see the truth of that.'

Scipio held Regulus's gaze for a second longer, the hatred passing between them palatable, an almost physical force that marked the permanent division between them. He turned on his heel without another word, casting one last glance at Longus before storming from the room, a deafening silence left in his wake.

Atticus stood back from the door as he heard the sound of approaching footsteps on the other side. He reached up and touched the scar on his face, fingering it lightly as he traced the length of it along his jaw-line. He had seen the wound for only the first time three days before after the *Aquila* had docked in Ostia, a foreign reflection staring back at him from a barber's polished copper mirror. Now he thought of it again, unconsciously continuing to touch it, thinking all the while of the person on the other side of the door who would also be seeing it for the first time.

The door opened inward and Hadria stepped back to push it past her, pivoting lightly on one foot as she did. Her expression changed quickly, so swiftly that Atticus, who was gazing directly at her, did not catch all the emotions displayed, surprise turning to elation and love, turning to concern at the sight of his wound. She rushed forward into his arms, pressing tightly against his chest, touching the heavy layer of bandages across his torso, then releasing the pressure of her embrace, fearful that she was hurting him. He pulled her close again, enfolding her slender body in his arms, whispering reassurances in her ear. She returned the embrace and her body began to shudder slightly, her tears warm and damp against his shoulder, the fear for him that she had thought to suppress rising again at the sight of his terrible wounds.

An hour later they lay in the solitude of her bedroom, the sounds of city barely audible through the opened shutters, the noise muted by the heat of the early afternoon. Atticus lay on his back, his eyes tracing the light reflected across the ceiling, his mind casting back to a dawn weeks before at the edge of Thermae and the glare of the sun on the waves. Hadria lay beside him, her finger tracing an imaginary line an inch above the scar on his face, recalling Atticus's words of moments before when he told her of how he was attacked. Hadria had listened, silently glad that she had taken the lead an hour before when she had led him to her room, the fear resurfaced and so vividly remembered giving her reason to value every moment and she had tempered their mutual anticipation and yearning with a tenderness that Atticus had never known.

Now Atticus lay replete, his mind drifting aimlessly until he suddenly glanced to the door, his brow wrinkling as if in annoyance and he stared at it for a moment longer before turning away.

'What's the matter?' Hadria asked, noticing his expression.

'I thought I heard someone approaching,' he said, looking

once more at Hadria. 'I was expecting a knock, a message from your father's house that Septimus had returned.'

Hadria nodded and her expression turned serious. 'I told him about us the last time he was in Rome,' she said. 'He was very angry.'

'I know,' Atticus replied and he told Hadria of his confrontation with Septimus on the *Aquila*.

'And you haven't spoken of it since?' Hadria asked, her tone one of concern.

'There is nothing more to say,' Atticus said irritably. 'Septimus will not change his mind.'

Hadria's forehead creased as she tried to divine her brother's inner thoughts. She could not be sure but she still felt her original conviction was sound, that Septimus did not want Hadria to lose another love in battle as she had her first husband. She spoke her thoughts aloud to Atticus, watching as his brow furrowed.

'That's why he told me to stay on deck before Tyndaris,' he said almost to himself, 'and why he was angry to see me when I went onto the Carthaginian galley to warn him.'

'What do you mean?' Hadria asked.

Atticus explained.

'So he's trying to protect you . . .' Hadria whispered, her words hanging in the air as Atticus remained silent, thinking of his friend. After their confrontation on the *Aquila* he had been sure of Septimus's position. Now, with Hadria's insight, he was no longer certain.

The Senate stood as one as Regulus entered the Curia, his preannounced request for a full audience ensuring that every senator of Rome was in attendance, their numbers swelled by tribunes and senior magistrates who had also been summoned at the senior consul's request. Regulus walked

311

slowly to the podium, indicating with his hand for the assembly to be seated. He stood silent for a moment; savouring the approbation of the Senate but also the renewed sense of a shared purpose that permeated the Curia, the narrowly averted threat to Rome infusing the Senate with a reunified aspiration that stood above the petty power-plays and squabbling of the daily debate. Regulus had experienced this level of concord before, immediately after the victory of Mylae, when all of Rome rose to its feet in triumph. He was a lowly senator then, anonymous amongst three hundred. Now he was senior consul and the united power of Rome was his to command.

'My fellow Romans!' he began, his voice reaching every man in the hushed chamber. 'We have reached a cross-roads in our fight with the *Punici* of Africa, a moment of truth when decisive action can and must prevail.'

A murmur of agreement rippled across the chamber.

'As you all know, a Carthaginian plan to invade this very city was exposed,' Regulus continued, indicating to Varro who stood in the wings, his first time in the Curia since announcing his defeat at Thermae, the tribune now bowing his head in acceptance of the splattering of applause from the Senate, 'and subsequently thwarted at Tyndaris.'

The Senate clapped again, this time towards the podium but it quickly abated as Regulus raised his hand.

'It was a bold plan, a decisive plan that, if it had succeeded, would have given the Carthaginians not only unconditional control of Sicily but also a new subservient state in their empire . . . a state named Rome.'

Many senators reacted with instinctive anger, shouting denial and cursing the Carthaginians who would dare such a thing. Regulus let them vent their antagonism, his eyes instead on those senators who remained silent, those who had understood the subtext of his words, many of them nodding their heads in pre-emptive approval.

'I say to you then, Senators of Rome,' Regulus shouted, overwhelming the cacophony of noise. 'That we reverse this plan of the enemy, that we take their initiative and infuse it with Roman audacity!' The Senate began to cheer. 'With Roman courage!' Regulus shouted, his voice struggling against the ovation, 'and with the power of this mighty Republic!'

As one the Senate stood to applaud, the noise reaching a crescendo as Regulus stretched out his arms to encompass the power surging around him.

'We will take this fight to the shores of Carthage herself!' he roared, his final words tipping the Senate over into complete support for their leader.

Varro stood proudly beside his father as yet another senator approached to shake his hand. Regulus had finished his speech over an hour before and only now was the Curia beginning to empty, the session extended to allow the senior senators of the chamber to publicly back the consul's plan, their orations infused with praise for Regulus and Varro and heavy with rhetoric that expounded the ideals of Rome, of how the overthrow of Carthage would bring civilisation to the shores of Africa. They were words that gave every tribune in the chamber cause to imagine their glorious fate in the approaching battle, but none more so that Varro, who saw his success at Tyndaris as only the beginning.

The crowd dissipated quickly and soon Varro's father drifted off with a group of senior magistrates, grasping his son's arm lightly as he left, his pride evident in every gesture. Varro walked slowly towards the colonnaded exit, the later afternoon sun creating blocks of light between the pillars through which droning insects traced lazy paths of flight. Varro stood still for a moment in one of the shafts of light, glancing briefly over his shoulder at the inner chamber and smiling slightly, the white brightness of the sun warm on his face. He turned again and was surprised by a figure standing in his path.

'Congratulations, Tribune,' the man said and Varro instantly recognised the voice.

'Thank you, Senator Scipio,' he replied and began to walk around him.

Scipio pre-empted the evasion and clasped Varro's arm, holding it firm. 'You have done well, Varro,' he said, a hint of sarcasm in his voice.

Varro shrugged his arm clear, irritated by Scipio's conde-scension. 'I have done what I set out to do,' he said. 'Return to Rome with my honour restored.'

'But what of our agreement?' Scipio asked, 'The Greek Perennis still lives.'

'For now,' Varro said dismissively, 'and as for our agree-ment, it would seem I was mistaken in believing I needed your help.'

Scipio's face coloured in anger, 'An agreement made cannot be broken,' he said, stepping closer until he was but mere inches from Varro's face, 'and you owe me.'

'I owe you nothing, Scipio,' Varro spat, 'and your power in the Senate is no more. I will take my revenge on Perennis, but in my own time, and certainly not on your command.'

Scipio was about to retort but Varro brushed past him, walking quickly but confidently away until he was lost from sight. Only then did Scipio's face contort into an expression of pure rage, his dismissal at the hands of an upstart like Varro striking at the very centre of his pride and honour.

'So they all believe my power is no more,' he whispered to himself, his mind summoning the memory of Regulus's equally vile contempt, the thought fuelling his anger and hatred. He had raised Regulus from obscurity, rescued Varro from disgrace and both men had turned on him, their success giving them a false sense of invincibility, a belief they could dismiss Scipio and all he had done. But they were wrong, Scipio thought, his face twisting into a malicious smile, and with the patience of a hunter he set his mind to devising a new plan, one that would rid him of his enemies and finally achieve the death of a Greek captain who was at the centre of his hatred.

Atticus wiped the fine mist of sea-spray from his face as he leaned against the forerail of the *Aquila*, his gaze sweeping over the ordered formation of galleys fore and aft, their number stretching the length of the black shoreline of Fiumicino. He looked to the galleys closest to the *Aquila* in the five-abreast formation, triremes all who made up the centre of the line, the prized van- and rear-guard positions all granted to the pre-eminent quinqueremes who accounted for nearly half of the three-hundred strong *Classis Romanus*, a immense fleet that had taken three weeks to assemble.

'Impressive . . .'

Atticus turned to find Septimus standing behind him. He was clad in full battle armour, the breastplate newly reshaped, the battle scars removed. Atticus nodded and looked to the fleet once more, a curious sensation in his chest as he repeated Septimus's description in his mind, the display of Rome's power mesmeric.

'Orders from the vanguard, Captain,' Lucius said, interrupting Atticus's thoughts again. 'The fleet is to heave-to at Ostia to allow the flagship and the senatorial galleys to take point.'

'Very well, Lucius,' Atticus replied. 'Inform Gaius and stand by at the helm'. Lucius nodded and walked quickly away.

'How are the new troops?' Atticus asked of Septimus, his thoughts now on his own galley.

'They're good men,' Septimus replied, 'all from VII of the Fifth.'

Atticus nodded, glancing past Septimus to the assembled ranks of his replenished demi-maniple on the main deck.

'So, our first stop is Brolium?' Septimus asked, changing the subject.

'Naples first,' Atticus replied, 'to pick up the transport ships that have been assembled there along with the replacement troops for the Ninth. Then we sail for Brolium.'

Septimus nodded, his thoughts straying to Marcus. The devastated Ninth legion had never been called to join the Second in fighting the Carthaginians to the south of Brolium but with the enemy now in full retreat and the replacement troops bringing the Ninth back up to full strength, they were the obvious choice to sail with the invasion fleet.

'We should be in Brolium in about four days,' Atticus added. 'Two days to re-supply and embark the Ninth and then a full week to Agrigentum where the Sixth Legion will board.'

Septimus nodded again, marvelling anew at the scale of the invasion force. Three years before four legions, forty thousand men, had crossed the Strait of Messina to invade Sicily, but that crossing had taken less than an hour over a mere four miles of calm coastal water. Now the invasion was striking at the very heart of the Carthaginian Empire.

A sudden clarion call blasted from the vanguard of the fleet, the sound taken up and amplified until it rippled across the length of the entire formation, the air charged with the blare of a thousand trumpets as the head of the fleet reached the harbour entrance of Ostia. The flagship *Victoria* emerged, flanked by a dozen other quinqueremes, their banners heralding the family names of the senators on board, over fifty of them in total, many of them junior in rank, eager to associate their names with the impending invasion.

Hamilcar paced incessantly across his room in the naval barracks in Carthage. He had spent all morning with delegates from the one-hundred-and-four, discussing with them the latest rumours arriving in the city from traders interacting with others who had been to Ostia. The rumours were of a gathering fleet, and of Fiumcino's shipyards' increased and insatiable appetite for raw materials; pine and oak, canvas and iron; of a brooding tension that was permeating the enemy military.

He strode to the window and looked out over the harbour, subdued in the heat of the mid-day sun. In the military port, and beyond in the commercial harbour, the assembled fleets of the empire remained at anchor, over two hundred galleys, with only the Sicilian fleet still on station in the hostile waters surrounding the contested island. The galleys looked to be sleeping, tugging lazily on their anchor lines as the current shifted beneath them, the energy and anticipation that had infused the crews and commanders when they first arrived in Carthage now lost to apathy and tedium.

Hamilcar was due to stand before the supreme council of Carthage within the hour, to outline his revised plan of campaign now that his proposed invasion was all but impossible. The massive fleet in Carthage's harbour was a constant strain on the city's resources, draining the grain warehouses and coffers alike and Hamilcar knew that a majority of the council, led by Hanno, were anxious to return the fleets to their home ports.

The first knock on the door went unnoticed by Hamilcar, engrossed as he was in his thoughts, his eyes having lost their focus as he stared at the galleys before him. The second knock broke his reverie and he spun around, calling enter as he did. The door opened and Himilco stepped in, the captain's face animated, his eyes darting to Hamilcar's desk and then scanning the room until he saw his commander. He walked quickly to him.

'My lord, I have further news of the Romans,' he said.

'Don't you mean rumours?' Hamilcar asked dismissively.

'No, my lord,' Himilco insisted. 'There is a Maltese captain outside who you must hear.'

'Maltese?' Hamilcar asked, intrigued.

'Yes, my lord. His ship approached the flagship *Alissar* in the commercial harbour and asked to speak to the commander. Once I heard his report I rushed him here.'

'Very well,' Hamilcar said. 'Show him in.'

Hamilcar studied the captain as Himilco escorted him in. The Maltese was tall but showed none of the bearing of a military man, his eyes alert and intelligent but without the hard determination of one who has seen battle.

'You have news?' Hamilcar asked, his gaze suspicious.

'Yes, my lord,' the captain began, 'from Naples.'

'Go on.' Hamilcar said.

'As you know, my lord, the Maltese are no longer welcome in Ostia so we are forced to trade with the Republic further south where local loyalty leans more to the drachma and the denarius.'

Hamilcar nodded impatiently. Malta had been a province of Carthage for over one-hundred and fifty years, but her traders acted independently to those of the city, sailing their vessels into nearly every port in the Mediterranean, ally and foe of Carthage alike, their singular loyalty to trade recognised by all. Only Ostia forbade them entry.

'And what have you heard?' Hamilcar asked.

'It is what I have seen, my lord,' the captain said quickly. 'A large Roman fleet sailing south from the city a week ago.'

'How many ships?' Hamilcar asked, his voice suddenly on edge.

'At least three hundred galleys, my lord,' the captain replied, 'escorting transport ships carrying legionaries.'

Hamilcar stood silent for a moment, his mind racing. 'Where were they heading?' he asked.

'The rumours in the city said Brolium on the Sicilian coast.'

Again Hamilcar remained quiet as he tried to discern the Romans' intentions. He stepped forward, his hand on the hilt of his sword. 'Why do you bring us this news?' he asked, searching the captain's expression.

'The Romans have already closed the port of Ostia to our ships,' the captain spat. 'If they expand their territory then who knows what rule of law will follow? We Maltese want only trade and for generations Carthage has given us a free hand. Given a choice I would sooner have the Romans bottled up on their peninsula.'

Hamilcar nodded but he remained cautious. This information, taken with the rumours thus far, seemed to indicate a massive offensive. But against where? Panormus? Syracuse? Either way, he now had vital information to share with the supreme council, information that would decide the next move of the Carthaginian fleet.

'Can we believe this message?' the councillor said, looking to his colleagues, uncertainty in his voice, his question answered simultaneously by a half-dozen others. Hamilcar stood silently as the debate swung back and forth amongst the twelve members of the supreme council, waiting to be addressed directly having finished his report. As always he looked to his father surreptitiously, searching for some unspoken advice, the intricate alliances and sub-groups of the council a mystery to Hamilcar, leaving him with little idea of who still supported him as military leader.

'Do you believe this message?' the suffet finally asked, looking at Hamilcar with hooded eyes.

'I have dispatched a galley to Thermae with orders for the captain to make contact with our spies in Brolium,' Hamilcar replied, carefully keeping all bias from his tone. 'If the Roman fleet do indeed dock there, then I believe we will have verification of the message. In the meantime I have interned the Maltese captain and his crew. If his report is false then we shall exact the real truth from his lying tongue.'

'If the report is verified,' the suffet said, 'what do you propose?'

'To learn of their final objective and then take the battle to them with our entire fleet.' Hamilcar replied boldly.

'To what end?' Hanno said with derision. 'To attempt to regain the confidence of this council?'

'No,' Hamilcar replied, anger in his voice. 'To wipe the Roman scourge from our seas.'

Hanno made to retort but the suffet held his hand up for silence. 'I agree with young Barca's plan,' he said after a moment's pause, looking to each council member in turn. 'With such a Roman fleet at sea we must act decisively.'

Some of the council members nodded in agreement while more looked stonily ahead, Hanno amongst them. The suffet marked the division and, conscious of the need for agreement, turned directly to Hanno.

'This reversal of Barca's invasion plan,' he said. 'You no longer have faith in his ability to command?'

'No, Suffet,' Hanno replied, 'I believe Barca has been blinded by his own ambitions.'

Hamilcar bristled at the remark but held his tongue, catching his father's expression of warning in the corner of his eye.

'Hamilcar Barca is our most able commander,' the suffet began, 'but perhaps Hanno is right, perhaps he is too determined, too aggressive. I propose that you, Hanno, sail with the fleet to ensure that assertiveness is tempered with experience.'

Hanno nodded in agreement, knowing he could do little else. To refuse would invite accusations of cowardice. The suffet noticed Hanno's allies also comply and he quickly called a vote, one that was carried easily.

Hamilcar saluted to the council before turning on his heel to leave the chamber. He caught Hanno's eye as he did, seeing there the latent hostility he felt surging through his own veins. Hamilcar closed the chamber door and stood silently for a moment, fully realising that battle-lines had now been drawn not only in the sea but also in the council of Carthage itself, battle-lines that Hamilcar had to cross if he was to destroy his enemies. A cold determination crept onto Hamilcar's face as he savoured the thought. Gone now was the subterfuge, the snares and planning that had consumed him over the previous months, replaced with the clarity given only to a warrior when he stands, sword in hand, upon the battlefield, his vision filled with the sight of his mortal enemy.

CHAPTER FIFTEEN

The rough hewn hawser dipped and raised with the even stroke of the *Aquila*'s oars, the sea-water dripping from the fibres of the rope with every pull, creating a cascade that fell in time with the drum beat of the trireme. Atticus leaned over the aft-rail and took a grip on the rope, testing its strength, feeling the tension within. He looked back along its length, following the lines as it fell to the sea and then rose again to the bowsprit of the transport ship fifty yards behind. A crewman stood on station there and he waved across as he noticed he was being watched, a wave Atticus returned before turning away once more.

Lucius approached him from the helm. 'Cape Ecnomus,' he said pointing over the starboard rail. 'We're about eight hours out from Agrigentum.'

Atticus nodded in return and then turned his attention back to the line of his galley. The *Aquila* was near the centre of the long line of triremes that stretched from the shore, each one towing a transport ship, an ignominious task ordered of the third squadron the day before when the wind suddenly dissipated, becalming the sail-driven transports. Now only the command ship of the third squadron, the *Orcus*, was without a tether, Varro's quinquereme sailing a full ship-length ahead of the line as if in an effort to distance itself from the trireme dray-horses.

'Eight hours out,' Atticus said as Septimus approached from the main deck, a slight sheen of sweat on his forehead, a wooden training sword loose in his hand, a weapon he had been rarely without over the previous week as he trained his new men to full battle-readiness.

'Still no sign of Marcus?' Septimus asked, indicating the transport ships behind.

'No, I haven't seen him,' Atticus replied. 'The Fourth must be on one of the ships on the flanks.'

Septimus nodded, 'He's there somewhere,' he said, his eyes scanning the decks of the ships nearest to the *Aquila*. Each deck was crowded with red-cloaked legionaries, many of them leaning out over the rails, their sea-sickness staining the hull, their faces pale and drawn from the week long passage down the east coast of Sicily.

'Signal from the first squadron,' Corin shouted and Atticus looked to the mainmast, waiting for the lookout to decipher the full message, a sudden feeling of unease sweeping over him as he watched Corin spin around, his expression one of pure dread.

'Enemy fleet ahead!' the lookout roared and Varro felt a sudden knot develop in the pit of his stomach.

'Confirm that message!' he roared up the masthead as he walked quickly to the helm.

'Signal from the first squadron is confirmed!' the lookout shouted. 'An enemy fleet has been sighted.'

Varro looked to the sea ahead but could see nothing beyond the first and second squadrons a half-mile ahead. They were sailing in arrow formation, each squadron forming one side of the spear-point with the two command ships at the apex, the *Victoria* under Regulus at the head of the first squadron and a quinquereme under Longus at the head of the second.

Varro had been given command of the *Orcus* on the day the fleet had sailed from Brolium, the singular honour of commanding the third squadron bestowed upon him in recognition of his part in thwarting the Carthaginians' plans to attack Rome. It had been a proud moment for Varro, standing on the main deck of the *Victoria* as Regulus announced the promotion before the assembled tribunes and senators, the consul speaking highly of Varro's courageous action at Thermae which had saved so many *hastati* of the Ninth in addition to his capture of the pirate galley that had led to the exposure of the enemy's subterfuge.

Now however, sailing a half-mile behind the consuls, Varro felt suddenly cheated. The *Orcus* was a powerful galley, a ship that belonged in the van of the fleet, destroying enemy triremes as the Roman quinqueremes had done so easily at Tyndaris. Instead Varro was leading a fleet of hulking transport ships and obsolete triremes, a reprehensible command that would ensure that the glory of the battle ahead would fall to other, lesser men.

Varro walked slowly to the foredeck; his gaze locked on the Roman formation ahead, the distance opening with every passing minute as the vanguard accelerated to battle speed. He looked beyond them to the horizon, seeing for the first time the dark shapes of the approaching enemy, their naked mainmasts like a wave of scorched grass against the sky. Varro's dark mood deepened at the sight, his eyes sweeping across the enemy line, estimating their numbers to be less than a hundred, a pitiful force against the three hundred galleys of the *Classis Romanus*. Success for the Roman fleet was assured, a near slaughter given the odds and Varro cursed the fates that robbed him of his part in a victory that would be gained on such easy terms.

The tribune was turning away from the sight but a flicker of darkness at the edges of the Carthaginian line made him turn once more, his mouth falling open slightly as he watched the enemy line extend on either side, the dark wave of galleys breaking towards the shoreline and the horizon to the south until it filled the entire seascape ahead, Varro's dark mood dissipating without conscious thought to be replaced with a cold dread that filled his entire soul.

'Battle speed!' Hamilcar shouted, his heart racing as the line of enemy galleys unfolded before his eyes, a wedge of galleys that swept north and south; a formation his patrol galleys had sighted the day before. He ran back to the aft-deck, weaving through the scurrying crew as the *Alissar* was made ready for imminent battle. Himilco walked briskly towards him as he reached the aft.

'Signal the fleet,' Hamilcar said. 'Advance the flanks!'

The captain saluted and ran to the aft-rail, issuing the order to the signal-men who quickly dispatched the message that would ripple down the three hundred and fifty-strong line of galleys in a matter of minutes.

Hamilcar looked to the shoreline not five hundred yards off his port quarter. Ahead was Cape Ecnomus, Roman-held Sicilian land and a point on a map Hamilcar remembered examining months before. At the time he had envisaged his land forces striking east across that very Cape, cutting off the city of Agrigentum from rescue, the Carthaginian flank protected by the army of Syracuse, the Romans in chaos and on the brink of surrender with the news that their vaulted city of Rome was on its knees.

That vision had been ripped from Hamilcar's mind on the

day the Romans had attacked Tyndaris. Hamilcar still wondered how the enemy had uncovered his plan. Belus's disappearance must be connected somehow but he was unable to link the two positively. The goddess Tanit had a hand in Hamilcar's fate, of that he now had no doubt, her hand of fortune lifting from his shoulder at Tyndaris only to fall once more upon him with the deliverance of the Maltese captain's report, the Carthaginian spies in Brolium initially confirming the fleets arrival and then revealing the true objective of the enemy fleet, the Roman town awash with the rumour as the legionaries boarded the transport barges, their destination; the shores of Carthage.

The Romans had indeed reversed his strategy, turning the blade until it now pointed directly at Carthage, their base at Agrigentum a close enough jumping-off point to Carthage as Tyndaris had been to Rome. It was a conceit that drove Hamilcar to a near frenzy of anger, a blatant arrogance that typified the Roman foe, the self-assurance that made them believe that the order of superiority could be so easily reversed. Carthage was not Rome. She was not the sleeping prey the Roman city had been, she was a leopard lying in wait, ever-fierce, ever-prepared to defend her progeny against any who would dare to attack.

The *Alissar* began to forge ahead at Hamilcar's command to advance the flank, an invisible tether drawing out the galleys behind her, the manoeuvre mirrored on the seaward flank until the Carthaginian formation resembled a crescent moon. The lines were re-dressed quickly, deft touches that marked the fine seamanship inherent on every galley of the fleet. Hamilcar looked back along the formation, his gaze picking up the flagship *Baal Hammon* in the centre of the line. She was sailing slightly ahead, no doubt by order of her commander Hanno, the councillor's arrogance demanding the prominent position in recognition of his titular command of the fleet. Hamilcar's strategy to defeat the Roman fleet had begrudgingly been accepted by Hanno before the fleet sailed, the councillor recognising the formidable logic of the plan. The agreement had created an uneasy truce between the men; their mutual animosity set aside, neither man willing to risk the fate of Carthage and, as Hamilcar stared across at the *Baal Hammon*, he felt his confidence rise, knowing the might of Carthage was for now united under one banner, one cause. Death to the Romans.

Regulus felt the deck rise and plunge beneath his feet and he gripped the side-rail on the aft-deck for balance as he stared ahead at the oncoming Carthaginian line. The false wind created by the galley's speed blew fresh onto his face and he breathed deeply, drawing in the salt-laden air, tasting it as if for the first time. A lifetime ago he had commanded a legion in the field, had tasted battle, both bitter defeat and sweet victory. It was a time he had long forgotten, the memory fouled by the listless air of the Curia and the leaden air of the bathhouse. Now a new memory was being forged, a latent vigour re-discovered and Regulus looked to the forces that were his to command.

The main deck of the *Victoria* was crammed with troops, a full maniple, the I of the Fifth, in addition to a further sixty legionaries of the *praetoriani*, each man a veteran, every soldier on board the flagship battle-hardened and ready, their swords drawn in anticipation. Regulus looked once more to the Carthaginian fleet, wondering anew what skill the enemy possessed that allowed them to anticipate the approach of the *Classis Romanus* and assemble such a host against it. They had appeared as if from nowhere, their battle-line fully deployed and prepared and Regulus had realised that near disaster had only been averted by the fact that his fleet was already deployed in an aggressive posture. It was a formation Regulus had insisted upon only days before for the protection of the helpless transports and he looked skyward; a whispered prayer on his lips to Mars, the god of war who he believed must have had a covert hand in his decision, his guiding hand granting Regulus the opportunity to take the fight to the enemy.

'Captain,' Regulus commanded to the man at his side. 'Order attack speed and signal the third squadron to stand fast.'

'Yes, Consul,' the captain saluted and issued the orders over his shoulder, turning once more to stand tall beside his commander, the flagship accelerating to twelve knots, her clean lines and unblemished hull causing her to skim over the gentle swell, steadying her deck. Regulus left go of the rail and moved to the helm, his eyes darting to the lead ship of the second squadron, picking up the figure of Longus standing apart on the aft-deck. He looked over suddenly at Regulus, as if he knew he was under scrutiny, and he nodded to the consul, a brief but confident gesture that Regulus returned.

The spearhead created by the convergent lines of the first and second squadrons flew onwards, the helmsmen of the lead ships keeping the formation in perfect balance, their thrust directly towards the centre of the Carthaginian line. Regulus watched the I of the Fifth walk forward to take position behind the *corvus*, his gaze tracking up the height of the raised boarding ramp. It was a fearsome weapon, poised to strike and Regulus felt the anticipation of battle unfurl itself within his heart as the men of the Fifth roared a war cry in answer to the call of their centurion.

The consul looked beyond the *corvus* to the enemy line less than four hundred yards ahead. The breath in his throat stilled for a heartbeat, his eyes darting left and right and he ran once more to the side-rail to gain a better line of sight. Now he was certain and Regulus felt his heart rate rise as elation surged through him. The Carthaginian formation was as yet unbroken but it had become concave, as if the centre was recoiling before the Roman thrust, an instinctive reaction to an aggression they had not expected of the Romans, the Carthaginians obviously believing that they would catch the *Classis Romanus* unawares.

Regulus locked his gaze on the centre of the Carthaginian line as the gap decreased, anticipating what he was about to witness, praying that he was right, knowing that victory would be assured. He raised his hand up and clenched his fist, holding it still above his head, the muscles in his forearm trembling with the force of his grip, his entire being focused on one galley, a flagship, sailing slightly advanced of the line. Regulus waited, the seconds passing as the oars fell and rose in unison.

The change happened suddenly and Regulus roared in triumph, his fist slamming down on the side-rail, a death knell for the *Punici*. The Carthaginian flagship was turning, her deck keeling over violently as the galleys around her reacted in kind, the Carthaginian line disintegrating into confusion and fear within seconds, the roars of defiance and aggression on board the Roman galleys turning to baying cries of triumph and mercilessness.

'Maintain attack speed!' Regulus shouted, striding to the helm. 'Hunt them down! Prepare to release the *corvus*!'

The command was quickly passed along the deck and outward to the other galleys of the spearhead, the legionaries hammering their shields in affirmation of the order. Regulus drank in the sound, feeling his Roman heart match the beat of ten thousand blades raised at his command.

The enemy centre was now fully turned, fleeing before the Roman spear, the gap of three hundred yards a pitiful defence against the unleashed Roman advance. Regulus was staring once more at the Carthaginian flagship, his gaze now sweeping her aft-deck, trying to single out the cowardly enemy commander who believed he could run from his fate, the consul's fixation blinding him to the enemy galleys beyond the centre of the Carthaginian line.

'They're turning!' Corin shouted from the masthead, the excitement in his voice impossible to contain. 'The enemy are in retreat!'

Atticus ran to the foredeck to gain a better view, passing quickly through the serried ranks of legionaries on the main. He skirted around the newly replaced *corvus*, his shoulder brushing against the cumbersome ramp as he did and he mumbled an incoherent curse, his eyes never leaving the sea ahead until his legs struck the forerail. He glanced down, the surging water breaking over the ram echoing a rhythmic splash and he placed his palms on the rail, leaning his upper body forward as he stared once more ahead. The lead squadrons were over a mile away and beyond them was the enemy line, its aspect in complete disarray as the galleys turned away from the fight.

'Something's wrong,' a voice said beside Atticus and he nodded to his second-in-command.

'No collisions,' Atticus remarked.

'And I've never known the Carthaginians to run before,' Lucius replied. 'Not before the battle's even started.'

'Lucius,' Atticus began. 'Get aloft. Do a full sweep.'

Lucius nodded and turned, sidestepping past Septimus as he went.

'They're in retreat?' Septimus asked, removing his helmet and rubbing his forehead with the back of his hand.

'I'm not so sure,' Atticus replied and Septimus looked to him.

'It's not like the Carthaginians to break so easily,' Atticus continued.

'But they are turning from the fight,' Septimus insisted.

'Without panicking,' Atticus said, his gaze now sweeping across the entire seascape ahead. He turned to Septimus.

'Have you ever known an enemy to retreat suddenly in complete order?' he asked.

Septimus was silent for a moment, his head turning to the Roman attack. He shook his head. Something was wrong.

Hamilcar slammed his fist onto the side-rail as he watched the centre of his line turn in full retreat, the two hundred galleys of the Roman spearhead never pausing as their head-long attack transformed into a full pursuit. The lead galleys of the Roman formation were quickly in line with the *Alissar*'s advanced position on the landward flank, granting Hamilcar a perfect view across the half-mile distance, his professional eye immediately recognising the classic Tyrian design so loved by the Carthaginians in the new Roman quinqueremes. The reports from Brolium on the strength and size of the Roman fleet had been extensive and within seconds a malicious smile spread across Hamilcar's face as he counted the larger hulls in the formation.

'Two points starboard!' Hamilcar ordered the helm and the *Alissar* turned quickly to her new course, the entire land-ward flank responding immediately, separating Hamilcar's attack force from the galleys of the centre as they fled west away from the Romans. Hamilcar turned his gaze south-wards once more, seeing through the single ranks of the Roman formation to the opposing flank of the Carthaginian line, watching as their aspect changed to mirror his own course. He looked ahead once more, finally focusing all his attention on the true target of his attack, the soft underbelly of the Roman fleet.

'Aspect change on the flanks!'

Varro looked up to the masthead, turning away from the sight of the Roman pursuit for the first time, his mind quickly deciphering the call, his brow creased in confusion. The sight of the extended Carthaginian line had shaken him but he had quickly buried his apprehension, the resolute signals of attack from the *Victoria* giving him confidence once more and he had cheered with the rest of the crew as the enemy centre turned in retreat.

Suddenly he was unsure once more and he looked to the enemy galleys closest to the shore. They were advancing, flanking the Roman spearhead, the lead galleys already turned to a course directly aimed at the centre of the third squadron, the galleys behind the vanguard sweeping out to form a line of battle. Alarm instantly swept through Varro, his gaze locked to the galleys in the centre of the line, quinqueremes all, ships that outmatched every galley in the third except the *Orcus*. They could not stand. There was no hope. The first and second squadrons were sailing further away with every passing minute, isolating Varro, cutting him off, abandoning him to the Carthaginian jackals.

Varro looked to the shore less than a mile away, a series of inlets and jagged headlands. If the *Orcus* could reach it first there was a chance they could fend off any attack, the shoreline protecting his rear. He spun around, searching for the captain, seeing the line of triremes still tethered to the transport ships. He froze for a heartbeat. There was nothing he could do for them. The enemy galleys were too strong, too numerous. To stand and fight was to die and Varro was not willing to die for some forlorn cause. Fleeing was the only option for him; for everyone.

'Captain!' Varro shouted, finally seeing the man. 'Attack speed. Make for the coastline!'

'Yes, Tribune,' the captain replied and quickly issued the orders. 'What will I signal to the rest of the squadron?' he asked as the *Orcus* broke formation.

Varro looked to the line once more, weighing his options. If they all cut loose and ran the confusion would better hide the *Orcus* from the enemy. He turned once more to the captain. 'To Hades with them.'

Atticus watched the Carthaginian flanks complete their turn around the rear of the advancing Roman spearhead, Lucius continually shouting down aspect changes from the mast-head, the second-in-command's voice level and unhurried. Atticus glanced briefly to the ship tethered to the *Aquila*, calcu-lating the maximum speed his galley could drag the dead weight against the distance and speed of the approaching Carthaginian line. They could not run, not without cutting loose and condemning the entire Ninth legion. The triremes of the third squadron would have to stand and fight.

'The *Orcus* is breaking formation!' Lucius shouted, tension in his voice for the first time.

Atticus ran to the side-rail and looked to the command ship, the quinquereme already accelerating to attack speed, her course cutting across the Roman line as she started to flee. A ferocious anger surged through him as he spotted Varro on the aft-deck, the tribune standing tall by the helm, his back turned to his own line as he stared at the approaching enemy attack.

'Varro!' he roared, but the tribune stood unmoved.

'The *Pomona*!' Lucius shouted and Atticus spun around to

look at the trireme two ships further down the line. She had cut her tether and was falling into the wake of the *Orcus*, following the command ship in headlong flight. Within a minute a dozen more galleys had broke from the formation, the crack of axe blows resounding through the air as lines were cut and more transport ships were cut loose, panic quickly sweeping through the ranks, the sight of the command ship flight unleashing the survival instinct in every galley.

'We can't run!' Septimus said as he ran onto the aft-deck, his eyes sweeping past Atticus to the galleys on all sides, confusion transforming to outright panic before his very eyes. 'The Ninth!'

Atticus looked to the ships again, the sails of the released unfurling in a futile attempt to gain some headway in the tepid breeze, their hulls turning slowly, barely making steerage speed. A sudden crunch of timbers cracked through the air as two galleys collided, the total chaos turning Roman against Roman as they sought to escape.

'By the gods, Atticus,' Septimus said, grabbing his friend by the shoulder and spinning him around, his face a mask of terror for the lives of the Ninth. 'We have to do something!'

Atticus stared at Septimus, his mind racing, a thread of panic reaching up and clawing at his spine. Lucius arrived on the aft-deck, his eyes dark with anger and frustration. Atticus looked to the *Orcus*, the command ship holding a direct line to the coast. Varro had destroyed the squadron, had broken its back as surely as the *Punici* would have done. Every galley was fleeing. It was every man for himself and no one man could stand alone, no one galley could stop the Carthaginians. Atticus looked down to the deck beneath his feet and then raised his head as he looked along the length of the *Aquila*. She was a fine ship.

He turned to Lucius, his eyes hard and cold.

'Sever the line,' Atticus said, his voice steady, a captain of the *Classis Romanus*. 'Attack speed'.

Regulus watched the runner sprint onto the aft-deck of the *Victoria*, his head darting left and right, searching for his captain. He spotted him and ran to his side, speaking quickly, pointing over the aft-rail. Regulus saw the captain turn, his expression apprehensive.

'What is it?' Regulus asked, walking towards the captain, turning his head for a second to the enemy ships fleeing before his own.

'The enemy flanks,' the captain said, 'the masthead lookout reports they did not turn.'

'What's their course?' Regulus asked, suddenly uneasy.

'They've turned into the third squadron, Consul,' the captain replied, his own anxiety evident in every word.

'The third squadron . . .' Regulus whispered. The Ninth legion, ten thousand men. Only a single line of triremes stood between them and the enemy. He cursed loudly, striding past the captain toward the aft-rail. He had never thought to look beyond the enemy centre, too elated that they had turned so easily. He looked to the third squadron a mile and a half behind. Approaching fast to on its flanks was the Carthaginian attack, a now solid line of advance, at least a dozen quinqueremes in each line. It was impossible to make out any detail in the Roman formation but Regulus thought it was in disarray, as if Varro was redeploying his forces to make a stand against the enemy. It was a valiant attempt but Regulus knew any such stand was doomed without the assistance of some of his forces.

'Captain!' he shouted, glancing over his shoulder. He would cut his force in two, sending one half back to relieve Varro's galleys. It would mean the escape of many of the Carthaginian centre but the transports had to be protected at all costs. The captain appeared beside him. Regulus turned.

'Signal Consul Longus,' Regulus began, 'order him to take the second . . .'

'The enemy are turning!' a voice shouted out and Regulus looked to the waters ahead. The entire Carthaginian line was turning once more into the attack, every galley, a fluid co-ordinated manoeuvre as if some unseen hand had swept over their line.

'Mars protect us . . .' Regulus whispered as the full realisation of what he was witnessing overwhelmed him. There was never a retreat. It was a trap, and the Roman vanguard had taken the bait completely, leaving a vital part of the fleet vulnerable, risking a loss that would prevent the invasion of Carthage, the death of ten thousand legionaries.

Hamilcar glanced left and right as the last of his galleys slipped into formation, completing the battle line, creating a sweeping wave fifty ships wide bearing down on the Roman line at seven knots. The seaward flank was a mile to the south, its line equally formed on a convergent course with Hamilcar's galleys and the Romans trapped between them.

'Attack speed!' Hamilcar ordered and the *Alissar* bucked beneath him, taking on the extra knots with a savage intent that matched the will of its commander. Hamilcar moved once more to the side-rail to gain a better view of the Roman squadron a half mile away, his elation growing with every passing oar-stroke, the decreasing distance confirming the masthead's earlier report that the enemy were retreating. The line was in complete chaos, with galleys fleeing north towards the coastline and east, away from the line of attack. Only the transports remained relatively unmoved, the fickle insipid wind making a mockery of their attempts to manoeuvre by sail. Hamilcar had been ready for a fight, had already accepted in his mind the loss of many of his galleys, even the quinqueremes that would be vulnerable to attack as they rammed the transport ships. Now that fight was dissipating before his eyes, the shield wall drawing back to lay bare the unprotected.

Hamilcar looked back over his shoulder to the rear of the Roman spearhead, the enemy galleys slowly fanning out to counter the re-turned Carthaginian line that threatened to envelope them. Hanno had timed his counter-stroke perfectly. He had executed the first part of the plan exactly as requested and so now, for the first time, Hamilcar felt confident that Hanno would follow the second part of his plan, the order that dictated how the councillor would engage the enemy vanguard.

His back protected, Hamilcar brought his full focus back to the transport fleet and its retreating escort. He felt his elation surge again and he closed his eyes, breathing in deeply, sifting the smells in his nostrils, the clean salt, the stale dry land and underneath, something else, a smell he could almost imagine, a smell of sweat and bile, the fear of the ten thousand men trapped in floating timber coffins.

'Enemy galley on intercept course!'

Hamilcar snapped open his eyes and looked to the masthead, seeing the outstretched arm and following the indication to the sea ahead. A lone trireme was approaching, her bow reared up in attack speed, her foredeck drenched in spray from her cutwater as she sliced through the gentle swell. Hamilcar looked to her flanks, to her rear and beyond, searching for other galleys, for the attack she must be leading but there was none. The trireme was alone, a single galley against a line of fifty. Hamilcar's mouth twisted into a snarl as he stared at the lone galley, admiring the bravery of the suicidal charge but dismissing it instantly.

'Hold your course!' he shouted to the helmsman.

Hamilcar had seen how the Romans attacked their prey many times, striking them head-on, holding them firm before releasing their cursed boarding ramp. But the approaching galley was a trireme, sailing into a pack of quinqueremes and Hamilcar knew the *Alissar* would brush her aside with barely a check. He smiled at the prospect, his hand gripping the side-rail in anticipation of the hammer blow to come.

'Steady,' Atticus said as he placed his hand on Gaius's shoulder, the helmsman gripping the tiller with a force that turned his knuckles white.

The solid line of Carthaginian galleys seemed to stretch forever before the bow of the *Aquila*, the quinqueremes in the centre a terrifying combination of speed and brute strength, their hulls dwarfing the smaller galleys on the flanks and the single galley that sailed towards them.

Atticus looked to the main deck and the sight of Septimus forming his men into protective ranks. The men moved with grit determination, their faces grim under iron helmets and cheek-plates, every sword drawn for the fight to come. Atticus checked his own weapon by his side, drawing the blade an inch out of its scabbard, feeling the familiar weight before slamming it home, his attention returning once again to the enemy.

Atticus counted to the centre galley, the lead ship, its mast-head banners unfurling languidly behind and in an instant he was transported back to Tyndaris weeks before, remembering those same banners on a fleeing quinquereme, Hamilcar Barca's galley. Atticus ran to the side-rail, locking his gaze on the masthead of the enemy galley, confirming what he believed, realising that his target was ever more deadly because it carried the military commander of Carthage.

Atticus stood back from the rail and moved to the centre of the aft-deck, his eyes sweeping once more over the deck of his ship. Corin had descended from the masthead and he stood with the rest of the crew on main deck, the men in a tight knot as Lucius issued final orders to each man. The legionaries beyond were in their own ranks but Atticus noticed glances being exchanged between the two groups, expressions that marked their shared fate, Roman and provincial citizen alike.

Septimus stepped away from his men and strode to the aft-deck. 'They're ready,' he said, his expression grim, unrelenting.

Atticus nodded, 'Expect two attacks at least,' he said, tension in his voice for the first time as the distance to the enemy fell below four hundred yards. 'My crew will try and hold the aft, you hold the main.'

Septimus nodded, looking at Atticus closely, seeing the shadow of uncertainty in his friend's face.

'This is something,' he said and Atticus gave him a quizzical look.

'I said we needed to do something,' Septimus explained, a slight smile reaching the corners of his mouth, 'and this is it.'

'We had to give the Ninth some chance . . .' Atticus said, glad that Septimus understood his order to charge the Carthaginian line. He looked to the advancing enemy, the odds overwhelming and he turned to his friend.

'About Hadria,' Atticus began, unsure of what he was about to say.

Septimus looked at Atticus, holding his gaze. 'She told me,' he said, the shadow of an emotion sweeping across his face, 'that she won't give you up.'

339

'And you can't accept that?' Atticus asked, silently willing Septimus to relent.

Septimus looked to the waters ahead, each drum beat and oar stroke taking the *Aquila* closer to certain defeat and the very fate he had wished to shield his sister from, the loss of another love in battle. He turned once more to Atticus.

'Not today,' he said and walked back towards his men, his hand reaching for his sword and drawing it with one sweep of his arm, the metal singing against the scabbard.

Atticus watched Septimus for a moment longer. Not today, he thought and he drew his sword, the grip of the hardwood hilt solid between his fingers. He caught Lucius's eye, nodding to him in command, the older man nodding back imperceptibly before ordering the crew to make ready.

The *Aquila* sped on, her two hundred oars never faltering, the banner at her masthead whipping out to release the eagle in flight, the seventy-ton hull like an arrow set loose from the draw, skimming the wave tops, taking deadly aim. Atticus stepped back to the helm, seeing Gaius's hard stare, his gaze never wavering and Atticus took strength from the helmsman. He looked to the enemy. Two hundred yards.

'Ramming speed!'

One hundred yards, thirteen knots, the enemy surging forward, the edges of the line disappearing as all focus turned to the centre, the drum beat crashing out, the oars slicing through the air and surging through the water.

'Steady *Aquila*,' Atticus whispered, placing one hand on the tiller behind Gaius's grip, his vision filled with the sight of the charging behemoth bearing down.

Fifty yards.

'All hands, prepare to be boarded!'

Forty yards. Thirty.

'Now, Gaius!' Atticus roared and threw himself against the

tiller, the helmsman surging with him, their every strength throwing the rudder hard left, the *Aquila* responding in opposition, her bow slicing right into the path of the flagship, her hull turning in seconds to create a solid wall of timber, iron and men across the enemy front.

CHAPTER SIXTEEN

The *Alissar* struck the fore section of the *Aquila* with all the force of her one hundred ton hull, her eleven-knot momentum driving the ram cleanly into the *Aquila*, punching through the seasoned oak, the blunt-faced fist propelled deep into the slave deck of the trireme. Sixty yards along the hull, the second quinquereme struck, her ram taking the *Aquila* deep below the waterline, flooding the lower hold, the splintered timbers of the *Aquila* clawing at the lower cutwater of the quinquereme as if desperately trying to stay the blow.

Hamilcar regained his feet and charged to the front of the aft-deck, scarcely believing the sight before him. A huge crash and screech of timbers made him spin around in time to see two of his galleys collide, a quinquereme turning into the path of another as it swerved to avoid the aft-section of the Roman ship. He swore at the top of his lungs, cursing the idiotic captain who had caused the collision, cursing the Roman galley that shattered the centre of his line. He looked to the trireme, his gaze sweeping her chaotic decks, the galley somehow familiar but the thought cast aside as fury overwhelmed him, his sword leaping from his scabbard without conscious thought. He ran to the main deck, gathering his crew as he did, leading them on, a gathering storm, surging towards the fore and beyond to the enemy deck.

'It's the *Aquila*!' the masthead roared and Varro whipped his head around, watching as the trireme was rammed by two of the enemy quinqueremes. The sight transfixed him, his mind flooded with doubt, anger and confusion.

'We have to help them!' a voice shouted beside him and the captain's call was taken up across the deck. Varro snapped around, his expression furious.

'Hold your course!' he roared, striding over to the captain.

'Helm! Collision course!' the masthead roared, his voice manic.

Varro and the captain looked directly to the water ahead, to the three Roman galleys that had turned and were sailing directly across the *Orcus*'s line and towards the Carthaginian attack, their crews having also seen the *Aquila*'s lone charge, the sight spurring all to follow.

'Helm, evasive course!' the captain shouted and the *Orcus* turned to starboard.

Varro looked to the helm and beyond to the ragged anarchic formation that had once been his squadron, his gaze immediately picking up the sight of a dozen more galleys turning into the fight, the sound of shouted orders and angry calls for support gathering every ship to the fight, the effect rippling down the line with other Roman galleys turning directly into the seaward enemy attack.

'Tribune,' the captain said, his face stern. 'Your orders.'

Varro turned to the captain, his eyes darting beyond to the empty sea ahead and the coastline. It was close, minutes away.

'Your orders,' the captain repeated.

Varro put his hand to the hilt of his sword, fighting the urge to draw the blade, to run the captain through, to escape.

343

He looked at the captain directly, seeing the challenge in his eyes, the naked contempt for Varro's indecision.

'Hard to port,' Varro growled and the captain instantly reacted, shouting the command to the helm, the *Orcus* turning once more, this time into the face of the oncoming enemy attack.

Varro watched the scene change before the bow of his galley, the coastline giving way to open sea and then the Carthaginian formation, a gaping maw in the centre of their line, a savage tear caused by the *Aquila*.

'Perennis,' Varro whispered, all his hate and fear forged into one man, the Greek captain who seemed set to ruin his fate once more, the *Aquila*'s lone attack exposing Varro's retreat in all its shame. There would have been others to blame after the battle, the captain of the *Orcus*, of other galleys, men lost in a chaotic fight against overwhelming odds whose deaths Varro would use to tangle and bury the truth, but now that confusion was gone, replaced with the clarity of attack, the entire Roman third squadron taking the fight to the enemy. Varro's order to retreat would be remembered, reported, his reputation ruined forever. One man had precipitated this, one man who had come so close before. Varro turned to the captain once more.

'Steer a course to the *Aquila*,' he said. 'We will go to her aid.'

'Yes, Tribune,' the captain said, concurring unequivocally with the order. The *Orcus* was the largest galley of the squadron, only she could pass unmolested through the open centre of the Carthaginian line and save the brave men of the *Aquila*.

Varro caught the captain's expression of approval and he turned away, hiding the rage that rose unbidden to his face.

'Vitulus!' he shouted. The guard commander ran to the tribune.

'We will soon board the *Aquila*,' Varro said, his voice low and menacing. 'There will be confusion, chaos, many will be killed. Make sure one of those is Perennis.'

Vitulus nodded, his eyes cold as he saluted the tribune, stepping back to draw his sword, his gaze following Varro's as both men turned to the sea ahead.

The Carthaginian warriors flooded onto the port-side fore and main decks of the *Aquila* in a savage wave of iron and fury, their war cries screaming hate and death to the Romans, their momentum a relentless force that swung towards the tightly packed semi-circle of legionaries backed up to the starboard rail. Septimus shouted the release of *pila*, the spears striking the mid and rear ranks of the Punic charge, the front line too close to maul, the Carthaginians bearing down behind their shields as they ran across the ram-tilted deck towards the Roman shield wall.

'Steady the line!' Septimus roared, no other command to give, the sea behind them an enemy as merciless as the *Punici*.

The Carthaginians struck the legionaries with an incredible force and the Roman line buckled and caved, the men behind pushing forward against the front, heaving the formation back into shape with the desperate strength of sixty against two hundred. Septimus struck out with all his might, driving his sword home with a ferocity born of a forlorn hope, his roar giving vent to all his bravery, all his strength, the men to his sides matching his savage aggression, giving no quarter, expecting none, remorseless enemies on all sides.

The Carthaginians surged around the Roman shield wall, enveloping it, hemming it in against the fragile starboard rail, sensing the kill, their blood-lust unleashed while others ran towards the aft-deck, a baying pack of wolf-hounds searching for prey. Atticus stood unmoved; the crew of the *Aquila* to his back, Lucius and Gaius to his side, anger wrought on every face, knowing their ship was dying beneath them. The Carthaginians gained the aft-deck, spreading out, never faltering as they ran onwards. Atticus raised his sword, holding it high, the unsullied forged iron blade light in his hand. He summoned up his will and let fly with a roar: '*Aquila!*' The call unleashed his crew and their war cry surged out before them as they ran full-on into the Carthaginian charge, Atticus running deep into the enemy ranks, sweeping his sword down into enemy flesh, the blade drenched with blood that fell to the deck of the dying galley. The crew were swallowed by the Carthaginian horde, the fight on all sides as Atticus held his ground at the centre of the aft-deck with a small knot of men, every man fighting with a demonic fierceness that defied the greater strength of the *Punici*.

Beyond the decks of the *Aquila* the Carthaginian flanks struck the ragged attack of the Roman third squadron, the galleys colliding head-on, the quinqueremes breaking through, the Carthaginian triremes held fast, the Romans streaming across boarding ramps as the battle descended into single combats. A single Roman quinquereme slipped through the line, tearing through the water at twelve knots with the ranks of a full maniple forming on her decks, their shields raised and swords drawn, the standard of a Roman tribune flying from the masthead.

The *Baal Hammon* reversed oars, her ram at first resisting the pull, the splintered hull of the Roman trireme clawing at the bow of the Carthaginian galley. Hanno watched the death throes of the enemy ship from the aft-deck, his gaze darting left and right, to the archers on his own galley who ceaselessly rained death on the Roman decks, the legionaries hidden behind shield ramparts, forestalling the certain death that awaited them and their ship.

Hanno looked beyond the galley to the fight at large, the lines of battle now a tangled net. He suddenly thought of Hamilcar's strategy, the plan Hanno had agreed to before the battle, to feign retreat and then counter-attack but to avoid a full engagement against the *corvus*-armed Roman galleys, Hamilcar warning Hanno that the enemy could not be beaten on their terms, that the ramp still held sway in open battle. Hanno looked to the sinking trireme before the *Baal Hammon*, the Romans dying before his eyes, the quinquereme, finally released, turning quickly to seek new prey. He smiled derisively. Hamilcar was a fool, or worse he was hoping to take the lion's share of the victory, his strategy a clever ruse to minimise Hanno's impact on the outcome.

The *Baal Hammon* came full about and Hanno was afforded a wider view along the length of the battle. Carnage was everywhere, the sea strewn with wreckage, rammed Roman galleys amidst Carthaginian pyres, the galleys set aflame by victorious legionaries. Half of the fleet on each side was engaged, most of the galleys fighting in desperate ship-to-ship battles, the Romans fighting to take Carthaginian decks they had boarded across the infernal ramps.

Hanno felt a sudden sliver of doubt as he stared at the dozen fights closest to the *Baal Hammon*. The Romans were prevailing in every clash where they had managed to deploy their boarding ramps, the Carthaginians only succeeding when the ram had decided. In close quarters, with little sea room, the Roman tactics had the advantage and the words of Hamilcar's warning echoed once more in Hanno's mind.

Atticus punched hard with his *hoplon* shield, the copper boss slamming into the Carthaginian's chest, driving him back, robbing him of his balance and Atticus lunged forward, striking low, his blade tearing through the enemy's groin, the Carthaginian falling even as Atticus withdrew his sword. Lucius stood to his side, the seasoned veteran drawing on the strength of a thousand fights, his sword arm never tiring, his thoughts still firmly locked on sweeping the Carthaginians from his ship and somehow saving her from the sea's grasp.

Atticus felt the side-rail slam into his lower back as he back-stepped away from a furious assault, the Carthaginian soldier's blade a blur of iron in a deadly sequence of sword-strokes, Atticus's arm going numb under the shield that bore the brunt. He stabbed out with his sword, a desperate jab to force his enemy to relent and through sweat-stained eyes he saw the Carthaginian block left with his shield, giving Atticus the opening he needed. He pushed forward from the rail, his sword instinctively following a series of strikes, the years of single combat commanding his every action, every move and the Carthaginian gave ground slowly until he backed into another fight, forcing him to stand firm. The Carthaginian responded with a frenzied counter-attack and Atticus turned his shield once more in defence, his eyes locked on the Carthaginian's, seeing the fury there, the eyes anticipating the sword. Atticus shortened his defence, closing the distance to beneath a sword-length, breaking the Carthaginian's assault and Atticus pushed forward until the two were chest to chest, the stink of sweat and aggression filling his senses. Atticus ignored the continued blows on his shield, the close quarters negating their strength and he swung his sword out low and wide, bringing the blade in behind the Carthaginian, sweeping it back until it sliced into the enemy's hamstring, the Carthaginian screaming out in pain as his tendon split, his leg buckling under his own weight and he fell to the deck, dropping his sword to reach for his wound, his face a mask of agony.

Atticus jumped back, bringing his sword up quickly, the fight pressing in on all sides as two Carthaginians quickly stepped over the man he had downed, their swords charged against Atticus, their expressions malevolent, taunting, their quarry singled out before them. Atticus brought his shield up to his shoulder, his sword dropping low for the first attack, his eyes darting from the first man to the second, crouching slightly to coil the energy of his legs, ready for the lunge. The two Carthaginians moved in, one of them smiling viciously and Atticus smiled back, his eyes ever cold. He paused as the moment to attack neared and he tightened his grip on the hilt of his sword. He was about to charge but he checked himself, realising a sudden unease on the faces of his attackers, their eyes no longer on Atticus but to a point behind him and they began to back off.

Atticus glanced over his shoulder, the breath that he had held releasing as the sight before him overwhelmed his mind. The *Orcus* was less than fifty yards away, her *corvus* already partially lowered, the serried ranks of a full maniple drawn up behind, a solid wall of shields above which iron helmets and cheek-plates framed hostile and determined faces. The *Orcus* closed the gap in seconds, her oars dipped and held to slow the galley and the bow of the quinquereme struck the stern of the *Aquila* lightly, the *corvus* falling firmly onto the aft-deck, the spikes hammering into the timbers.

The legionaries flooded across, forming a line, the strident commands of a centurion marching them forward. The Carthaginians faltered then quickly turned into the new threat, a ragged few joined by scores in a matter of seconds, the *Punici* slamming into the shield wall, hammering with all the frenzy of hate against leather and brass.

Atticus called the remaining crew of the *Aquila* to the rails to continue their fight on the flanks, wary that in the confusion of battle the armourless crew might be mistaken for Carthaginians by the legionaries. He looked to the main deck and the embattled men of Septimus's command, his attention drawn away from the *Orcus*, never seeing Vitulus run across the *corvus*, his own gaze looking beyond the front line of the legionaries, searching for his prey.

'Hard to starboard! Withdraw oars!' the captain of the *Baal Hammon* roared and Hanno leaned into the turn as the quinquereme swung to avoid the fall of a *corvus*, the Roman quinquereme sweeping past the bow, the cutwater of the *Baal Hammon* slamming into the extended oars of the Roman galley, snapping the fifteen foot spars like twigs underfoot, until the counter turn of the Roman ship dragged the remaining oars out of reach.

'Attack speed!' the captain called again, his eyes searching for open water, the second narrow escape from boarding tearing at his nerves. Hanno felt a contagious panic spread over his galley, seeping into his own mind, the complete dominance of the Roman quinqueremes over the equally sized galleys of his own fleet a terrible realisation that had suddenly thrust the *Baal Hammon* into the fight of her life.

The *Baal Hammon* had rammed and sank two Roman triremes, charging them down and striking them deep with a strength they could not defy and Hanno had praised his decision to fully engage the enemy, sensing victory with every Roman who fell under the ram of his quinquereme. But beyond his own galley, Hanno had suddenly witnessed the real truth of the battle, the Romans triremes like jackals hunting down prey, attacking creatures their own size with a savage sabre-toothed weapon that conquered relentlessly. And amongst them the larger quinqueremes, attacking the command galleys, the Carthaginian crews overwhelmed and slaughtered.

The *Baal Hammon* found clear sea and the captain brought the galley around once more, the tangle of butchery that was the battle-line spread out before the bow once more, the helmsman holding his course, waiting for the command to re-engage. The captain looked to Hanno, his expression questioning, his eyes devoid of the confidence that befitted the captain of a flagship. Hanno looked beyond him, immediately seeing a number of Roman triremes holding fast to Carthaginian galleys, stationary in the water, perfect targets for the *Baal Hammon*. Hanno hesitated however, knowing that to ram the triremes was to expose his own ship to the threat of being boarded by another, a fight he knew could not be won and for the first time the unthinkable crept into his thoughts, the unendurable truth he had realised earlier but had buried beneath his honour.

The Roman line swept ever forward, the Carthaginians falling before the onslaught, the rear ranks stepping forward as the front stepped back, creating a solid press of men before the legionaries, the Roman blades wreaking a terrible carnage. Atticus stood at the starboard rail, many of his crew at his side, turning the outer flank of the Carthaginian host, giving them no pause, the press of men increasing in the centre until the Roman line concaved, the sides of the line moving forward even as the centre came to a halt.

Vitulus stood behind the starboard flank of the line, stepping forward slowly as the line advanced, his eyes never leaving the sight of the Greek captain standing only yards away, the gap closing with every Carthaginian slain. He readied his sword and moved to the rail, pushing forward until he reached the front line of the attack, slotting his shield to the end of the line, striking his blade forward with intuition; the instinct learnt during the years spent in the legions never leaving him.

The Greek was but feet away, oblivious to the advancing wall, his eyes locked on the combat before him, his sword striking the shield of a Carthaginian warrior. Vitulus recognised the sailor to the captain's left, the older man standing closer to the Roman wall, an obstacle Vitulus would avoid. He pushed forward, breaking out of the line, using his shield to push the Carthaginian before him away from the rail and into the maelstrom of the centre. Vitulus readied his sword, drawing the weapon back, his shoulder tensing as it reached the height of its arc, the blade pointing almost directly down, poised to stab forward, waiting for a path to open, for a moment when the captain would be exposed. He saw one and lunged without conscious thought.

Lucius saw the blade from the corner of his eye, his weapon whipping instinctively away from the Carthaginian to his front to block the sword swiping behind him, the clash of iron jolting his forearm, the strength and direction of the sudden attack shocking him, knowing how close his captain had come to death. He turned in an instant, his sword already recovered, his mind screaming restraint as he suddenly spotted the red cloak of a legionary.

'We're Roman!' Lucius shouted, the attacker's face inches from his own, the expression of rage twisting the features of the legionary. The soldier spat back in fury, striking again with his sword, Lucius parrying the blow but staying his counter-strike, bringing his shield up in defence but keeping his sword at bay. He broke off and made to roar again, to breach the obvious trance that consumed the Roman soldier but the words died on his lips as he recognised the legionary for who he was. Vitulus noticed the change in Lucius's expression and attacked without hesitation, driving his sword through, bringing his shield to the fore. Lucius tried to react, his sword sweeping back up into the fray, his soul consumed with hatred for the assassin but Vitulus's strike was too quick and the hammer blow of the sword drove the air from Lucius, the blade slicing unchecked into his stomach until the pommel punched against his skin, knocking Lucius back. Vitulus stared into Lucius's face, hold his gaze, seeing the hatred there, the emotion overwhelming the agony of the strike. The legionary held the gaze for a heartbeat and then twisted the blade, Lucius's expression collapsing into a mask of pure pain as Vitulus withdrew the blade, the sailor falling to the deck, a scream dying in his throat.

Atticus felt a weight fall against his legs and he glanced down, a cry of anguish escaping his lips as he saw Lucius beneath him, the sailor holding his hands tightly across an appalling wound, blood and viscera spilling from between his fingers, his eyes wide in terror and pain. Atticus made to crouch down but a hidden instinct caused him to look up and he immediately recognised Vitulus, his sword drenched in blood, the legionary's eyes suddenly shifting from Lucius, catching Atticus's stare. Vitulus reacted instantly, his sword darting forward with incredible speed. Atticus sidestepped, slamming his shield down to strike the top of Vitulus's sword, the legionary bringing his own shield around to parry the counter-strike from Atticus.

The first blows landed, the two men immediately backed off, finding their feet on the blood-soaked and body-strewn deck, fighting for balance as the tide of battle broke beside them, the Carthaginians checking the advance of the Roman wall, the sheer weight of numbers concentrating the slaughter along an immovable front line. Atticus charged into the attack, his mind wiped of all thought save one, his sword moving without conscious reason. Vitulus stood his ground, his shield absorbing the assault, his own sword stabbing forward, seeking a breach. Atticus ignored the sword strikes on his *hoplon* shield, his anger consuming him, the desire for revenge allowing him no respite. He pushed forward, stepping over his friend, forcing Vitulus to step back, the rail to their sides denying them room to circle.

Atticus pushed forward two more paces and then suddenly checked his advance, holding his ground as Vitulus began a counter-attack, his body already poised to step back, knowing how Vitulus would press forward, staying his own attack as he waited for the moment he knew was coming. Vitulus advanced, his attack instantly transforming into the innate sequence of the legions, the shield shoved forward, the sword striking out, the shield pushed forward again, the predictable rhythm that was so lethal when used in formation. Atticus drew Vitulus on, inch by inch, his anger screaming at him to strike but his instinct restraining his sword arm. He watched the rhythm take hold of Vitulus, the legionary's expression turning to triumph as Atticus retreated further, the Roman shield pushing him back, the pressure unrelenting.

Atticus allowed the shield to push him back one final time, parrying the sword strike that followed, waiting for Vitulus to commit to the next shield thrust, his predictability becoming a fatal weakness in single combat and Atticus suddenly twisted his entire body as Vitulus shoved forward, the legionary falling as the resistance against his shield disappeared, his sword arm stretching out to regain his balance. Atticus continued his turn, spinning his body completely around, his sword following on a wide arc, the momentum building, the strength of his entire body behind the blade as he came full about, Vitulus's exposed midriff drawing the tip of the blade. Atticus punched home the strike and the blade slammed into Vitulus below the ribs, the force of the blow accelerating his fall, the blade vanishing to the hilt before sliding out again, the legionary dead before he hit the deck.

Varro watched the fall from the fore-deck of the *Orcus*, his disbelief giving way to rage, the triumph he had felt swelling up only seconds before as Vitulus pushed home his attack now replaced with a fury that seemed to contract every muscle in his body. An intense urge overwhelmed him and he drew his sword without conscious thought. He ran across the *corvus*, his gaze never leaving the Greek spawn of Hades who defied him, whose every breath mocked Varro's honour. He stopped amidst the dead strewn across the aft-deck of the *Aquila* behind the Roman advance, Carthaginian and legionary, a tangled slaughter of bodies. The Greek captain was kneeling over another man, the fight raging to their side, the Carthaginians refusing to relent under the pressure of the shield wall. Varro felt the bile of hatred course through him and he raised his sword.

'Perennis!' he roared, his voice cutting through the air.

Atticus's gaze shot up, seeing the tribune standing only yards away, Varro's eyes boring into him. Atticus rose to his feet. Seconds passed, a sudden pause in the vortex of battle as both men became locked in deadly enmity, Atticus slowly lifting a hand to his face, touching the scar there, his hand falling away, his eyes following to rest on the dying figure of Lucius. Varro charged with his sword before him, a slow, almost hypnotic movement as if time had slowed for both men and Atticus stepped forward, throwing his shield to the deck, the grip on his sword tightening.

Varro surged forward, a scream surging from his throat as he rushed to the attack and Atticus roared in defiance, a war cry of his ancestors as he ran to meet the Roman, the two blades clashing in a blur of iron and terrifying hatred. The fight descended into a brawl, both men lashing out in unforgiving fury, each strike parried and immediately reversed, neither man pausing.

The balance gave way within a minute, Atticus's experience and battle-hardened strength coming to the fore, the pure hatred of Varro's attack not enough to overcome a more-skilled opponent. Varro stepped back, his mind registering for the first time the escalating pain in his sword arm, the muscles burning, his counter-attacks regressing more and more to a desperate defence under the crushing onslaught. The Greek captain came on, never relenting and Varro felt the first threads of panic encircle his heart as he stared at the harsh determined expression of his opponent. His hatred suppressed his fear, forcing him to think and he immediately went on the offensive, knowing only one attack could save him against the better swordsman. Revenge filled his soul as the fight came to closer quarters, Varro pushing forward with all his strength until the two swords were locked between them, the pommels intertwined. Varro leaned in further, looking over the interlocked blades, his face only inches from his enemy's, the green eyes of the Greek never leaving his own. Varro held the gaze, a malicious smile creasing the edge of his mouth, almost tasting the victory to come as he reached down with his free hand.

Atticus held the tribune's gaze, anger tensing every fibre of his body, the sword blades shifting slightly, metal grinding against metal as Atticus readied himself for a final lunge to separate the weapons and finish the fight. He saw Varro's lips curl slightly at the edge of his mouth, a vicious smile that spoke of some inner madness and as Atticus returned his focus to the Roman's eyes, he saw them flicker slightly, darting low and left. Atticus reacted instantly, his own hand reaching out unbidden, his eyes dropping to follow Varro's glance, seeing the deadly blade.

Atticus grabbed wildly for the dagger, his hand grasping Varro's, his fore-fingers reaching over the pommel onto the blade, the edge slicing his flesh. He forced the knife up, turning

356

the blade away from his stomach, the tip brushing against his tunic as he pushed the knife ever upwards. He looked to Varro's eyes once more, seeing beyond the hatred there to the emerging fear. Atticus pushed harder, the muscles in his arm bulging, his grip tightening, the blade cutting deeper into his fingers, the pain ignored as the blade came up past his chest. Atticus held it there, feeling Varro's arm tremble under the strain. He stared at the tribune again, nodding slightly as he witnessed the naked terror in Varro's eyes.

Atticus eased the knife forward until the blade touched the skin of Varro's neck. The Roman pushed back with one last effort but Atticus pressed on, the knife piercing Varro's skin, bright red blood spurting out, splashing across Atticus's face. The pressure against the knife held as Varro dropped his sword and reached up with his other hand. Atticus stood back, the knife still pressed across Varro's throat and with a sudden swipe he whipped the blade across, slicing deeply, Varro's hands immediately clutching his throat as blood gushed through his fingers, his mouth open in silent fear, his eyes wild, unseeing.

Atticus watched as Varro swayed and he shot out his arm, grabbing hold of Varro's chest-plate, suddenly abhorring the idea of the Roman's body defiling the *Aquila*'s deck. He hauled him to the side-rail and held him there for a second as he looked at his enemy one last time before throwing him over the side. Varro struck the sea eight feet below and sank beneath the water, surfacing a moment later, one hand still on his throat, the other flailing the water, his face a mask of absolute panic, his armour dragging him down, his blood staining the sea around him. He reached out to the hull of the *Aquila*, grasping for a hand-hold but the smooth timbers betrayed him and he slipped beneath the surface, the sea returning to calm as Atticus looked on dispassionately.

*

'Enemy galleys approaching!'

Hamilcar shot around, running to the side of the foredeck of the *Alissar* to gain a better view of the sea behind. Scores of Roman galleys were approaching, the bulk of the spearhead. Hamilcar looked to the horizon beyond them, seeing the grey palls of smoke that marked each burning galley and he cursed Hanno's name, realising the councillor had defied him and that that defiance had turned to failure, costing Hamilcar the time he had so desperately needed to overwhelm the Roman transport fleet. He turned and looked beyond the stricken Roman trireme, his gaze sweeping over the seascape, his galleys locked in combat, a lone few having broken through, a pitiful number of transport ships sunk with the others scattered across the horizon.

Hamilcar looked once more to the approaching Roman vanguard less than a mile away. They would be upon him within minutes, an overwhelming force that could only end in defeat and capture for the remaining Carthaginian galleys in the fight and his eyes fell across the fight on the Roman trireme transfixed to the ram of the *Alissar*; the battle-lines clearly drawn by the shield walls of the Romans, one across the aft-deck and a defensive semi-circle on the main, the quick victory Hamilcar had expected turning into a bloody stalemate with the arrival of a Roman quinquereme. His indecision lasted a second longer and he called the captain to his side, the order catching in his throat as he cursed his fate.

'Sound the withdrawal,' he said, his heart consumed with thoughts of the consequences that would follow his decision. 'Full retreat.'

The trumpet calls of retreat were followed an instant later by triumphant shouts, the Roman lines surging forward as the Carthaginians ran to the two quinqueremes, many of the *Punici* dropping their weapons in their haste, the men leaping across to the foredecks to escape the unleashed legionaries. The rowers of the Carthaginian galleys began to backstroke, slowly withdrawing their rams, the sea-water gushing in around them, filling the lower holds of the *Aquila* as retreat rapidly descended into rout, the Carthaginians left on the *Aquila* trying to jump the ever-increasing gap, many falling to the water below, easy prey for the hungry sea.

Septimus led his men to the foredeck of the *Aquila*, attacking the bottle-neck of retreating men; giving no quarter to an enemy who had offered them less and the fight became a desperate slaughter as the Romans purged the *Aquila* of Carthaginians, the remnants throwing themselves into the sea to avoid the vengeance of a merciless foe. Septimus called his men to order, breathing heavily, his blood-soaked sword falling to his side, his gaze drawn to the retreating Carthaginian quinqueremes and beyond to the Roman vanguard.

Septimus suddenly became aware of the desperate screams of panic beneath him as the battle noise on the foredeck abated and he looked across the *Aquila*, noticing the tilt of the deck that was worsening with each passing second, the Carthaginian rams that had supported the *Aquila* supplanted with an unstoppable flood of sea-water.

'Every man to the *Orcus!*' Septimus roared, his men reacting instantly and they ran the full length of the *Aquila* to the *corvus* of the Roman quinquereme, the legionaries of that galley following without hesitation. Septimus took up the rear, ensuring that every injured legionary was taken aft, his eyes sweeping the decks, ignoring the dreadful screams of the dying rowers chained to the dying galley. He reached the aft-deck and immediately spotted Atticus, the captain kneeling at the side-rail with a man's head on his lap. He ran to them, recognising the pale bloodless figure as Lucius.

'Atticus,' Septimus called. 'Is he . . .?'

Atticus looked to Septimus, a haunting expression of grief etched on his face. 'Get your men off,' Atticus said, 'and hold the *corvus* for me.'

Septimus nodded, turning to the last of the legionaries waiting for their chance to get across the boarding ramp.

Atticus leaned over, his face inches from the man he had served with for so many years, his trusted advisor and mentor, his friend.

'Lucius,' he said. 'We need to go.'

Lucius opened his eyes and gazed across *Aquila* before looking up at Atticus.

'She's dying, Atticus,' Lucius said, his voice cracking, a trickle of blood forming at the edge of his mouth, a massive pool of blood covering the deck beneath him.

'I know,' Atticus replied, forcing his own eyes to look out over his galley, accepting and facing that truth for the first time.

'Leave me here,' Lucius said, his eyes pleading. 'Leave me with her.'

'No I can't,' Atticus replied. 'There's still time. I . . .'

'No,' Lucius said, shaking his head. 'There's no time, not for me, and I don't want to die on some blasted quin.' He tried to laugh and blood coughed from his mouth, staining his lips. He gasped for breath. 'She shouldn't die alone,' he said.

Atticus nodded and held out his hand. Lucius grabbed it, the strength of a lifetime's friendship and respect making the grip firm. Atticus laid Lucius's head gently on the deck and stood up, holding his gaze for a second longer before turning and walking to the *corvus*, Septimus already across, the *Orcus* ready to pull away.

Atticus stopped for a heartbeat and looked down at the

deck of the *Aquila* and then back along her entire length, the galley sinking rapidly by the bow. He nodded to her and jumped onto the *corvus*, the ramp rising even as he walked across and the *Orcus* got underway, the quinquereme turning as the first galleys of the Roman vanguard swept past, many of their crews looking to the sinking trireme, at the many slain on her decks, Roman and Carthaginian, wondering what ferocity had gripped the solitary ship. Atticus stood with Septimus on the foredeck of the *Orcus* as the quinquereme accelerated to battle speed, her course turning into the wake of the fleeing Carthaginians while Atticus watched once over his shoulder as the *Aquila* slipped beneath the waves.

EPILOGUE

The muted sounds of a thousand voices, of shouted commands and a multitude making ready was carried on the soft breeze that blew into Regulus's room in the barracks overlooking the harbour of Agrigentum. He glanced down at the parchment on the table, reading again the last lines of the written report, satisfied the man standing before him could add no more. He looked up, studying the captain's face, searching for any signs of subterfuge. There were none.

'You're dismissed,' Regulus said and the captain of the *Orcus* saluted and turned on his heel, leaving the room quickly.

'His report confirms it,' the young man seated by the far wall said, standing up as he spoke. 'Varro attempted to flee and only engaged when the *Aquila* forced him to. Along with the statements of the other captains the evidence is overwhelming.'

Regulus nodded but remained silent, turning his head to stare out the window to the harbour of Agrigentum, to the ranks of galleys and transport ships, the preparations to sail at a frenzied pitch. He turned back.

'I agree, Longus,' he said, 'but the captain of the *Orcus* also states that Varro ordered him to sail directly to the *Aquila*'s aid and we know that Varro was lost in that fight.'

Longus made to respond but Regulus held up his hand.

'He died trying to save those men, Longus,' Regulus said.

'But his cowardice almost cost us the Ninth Legion,' Longus protested. 'Whatever bravery he subsequently showed.'

Regulus lapsed into silence again, his mind already decided on the matter. To denigrate Varro was to call into judgment his own decision to appoint the tribune as commander of the third squadron and it was a sign of weakness that Regulus had to avoid at all costs. The invasion would begin within days and last several months, a long time for Regulus to be absent from the Senate chamber and he could not have any doubt of his abilities to command fermenting in the Curia.

Regulus looked to Longus again, ready to call the last meeting when a sudden thought occurred to him, a thought that made him uneasy. To quash all record of Varro's cowardice was a calculated move to protect himself rather than a noble deed for Rome and Regulus realised that a part of him had become like the man he most despised, Scipio. He brushed the thought aside, burying it quickly, not ready to admit that he had made the needs of Rome subservient to his own.

'Send in Captain Perennis,' he said and Longus nodded, wondering at the senior consul's suddenly strained expression.

Atticus walked into the room and stood to attention before Regulus, Longus walking around the table to stand at the consul's shoulder. Regulus studied the man before him, the vicious scar across his jaw-line, the hard determined features, his green eyes almost unfocused in their intensity. The consul had seldom seen a more charged expression, as if latent fury was but a shade beneath the exterior and Regulus silently confirmed his earlier decision.

'You are to be commended, Captain Perennis,' Regulus began, his voice expansive, his expression affable. 'You have done Rome a great service, showing courage and daring against a determined enemy.'

The consul paused, waiting for the captain to accept the complement but the young man stood unmoved.

'Rome has found in you a son she can be proud of,' Regulus continued, 'and I hereby promote you to the newly formed rank of *Praefectus Classis*, Prefect of the fleet, reporting directly to the commander of the *Classis Romanus*.'

Again Regulus paused, waiting for a reaction. He glanced at Longus, his expression perplexed but the junior consul merely shrugged in reply, unable to explain the captain's apparent indifference. Regulus turned once more to the captain.

'This is a singular honour, Perennis,' he said, a slight note of irritation in his voice. 'You will be the only Prefect who is not a citizen of Rome.'

A silence drew out once more.

'Perennis?' Regulus snapped, standing up suddenly. 'Do you have anything you wish to say?'

Atticus remained silent for a moment longer before turning his gaze directly to the consul. 'Rome victorious,' he said, striking his chest with a fist in salute, snapping back to attention before turning around and walking from the room.

Atticus paused in the courtyard of the barracks. He turned his face briefly up to the sun, closing his eyes against the light as he breathed in deeply, his mind overwhelmed by a dozen thoughts. The senior consul had been hearing reports all morning from many of the captains in the fleet, no doubt in a bid to create a complete account of the battle and although there was no indication that anyone had witnessed Varro's death, Atticus had prepared himself for the worst when the consul's summons had arrived, imaging a scenario that had been completely shattered by Regulus's offer of promotion.

Atticus lowered his gaze and saw Septimus approach, the centurion in full battledress. His brow creased in puzzlement. 'What brings you here?' he asked, having left Septimus an hour before on the *Orcus*.

'The legate of the Ninth requested to see me,' Septimus replied, indicating over his shoulder.

'What about?'

'Nothing important,' Septimus said and he looked intently at Atticus. 'Well?' he asked.

'Promotion,' Atticus replied off-handedly. 'To a new rank, Prefect of the fleet.'

Septimus looked relieved and he clasped Atticus on the shoulder. He left his hand there for a moment, studying his friend, surprised to see none of the relief he himself felt. Atticus looked up over his shoulder to the windows of Regulus's office, the consuls reverting to shadowy figures in his mind's eye, indistinctive men, Roman commanders.

'Who are these men?' he asked, almost to himself.

'Who?' Septimus asked, causing Atticus to turn back.

'These Romans,' Atticus replied, confused emotions giving an edge to his voice. 'These men we fight for. By the Gods, Septimus, I don't know who the enemy are anymore.'

Septimus removed his hand. 'I know who they are,' he said, remembering the fury that had gripped him when he threw his sword after a fleeing Carthaginian galley. 'The *Punici*, Atticus. They're the enemy.'

'The Carthaginians?' Atticus replied. 'Men who fight with honour. Men who face their enemy regardless of the odds, who never shirk from the fight.'

'Would you rather fight for them?' Septimus asked, anger compounding his confusion at Atticus's words. 'Look around you, man. Look to your front. I'm Roman and I fight with honour. Fight for that Rome, not for men like the consuls.'

'I do,' Atticus replied, all his frustration and loss rising to the surface. 'I sacrificed the *Aquila* to save the men of the Ninth, to save Roman men, and how is that repaid, how was Lucius repaid? Attacked from behind by a Roman.'

Septimus's retort died in his throat at the mention of Lucius, remembering the older man, the gruff sailor who had never hidden his dislike of legionaries but who had always shown Septimus respect.

'I won't forget why Lucius died,' he said, 'and I'll make sure men like Marcus and his command knows too. They're honourable men, Atticus. They won't forget.'

Atticus nodded and Septimus held out his hand in comrade-ship, holding it steady.

Atticus noticed the gesture and looked to Septimus, seeing past his uniform to the man, the Roman, who had become his friend. He remembered Marcus, the centurion of the IV Maniple, and remembered why he had sailed the *Aquila* to her doom, knowing then as now that he could do nothing less for the legions. Thoughts of the *Aquila* turned his mind once more to Varro, the poisoned viper that had hidden amongst the honourable men he served with, a whoreson spawned from the very corruption that festered in the heart of the Republic and yet again Atticus knew of one amongst them, Duilius, a new man, an outsider in many ways, but an honourable man, a Roman.

Atticus's eyes refocused once more and he looked to Septimus's proffered hand, the conflict raging unabated within him, the loss of the *Aquila* and Lucius too raw to allow him to think clearly. In seeing Septimus he thought, as many times before, of Hadria, of his love for her and his friend's refusal to accept that relationship. Hadria was sure of her brother's motives but Atticus could not grasp that same conviction, his friendship for Septimus tainted by the actions of his fellow Romans. Not today, Septimus had said and Atticus turned that resolution to his own conflict. In Septimus he had an ally and a friend and he took his hand, the grip firm between them. In time, Atticus thought, he might discover the same loyalty to Rome that Septimus took for granted, but not today.

Hamilcar walked quickly down the gangway of the *Alissar* onto the docks of the military harbour, pushing his way through the press of men on the quayside, stepping over the injured and dead alike who littered the narrow walkway. He sighted the *Baal Hammon* on the far side of the harbour, knowing she had only recently docked; Hanno's section of the fleet only an hour ahead of Hamilcar's on the flight south to the safety of Carthage. Hamilcar walked on, realising that Hanno was now long gone, no doubt to the council chamber to announce the defeat in terms that exonerated the councillor.

Hamilcar had thought of little else over the previous days, replaying every moment of the battle in his mind, searching for the point when victory assured turned to ignominious defeat, re-examining his strategy again and again; every time his conclusion gathering greater conviction. Hanno's retreat had cost Carthage the battle. Hamilcar rounded a corner into the city proper, the breath catching in his throat as he sensed the palpable fear in the city. Panic seemed to emanate from every man, woman and child on the street as anxious eyes turned north to the horizon and the certain Roman invasion to come. He stopped dead, nausea threatening to overwhelm him as the shame of that fear struck home. He stepped forward again, his gaze focusing on the street ahead that would lead him to the council chamber.

Suddenly he stopped, the shame he felt instantly replaced

by anger and a spasm of bile rose in his throat. Not twenty feet away, in the shadow of an awning stood Hanno with a squad of soldiers fanned out before him, their faces grim, their eyes sweeping the street. They were looking for him, Hamilcar realised and he reached for his sword, silently cursing Hanno, vowing to take as many of his henchmen as he could before death claimed him.

Hamilcar strode forward, people scattering before him as they saw his drawn blade. One of Hanno's men spotted Hamilcar and pointed, his call alerting the others and Hanno turned to stare at Hamilcar. He walked out from behind his men and approached Hamilcar alone.

'Put down your sword, you fool,' he hissed and Hamilcar hesitated. 'I need to talk to you.'

Hamilcar looked warily beyond the councillor to the squad of soldiers, each man unmoved. He sheathed his sword.

'Follow me,' Hanno said and walked back towards the *Baal Hammon*, Hamilcar falling in behind him, his mind racing but unable to comprehend Hanno's actions in the short time it took to reach the quinquereme.

Hanno walked to the aft-deck and ordered it cleared, leaving the two men standing alone.

'How many did you lose?' Hanno asked, his head bowed, his voice an angry growl.

'Thirty-eight,' Hamilcar said.

'Fifty-six,' Hanno replied and walked away two steps.

'Mot protect them,' Hamilcar whispered, 'over ninety galleys. Lost.' He lapsed into silence.

'This is your fault!' Hamilcar suddenly spat, anger coursing through him. Hanno spun around.

'Listen to me, Barca, and understand this,' he said, stepping forward once more until he stood inches from Hamilcar. 'Either we stand together or this defeat destroys us both.'

'If you had followed my strategy . . .' Hamilcar began.

'No one knows of your strategy except me,' Hanno spat back, cutting Hamilcar short, 'and I will deny everything.'

'Even before the supreme council?' Hamilcar asked, staggered by Hanno's audacity.

Hanno smiled; a joyless grin that spoke of his confidence.

'I will deny it, Barca,' he said, 'and my counter-accusations will sully us both.'

Hamilcar stepped back, his previous conviction in tatters. He could see Hanno's reasoning. It was one man's word against the other's and the infighting would destroy them both. Only a united front could save them, an equal share of the blame quickly forgiven by both factions of the supreme council with the threat of Roman invasion looming on the horizon.

Hamilcar turned away from the councillor and walked to the side-rail, a heavy weight in the pit of his stomach. He looked upward to the Bysra citadel high above the city, studying its towering height and he felt the wellspring of might that was Carthage surge through him, his heart taking strength from the ancients who built the formidable fortress, the founders of Carthage who sailed from the shores of Tyre so many generations before.

Hamilcar had failed to stop the Romans at Ecnomus, defeated by fate and the fallibility of lesser men. Now the battle-lines would be drawn on the very shoreline of Carthage, a boundary that no enemy had crossed in over a millennium and Hamilcar vowed, from the very depths of his soul, that the unconquered city of the *Punici* would not fall.

Atticus rubbed his hand along the side-rail, his fingertips examining the fine grain of the hardwood made even by the plane of a carpenter only months before, the craftsmanship as yet untouched by the harsh elements of the sea.

'Answering standard speed, Prefect.'

Atticus turned and nodded to Gaius, looking to the fifty galleys of his command that sailed in formation behind the *Orcus* as he walked over to the helmsman.

'Steady as she goes, Gaius,' he said, the helmsman nodding, his gaze ever-sweeping across the sea ahead, observing the position of the other squadrons of the *Classis Romanus* and the transport ships that sailed in their care.

Atticus looked out over the deck of the quinquereme; the legionaries formed in ranks on the main, the *corvus* standing ready on the fore, Corin aloft at the masthead and for a moment Atticus could almost imagine the galley to be the *Aquila*, his eyes looking unconsciously to the main, expecting to see Lucius walking amongst the crew, shouting orders that carried to every corner of the ship. He shook the thought aside, forcing his mind to slip back into the rhythm of command and he scanned the galley with a critical eye, checking the line of her course, the tautness of the running rigging, the rise and fall of her two hundred and forty oars. Atticus nodded slowly to himself. The *Orcus* was a good ship.

'Legionaries are all present and correct, Prefect,' Septimus said as he approached the helm and Atticus smiled. His new position outranked Septimus but he was sure the centurion was only using the title to taunt him, perhaps knowing that Atticus had no intention of telling his friend how to command his own men.

'Very well, Centurion,' Atticus replied facetiously. 'Stand by the helm.'

Septimus nodded and stood beside Atticus, both men facing out to the sea ahead, the two of them lapsing into silence.

Atticus looked to the transport ships ahead, almost sensing the pent-up anticipation of the men sailing in them, the legionaries of the Sixth and Ninth. He glanced at Septimus, wondering if his friend knew that Atticus had found out that at Septimus's meeting with the legate of the Ninth he had turned down an offer to command a maniple of that legion, requesting instead to remain with the former crew of the *Aquila*. It was a decision Septimus had yet to disclose openly and Atticus was now beginning to believe that he never would, the motives of his decision remaining a secret.

'What do you think?' Atticus asked as he noticed Septimus was looking directly at the transports.

'About the invasion?' Septimus asked. He paused for a second. 'I think we're facing the fight of our lives.'

Atticus nodded and looked to the sea ahead, filled with the ships of Rome; the *Classis Romanus* and twenty thousand men of the legions, the unfettered might of the Republic. Beyond the horizon lay the brooding shore of Africa, stronghold of the *Punici*, their ancient homeland and Atticus realised that Septimus was right. The Carthaginians had been beaten but they were far from conquered and the ferocity they applied in Sicily was but a shadow of the viciousness they would wield with their backs to the walls of Carthage.

HISTORICAL NOTE

The Battle of Cape Ecnomus took place in 256 BC off the south coast of Sicily when a Carthaginian fleet engaged a Roman fleet poised to sail south to invade North Africa. The number of ships and men involved are truly staggering, with Polybius stating that 350 Carthaginian ships faced 330 Roman, with upwards of 250,000 men engaged in battle. Modern scholars have challenged these figures but nevertheless their estimates have only reduced the size of each fleet by about 100 ships which still allows for Ecnomus to be ranked as one of the largest naval battles in history.

The Roman fleet was commanded by Marcius Atilius Regulus and Lucius Manlius Vulso (Longus) while the Carthaginians were commanded by Hanno (who actually led one of the flanks) and a commander named Hamilcar. (Not Hamilcar Barca as I have written. Again Barca has been brought into the conflict earlier than recorded for narrative purposes.)

The deployments of the two fleets are similar to those described, with the Romans sailing in a triangular formation and the two consuls sailing at the apex of a spearhead while the transport ships were towed in line abreast at the rear. The Carthaginians sailed in line abreast formation with the flanks (particularly the landward) advanced, their simple plan being to draw in and then engage the Roman spearhead in the centre while flanking the main force to attack the more vulnerable transport ships.

Initially the Carthaginian plan worked, with their centre withdrawing in the face of the Roman spearhead until a significant gap had opened between it and the Roman transport ships. They then re-engaged, holding down the Roman centre while their flanks attacked. The Roman galleys towing the transport ships (primarily carrying horses) cut their tethers and engaged the flanks, the battle in essence breaking into separate actions.

The decisive moment came when the Carthaginian centre disengaged and fled, allowing the Roman spearhead to turn and sail to the assistance of the beleaguered rearguard and like many battles, the Carthaginians suffered their greatest number of casualties near the end of battle as their formations collapsed in retreat. In all, the Carthaginians loss 94 galleys, 64 captured and 30 sunk while the Romans lost 24 galleys, a decisive win.

At Ecnomus, as at Mylae, the *corvus* played a vital part with the Carthaginians failing to find an effective tactic to counter the simple boarding device.

The majority of galleys in both fleets were quinqueremes, the smaller galleys becoming less important in the order of battle, and Polybius reports that the consuls of Rome sailed in two sexiremes, or 'sixes'. Given this change it seemed fitting that Ecnomus would be the last battle for the *Aquila*.

Immediately after the battle the Roman fleet sailed to the Sicilian coast to rest and regroup although they did not delay long. Victory at Ecnomus had driven the Carthaginian fleet to their home waters off Africa and the Romans were eager to follow. What lies ahead, however, will shake the very foundations of the Roman Republic.

The enemy fleet are far from beaten and to their backs is the city of Carthage, an impenetrable fortress that has not fallen in 500 years. The war will rage on with Atticus and Septimus in the vanguard, not realising that their greatest defeat lies ahead, a loss that is unequalled in history.